To Tor[...]

KU-674-125

With Best
Wishes. & Good
Luck.

From. D. Francis.

Tony Cooper

61 Lyde Road
Yeovil
Somerset.

THE WITNESS OF CANON WELCOME

BOOKS BY ERNEST RAYMOND

Novels :
GENTLE GREAVES
WE, THE ACCUSED
THE MARSH
FOR THEM THAT TRESPASS
THE KILBURN TALE
A SONG OF THE TIDE
THE FIVE SONS OF LE FABER
THE LAST TO REST
WAS THERE LOVE ONCE ?
THE CORPORAL OF THE GUARD
TELL ENGLAND
A FAMILY THAT WAS
THE JESTING ARMY
MARY LEITH
NEWTIMBER LANE
THE MIRACLE OF BREAN
CHILD OF NORMAN'S END
ROSSENAL
DAMASCUS GATE
WANDERLIGHT
DAPHNE BRUNO I
DAPHNE BRUNO II
MORRIS IN THE DANCE
THE OLD TREE BLOSSOMED
DON JOHN'S MOUNTAIN HOME

Trilogy :
ONCE IN ENGLAND
  comprising editions of
    A FAMILY THAT WAS
    THE JESTING ARMY
    MARY LEITH

Biography :
IN THE STEPS OF ST. FRANCIS
IN THE STEPS OF THE BRONTËS

Essays, etc. :
THROUGH LITERATURE TO LIFE
THE SHOUT OF THE KING

  With Patrick Raymond :
BACK TO HUMANITY

Plays :
THE BERG
THE MULTABELLO ROAD

THE WITNESS OF CANON WELCOME

by

ERNEST RAYMOND

CASSELL & COMPANY LIMITED

LONDON, TORONTO, MELBOURNE, SYDNEY,

WELLINGTON

First published 1950

Set in 10-pt. Basherville type and
Printed in Great Britain by Wyman & Sons Ltd., London, Reading and Fakenham
F.1050

FOR

DESMOND AND MARGARET FLOWER

PART I

CHAPTER ONE

If you go northward from the Angel, Islington, towards the Great North Road, you will pass, as you climb the Northern Heights, the church of St. Boniface Martyr, Hamden Hill. And if you have an eye for such matters, you may wish, as you pass, that this handsome church stood on the top of the hill, for then, surely, its tall spire would be visible from a hundred points in the heart of the city. But it is not so placed ; nothing is perfect in this world, and certainly not in North London. The church stands quite a little way down on the southern slope. When our fathers built it in 1849 London was already spawning over every field and park on the hillside, and they had to pitch their church where they could. But they built what they conceived to be a noble structure for the thousands of new-comers to the ancient village of Hamden-on-the-Hill. They built in the Gothic, or so-called " Christian " style, and their church stands as a monument to their orthodoxy in religion and architecture, and to their faith, somewhat too optimistic, in the continuing piety of North London.

It has a square tower fully a hundred feet high, with angle pinnacles which carry it to a hundred and thirty feet and, crowning this fine tower, an octagonal spire whose apex and steeplecock enter the upper air at a point nearly two hundred feet from the ground. It has a steep roof over its long nave, and a lower one of the same pitch over the chancel ; and there is nothing but the machine-made cut of windows and ornaments, and the slightly tired air of the whole building—an air of duty rather than delight—to tell you that it wasn't built six hundred instead of one hundred years ago. In intention an exceedingly religious building, it stands within its garden, and behind its railings, somewhat isolated from this present irreligious age.

Could you bestride the roof, or climb the spire and join the steeplecock, you would see as you looked southward down the hill the larger part of the parish over which the church presides—and a great deal more on a fine day. Let the sun be genial, and the blue mist a lucent veil, and you would see nearly all the vast wilderness of London smoking and shining, seven hundred square miles of it, in the bottom between the hills. The road beneath your eyes would run like a thrown rope into the midst of this boundless agglomeration, there to lose itself in a tangle of streets and thoroughfares, byways and bridges and viaducts.

Our parish is but a handful picked out from this far-thrown dump, but it is an oddly-mixed handful. There are two very different samples in it. Around the church stand a few grey brick mansions, a few truncated stucco terraces, and in and among these a congregation of rough-cast villas, each with its narrow garden cut out from some old estate. You may even see in one garden or another a stately old oak that long ago stood alone in a gentleman's park. That is one sample. But the parish of St. Boniface Martyr is not all quiet and verdant and respectable like this. Not at all. These middle-class homes, large and small, cover perhaps a fifth of the parish acres and a tenth of the population—an Upper Tenth sitting appropriately enough half-way up the hill and comfortably close to the church. The remaining nine-tenths lie lower down. Take the road down hill, and in a minute you have exchanged the little retired houses, withdrawn behind their shrubs or fences, for long, tall blocks and terraces thrust hard against the pavement. All are dark and frowning, after a hundred years of London smoke, so that the streets seem to be long, grey canyons stretching on and on, without change or hope of change, like the lives of many who walk the dank pavements between their walls. Mostly they are Victorian terraces, but along the immemorial highways you may distinguish, despite the uniform black with which the soot has painted them, Regency terraces and eighteenth-century terraces, and even an old lost cottage of yet earlier date.

Where the hill flattens out among these dark, tarnished streets is the great Railway Motive Power Depôt, known to all its dusty slaves as the Hebron Town Loco : a huge area of engine sheds, machine shops, tool stores, coaling plants, ash-lifting plants, and water cranes, with a coming and going, day and night of drivers, firemen, cleaners, coalmen, sandmen, and shunters. Daily and nightly the hundred and ten engines raise their steam in the running sheds and step out of them, like horses from their stables, to travel the long mile to the strident and steaming Terminus and there be harnessed to waiting northbound trains. The whole

2

district around the depôt smells of their smoke, and in this pungent air you will find, because of the nearness of the railways, tall, cliff-like warehouses, depositories, factories, and breweries, together with coal merchants' wharves smelling of coal-slack and builders' yards smelling of timber.

Smaller streets branch like radial veins from the main roads —long, curving streets, all in their Victorian dress of stock-brick and stucco—stock-brick and stucco, line upon line of it, street upon street, as far as foot can tread in a month of days. The shops in these smaller streets are full of instruction for those who have a mind to ponder them : odd furniture shops, wardrobe dealers, fish friers, bagwash laundries, cut-price stores, and the surgeries of young doctors with strange oriental names. You may, for example, be surprised at the number of hairdressers. Chapels and meeting houses are many, but not so many as the hairdressers. Is it that the hairdressers offer the local youth, male and female, an easier sense of salvation ?

Hebron Fields this district of North London has been called ever since men dwelt here and gave names to their meadows, roads, and tracks. Some of the old names survive to this day, attached to long streets or to cobbled and haggard alleys. They pluck at your coat as you pass by, and speak, not without sadness, of the old, sweet landscape that lies beneath. Sloe Lane you may see, and Millbank End and Hedge Row and Manor Rise ; and you can stay and drink at corner taverns which, however hideous their modern incarnation, carry such names as The Gentle Shepherd, The Sportsman and Gun, The Angler's Pitch, and The Plough.

The parish of St. Boniface, as has been said, grasps at a segment of this boundless dry desert of streets ; and this segment includes, rather unfortunately, the part known as Friars Circus. Friars Circus it may be called, but anything less monastic, anything less devoted to religion and good works, it would be hard to find between here and the Lower Thames. Down by the river, for sure, there are equally irreligious spots but none, I think, much worse. Four roads fall down the slope to converge upon the Circus, and three more approach it from the flat south to complete the asterisk. The seven points which thus abut upon the open centre are known to all the Wide Boys of this neighbourhood (and they are exceedingly wide) as The Corners ; and much malfeasance do they practise or concoct at these corners, singly, in couples, or in gangs. Friars Circus, down in the Fields, is the heart of this segment of St. Boniface's parish, but, alas, the heart is weak. Like the heart of man, as the sad Jeremiah saw it, it is deceitful above all things and desperately wicked. Often the Wide Boys, in affection for the Corners as their Club Lounge, or in gratitude for much profitable practice there, refer to them as The Corns, and this is a better name than they know. It carries, though they perceive it not, an even better metaphor than " the heart ", because these low parts cause many twinges to the quiet and respectable part up above. Indeed the story I am going to tell you is perhaps a tale of the twinges.

§

Let us leave the Fields and the Circus shining like better places beneath the sun of an April morning and climb the hill again to the church. On the north side of the church, and within its small demesne stands the Vicarage, a large rectangular cream-painted house under a hipped slate roof. The garden about the house is brilliant to-day with red and yellow tulips, white narcissi, blue grape hyacinths, and the gold of young privets ; it is a well-tended garden because the living of St. Boniface Martyr is a fat one (so far as any living in these days can be said to have any flesh on it), and the Vicar is often successful in certain quiet dealings on the Stock Exchange, so he can well afford a jobbing gardener. His vicarage is very much a part of the greener and more comfortable world on the hill-slope above the Fields, and it is wholly fitting that it should be garlanded with flowers to-day because this is one of the happiest days of his life.

You can enter the garden through wooden gates in a high brick wall or through the gates in the railings of the churchyard ; we take the latter path that we may profit by a notice board which, standing above the railings, faces the passer-by. It says :

WORDS TO THE WAYFARER

TO-DAY'S THOUGHT

The Wisdom of This World
is
Foolishness with God

4

Having given hospitality to the thought, like the wayfarers we are, we pass through a little gate in the churchyard shrubs into the Vicar's garden and, though all his doors are shut, into his long dark hall and his large, bright study.

The Vicar, Canon Humbert Welcome, is seated at his wide mahogany writing-table. This is a handsome piece of furniture in the centre of a comfortable and not unhandsome room ; and on its large leather blotter is quite the handsomest letter the Vicar has received for many a day. He himself, though not tall, is a tolerably handsome piece of furniture and one which sits well in his place in the picture. The first thing you observe about him is the crimped silver hair which waves away from a central parting and is brushed up in wings over his ears. A woman's glory may be her hair, but the hair of an Anglican canon can be his glory too, when it is silver and wavy and makes wings above the ears. A small bird-like nose projects from the midst of his round, soft cheeks. The cheeks are pleasantly pink and unscored, because his years, so to say, are younger than his hair. He is fifty. There is a comfortable roundness about his body too, and one imagines it pink and smooth like the cheeks, but at present it is enclosed in a Sarum cassock and cincture—not that he intends to conduct service on a sunny Monday morning, but because a cassock, besides being a robe which renders you remarkable in the street (and is therefore good publicity), is also the laziest garment on earth. A clerical collar, a cassock, and a cincture quickly tied ; and you can say to the world, like George Herbert of old, " Come, people ; Aaron's dressed."

The handsome letter under his eyes is headed *Who's Who*, and he reads again (for it is sweet reading), " Messrs. Adam and Charles Black will be glad to have the form overleaf completed and returned to them for insertion in the next edition of *Who's Who*. . . . A proof of the entry will be sent for correction before publication and annually thereafter." He turns to the form overleaf and considers again the panels allocated to Name and Title, Decorations and Orders, Present Position, Education, Career, Publications, Clubs.

And now he rises and walks up and down his tired carpet, for the delightful occupation of assembling details for this brief biography. Always he walks up and down when he is composing a sermon, but that, far too often, is a wearisome task ; this labour to-day is a delight. What high-sounding things can he enter in about his Present Position and his past Career ; and what—without stretching the word too far—could go in as Publications ? His mind sweeps the last thirty years for appointments and rewards and activities that would look well in print. Very pleasant, nay, exciting it is to visit the past like this and to pounce upon one fine flower after another for a really handsome nosegay. " Prebendary of North London. . . . Proctor in Convocation. . . . Rural Dean of Hamden—what else ? Member of Diocesan S.P.G. Committee, Clerical Assistance and Pensions Committee, Diocesan Board of Finance—anything else ? Yes, Public Morality Council. . . . Street Offences Abatement Committee—something else, surely ? Governor of Hamden High School (C. of E. Girls School Trust) . . . Vice-President of Hamden and Stangate Literary Society—or is that too local and small a distinction ? "

He halts by the window and gazes out at the flower show in the garden. But he is not seeing the tulips and the narcissi ; he is looking into the garden of the future and wondering what fine buds may be ready to blow there. This letter from the publishers of *Who's Who* (excellent men) must mean that they consider him a marked man now that the Bishop has nominated him to a prebendal stall. Only fifty, and he is no longer the Reverend Humbert Welcome, but Canon Welcome. Of course " Canon " is not strictly accurate because unfortunately the honorary canons of this diocese have the title of Prebendary, but most of the other prebendaries suffer their faithful to call them " Canon " and to remain in ignorance of the fact that honorary canons are a cheaper line of goods than canons-in-residence. If he's a canon at fifty, why not an archdeacon in gaiters at fifty-five, or even—a lovely bloom, this—a bishop ? There's a sporting chance (if that word is legitimate) that he may reach the episcopal bench now that he's got going. . . . After all he's a Cambridge man, with an M.A. degree at a time when more than half the clergy are coming from theological colleges and have no degrees at all. And he's something of a scholar ; he can write on this pleasant form, " Corpus Christi College, Cambridge, 2nd Class Theological Tripos, Lusus Greek Testament Prize." And thanks to some splendid " tips " from old Marcus Brumley, shrewdest of stockjobbers, he's amassed enough capital to be able to push his way (the expression slips out) among the people of influence and power.

" The Right Reverend Humbert Welcome, D.D., Bishop of

——" Oh, the bright flowers that range themselves around this noble bloom ! Rochet of fine lawn with billowing sleeves, shining pectoral cross, bejewelled episcopal ring, " My Lord " on the lips of junior clergy, young men kneeling to receive his blessing. . . .

When one has composed phrases that seem good, one longs to write them down, and he hastened back to his desk to embellish the form with all the titles, degrees, and dignities that he'd assembled as he walked. But even then he did not feel that the panel given to Career was sufficiently full and decorative, and he turned the pages of his own out-dated volume of *Who's Who* to see what other canons and prebendaries had written. He was much helped by their compositions. Hardly one but had made the most of his career for the eyes of the world. " Twice lectured in Canada from coast to coast at the invitation of the All-Canada Church Society " said one ; and another : " Has travelled widely in Europe and the East " ; and another : " One of the first clergy invited by B.B.C. to broadcast. Has preached to great audiences all over the British Isles advocating a Return to Christ."

Inspired to similar creation himself Canon Welcome wrote " During the War went five times to the Front to organize lectures for Officers and Men. Received the special thanks of the King of the Belgians." This related to a parade in a barn where he with twenty others was presented to King Albert who, on being quickly told what he was doing in Flanders, said " I thank you " and passed on.

Publications ? He had not published anything in the sense of having had anything accepted, paid for, and produced in book form by a publisher, but since all the other parsons in *Who's Who* who were in a similar difficulty had filled up this column, so far as he could see, with all manner of rubbish, he resolved to find *something* which he could put down to his credit. Instructed by their methods, he wrote, " History of St. Boniface Martyr, Hamden Hill "—a pamphlet which he'd had printed and which could be taken from a table in the church on payment of threepence : " Little Lessons for Little Folks "—a Christmas booklet which years ago he'd had put together at some expense as a prize for his Sunday School children ; " To Your Tents, O Israel "—a sermon which he'd preached at the time of the Archbishop's appeal for a Return to Religion, and which, since his congregation had said it " ought to be published "—and he thought so too—he'd sent to the *Hamden and*

7

Hebron News; and "Articles in *Church Times, Guardian,* and many other journals". The many other journals were the *Times* and the *Hamden and Hebron News* to which he wrote whenever a suitable opportunity presented itself.

Steps on the gravel. Door bell. Door opening to some woman. "Is it possible to see the Vicar?"

Confound the woman! Would these people never learn the value of his time and the pressure of a vicar's work? Coming to disturb him in the morning which he always devoted to work. Of course at the moment he wasn't . . . but the principle remained. Ask the woman's business—tell her to call at the proper time—make her understand—send her away——

But, good God, was it credible? Amy—Amy, his wife whom he'd instructed ten thousand times that his mornings were not to be disturbed—she was actually parleying with the woman, and—yes, impossible! oh, maddening disobedience, infuriating disbelief—she was going to bring the creature in. Here were Amy's steps coming to his door. And for twenty-two years he'd tried to make her understand that his mornings were sacred. Twenty-two years he'd been trying to train her, and here she was, coming *in.*

His door opened nervously, irresolutely. And the foremost parts of Amy appeared round its edge. " I'm sorry, darling, but——"

He slammed his fist on the writing table. " Oh, my heaven above ! Oh, merciful saints, and God in his pity ! " He drooped his head between his hands like a man who has no further hope in life. He sighed like a toy balloon that is undone and empties and dies. " God . . . God . . . God. . . ."

Amy came quickly into the room and shut the door, lest the visitor heard. One hand dropped from the Vicar's suffering brow and folded over the letter from *Who's Who.*

" I'm sorry, dear," Amy repeated, " but——"

" Have I ever said that I'm not to be interrupted in the morning? Have I said it ten thousand times in twenty years? Twenty years. It's useless. I give it up. Nobody believes I mean it. Here am I, engaged in profoundly important work, and all my powers of concentration are shattered. All the necessary atmosphere is dispersed. I shall have to create it all anew, and begin everything from the beginning again. When will anyone understand it? Who is this woman?—this pest? Can't you—— ? "

" She's a Mrs.——"

" Can't you explain to her that I have working-hours which are sacred ? Has there ever been a woman yet with any sense of ordering and arranging her time ? Never. They have no system of work themselves and can't imagine that men have. They say that Woman's work is never done, and they're right ; it's never done because they don't do it if there's any chance of gossiping instead. Will no one ever learn that a clergyman's time—— ? "

" But, dear, this woman is——"

" Let me speak. Do let me speak, *please* ! That a clergyman in his working hours can no more be disturbed than a dentist or a doctor. Would anyone burst into a dentist's room when he's deep in a patient's tooth ? Would they come crashing into a doctor's surgery when he's examining some woman naked on a couch ? No—*oh*, no—but a clergyman doesn't matter. He's nothing to do all day. Never have I been busier than— and, as you know I've a Staff Meeting here in an hour's time. A tremendously important Staff Meeting because of the Strike. Perhaps the most important Meeting of my career."

His irritation was not helped by the fact that his wife, at forty-eight, and at half-past nine in the morning, looked more than ever bulky, voluminous, shapeless and undesirable. More than ever this morning did her masses of bosom seem to be shored up in front of her and only saved from collapse by the corsets under her cream blouse. More than ever did her stomach, under her blue skirt, seem to resent the correction of her belt and to be pushing that nuisance upward so that it could thrust itself forward as it wanted to. A pain of frustration sank his heart ; and his eyes, in search of further pain, rested on her thinning grey hair, on the veining and mottling of her skin, and on the dewlap that now sloped down from her chin to her neck. " Like the wattle under the throat of a turkey," he thought.

He turned his eyes away. Amy had grown very ugly. Where, in yonder massy, ruddy, grey-haired woman, was the slim, peach-faced girl he had married twenty-two years ago ? Of course he too was somewhat rounder than he used to be, but it didn't matter in a man. And his hair was grey too, but silver-grey, and an ornament. Amy was ugly now ; there was pleasure no more in kissing her ; it was a duty best done quickly ; and he—well, he was only fifty, and he still hungered.

And yet he loved her—loved her even when, as now, he

9

was scolding her and suffering an ache of disappointment because he could desire her no more. How could he do other than love her, after their twenty-two years together, and she so loyal and dutiful ? The very fact that she was a simple, unsophisticated, chattering woman meant that she believed in his show of goodness and hard work and in her duty to love and aid him, and that she praised his talents and labours in the streets.

Oh, yes, he loved poor Amy. A good wife. It was not her fault that she was grown very ugly. Domestic affections were one thing, and a powerful man's hunger another. Especially in an ordained priest who could never, if he had any conscience at all, let his body follow his thoughts.

Forget that a good wife's body is useless : the pain is too great. " Who is this woman ? At half-past nine on a Monday morning. I never heard of such a thing ! Where are her housekeeping tasks ? Has she no breakfast things to wash up, no beds to make, no shopping to do ? Why can't she let me alone ? Why can't you tell her to go away ? "

" I hardly liked to. She is that woman who——"

" That's what I complain of. Rather than inflict a faint hurt on some foolish woman's feelings you sacrifice me. Always I am the one to be sacrificed. I should have thought your business was to protect me from these intruders, not to offer me up as a sacrifice to them. It makes no difference who the woman is. I don't care if she's the Queen on her Throne. I see no one in the mornings. There are only two exceptions, as you know : if the callers come from the Press, I do not, for the sake of the parish, turn them away ; or if their business is likely to bring any money to our funds, I must sacrifice myself rather than that the Church should suffer. . . . Or, of course, if they're sick and dying."

" I thought perhaps she might be someone wealthy whom you wouldn't wish to turn away. She's that rather beautiful woman who's been in church the last few Sundays, and whom you noticed and asked about."

" Oh . . . ! " The stout barrier of indignation with which the Vicar had surrounded himself turned to vapour at the word " beautiful " ; it trailed away in a diminishing cloud. But he didn't want his wife to know this. It is always better, if you've indicted someone unreasonably, to leave them there in the dock. " Oh . . . *that* woman, is it ? "

" Yes, the one you called ' The Tired Beauty '."

" Did I ? " said the Vicar, well remembering that he did.

" Yes, you said how slim she was for her years, and how beautifully she wore her clothes. Don't you remember ? You guessed she must have been an actress once because she moved so beautifully. You said she looked very well-to-do, and might be good for a subscription."

" I was joking. Naturally. Joking."

" Of course, but I thought——"

" There are no ' buts ' about it. And no ' I thoughts ' either. Because the woman seems a lady and well-to-do, you're afraid to ask her her business and, if it's not urgent, tell her to arrange an interview, as she would with her dentist. No, you'd rather sacrifice me at any time. I give it up. Oh, for God's sake don't start weeping. I haven't said anything. I'm sorry if I sounded rude, but this business of being interrupted in my hours of work drives me mad. If this woman is there, and you've let her suppose I'm at home, I'd better see her. But it's very disturbing." He rose from his table and stood before the fire-place, thrusting both large plump palms between cincture and cassock. " Bring her in. And please don't look as if you'd been crying. I don't want her to think I'm a bully. That's the last thing I am."

She—The Tired Beauty. It *was* disturbing, but not in the way he meant to imply. It was his heart that was disturbed, and his breath a little, as Amy went out, carrying the most gracious smile to this guest, and as he prepared an even sweeter one for her. Who was she ? Her black hair, strained down either side of a narrow, perfectly moulded face to the silken chignon at the nape, her extreme pallor, her large eyes fixed on him at lectern and in pulpit, her weary grace of movement —all these things had lodged their shafts in his heart these last few Sundays. And now she was come to him : she was at his door, and he was going to speak with her.

§

She came in, an expensive and scented zephyr preceding her, and Amy following behind with the words, " This is Mrs. Buxton, dear." Amy retreated and closed the door on them.

His smile, as he stepped forward into the fragrance, was more than welcoming : it seemed to lay a pastoral and affectionate hand upon her shoulder. " How do you do, Mrs. Buxton ? "

The white, hollowed face, between the tight-drawn hair,

11

went a little to one side with all of an actress's grace. " How
do you do ? " she echoed in a voice so level and low that
it reminded him of dusk on a summer night. It sorted well, this
low smooth voice, with the dark smoothness of her hair, the
emeralds in her ears, and the twilight blue of her eyes. These
eyes seemed to lie in a smoky haze beneath the pencilled brows
and the lids black-weighted with mascara. The only thing
that was perhaps a little out of key with all this low-toned
softness was the careful vermilion of her lips. Mrs. Buxton
must have laboured long upon her face this morning before
bringing it to him. He wondered whether, as a vicar, he ought
to approve of all this artistry ; as a man he had no doubt that
it was most effective and disturbing.

" Won't you sit down, Mrs. Buxton ? "

" Oh, thank you so much, but I mustn't keep you." She
dropped to the cushion of a chair with a movement so well
controlled, and yet so natural, that he guessed it had been
learned in a school of dramatic art. " It is so very kind of
you to see me. I'm sure you're terribly busy. It was Dr. Bettersby who suggested I might call. I already know one of
your clergy, you see : Dr. Bettersby, and what a brilliant man.
I'm sure his talk is an education in itself." Not striking sentences, not dramatic ones, not emotional ones ; but the slow,
deep, earnest voice in which she delivered them would have
served for Lady Constance in her grief for her child, or for
Lady Macbeth in her sleep.

" Yes, Bettersby is a good scholar. But what can I——?
No, first let me ask you a very impertinent question." Hands
thrust into his cincture, he smiled disarmingly. " May I ? "

" But of *course* ! The only exciting questions are impertinent
ones." And she folded her long, slender hands over her lap,
in readiness to answer it.

" I noticed you in church last Sunday, and I suspected you
were an actress. Did I guess right ? "

The smile about her lips was beautifully restrained. It was
only the hint of a smile since the high rule of art was to leave
the imagination of your audience room to play. " Why did
you think that ? "

" Because you know how to move. Not one woman in a
hundred knows how to move. Most of them cannot even walk ;
they waddle. You have learned dancing and miming, I think."

" How clever you are ! What an eye you have ! "

" I am right then ? You were an actress ? "

" Ages and ages and ages ago. But that's all over and done with. It's nearly twenty years since I was on the stage. I'm an old woman now."

" Oh, come, come ! That's ridiculous."

" But I *am* ! I am forty-six."

" And that I find very hard to believe."

" Nevertheless it is so. Most regrettably I married when I was twenty-nine, and that put an end to my career. My husband couldn't bear the thought of my going back to the stage."

" He—he is dead ? "

" Yes, he died nearly two years ago. He was more than twenty-five years older than me, you see, and he wore himself out making ever more and more money."

Like hawks that had slipped control the Vicar's thoughts flew to his church funds. And to his Easter offering. " He was a merchant, your husband ? "

" A manufacturer. Cosmetics. All the money he left me came out of the vanities of us women. You can make three and four and five hundred per cent. profit out of toilet preparations, if you pack them in nice enough boxes and call them silly enough names. ' Misty Rose Dust ', and ' Madonna Lily Milk ' and that kind of thing. So idiotic we women are ! "

But that, thought the Vicar, was not sufficient reason why the clergy should decline a portion of the three hundred per cent. profit. Such a thought was not for publication, so he continued, " Will you go back to the stage now ? "

" Oh no. There is no place for me now. I am forgotten. Completely forgotten."

" Surely not ? "

" But yes, my dear. I had some success in my day, but not enough to be remembered. I've acted in plays by Pinero and Sutro and Henry Arthur Jones. I knew Sir Arthur Pinero well."

" Indeed ? How very interesting ! And what was your stage name ? "

" Lilian Eadie—but you won't remember it."

The Vicar did not remember it, and so only nodded pleasantly and left her in hope. " Oh, yes ? "

" Lilian Eadie is naturally my maiden name, and that was really why I became an actress. What else could one do with a really delightful name like that ? I'm thinking of returning to it. One can't go on being called Mrs. Buxton. It sounds

so corpulent." She trilled a laugh like a roulade. " I hope if
we get to know each other you'll always call me Lilian Eadie."

" Lilian Eadie suits you splendidly. It has a slender and,
well, graceful sound, if I may say so. May I ask, have you
come to live here ? "

" Oh, dear me, no ! I live miles and miles and miles away
from here. In the tiniest little service flat high above the world
in Chelsea. Perhaps one day you and your wife, if you have
nothing better to do, will come and have a little dinner with me."

" But how comes it you—— ? "

" I know what you're going to say ! I was ever so lonely
up in my tiny flat so I went to church at Holy Trinity, Sloane
Street. You were preaching, and I was so impressed that I
came to your church to hear you again. It was the most
wonderful sermon I ever heard. It was one of the great experiences of my life."

The Vicar remembered the sermon. It was certainly a good
sermon because it was one he often preached in a strange
church, and he'd preached it so often now that he'd got it into
perfect shape, knew it by heart, and could deliver it with hardly
a glance at his notes. " Really? What could the sermon
have been ? "

" Oh, I don't remember exactly what it was about, but it
was an experience. And now I want to come to your church
always. That's not very wrong of me, very naughty, is it ? "

" Most assuredly not. You must go where you feel you get
the greatest help."

" Well there's no doubt about where that is. But, oh dear,
oh dear, I'm so afraid, so afraid ! "

" Afraid of what ? "

" So afraid we shall lose you soon."

" What do you mean ? " He frowned in mock anger. " I'm
going to live a long time yet."

" Oh, I didn't mean that ! You didn't really think I meant
that, did you ?—you who look so incredibly young. Oh, I'm
saying dreadful things ! I must go before I say something that
sounds even more silly. I just meant that they're sure to make
you a bishop."

" Oh no, dear lady ; no, no." He laughed at the absurd
idea. " That's the last thing I should expect. That's "—yes,
he said it before he could stop himself—" that's the last thing
I want."

" But you'll have to do it for the sake of the Church. Nobody with a power like yours should be less than a bishop."

Now, Canon Welcome, like most competent men, was as shrewd as need be, and knew that the people of the stage, young and old, caress you with exaggerated flatteries, first because they love you while they are talking to you, and want you to love them ; secondly because a sentence, when it is in the superlative mood, and simple and clean as an arrow, makes a better line to speak than one bedevilled with qualifications ; and thirdly because their traffic is not with reality but with something more beautiful, which it is their business to body forth in low, pregnant voices. All this he knew, but none the less found it very pleasant to be told that nobody with a power like his should be less than a bishop.

" No, my dear Mrs. Buxton—my dear Lilian Eadie," he protested, looking out of the window, as at the future with its flowers. " There are many far abler and far better men than I with a much greater right to be bishops." True, but he hoped she wouldn't believe it.

" I don't believe it," she asserted, curving one pencilled eyebrow upward in mischievous flattery. " That's just your modesty." He was relieved that she should think so. " But look at me chattering here when you're so terribly busy. I really came to ask if there was any work you could give me to do."

" I am sure there are many things we can ask you to do." And, as he said this, he wondered whether, with those cochineal lips and heavy, blacked eyelashes, he could introduce her to the Girls' Friendly Society or the Mothers' Union. Hardly. Perhaps the Finance Committee. " We will certainly find something for you to do. Perhaps you could visit for us."

" Oh, but don't send me into any dreadful part. Dr. Bettersby tells me that you've got some streets and alleys that are just *too* awful."

" That's right : some of the worst in London," said the Vicar proudly ; for he, too, was enough of an actor to crave, the clean, superlative line. " It's odd that a highly respectable parish like ours should include such a grim little cesspool as Friar's Circus and the streets around it. I always say that the very dregs and lees of humanity seem to have settled in a kind of sediment down there——"

" Oh, dear ! " exclaimed Mrs. Buxton, in a voice like the dusk of evening. " It sounds terrifying."

15

"Yes, I have everything in my parish from an earl to a pearly king, and dozens of old lags and one ex-murderer."

"Oh, please then, if I'm to visit, may it be the earl? I'm terrified of murderers."

"I'll discuss it with the other clergy——"

"Somebody else must convert the murderers. I'm sure you could do it if you tried. You could do anything."

"I'll discuss it this morning. We have a Staff Meeting in a few minutes."

"*Oh!*" She let forth a little stage scream. "I'm keeping you. I'm keeping you from frightfully important business. I ought to be *ashamed* of myself. You're wishing me at the other end of the world." She rose from the cushion of her arm-chair as silently and gracefully as a swan's neck from its place of rest between its wings. "I'll take myself off at once. How you must hate all pestering and talkative females!"

"Not at all, not at all."

"Oh but yes; we're the plague. Let me disappear at once. But first may I say this: your preaching is so wonderful, so marvellous, but—oh, it's dreadful of me to suggest it, but I do wish you had vestments and incense and all the tra-la-las." She swept a beautiful thin hand through the air, palm upward, as if that sufficiently explained the tra-la-las. "Besides, think of yourself in a cope. You'd look, if you'll forgive me, quite ravishing. And that nice Dr. Bettersby. And your beautiful young curate, Mr. Clay. Not that either of them have quite your *presence*—especially Dr. Bettersby; he's so like a dried, but nice, fig. Still, a cope covers everything. Every man looks a heavenly creature in a cope."

"There's nothing I should like better, my dear lady, but——"

"I knew you would! I knew it! You're an artist."

". . . but there are laymen in my congregation who wouldn't permit it at all. They'd depart."

"Ah yes, I know. One's public. One cannot lose one's dear public. But I'm still talking! I must go. Look, here is my card. Write and tell me what I can do. I'll do anything—anything except murderers."

"I shall not fail to write to you." And as a dentist escorts his patient, or a lawyer his client, he went with her to the front door and smiled and bowed till she was out of his garden.

Returning well-pleased with all that honeyed flattery, he saw the closed door of the dining-room and, knowing that Amy was behind it, remembered how tetchy and ruthless he'd been with her. He remembered the sudden damping of her eyes and a mountain of pity swelled up in him. " God, I hate myself ; I hate myself, sometimes. It's cruel, brutal. . . . She's good. Never a better wife. I'm irritable and selfish and rude. Roaring at her. Men are loathsome things. Oh, hell, hell . . ." which expletive was Christian in feeling if not in phrasing—though maybe the word was exact, if unselfishness and kindness are the kingdom of Heaven and selfishness and cruelty hell.

Obeying an impulse, he went into the room, saw her seated at the big dinner table over some tradesmen's bills and kissed her on her grey hair.

He did not enjoy the kiss but he pressed it down.

" Sorry if I was rude, Magpie." Such had been his pet-name for her ever since she'd been a slim dark girl in a black and white frock. " But I was most terribly busy at the time. You know what my mornings are."

" Oh, that was nothing." She smiled from behind the instant tears. " Nothing so long as you still love me a little. Sometimes I think I'm no more to you now than a convenient old housekeeper."

" Now don't be a silly old magpie. Who else should I love if not you ? I'm just a disgustingly irritable old man, and I think I get worse and worse as I get older. I'm hateful. Now I must go. I'm the beastliest of men."

He patted her fat shoulder and went. And he walked back into his study well pleased that he had given her a long kiss and a shoulder-pat. An appropriate line of poetry sprang into his mind—" Oh, that was right, lad, that was brave." And as he closed his door and returned to his table he thought, " I may not believe in all the dogmas, but I do most terribly believe in kindness and pity and unselfishness. I have the substance of the matter in me."

This was always his grain of comfort when he doubted whether a man who believed little of the Creed and less of the Thirty-Nine Articles should remain a vicar and a prebendary. A decent man is not happy when he drinks the cup of his own hypocrisy, and he makes haste to dilute it.

" Yes, I have the substance of the matter in me," he decided ; and went back to the letter from *Who's Who*.

17

CHAPTER TWO

Two men were coming up the hill towards the Vicarage ; both clergymen ; one middle-aged, the other just as young as an Anglican priest can be.

The middle-aged one was long and thin with keen, blue, blinking eyes, a large red, peeking nose which seemed frost-bitten even in this shining April sun, a long red chin to match the nose, and long, loose, stringy limbs. On his narrow frame and limbs hung a black suit of old-fashioned priestly cut, the jacket square at base and neck and the waistcoat buttoning right up to the clerical collar. He wore a black Homburg hat, and because his skull was as long and pointed as a Rugby football, the hat, a size too small and a thought too high, seemed to rest uneasily on this lofty crown, tilting forward over his brow and leaving his occiput to protrude behind.

He was talking much, and at speed, to his young companion as they trudged up the hill ; and his nose leaned forward, and the keen eyes blinked at pavement or gutter, as he scattered his words like seeds by the wayside. It was as if his hail of talk was addressed rather to the pavement than to his companion.

This middle-aged, peek-nosed, bright-eyed talker was Dr. Bettersby, and one may ask how it was that a man of his years, title, and scholarly attainments was no more than an assistant priest to Canon Welcome. The answer is that he was not a full-time curate but only an occasional helper. For fifteen years Principal of the Theological College, Leaminster, he had recently retired to the large house and garden on Hamden Hill which his wife had inherited, together with an adequate income, from her father, old Colonel Hanover. And since old Colonel Hanover, deeming it his duty to his men (as he regarded the rest of the parish) to attend the padre's church parade, had been a regular attendant at St. Boniface Martyr, often carrying a collection plate, it was natural that his successor in the old grey house, being a clergyman, should give some help to St. Boniface. Besides, parsons, even when they inherit a competence, do not easily abandon their rightful and prominent place up in a chancel or before an altar. Dr. Bettersby still indulged his habit of prominence by helping Canon Welcome on Sundays and feast days, and in times of national excitement or crisis. But most of his days he gave to his garden and he would tell you that, as an old Theological College Principal, he had followed with an admirable exactitude the example of Diocletian the Emperor who at the age of fifty-nine retired from the fruitless task of persecuting Christians, and took to growing cabbages instead.

The clerical dress of his young companion belonged as clearly to a new generation as Dr. Bettersby's to an old one. His big, broad, somewhat too plump body was vested in a suit of pale grey flannel, and the only clerical element was at the neck where a stiff white collar, buttoned at the back, and a black silk stock, contrasted with the light and sporting grey. With his round, boyish face shining above the black stock the Rev. Timothy Clay was as palpably an ordinary curate as Dr. Bettersby was an exceptional one.

And so they came up the hill, Dr. Bettersby talking to pavement, kerbstone and gutter ; Timothy listening.

" It is nonsense, my dear Timothy. I repeat for your instruction that it is nonsense. The Kingdom of God, we are rightly informed, is not of this world, and for that incontrovertible reason I am and always have been utterly sceptical of clerical sorties into the arena of politics. What has the Rural Dean of Hamden to do with a strike of half a million railwaymen ? Are they the least interested in what he has to say ? Is Euston waiting upon his word, or Grantham, or Crewe ? I trow not."

" I suppose he thinks that as rural dean——"

" But, my dear boy, what is a rural dean ? What at any time in the Church's history was the significance and importance of a rural dean ? It has been my wretched task for fifteen years to inoculate twenty centuries of church history into some hundreds of unhappy young men, and I do not recall that I have once had occasion to mention a rural dean. Our brother, with his invincible need to believe in his own importance, against all reality and common sense, interprets his rank and title with a seriousness and a self-satisfaction that are easier to understand than to underline. Were the scales to fall from his eyes as, thank God, they long ago fell from mine, he would perceive that in this present age all clergymen are faintly ridiculous, but there's something more than usually ridiculous in a rural dean. You with your young fresh eyes perceive that, surely ? "

" No, I'm afraid I hadn't thought of it, sir—no."

" Goodness gracious ! Is it possible ? But I suppose they dimmed your clear vision for ever in the chapel of your public school. That is practically all that the chapels of our public schools do achieve. It'll be years before you find yourself able to see clearly and without the refracting spectacles with which your chapel equipped you—if you ever are able so to do—which I trow not. And I beg of you not to keep on calling me ' sir '. It points too clearly to the fact that in your eyes I am already marching into decrepitude. I am not. I never felt better in my life. Certainly I can number some fifty-nine years of life, but that is merely an arithmetical measurement. In heart and spirit I am contemporary with you, and about twenty-four. ' Bettersby ', therefore, is all I seek from you."

" Very good, sir. I will remember."

" Ten o'clock. Our brother must be waiting for us. Well, if it pleases his boyish spirit to consider this a Council of War, let us not, who have been boys ourselves, deny him this small pleasure. But in all other respects, my dear Timothy, we shall be wasting our time. Here we are, two active young men, sentenced to a desolating hour in a room inaptly denominated a Study, while our brother holds forth on the Church's Witness in a time of civil strife. It will be the more desolating since he has no clear idea what the Church's Witness is, nor, if he had, would he desire it proclaimed with any disturbing clarity, and therefore his trumpet gives forth a most uncertain sound. I have never yet, at the close of one of our excellent brother's discourses, whether delivered in the pulpit or the study, risen from my seat without a measure of incertitude as to his meaning —an uncomfortable and headachy feeling which is only partly relieved by the thought that I can now go, and it is no longer necessary to wrestle with incoherence. You get my meaning, perhaps ? His only good sermons—I say it openly, since I will not speak other than the truth—are those that have been written by me ; by which I would have you understand those written by him after he's inveigled me into a discussion on the subject, so as to know what to say. That, I surmise, is why I have been bidden to this conference this morning."

" Oh, I think there's more to it than——"

" He would do better, my dear Timothy, not to suck my brains, or the brains of any other clear thinkers, in this fashion. Much better. He has, you see, the inestimable advantage over some of us in that his vague and ponderous generalities might mean any of six different things, and since there are at least six different points of view on any Anglican issue, he satisfies all of them. He will go far. I count a man greatly blessed in the Church of England if he is unencumbered by any dangerous lucidity. Let me give you, dear boy, a modicum of advice : avoid lucidity like the plague. It has been my undoing. It has cost me, I have no doubt, many a preferment, and the titles and temporalities attached thereto. The Bishop of Leaminster was good enough to say that my habit of expounding to young ordinands the harshness of reality with some point and sting was destructive of their idealism and enthusiasm. He called it cynical and suggested that it was ill-suited to tender young men in their twenties. Such is the episcopal view of education."

" But you *are* a cynic, aren't you, Dr. Bettersby ? "

" Drop the ' Doctor '. ' Bettersby ', plain ' Bettersby '. Am I a cynic ? Only if an urgent craving for clarity of vision, accuracy of thought, and precision of statement force me to say that I perceive neither pleasure nor sense in being summoned to the Vicarage this morning for what our brother is pleased to call, in a vein which he would have us think humorous, but which is really pompous, an ' extraordinary ' meeting. It is only extraordinary in the sense that he conceives it will have any value and bear fruit. Personally I have no objection to his spending his week-days in a merry-go-round of noisy and fatuous activities, and calling them pastoral work, so long as he doesn't want me to mount one of his horses. I can perceive, you see, that they are not living horses but only creatures of wood and gilt, and that they go round and round, and up and down, without arriving at any point except the place at which they started. An admirable metaphor, I think ? "

" Yes, but a little unfair. And, for you, a little imprecise."

" Imprecise ? Certainly not. Or hardly at all. Would you not say that for most of his time, and certainly in his discourses, he goes up and down and round about, making a merry din the while, but arriving in the end at nothing new ? Yes, surely you would ; you are an intelligent lad. Dear me ! This hill ! How do you like having to climb this abominable acclivity whenever you take a service or attend our brother's play-time—— ? "

" It doesn't trouble me, sir."

" I confess I look forward to his roundabouts this morning with something approaching physical anguish. I could with some satisfaction have rested this morning. Last night my wife and I took dinner with that excellent woman, Mrs. Buxton —have you met her yet ? She has only lately appeared in our congregation, but desires to become a pillar. She asked me how to become a pillar, and I told her to take her trouble to our brother who is surely a specialist on the subject. You should cultivate her. She has an exceedingly well-appointed little flat in Chelsea, high up above the sins and follies of this world, and she serves a meal that is eatable. Her wine will pass too—which is strange in a woman who alives alone, but I take it the late Mr. Buxton educated her. The port was particularly attractive. Clara and I spent a completely unwasted evening there. The Buxton and I sat side by side, and our talk, I think I may say, was good. She ended by asking me to call her Lilian Eadie. Like her wine, our talk had body and bouquet. At times it was a dry wine, and at times sparkling."

" Really ? What was it about ? "

" Mainly about persons, my dear boy, and not, alas ! very charitable. No, I fear I must admit that it was more accurate than flattering. There was a certain lack of warm humanity in my comments on our brother but a beautiful precision of statement. Still, what would you ? Among intelligent people the truth is the only acceptable currency. And surely religion and the naked truth must be able to dwell together, whatever the dear Bishop of Leaminster may say. Like righteousness and peace they should kiss one another."

" Yes, yes," laughed Timothy, " but in that particular psalm it was *mercy* and truth that met together."

" An excellent retort, my dear lad. Quick and to the point. Yes, we must be more merciful. Mrs. Buxton and I were a little wanting in that beautiful quality last night. I regret it. ' I will have mercy and not sacrifice '—alas, alas ! we indulged in sacrifice rather than mercy. Here we are : ' The Wisdom of this World is Foolishness with God.' An excellent talk, my dear boy. I enjoyed every moment of it. For once I was only conscious at intervals of the steepness of this interminable hill. Now let us go in, like good Christians, to the martyrdom."

"Come in, Betts, old boy. Come along, son Timothy." Canon Welcome, standing before the fireplace, hands at rest between cincture and cassock greeted his clergy with genial smiles and genuine pleasure : he liked to love all his fellow men, except the few with whom he had quarrelled. "Sit down, both you lads, for a moment. That's right, Betts, take your usual chair. I have a surprise for you. You will meet our new brother this morning. I have asked him to come so that we can all get to know him."

"Who is he?" asked Bettersby, leaning his long frame far back in his low chair. "This is important. This is serious. What, pray, are you loosing among us?"

"He's a man called Baynes. Peter Baynes. He has not yet come into residence, of course, but he has found somewhere to live—and where do you think it is?"

"Within the bounds of the parish, I trust?"

"Most certainly within the bounds of the parish. Most emphatically so." And he twinkled at them, as one who is hiding a mystery.

"Well, where? Is it somewhere remarkable?"

"You may think so."

"Then tell us, please."

"In Maker Street."

"*Maker Street?*"

"Even so."

"Good heavens! Good gracious me!"

"Yes, in Maker Street, within a stone's throw of the Circus and the Corners."

"But why? Why this heroism? Maker Street is about the fourth worst street in the parish. He will be murdered in his bed, I take it."

Canon Welcome drew his hands from behind the cincture, and in one movement spread them apart and shrugged his shoulders. "He says that if he's going to work among the bad lads of that district he'd better live among them. He's lodging in a perfectly respectable house, with a Mrs. Anscombe, the relict of a brewer's labourer."

"Ah, well, it's good to be young and brave."

" Young ! My dear Betts, he's not young. He's exactly the same age as I am." Canon Welcome turned to Timothy. " Sorry, Tim, old boy, not to be able to provide a young companion for you, but both the Bishop and I think it best to have an older man in charge of a mission church."

" I quite see that, Vicar," said Tim, though in truth he was wondering why a young man couldn't do as well down there as some old buffer of fifty. " I quite see. Naturally."

" But how comes it," asked Bettersby, " that at fifty he has no cure of his own ? "

" Because, my dear Betts, he's only been about five years in Orders. He's only served in one curacy before this : St. Edmund's, Highbury."

" Not ordained till forty-five ? What was he before he took Orders ? "

" Well "—the Vicar coughed, to clear his throat and open a passage for strange news and to gain a few seconds while he summoned the strength to utter it—" he was the manager of a small boot shop."

" Oh ! " The doctor's dismay escaped from him before he could arrest it.

" Yes." And quickly, like one who, unloading dubious goods, thinks it best to unload the lot at once and give the recipients one shock instead of many, the Vicar added, " A boot shop in Hackney."

Dr. Bettersby bowed as though no information could be less unexpected. " Hackney. Then he is not, I take it, a man with a degree ? "

" No, Betts."

" Not a university man ? "

" No. Frentham Theological College."

Dr. Bettersby nodded again, lips compressed ; and there was silence in the study like the silence in Heaven when the seventh seal was opened. Nobody said aloud, " Then, what with the boot shop and the Theological College, our new brother is not a Gentleman ", such measurements being no longer in fashion, but the thought was in the minds of all three. The Vicar, thinking that the silence had persisted long enough, expressed the thoughts of them all in publishable terms. " Yes, his origins are humble, but that may be a help to him rather than a hindrance in a mission district like Little Bread Street. He did good work among the poor at St. Edmund's, according

24

to Platt-Brown, his vicar ; and the Bishop thinks it's time he had a small charge of his own."

" But there are others besides the poor in the Little Bread Street area," said Bettersby grimly. " Don't forget there's such a place as our Circus."

" Yes, he's got the Circus and the Corners, and we'll see what he can do with them."

" God help him."

" God help him, certainly. I like him. I like him immensely. An excellent fellow. Well, gentlemen, I think it's not necessary to wait for him. Shall we . . . ? "

And the others, knowing what these two syllables meant, promptly rose.

Canon Welcome interlaced his fingers before his breast and bent his head. " O God, forasmuch as without Thee we are not able to please thee, mercifully grant that thy Holy Spirit may in all things direct and rule our hearts. Now lie back in your chair, Betts, old man ; and put on your disgusting pipe if you want to, Timmy. I'll stand here. Well, gentlemen, as you know, there's a very special subject I want to discuss with you today. Apart from that there's only the preaching to be considered. I will preach on Sunday morning ; and you, son Tim, in the evening."

Tim gulped. But he managed to say, " Yes, Vicar," before swallowing and moistening his lips. And he thanked Heaven that the eyes of the others could not pierce beneath his black stock and see the speedy pulsing of his heart. The Vicar's words had sentenced him to a torture of stage-nerves from Saturday next to Sunday evening, twenty-four hours of gulping swallowing, sighing, and hapless abstraction from the world. Still, there were six more days before this tribulation need begin ; six days before he must lie upon the rack. " Very good, Vicar."

The Vicar, however, had perceived the symptoms, for he himself, even after twenty-seven years of preaching, could still feel his heart sickening, his mouth souring, and his bowels coming loose before an important cathedral sermon or after-dinner speech. And because he liked his young curate, and because his stores of pity were tapped, he offered him warm words of encouragement. " I'm sure you'll be very eloquent. You always are. His sermons are much appreciated, aren't they, Betts ? "

" I'm afraid I have but seldom sat under him, Vicar."

" That's your loss then. He's going to make a fine preacher, our Tim. Now, this strike. It's a very serious business. Very serious indeed. And the question is, what is the Church going to do about it."

" Yes, what ? " said Bettersby.

" I feel we must clearly do something. The Church cannot keep silent at a time like this. There are immense moral issues involved."

" Such as ? "

" Well, such as . . ." but the Vicar could not, at such abrupt notice, think what they were, and he tried to remember the *Times* leader of that morning. " Such as the duty of the railwaymen to the community, to their brothers and sisters——"

" And the duty of the community to its railwaymen ? "

" Oh, certainly. Most certainly." The phrase sounded unexceptionable. " But the men cannot be allowed to hold the community to ransom——"

" In other words, they may not use the strike weapon ? "

" Oh no, I wouldn't say that. I didn't say that." He began to feel exasperated at this arguing with him, this forcing of him to give substance and strong outline to something that he'd rather leave shadowy and gaseous. " But the men behind this strike really cannot be allowed to capture control of the country's government. They cannot be allowed to shift the centre of gravity from Parliament to the headquarters of the great trade unions. That's what I contend they are trying to do." The *Times* leader was coming back to him in full power. " And that, as I see it, is the end of representative government. It is to undo in a moment what our people have taken a thousand years to build. I must say I feel very strongly about it. Very strongly indeed. I feel it's the manifest duty of every right-minded citizen at a time like this to exert himself with the object of keeping the public mind firm and steady——"

" But firm and steady in what ? "

" In what ? Oh—well—in—in support, I suppose, of the government and representative institutions. Yes. I must say I feel very strongly that we all have a duty. I think you, Tim, should be in the Citizen Guard, which I see they are forming in case of trouble. I think our younger clergy should set the example to other young men."

Tim, a generation younger than his vicar, was not so sure

26

that he was on the side of the Government, but he didn't say so. He just nodded and grinned sheepishly and non-committally.

"And for us older clergy," continued the Vicar, now walking from the fireplace and looking out of the window at the flowers because he was annoyed with Bettersby and didn't want to look at him, "I feel it's incumbent on us to proclaim with no uncertain voice the Church's Witness in the matter. I feel it most strongly, Bettersby, whatever you may feel about it. Who was it—Jeremy Taylor—who said we must preach to the times?"

"Preach to the what?"

"To the times."

"Oh, I see. Oh, well, as long as it's not to the *Times*——"

"*Tst, tst!*" Canon Welcome was not at all patient with this laboured and unnecessary joke; it carried a faint suggestion that Bettersby thought him self-important and silly; and he announced rather acidly, keeping his eyes away from the scoffer, "To the times, I said. And I do not see, I confess I do not see, how it is possible for me to avoid a public expression of my mind. I feel I ought to speak on an issue which in my view raises the whole question of moral obligation in public affairs. I feel it most strongly. Yes. I feel it my duty." So he repeated because he was longing to do this duty. "I don't know what my business is if it's not to uphold the supremacy of moral principles. *You* think I ought to say something about the Crisis on Sunday, don't you, Tim?"

"Yes . . . oh, yes . . . surely . . . say something. . . ."

"It's not as if I made a habit of venturing into politics. That I should deplore." Liking, and even loving, his young curate, he had to defend himself before him lest Bettersby's disappointing and hurtful cynicism should have shaken the lad's faith in his vicar. "As a rule I dislike and avoid allusion to events whose only proper discussion is on the platform or in the press. In ninety-nine out of a hundred sermons I limit myself to the fundamental articles of our faith. Controversial in some measure a fearless exposition of our faith is bound to be, but I don't think anybody could accuse me of being gratuitously or offensively controversial. It's only in an hour as grave as this—as *exceedingly* grave, I think I may say—that I—oh, surely, Bettersby, it can't be your view that there's nothing we can do. *Nothing?*"

"We can do many things, but whether they will achieve anything I doubt. The time has passed when people took religion seriously and burnt each other. A pity, but so it is."

The bell rang very distinctly. It was followed by a sharp knock on the front door.

" Ah, that must be our new brother," said the Vicar, glad to swing back from umbrage to *bonhomie* ; but he added a trifle apprehensively, " I—er—I must warn you boys that he's no—no Apollo."

The maid opened the room door. " Mr. Baynes, sir."

" Ah, Baynes, come in, my boy. Come in and meet Bettersby, my very good colleague ; and Timothy, my young son in the faith."

The new curate came in. He came somewhat diffidently, looking round upon them all, as if this encounter, or any encounter, shivered his shyness. Bettersby muttered to himself, " Holy Saints ! " and, catching Tim's eyes, provided for him a despairing lift of eyebrows and shoulders, and a despairing spread of his hands. He was trying to remember an apt quotation which was hammering at the door of his mind ; and suddenly he possessed it. It was " In did come the strangest figure."

About as tall as the Vicar, Baynes was coarsely and heavily built, his body the shape of a hogshead, broader round buttocks and belly than round shoulders and thighs. The thighs, however, were thick—thick enough to cause a slight waddle in his gait, after the fashion of Dr. Johnson. On this clumsy figure his dark suit hung baggily. The clerical stock sprang from his waistcoat at its junction with the clerical collar, and his pale grey socks displayed their crumples between the turn-ups of his trousers and the tops of his shoes. The shoes themselves were square, cheap, and trodden down, and Dr. Bettersby's eyes dropped to them with the obvious thought, " Surely the ex-manager of a bootshop could manage something better than that."

Timothy was hard put to it to keep a laugh behind his lips and his nose.

The face matched this barrel-shaped body in so far as it was broader across the cheeks than across the brow. The nose was a remarkable feature ; it was, the doctor said afterwards to his wife, a preposterous feature : an acute angle stretching from the face upwards and sideways. The grey eyes on either side of it were apologetic and sad, as if ashamed of it for a neighbour.

28

Canon Welcome beamed upon everybody. Sensitive to the general disappointment and therefore somewhat ashamed of his production, he tried to jolly things up a bit. "Yes, that's our Tim, Baynes. The Baby of the Chapter. You'll like him; he's a good lad and keeps us all young. Find a chair, old boy. I've been telling them about your 'prophet's chamber' in Maker Street."

"Oh, yes?" Baynes sat on a stiff chair, splaying fat, coarse fingers like two white starfish on his knees. Apparently he could think of nothing else to say, but as all waited, he added, "It's nice and close to the Little Bread Street Chapel."

"Which room is it?" asked Bettersby. "I know those old houses in Maker Street."

"It's the front room on the ground floor. Mrs. Anscombe has only two rooms altogether."

"Ground floor front! And flush with the pavement! Merciful heavens, you'll be burgled for a certainty. They're experts at parlour-jumping down that way. Get the back room my boy; get the back room. Or else lock up your treasures."

"I have no treasures," said Baynes, and for the first time a shy, tolerant smile, as of one who likes to be laughed at, lit up his face. That shy, awkward smile showed his extreme unease among these three gentlemen. They had Oxford and Cambridge degrees, and the thin one with the long, blue nose was a great scholar and doctor of divinity.

"You'll probably be murdered," said Bettersby, considering the question further in the comfortable depths of his chair. "Yes, that's what I think it'll be. The last two priests who went to live there were coshed on the head as they walked home, and died in some pain."

"Oh, really, Betts!" protested the Vicar.

"Well, perhaps that's an exaggeration, but keep clear of Hay Street, Baynes, and of Gravel Lane. The Bad Lads there pride themselves on having a short way with coppers and parsons."

"They're not all bad," said Baynes.

"They're certainly not," corroborated the Vicar. "The Circus area may have plenty of riotous elements, but more than half the residents are peaceful and good."

"I meant the Bad Lads were not all bad," corrected Baynes. "I rather like them."

"Oh, well, then. . . ." Bettersby could only accept this statement as one would accept the assurance of a man that he enjoyed a cup of weed-killer. "Oh, well. The Lord watch over you."

"Yes, and keep you away from any terror that walketh in darkness," beamed the Vicar, "and from the arrow that flieth by day. Now let's get to business. This is splendid. It is splendid, Baynes being able to join us this morning. We were discussing what, as Christian leaders, we can do about the strike, Baynes. Betts is of the opinion that we can do nothing. Our Timothy with engaging modesty has so far offered us no counsel, but I have most strongly, most emphatically, expressed the view that we . . . that we ought to do something. You agree, I expect, Baynes ? "

Baynes nodded once, but said nothing.

"Of course. I knew you would. Betts, do you think we could announce a Service for Strikers ? "

"A what ? " Bettersby looked extremely doubtful.

"A special service for the men and their families."

"You could *announce* it, of course."

"You mean no one would come."

"I wish I didn't mean that, Vicar, but I do. It seems to me that to think anything else would be pleasant but deficient in any perception of the realities."

"Well, how about a service in the street ? Near the gates of the depôt. If the men won't come to the church, shouldn't the church come to them ? " As this sounded well, he turned to the silent Baynes. "Don't you think so, Baynes ? "

Baynes accorded this a brief, truncated nod, but said nothing. And he continued to sit there very erect, hands on knees, not unlike a Buddha in the depths of divine contemplation.

"You'll get a few people at an open-air service," said Bettersby, "but it won't be the railwaymen. It'll be a few idlers, a handful of grinning and rude young men, one or two gaping women, and a supply of children, constantly changing. Probably on roller skates."

"You think so ? "

"Alas, I'm sure of it. Quite frankly I state my view that a service at the depôt would only advertise our weakness."

As the Vicar felt there was truth in this, he only pressed his lips together in thought and nodded several times.

And Bettersby went on : " I should say the only thing you can do is this. Preach in the church on Sunday morning, taking the strike as your subject and advertise the fact wherever you

30

can—in the streets and wherever else it is the habit of idle rail-waymen to swarm. Then you will at least have the usual con-gregation."

The words " advertise it wherever you can " had given the Vicar an immediate pleasure. He saw in a vision the double-crown posters with his name in heavy type : CANON HUM-BERT WELCOME. He saw the same advertisement in the local papers and, possibly, in the *Church Times*. " You think so ? And advertise it widely ? Yes, perhaps that's the only way. In addition to bill-posting you, Tim, could organize your scouts to deliver flimsies from house to house. I might even arrange for sandwichmen to parade before the pickets and the loafers at the depôt. Yes, I will certainly do that. I hate all this publicity, but in this noisy age we have to fight the world with its own weapons. But wait." He turned again to Bettersby, the father of the idea. " Aren't men of that sort more likely to come in the evening ? "

" It's so unusual for them to come at all that I should say that, being out of work, they're more likely to come in the morning than the evening."

" Yes, there's something in that. There's certainly some-thing in that," said the Vicar, who wanted to preach this topical and striking sermon before his more influential morning con-gregation. " Very good then ; that is settled. I preach, and we all do our best to bring the service to the notice of the strikers." Seeing that Baynes still sat like a stranger among brethren, Canon Welcome, always good-hearted and compassionate, turned to him. " What do you think, Baynes ? You have great experience of the poor. Are we on the right lines ? "

Baynes seemed to come out of a dream. He blinked several times at the Vicar, then smiled and lifted his heavy shoulders, as one who hardly liked to advise his seniors. He raised one starfish hand, scratched his head with a half-smile and dropped the hand back to his knee.

" Come, don't be afraid to tell us, Baynes. We're only learners like you. What do *you* think ? "

" I'm sure you're right up to a point, Vicar. We must pro-claim what we believe in, but as a rule the results of any sermon are so transitory. My experience is they last about an hour—"

" Couldn't agree more," put in Bettersby, nodding enthu-siastically at the carpet. " My sole criticism would be that your estimate is a shade on the generous side."

31

" —and all the real work has to be done after."

" Yes, of course," agreed the Vicar. " Of course. What do you mean ? "

" I mean that after preaching there's nothing to do but try and establish cells of real Christians who will infect the rest."

" Cells ? "

" Yes, people who will go out and live the life among them."

" Oh, quite ! Oh, absolutely ! Oh, yes, beyond question ! Of course, of course. But you agree we must proclaim it first ? "

" Naturally."

" That's what I'm saying. Good. That's fine. And that's all, I think, we can discuss at the moment," said the Vicar, knowing that he could proclaim the life eloquently, but anxious to escape from this dangerous talk of living it. " All right, then boys, that's settled. A difficult and rather unwelcome task, but I'll do my best. All that I ask of you now is your prayers—*and*, of course, that you do everything possible to bring the sermon— or rather, the service, to the notice of everybody."

CHAPTER THREE

WEDNESDAY broke bright with promise. The posters would be up on hoardings and boards, and the sandwichmen in the streets. Since the staff meeting he had put in much careful creative work on the advertising of the sermon because, when an artist is pleased with an imagined picture, it is not a task but a need to create it. He had designed the advertisement himself, throwing all the weight upon the name, CANON HUMBERT WEL-COME ; he had run with the design to the printers and to the office of the *Hamden and Hebron News*, and there spent a good measure of parish funds upon it ; he had hurried on to the bill-posting agency and there arranged that a powerful flow of posters should be directed towards the Fields and a patrol of sandwichmen should walk the gutters around the railway depôt like Joshua's trumpeters encompassing the walls of Jericho.

This large advertising in Hebron Fields was less, perhaps, to please his pride than to ease his conscience. Visiting in his parish was not an activity in which he delighted at all, and if he did suddenly feel the need to make a show of pastoral visiting, it was not to the Fields, and certainly not to the Circus and the Corners, that he would address his steps. And this not because he was afraid of any hooligans, gangsters, or shrill-voiced beldames but because, while full of hearty affection for people who would come to him, he had not that urgent love of souls which would drive him into dismal and depressing byways to look for them. To paste posters about the streets, to have hand-bills thrust under doors, and to pay for a curate in the Little Bread Street chapel lessened his guilty sense of having neglected this difficult and (in one part) dire region. Posters, handbills, and Baynes were his substitute for visiting.

His breakfast coffee was hardly cold in his mouth on this happy Wednesday before he had slung his priest's cloak over his cassock and gone hatless into the morning. At the door he had called to Amy, " I must go visiting. I have a lot of visiting to do today " ; which was exactly true, but it was the shop-windows and the hoardings he was going to visit, not the people. In a sense he was going to visit himself up there in big type on the bills.

The priest's cloak was a picturesque garment, of almost

33

circular cut, which fell to ankle length and was fastened at the breast with a chain and clasp. He was well aware that it hung with grace and a charm of contrast beneath his round friendly face and his silver hair. Therefore no hat. It always pleased him that as a priest he was able to wear this distinguishing, arresting, and (to state it frankly) theatrical garment without being accused of a vulgar exhibitionism. But since the April day was bright and warm, and the cloak accordingly was little necessary we for our part may discern a kinship between it and the double-crown posters ; they both advertised the Vicar to the streets. In this distinguishing cloak he was, we may say, his own sandwichman.

Going down the hill and into the littered streets of the Fields, he came first upon the railway depôt. It was silent. That which as a rule was a lake of many noises was now a lake of silence. Its gates were shut as in a lock-out, and idle men stood about them on the cobbled carriageways, their lips almost as grim and silent as those locked doors. Under the sky there was no sighing, whistling, or clangour of engines as they sauntered towards the Terminus ; in the sheds no hissing of stabled monsters full of steam ; and in the machine shops no whirring of wheels, slapping of belts, or shouts of foremen and chargehands. No smoke leaped in low, coughed clouds from standing funnels or streamed into the air from the high chimneys. The coal-hoppers, the ash-plants and the water columns stood as lonely and silent as idols in a desert. It was as if an evil fairy had put everything to sleep within its walls, or the blight of War had passed over it.

Further on, the iron viaducts, three or five abreast, slanted over the streets, darkening the white-tiled passages beneath them, and they too were silent. No trains, passenger or goods, rumbled, drummed or thundered over them ; the signals on their gantries, set at *Stop*, were lifeless and still. This deep silence of the railroads was a clean thing, and the streets, as if adapting themselves to it, were strangely clean too. For days no smuts had fallen from hurrying and snorting funnels to soil the pavements and blend with the April rains into a black, greasy film.

Once beyond the arches he was well within the Fields. And how different were these crowded streets from the quiet and empty hillside road in which his vicarage stood among its cluster of trees ! Here, on on every length of pavement, were swarming children, wrangling mothers, thronging shoppers, idling men, groups of shawled and gossiping women, innumerable small boys whose chief occupation, it seemed, was to ask you the time as

34

you passed, and, ever and again, some new, curried smell. Some
of the women's faces above the shawls or the cheap coats were
dark and Jewish, for his segment of the Fields included a fringe
of London's north-eastern ghetto. On many a bill-posting site
he saw his name, CANON HUMBERT WELCOME, shouting
at the people, but none of them, neither loafing men, nor chattering women nor happy children, turned an eye towards it.
They did, however, look at him, as at something unfamiliar,
when he passed by in his cassock, cloak, and silver hair.

It was disappointing, but in Graeme Street he saw approaching
him an ample and leisurely figure which lit up a whole chain of
hopes in his heart. With coat thrown open, hat pushed back,
hands in pockets, stomach protruding, and eyes turning left and
right to absorb the scene, it was clearly the easy, careless, corpulent
figure of Norman Leeds, editor of the *Hamden and Hebron News*.

" Aha, Norman ! " he greeted him. " What are you doing
down here in my parts ? Seeking copy ? Doing an article on
the Strike ? "

" That's just about it, Mr. Welcome. Seeking inspiration for
a leader on Friday."

" Then we're a pair. I'm visiting, of course—this is my
parish—but at the same time I'm trying to get this strike into
some sort of perspective. I publish *my* leading article in my
pulpit on Sunday morning. Perhaps you saw that I've put an
advertisement of it in the *News* ? "

" No, I'm afraid I didn't see that. Oh, you're going to
preach on the Strike, are you ? "

Then neither had he noticed the posters in the streets. Disappointing . . . very.

" I certainly am. I think I ought to, don't you ? In an hour
like this the Church should issue a Call to the Nation, I feel ; it
should proclaim its Witness—don't you agree ? "

" I agree completely, if it's going to proclaim the wickedness
of a few men trying to strangle a whole nation."

" Oh, I shall speak frankly. I was wondering if—"

" Give it 'em hot, I should."

" Oh, I shan't mince matters, I promise you." Very important to stand well with an editor. " If one's going to preach
at all, I think one should preach with the gloves off. I was
wondering if——"

" Let 'em have it hot and strong."

" Yes, yes. I feel very strongly with you that—er—that. . . ."

" That what ? . . . Give it 'em where it hurts."

" That this sort of thing can't go on. And I was wondering if you'd care to put in a note about this service on Sunday. I wouldn't suggest taking up your valuable space with anything about my humble self if I didn't think this was a matter of some topical interest. I remember you once asked me to tell you if I was having a service which was in any way ' news '."

" My dear chap, I'll certainly give it a puff if you want me to."

" I didn't quite mean that. Not a ' puff ' exactly. I never want to be ' puffed '—exactly. Actually I hate all this publicity-seeking—I recoil from it—but what else can one do in this screaming world ? Just a note, I thought."

" I'll not only put a note in about it, if you're going to tell these blighters where to get off, but, what's more, if you'll send the manuscript along, I'll print just as much of it as I can."

" I'm afraid I don't preach from a manuscript. Or only very rarely."

" O.K., then I'll send a reporter." (The Vicar hid his delight.) " I'm only too glad to, if you're going to let 'em have it. My leader unfortunately has to be more or less impartial—the owners insist on it—so if I can get the proper stuff in under cover of ' news ', why, that suits me ; that's just fine."

" I'm certainly going to speak my mind. No doubt about that."

" O.K., Mr. Welcome. And I'll feature it. I'll make a story of it, never you fear."

§

Canon Welcome's heart was high as he walked on. Perhaps the sermon was going to be a sensation. Perhaps it would even appear as a " story " in the London press. Only, if the editor's attitude was so hostile to the men, he'd have to attack them rather more strongly than he'd intended. One mustn't antagonise the press ; it had too much power.

The streets of his parish were many, and he walked on and on among them in a secret and rather guilty search for more and more glimpses of his name in heavy letters : CANON HUMBERT WELCOME. You might have supposed that, having seen one of the posters, he would be content ; but it was not so. The sight of one was so palatable a sweetmeat that, like a child, he must take another and another from the box till it was empty. And so on and on he went, in this unvisited part of his parish, with its tall Model Homes, and small loaded shops, its Trust

Buildings, Public Baths, common lodging houses, and great grinding and belling factories. And his feet brought him inevitably to that nodal centre which was the Circus, where seven of his streets met and kissed.

Did he imagine it, or did these streets really take on a furtive look, and sometimes a sullen look, as they got nearer to the seven Corners ? Were these dubious and ill-omened qualities only in the eye of the beholder who'd heard dark stories about these taverns and ancient houses ? Or did, perhaps, the furtiveness that was in him this morning, as he pursued his private and stealthy round, detect a kindred guilt behind the walls and the doors, even as deep answers to deep ? Certainly there were many young loafers here, propping up the house-walls with their cigarettes dangling from loose lips, but they were not necessarily the Wide Boys, too wide to work. They might be tube-cleaners, steam-raisers, or smiths' apprentices from the sheds and shops of the deserted depôt ; for, all said and done, there were as many honest as dishonest people in the Circus area, and their lads, while no better than the rest of us, were perhaps no wider. Dressy young girls pattered along on their high heels ; women's eyes followed him from doorways and windows, and many of them were dark Jewish eyes ; here two hurrying and laughing men spat upon a series of silver coins before dropping them into their pockets—customers, doubtless, just come from a street-bookie's stand ; and here at the crossways an urchin stood alone and watched three streets—probably a " corner man " on the look-out for cops and earning a shilling an hour from some gamblers huddled about a doorstep or in a tenement entry. But all these things could be seen anywhere in the Fields. Why should they look more sinful here ?

He was coming down Maker Street now ; and he passed the front window which would soon be Baynes's. Yes, easy to parlour-jump that window, stepping through it empty-handed and coming out again with trophies. It was a street of oddly mixed houses. After Baynes's small Victorian row there was a high tenement block called New Victoria Buildings, and then a terrace of narrow old Georgian houses that had lived a long two hundred years. Dignified and comfortable once, they were now given over to the poor ; children ran over them like maggots. He thought, as he walked by, of the griefs and gaieties, the ecstasies and terrors, which they had quartered in their long two hundred years. No. 17, as was well-known, was now a ' case ' or brothel and, fascinated by this knowledge, he glanced at its upper windows quickly and stealthily. And the thought came to him that the walls of those bed-chambers, which now harboured a nightly-changing traffic, must often in the centuries have been the last thing seen by dying eyes.

The posters were few in this part ; was it that the bill-stickers, after studying their religious contents, decided that they'd be wasted here ? Hardly one could he find. Still, he was well pleased with the display in the Fields as a whole and, even though he'd not seen a single person stop and read one he indulged himself with pretty pictures of a packed congregation on Sunday. And so, with his *amour propre* and his ambition comfortably anointed, he turned home again. He climbed towards the Vicarage by Northwood Hill, a steep incline with grey stucco houses on either side and a dim, inky road between.

§

Every morning he gave some time to the sermon. His mornings were free because he delegated to his curates all weekday services such as Matins and Litany, all urgent visiting, and all the unimportant weddings and funerals. As the G.O.C., he would say, he was almost entirely confined to Headquarters ; most unfortunately he had little time to accompany his subalterns into the Front Line. A vicar and rural dean had an immense amount of correspondence to attend to, and always a variety of addresses to prepare. So too in the afternoons : there was always a multitude of small activities to be discharged, not strictly ecclesiastical perhaps, but expected of a vicar or rural dean. This committee and that committee claimed him, this board and that council. It was sad, he would say, but his position involved, among other sacrifices, this surrender to secular and often trivial tasks ; but at least it meant that he left weekday parochial work in full control of his curates (and here he laughed generously) to the great advantage of the parish.

Committees and boards, he had long discovered, were the pleasantest ways of appearing to work ; and especially so if you were chairman, for then in your high place you enjoyed the feeling of authority, the interchange of gossip and laughter and jokes, and a sense of directing affairs ; and people witnessed you at work, or read about your activity in the morning, and so were able to believe you when you deplored your scant opportunities for parochial tasks.

Every morning, then, and an occasional hour in an afternoon, he was able to play with the sermon, altering it, touching it up, and polishing it ; and by Saturday it was in fine, exciting shape. But now a nervousness had begun to play a rataplan with his heart and an unpleasant game of inflation and deflation in his stomach and bowels. Such a nervousness only visited him when, the sermon or speech being important, he had written it all down and would have to act it if it were to appear extempore. And he clung to his reputation as a preacher who " hardly ever looked at a note ". This sermon had acquired the necessary importance because of those posters, and because of the big congregation which he was hoping might be there, and dreading might be there, and because of that reporter, and because Mrs. Buxton had said that his sermons were the great experience of her life.

He'd had to learn it by heart, and, when he learned a long address by heart, he walked always with the fear that his memory might suddenly fail him, his place in the manuscript be lost, a perspiration cloud his spectacles so that he couldn't read the manuscript even if he could find the place, and that thus he would go down in shame before the people without spar or rope to save him. The dozen hours before such a performance were a wrestle between his eagerness for the self-display and his fear lest a disaster earned for him nothing but pity.

But it was never very serious, this nervousness, nowadays : just an occasional gulp, a speeding of the heart, a failure of appetite, a little belch behind the hand, an inability to keep his thoughts on a book, and an increasing desire not to talk to Amy. He had been preaching too many years for these vigil nerves to be comparable with what poor young Timothy, not so many yards away, was certainly suffering now.

And this evening as he stood alone in his study, unwilling to read and waiting for the morrow, he had a moment of clear vision. Standing quite still behind his closed door, he saw that if only he loved his Master and His message more than himself he'd have no fears at all because his own glory would matter nothing ; but all his life, instead of losing himself in his subject, he had lost his subject in himself ; becoming, as it were, a producer who must project himself—his appearance, voice, and eloquence —before the people. Perceiving this so clearly, he felt sad and wished that he was a good man, a true priest, a simple saint, after the pattern he could see. He went to the window, where the blind was up, and gazed into the darkness sadly.

CHAPTER FOUR

Now it was Sunday and half-past ten by his study clock : he could justly cross the garden to the church. Always when nervous he set forth too early for the place where he must perform. With the sermon in his pocket, and one slight regurgitation, he evaded the eyes of Amy and slipped from the house. The church bell was ringing, but there was no one as yet in choir vestry or clergy vestry. So since there was no one to see him, he peeped from the clergy vestry door into the church. What he saw disappointed him. No great congregation assembling ; only a few faithful women in their usual places. Still, it was early yet . . . very early.

Back in the vestry he put on his fine cambric surplice, smocked and full in the folds, and going to the wall-mirror, squared the yoke on his shoulders, combed his silver hair, forced up the silver wings over the ears—and stopped as Timothy came in.

Timothy, though tall and broad as a Rugby forward, was white in the face, restless in his limbs, and uneasy with his breathing. His agony was upon him. He would know no release till about seven o'clock this evening, when his sermon would have been delivered without a catastrophe and the congregation would have risen for the last hymn. Then he would be as a boy let loose from school into the fields ; he would sing the last hymn with lustihood and fervour, praising the Lord, whether consciously or not, for the return of peace and the end of pain. Then would the lame man leap as an hart, and the tongue of the dumb sing.

The sight of Tim's nervousness strengthened the Vicar, because he felt proud that, even if he were a little anxious, he had long been superior to such suffering as this.

" 'Morning, Tim." He greeted him in cheeriest voice, partly to show how completely devoid of nerves he was, though about to preach, but even more because he longed to comfort and help the boy. " How's our Tim ? "

" Fine," said Tim, and a gulp caught even this monosyllable and tripped it up.

" Got a nice discourse for us this evening ? "

" Hope it's going to "—here he controlled a slight inflation—
" hope it's going to be all right."

" Sure to be." Canon Welcome laid an affectionate hand
upon his back and patted it. " You're going to be wonderful.
Don't you worry."

" I'm not worrying," said Tim, lying bravely.

" No. Well, there's no need to. They all like you immensely
and appreciate your sermons. They tell me so. You're going
to make a fine preacher one day, and that's not just blarney.
I mean it. I said so to the Bishop the other day. Always put
in a good word for you when I can with the Bishop. Any
nervousness you may feel now will pass away with practice. I
haven't felt any nervousness for years."

Tim smiled in gratitude ; a sick smile. And a little later
he went out to the privy.

This temporary incarceration of Tim enabled the Vicar to
look out again at the congregation. Good. It had swelled
considerably. The church was not full—it was too large, probably, ever to be filled again—but it was already, at ten minutes
to eleven, much fuller than usual. A few strange, awkward
men sat at the back. Strikers ? His eyes, sweeping the faces,
saw Lilian Eadie seated as near the pulpit as she could get.
Always a striking figure because of her exquisite clothes and
her trained grace of movement, she was dressed today in a frock
of deep blue which seemed to add to the mystery of her pallor,
her hollow cheeks, and her dark, gazing eyes. He saw Amy
sitting fatly in the Vicarage pew and marking places in her
Bible and Prayer Book. Amazing that Amy could believe so
simply all that incredible stuff in the Bible and all that the
clergy instructed her to believe. Amazing that she could believe
so simply in him. Twenty years in the same house, and she still
supposed that he believed all he preached, and that the vicar
of St. Boniface worked harder than any layman. She accepted
it as true enough when he described his work as " twelve hours
a day for seven days a week, and no trade union."

" A few strikers seem to have come," he said to Tim, who
was now back in the vestry, relieved of some, but not much,
of his trouble.

" What ? In the chur-urch ? " The gulp had tripped him
again. The railway strike, the possibility of national chaos,
the threat of starvation upon millions, a whisper of civil war—

all these were nothing to him, and would be nothing till about seven o'clock tonight. " There are a lot more outside."

" So ? " The Vicar swung round to him.

" Yes. Quite a crowd of them hanging around."

Canon Welcome's desire to see this crowd was not to be withstood, however much he might wish Tim to think him above such interest. " Aren't they coming in ? "

" They don't look like it. They're just standing around. Mostly out in the road." And he sighed heavily.

" Perhaps I could encourage them to come in." And he laughed as he quoted, " Go ye into the highways and hedges and compel them to come in." In surplice, but without scarf or hood, he went to the West front of his church. Yes ; little groups of men were standing on pavement and roadway, all in their Sunday mufti and mostly smoking cigarettes. They were men of all ages ; probably old drivers and middle-aged foremen, middle-aged fitters and boiler smiths, and young firemen, cleaners, assistants, and mates. The Fields, for once in a way, had come close to the church.

Did they seem a little sullen ? Hostile ? Why as they saw him in his white surplice did they turn their faces away ? Would they at the last minute toss their cigarettes aside and come in to hear what he was going to say ? Or was it possible that they were going to stage some demonstration—to heckle or barrack him ? He very much hoped so ; the idea was completely acceptable because of that reporter inside who would certainly telephone such a news-story to the national press.

Standing on the steps of his churchyard, he spoke to them in his heartiest manner—and sincerely, for at the sight of them he really loved them. " Good morning, boys."

Some grunted " 'Morning " ; others turned away.

" Aren't you coming in ? You're very welcome. *Come* on, lads. This is *your* church. I can promise you a nice service. And I'm going to speak about your strike, but you're not in the least obliged to agree with me."

Shy as children with a stranger, and as obedient, they either pretended not to have heard him, or threw their cigarettes away and slouched towards him.

" Good. That's fine. Come along."

And he led about twenty of these strangers into the church where they joined their fellows in the hindmost rows. Many

42

faces turned round as such a plenitude of boots and shoes sounded on the bare floor, and he felt very proud of these lost sheep which he was bringing into the fold. A good and successful pastor. Leaving them penned in their pews, he walked up the nave, pretending not to look to right or left, but really seeing all things. His service was now most agreeably attended.

One minute to eleven. " Ready, Tim ? " The two clergymen passed into the choir vestry. Boys and men stood robed in their places for the procession. A good attendance of choirmen—fine !—for this was not at all usual on a Sunday morning. All waited in silence. The Vicar stood with hands clasped for a prayer. The bell stopped ; the church clock struck in the tower ; and a sudden gladness, a happy, an almost breathless eagerness for his performance, overthrew the Vicar's nerves. He lifted his voice and sang " O Lord, open Thou our lips."

The choir responded, " And our mouth shall shew forth Thy praise."

" Let Thy priests be clothed with righteousness."

" And let Thy saints sing with joyfulness."

§

Now he was in the pulpit, hands clasping the lectern, eyes watching the congregation as they sang the last verse of the hymn.

A splendid congregation for these irreligious days, and he was amazed, and even appalled, that so many people should believe in him.

Of course it was largely a congregation of women who worshipped him, with here and there some dragged or directed children too young to disobey ; and a great proportion of these women were left and lonely persons like Lilian Eadie. What a relief it was to see in one or two places the hatless head of a man. But who were these men ? He distinguished Major Partridge, a retired officer with a sense of duty to the padre and Sir Layton Eaves, a high civil servant with a like sense of duty to the Established Church, and a few small tradesmen, some of whom, as he had long ago perceived, were there because they enjoyed their brief distinction as sidesmen or because to

43

be seen in church on Sunday brought business to their counters on weekdays. Where were the young men ? Where were the emancipated young women ? Where were the working men and women ? Why were only the salaried classes here, and those who didn't face the full blast of life ?

There were a few of these last today ; for there at the back, keeping close together for comfort in strange surroundings, and staring before them instead of singing the unfamiliar hymn, was the fringe of strikers with a rubicon of empty pews between them and the body of the faithful. Looking from them to the faithful, he wondered if there were one of these usual church-goers who was not a conservative voter and sharply critical of all undisciplined workmen. There were two groups before him : the Church, or that Remnant of it which survived ; and the world of harsh, real things in which those strikers dwelt. Yes, two worlds, and both within his parish : Hamden Hill and Hebron Fields.

While he was composing his sermon it had been the larger group, his familiar people, which had pressed upon his mind and so extracted statements which would please them. If it is yourself rather than your subject which you project before an audience you will inevitably give the majority what it wants, that praise may drown the blame. This sermon on the lectern would please his own people, but what about yonder silent men ? He felt momentarily afraid of that watching phalanx.

He had no doubt whatever that it was a splendid sermon. Its ingredients came from a dozen choice sources, for when Canon Welcome prepared a sermon, he robbed every apposite book, every relevant newspaper article, every brain that he could visit and dredge, and every other parson's sermon that descanted upon his subject with any pungency or pith. And all the fruits and flavours and adornment which he had thus garnered he put into his own dish and served without acknowledgment of their sources to his assembled guests. His arrangement of a sermon and his delivery of it, were alike excellent, because what you long to do well you learn to do well, and he had read surreptitiously every book on public speaking that he could find, and studied earnestly all the tricks, vocal and manual, of the greatest orators. As well as any actor he knew how to use his voice and his hands. He liked to make play with his hands because women had called them beautiful.

44

Confident then, that his sermon would be applauded by the majority, he was eager to begin.

§

> O Lord, stretch forth Thy mighty hand
> And guard and bless our Fatherland.

The congregation sang it for the last time, and the Amen after it, and sank down into their pews. The strikers, copying the rest sat too, but less happily, less comfortably. Canon Welcome closed his eyes. " May the words of our lips and the meditations of our hearts be always acceptable in Thy sight, O Lord, our strength and our redeemer." This said, he leaned one elbow on his lectern, as if completely at ease and independent of notes. He paused till the stillness was total and then said, " Our strength and our redeemer. That will do for a text. This is a grave moment, dear people. As I speak to you now, our nation is partially paralysed by a great strike, and the only true solution, as always, is that our Lord should come amongst us in strength and redeem the time. May I remind you how it all began ? "

This opening of his sermon was a thing he knew he would enjoy, because it made a dramatic story, and he had the art of telling it. Further, now that he had to mention certain times and dates, he was justified in lifting an elbow from the desk and glancing down upon it at something which he hoped the people would think a mere handful of notes but was really a *verbatim* manuscript. He braced back his broad shoulders and turned back the flowing white sleeves of his surplice for action.

" Thursday, ten days ago, the leaders of the railwaymen's union and of the Government met together to negotiate on the men's demand for a new standard rate of wages. Good. That is the way of a free people. But what was our surprise, our dismay, our alarm, on the next day, to read that the men's leaders had threatened to call a general strike at midnight if the Government did not make a new and more favourable offer by noon. Instructions had already been sent, we learned, to all branches of the railwaymen's union that there were to hold themselves in readiness to strike unless they received counter orders from their committee. This was not negotiation ; it was an ultimatum ; and the Government immediately announced

45

that all parleys were at an end till this ultimatum was withdrawn. The railwaymen's secretary, having received this response from the Prime Minister, came away from Downing Street and stated simply, 'The strike will begin at twelve o'clock tonight.'

"It was war. The Government made ready to fight the strike with all the resources of the country. They announced that all necessary motor vehicles would be commandeered for the distribution of food supplies ; that the great food routes of the country, some thousand miles of railway, would be kept open by means of volunteers ; that they hoped the crisis would be settled without civil disturbance, but they were prepared, if necessary, to use the armed forces, not only to handle the people's food but also to protect the volunteers and preserve the King's Peace."

The preacher paused on this fine sentence. He glanced down at his lectern ; then faced the stilled and staring audience again.

"By Saturday noon the great stoppage was complete. As from midnight the engine crews declined to take their engines out of the sheds ; the signalmen stayed in their boxes only till the last passenger trains had reached safety ; no man due for midnight duty reported for work ; on some lines at the stroke of midnight trainloads of milk, fish, and other perishable foods were left to decay where they stood ; and in some depôts even the horses were left in the stables with none to feed and water them.

"That was eight days ago. Eight days, and the strike continues with no weakening on the part of the men. On the other hand much has happened to frustrate and blunt the strike. Volunteers have offered themselves to the Government or the Companies in overwhelming numbers. They have offered themselves for all classes of work on the railways, driving, firing, loading, checking, unloading. Even as I speak to you, the food trains run."

Canon Welcome and a hundred thousand other men, in or out of pulpits, were drawing delight from the disaster because it provided them with such stirring lines to speak.

"Such is the field ; such the combatants. We are the Church, and have we not to ask ourselves, What is our position ? Are we neutral in this great controversy, or do we lean to one side or the other ? I have wrestled with this question in the last week ; I have prayed to God that He will guide me ; will you

46

also pray for me that He will ' open for me a door of utterance and give me the words that I should speak ' ? "

He gave a moment's glance at the verbatim manuscript beneath him.

" It has seemed to me after great thought that it was my bounden duty to quicken the public conscience by a bold statement of the Church's Witness. Bear with me then if I ask you this." Now he leaned upon the lectern as one who would speak quietly with friends. " If Christ were to come among us in strength at this time—that is to say, if the Christianity we profess were suddenly to become real and potent, how would it redeem the time ? First, it would surely compel us, for the sake of public and strikers alike, to assist in the collection and distribution of food, the maintenance of water supplies, sanitation, and street lighting, and the preservation of public order. And, in passing, perhaps I may say how infertile in ideas are those who are set to rule over us, how woeful is the want of vision in high places." Here, in this parenthesis, he was yielding to a temptation that visits us all, when we set our own fertile brains in contrast with the brains of those who have achieved high places. " Why, I ask you, are not fleets of boats and barges plying between the outermost docks and the last of the suburbs upstream, with the necessaries of life for our vast waterside population ? Why is not the Post Office flying the King's Mail on large machines to the main focal points and thence on smaller machines to the smaller centres, and thence distributing it among the local offices by the cars, sidecars, and cycles of ten thousand volunteers ? Such a service, I suggest could have been organized in two days or three.

" But that is by the way." He waved it to one side with a pink and graceful hand.

" I feel that you have all come with me thus far, since I have aligned myself neither with one side nor the other. Am I going to lose some of you now if I go on and pronounce frankly, fearlessly, aye, and fervently, what I assume would be the judgment of Christianity in its strength ? My brethren, those of you who are railwaymen, bear with me when I say I cannot but condemn the levity, the precipitancy, the rash foolhardihood "—always, when preaching, Canon Welcome tended to pile up his important words in threes—" with which this grave blow at the nation's life was delivered by those who lead you. Ask yourselves, has a strike of this magnitude ever been entered into with

47

quite such a reckless disregard of the public weal ? Common
justice demanded that at least a week's notice should have been
given so that tradesmen, business men, aye, and working men
and their wives, might have had time to prepare for the siege.
The Government counselled the railwaymen to postpone any
action for a few days, but they declined this respite to their
fellow countrymen. For this reason it looks to me as if the strike
were less a legal attempt to secure better wages than a revolutionary attempt by a few ambitious men to use your honourable
Trade Union organization as a lever for shifting the power of
Parliament over to their own hands."

There was a stirring of the men at the back ; an impatient
movement of bodies in lieu of lips. At once this hint of hostility,
by warming up his self-esteem, quickened his combativeness.
He leaned over the pulpit, held forth one minatory finger, and
declared with a new, warm emphasis :

" In so far as this is the truth of the strike then I must believe
that it is a matter of life and death for our country to defeat it.
There are some fifty million people in these islands, and only
some half million in the railway unions. Is the hundredth part
to capture control of the whole ? I think not. Our people are
not blind ; they are a shrewd people, and they can see that if
this lever works once, it will work again—and again and again—
and they will resist such bullying from anybody, as they have
done throughout their history, whether against kings, barons,
priests, or foreign enemies. Let them see that their ancient
freedoms are endangered, and they will fight this battle as they
fought the war with Germany, to the death——"

" Rats ! "

Not loudly but quite audibly a man's voice uttered this word
from the back of the church. The dreadful syllable was followed
by the sound of many feet as the man and all the others—a flock
of rams and lambs easily led into angry or dramatic action by
one born bell-wether—rose and trooped out of the church.
Nearly all the congregation turned to watch them go, and the
Canon, both angered by the opposition and delighted by the
incident, watched in silence till the disturbance was over. At
the south door the man turned and shouted—actually shouted—
at the preacher, " Inciting to bloodshed, that's what you are ! "

A shocked churchwarden rose to escort this brawling sheep
from the fold, but before he could reach him, the man had disappeared into the sunlight.

48

The Canon cast a quick sidelong glance at the reporter ; he was scribbling fast. Oh, good ! Canon Welcome's anger was washed away by a high wave of hope. In all the church just then there was no happier man.

When silence had settled in the church again he resumed, " A pity that my good friends did not stay to hear what I had to say. They would then have learned that I am not wholly against them. So far I have but said "—a pause while he found his place in the manuscript again—" I have but said that —I have but said that the Government must vindicate the democratic—no, the Government—yes, the Government and people must be under no illusion that this vainglorious attempt of the wilder men to impose their will upon the nation is a parting of the ways. The Government must vindicate the democratic principle of the right of the majority to rule.

" But having stated this plain fact without fear or favour, and having added that Government and people must have no hate in their hearts, I would go on to suggest a way in which a bridge might be cast across this desperate, dangerous, aye, and maybe disastrous, breach."

Elbows on the lectern (but in such a way as he could see his manuscript), fingers interlocked, eyes beseeching a sweet reasonableness from his people, he suggested that it was now largely a question of face-saving. The Government could not re-open the wages question till the men were back at work ; the Union could hardly order its men to return till they had something tangible to offer them. Here were two separate questions : the one political, the other industrial. Let the men concede the political point, and the Government declare that, if this were done, they would make some concession on the industrial point. Let the Government understand that the large-hearted British people were resisting the railwaymen only because they resented their leaders' methods, not because they disallowed their claims. They no more wanted their railwaymen to be treated unfairly than they intended themselves to be blackmailed.

When he had argued this at length and with admirable phrasing, he came erect, for his peroration was in sight. He was very proud of this peroration, having quite forgotten the various sources from which it came. Spreading his elegant hands in a persuasive gesture of appeal, he began :

" If this solution were accepted, my friends, the only victors would be the public ; the only defeated the fomenters of strife.

49

And, what is more, our dear England, as so often in the past, would have set an example and shewn a way to the world. Great Britain, because she leads the world politically, is always the world's testing ground. If revolution and tyranny were to get the upper hand here the effect would travel round the world like the shock of an earthquake. But if we show that, while refusing in our old fashion to bend our knees before any tyrant, we can yet, by our traditional methods of quietness, conciliation, aye, and ultimate compromise, quench the threat of revolution, our achievement will make for stability everywhere. And at the same time we shall have shown to the world, what I believe to be true, that the old harsh order is passing, and a new and more Christian one is born, an age in which all our working men will be given an economic status, higher, happier, aye, and assuredly juster than heretofore ; an age of complete social sanity that will bring a new benediction to mankind.''

§

Eager to meet some of the congregation, and hear some praise of his sermon, he left the vestry as soon as possible and walked down the nave to the south porch. Near the porch, Sladd, the verger, piling hymn books on a seat, desisted immediately from the task, ran forward, touched his cassock sleeve, and said mysteriously, " Those men are still here."

Sladd, though bald and seventy-one, liked a touch of drama no less than his vicar—or an excited child.

" What men ? "

" Them that walked out during the sermon, and the others that'd been waiting there all the time. And there's a lot more come up from the Fields. I walked out to see what was going on. Seems they got wind of the fact that one of 'em had shouted out at you, and that all the rest had walked out in that rude way. They been coming up ever since."

" Well, what of that, Sladd ? "

" I don't know, but they look a bit threatening to me."

" Nonsense ! Whom should they threaten ? "

" Who ? " Sladd looked at him and lifted his eyebrows as much as to say, *You* ought to know. " Well . . . it's you, sir, they're waiting for, if you ask me. I shouldn't go out just now, sir, if I was you."

" Good Lord, Sladd, I'm not afraid of them."

Eagerly he hastened to the porch and looked out—but for one person only. Yes, the reporter was still there. He was standing in the churchyard, staring at the men on the pavement and roadway, and obviously wondering if a news item was going to be given him. He hoped it was, but not more than the Vicar. Canon Welcome had little physical fear, but a large desire for fame. He walked straight out into the bright noon that disorder might beat around him and a news-story with a national appeal be provided for the reporter. He was not quite clear what he was going to do : perhaps speak to the men from the churchyard steps and receive some jeers and insults, or even a few stones. Had not St. Boniface himself been martyred by a mob of barbarians he was trying to convert ? And the present vicar of St. Boniface Martyr was quite ready for a small martyrdom, so long as he wasn't seriously hurt.

Some of the congregation stood around in the sunlight, chatting together and manifestly uninterested in anyone's martyrdom. Many smiled at him and thanked him for his sermon. Major Partridge, plumped like a marrow in his grey plaid suit, but with cheeks as red as a rose, turned from the Misses Pannett, to whom he was talking, to say, " A fine sermon, vicar. It was just what needed saying." And Sir Layton Eaves, who was standing alone, waiting for his wife to finish her causerie with Miss Greatrix, Miss Blayre, and Mrs. Oakley, said " Thank you, vicar. A most just statement. And delivered, if I may say so, with equal force and dignity." Clara Bettersby, who was listening, or pretending to listen, to Miss Greatrix's awful old mother, called out, " Splendid, vicar. I agreed with every word of it. Oh, why wasn't my silly man there to hear it ? " And even Amy, who was in conversation with Lady Barkhope and her lame daughter, turned to say, " Very nice, Humbert darling " ; and he wondered if " nice " wasn't a commonplace and inadequate word for such a sermon.

" Yes, yes," he agreed, anxious to get to the men and the martyrdom before the reporter lost hope and went.

But there was another in his path. Lilian Eadie swept up with both hands extended to clasp one of his and to hold it in a fervour of congratulation.

" Vicar ! " she exclaimed, her big eyes fixed on his, her voice deep and low, like the last light of evening. " Oh, Vicar ! It wasn't the sermon of the year ; it was the sermon of the ages."

" Oh now, come, come ! " he protested with a laugh. " That is saying rather too much. The ages ! Oh no ! That disposes of Demosthenes and Pericles and Cicero and a few others."

" I don't mind. I care nothing about Pericles. Nothing about Cicero. It was a *beautiful* sermon." Her voice dropped yet lower, and with a strong, velvety pressure, on the word " beautiful." She left the word, as it were, to sail and echo in the air. " I am uplifted."

" It was too long, dear lady. Thirty-five minutes is ten minutes too long."

" If it had been three hundred and five minutes it wouldn't have been too long."

" What ? Five hours of it ? " The schoolboy that still lived within the grave black cassock of the canon felt like protesting with some such crudity as " Oh, come off it ! ", but he remembered the cassock and limited himself to, " Oh, come ! "

" I could have listened all day. So amazing, so marvellous, so wonderful ! You make me realize what it is to have an education. No one educated me at all."

" No, my dear, *I* am not the scholar." In modesty, or, rather, in the appearance of it, one must demur against such flatteries. " Our Bettersby is the scholar. You should come and listen to him."

" Ah, but he hasn't your radiance."

" Radiance ? What do you mean ? " The word was so pleasing that he let the martyrdom wait a moment while he heard more.

" There is a light about you. He has immense learning and a wonderful vocabulary, and a nice bitter humour, but not light. Not light." Her voice was now deeper than dusk, as if to match this absence of light. It might have been the voice of Goethe as he died, saying, Light, light, more light. " Oh, no. Besides he's no actor."

" But, gracious goodness, you're accusing me of being an actor ? "

" No, no. No, darling. But you should have been an actor. How did you learn to use your hands like that ? All your power is in your hands."

For a second or two he wondered what in the name of sense this assertion meant. Pleased to have his hands admired, he was not sure that he wanted all his power attributed to them. He preferred that some of his power should be located in his head. It was only after deciding that the sentence was just a succession of pleasing words and signified nothing much more than that he used his hands admirably, that he felt quite happy again. " I'm glad you liked it," he said, smiling, but anxious to escape and be martyred.

" Like it ! I didn't *like* it, darling. It was an experience. One of the great experiences of my life."

A line which she'd delivered to him before, and in the same low tones—tones almost too full of feeling to be heard. A pity that she didn't remember she'd used it before ; it lost value if applied to every sermon.

" Look, Mrs. Buxton, I must——"

" Oh, call me Lilian. Do call me Lilian, darling. I'm used to everybody calling me by my Christian name. Buxton is impossible. Lilian Eadie. There ! "

" All right. Well, look, Lilian Eadie, I must go. I want to say a few words to all those men."

" Oh, but don't ! They look as though they were waiting to eat you. Oh, no, I insist not—*please* ! They were so terrible in church. I suffered agonies for you. In my acting days I should have died if anybody had shouted at me from the back ; I should have been transfixed ; I should have dried up completely. And you were unmoved. You just went on. That is in the great tradition. The show must go on. Oh, they were dreadful ! "

" Nevertheless I think I ought to speak to them."

" Oh, you are brave ! "

" Not at all. There's nothing to be afraid of. Now come and talk to my wife."

" I'd love to talk with so fortunate a woman. Lead me to her."

" Come, then. Amy, dear—you remember Lilian Eadie ?— you must get to know each other better."

" My dear Mrs. Welcome, *what* a sermon. How proud you must be of your husband. I was telling——"

He left her telling, and Amy listening, and walked towards the men in the road. And as he did so, leaving the fragments of his congregation behind him, he was conscious that he had walked out of an atmosphere of kindly praise and feminine adulation into one of antipathy, estrangement and suspicion. It was like quitting one's own country and meeting the altered face of an alien land.

The men, who had been arguing and grunting among

themselves, or standing aside and lipping their cigarettes in a solitude, fell silent and turned their faces towards him.

He halted on the churchyard steps and smiled benevolently upon them. The benevolence was wholly genuine. His heart had warmed towards them. Except in times of anger his heart warmed towards anyone whom he was approaching, and especially towards an audience whom he was about to address. And when as now the audience included fine rotund old weather-beaten men who'd served the State in their day, and young lads who despite brawny limbs and graceless Sunday clothes still held in his eyes the inalienable charm of youth, his heart quickened with nothing less than love. In such moments he would have liked to be a faithful, slaving, self-giving pastor to them all, a Vincent de Paul or a Curé d'Ars.

"Men," he called out, "will you listen to me?" All his congregation behind him left their prattle and turned his way to see and to listen. The reporter came forward, notebook in hand, but in this moment of love and longed-for sanctity, Canon Welcome had forgotten the reporter. "I wonder if you will let me tell you what I have been saying in the church. Some of you were angry with what I said and came out before you could hear it all——"

"You said it was up to the people to fight us as they fought the Jerries." Canon Welcome recognized the voice which had interrupted him in the church. "It was incitement to bloodshed ; that's what it was."

"Oh no, no! How could you think such a thing? You only think it because you are angry and want to believe the worst. I understand that so well ; I'm like it myself sometimes : angry with someone and anxious to believe they've said something hateful. I didn't mean that we must fight you men to the last, but that we must never yield to the method your leaders have adopted. That's all. It's not men we're fighting but a principle. I'm sure I expressed myself very badly indeed. And if so I am sorry."

"You're trying to break the strike ; that's what you're trying to do. You said it'd got to be broken. And what's it got to do with you? What do you know about it?"

"I'm not trying to break your strike. At least, I—I——"

"What d'you know about it? How'd you like to be a goods porter or a shunter on a quid or two a week? We got children, we have."

54

" But I'm on your side in the matter of wages. I said so to all my people. I said we could not stand by and see our railwaymen, who served us so well, denied a fair livelihood——"

" Look at that there house you live in. You never known what it is to see your kids hungry. You got all the money you want, packets—you have."

" Yah ! " called another voice. " And time some of it was taken from them. Why listen to '*im*? '*E* don't understand."

" I do understand—no, I mustn't say that ; I'm sure you're right, and I don't really understand. But I try to. I want to. If my words sounded harsh, then I blundered badly, and I ask your pardon. I wouldn't have hurt your feelings for all the world. Listen to what I said after you'd gone. I said——" and he fell inevitably into the words he had learned by heart, and virtue and power sank from him, because, even though he didn't want it, the words had pulled him back into an actor's rôle. " I said that we must shew to the world, what I believed to be true, that the old order was passing and a new and more Christian one was being born, an age in which all our working men would be given an economic status, higher, happier, and juster than ever before."

They were gazing up at him, but he could see that these words, fine though he had thought them in his study, had made no impression at all. They were just fine words, and no more. The only time he had been on the threshold of these men's hearts was when he had said, " No, I'm sure you're right, and I don't really understand," and " I am sorry."

Most of the men continued to stare up at him like dull children in a schoolroom, but the more hostile muttered something like " Pah ! " and " Blah ! " and " That gets us a long way, doesn't it ? " then turned as if in disgust, to drift down the hill. Defeated, conscious that there was a deep dyke between him and them which he could not cross, and with no more words in his heart, he could only add in a charged voice, " God bless you. God bless you all."

But the others were now following their leaders. Their backs were turned to this blessing. The tide of faces which for once in a way, had rolled up from the Fields to the gates of the church was being drawn home to its deeps again.

CHAPTER FIVE

CANON WELCOME's attacks of sanctity were seldom prolonged. And on this Sunday, even though the nation, according to his sermon, was poised over disaster and chaos, the sanctity terminated in the course of an admirable midday dinner. After this meal his round body, so far from feeling the wounds of martyrdom, was comfortably aglow. Cast into his easy chair, with feet up on a footstool, fingers interlaced over the rounded and slightly extended belly, and the door shut upon the quarrelling world, it lay as filled with warm satisfaction as a hogshead with wine. If there is such a feeling as a warm, glowing, sparkling peace, then that was the wine that was in him now : the flowing peace that comes from a sense of achievement, from remembering applause and words of praise, from digesting a tender portion of roast lamb washed down with Beaune, and from having nothing much more to do today, since Tim was taking the Catechism this afternoon and preaching at Evensong. And in the Vicarage it was accepted that, Sunday being such a tiring day, the Vicar must have his rest in the afternoon.

His eyes closed.

" . . . not the sermon of the year ; the sermon of the ages. . . ."

" He hasn't your radiance . . ."

" One of the great experiences . . ."

" Delivered, if I may say so, with great force and dignity."

Oh, ho, ah, hah, ah. . . . One hand left its lover to cover the yawn. Sleepy. Somewhat sleepy. Nothing more to do today except things which were pleasant. At Evensong he had only to sing the service in a voice that always pleased him and then sit back in his stall while Tim preached. How popular Timmy was in the parish, and he didn't feel in the least jealous of him. Why was this ? Partly because his heart was naturally expansive and generous, especially to anything young, and partly because he wanted to keep his church, and his collection plates, as full as possible while all the others failed to do so, and if a popular young curate was a box-office attraction, why, so much the better. Yes, 'sides he'd no need to fear Tim's reputation as a preacher. Tim's matter was fair enough, but his nervousness hobbled him to his manuscript like a donkey to a stake, and sometimes played the deuce with his delivery. Why, he'd known Tim obliged to suppress a hiccup in the course of a sermon.

In a day dream, behind his closed eyes, he saw the whole scene at Evensong tonight. Here comes Tim into the vestry, his big boyish face at the top of his tall broad body a little white, and his large powerful hands shaking as he hangs up his hat. And a stutter in his voice as he says, " Good evening, Vicar." And after that a long silent time, for Tim in his nervousness has arrived very early. There are still fifteen minutes to go, and for most of this time Tim has to stand like a big broad monument in surplice and scarf, saying nothing, but thinking terrible things. Once, and possibly twice, he breaks up the monotony by a protracted visit to the privy.

Poor Tim. . . .

Now they are in the chancel, and Evensong is sweeping them on a tide of psalms and prayers to the moment when Tim must mount the pulpit. A sweat is on Tim's brow, and a regular swallowing in his throat. Poor, poor Timmy. Canon Welcome's pity pours across the chancel to him. He sends up prayers for him in an access of sympathy. " God help him. Be with him. Oh, help him." He repeats these prayers with an even greater, a passionate, earnestness, as the last verse of the " hymn before the sermon " bursts out from all these unworried people, and Tim has to mount the steps of the pulpit. The boy goes bravely, like a man who will show no fear to the multitude as he climbs the scaffold. Oh, help him. Don't let him fail. Go on, Timmy boy ; you'll be all right.

Tim does not fail. He never does, and all those nights and days of nervousness are wasted. His is a very fair sermon, and very fairly read (has he not practised its delivery a score of times in the past week ?) They and the choir troop back into the vestries, and Canon Welcome pats him on the back.

" Very fine indeed, my boy."

" Oh, thank you, Vicar, thank you." Tim's face is rosy again, his eyes happy, his voice free and untrammelled. His evening, from now on, is a dance of delight.

" An admirable discourse, admirably delivered. Delivered, if I may say so, with great force and dignity."

Oh, ho, ah, hah, ah. . . . The yawn again.

Great force and dignity. What on earth did that mean when you came to think of it ? Only that old Eaves had liked his sermon that morning. So had Clara Bettersby. And Lilian Eadie.

Appalling to think that a vicar's outward aspect was largely moulded by women. His congregation was a mass of women. His churchworkers were a team of women. He stood, as it were, in a matrix of women, and they forced their pattern upon him. Because in their worshipping way they assigned to him a superiority, an authority, an omniscience, he became cocky, dogmatic, dictatorial and most unjustly self-satisfied. Almost all one's faults, come to think of it, could be attributed to the gravitational pull of all these endless, ancillary women. To begin with, there was Amy. She believed unquestioningly in every old dogma and in all current morality, and before her he had to believe too and say prayers at his bedside and go to church on his holidays. And to appear to be hard at work every morning. Then there was Clara Bettersby, a stout old conservative's daughter who believed in discipline for everybody. Before her he had to be a Tory and a gentleman. Then there was Ethel Greatrix, a long-toothed shark of a girl who worshipped him as a saint ; and before her he had to be saintly. There was her awful old mother who hadn't changed her views on any subject since her parents gave them to her in the eighties ; and before her he had to be a puritan, and a censor of the young, and to believe in the verbal inspiration of the Bible. And now there was Lilian Eadie : before her he had to be brilliant and highly educated and preach sermons that were an experience. And keep a radiance.

Ah, ha, hah, ah. . . . His hand lifted from his stomach again, but fell back before reaching the yawning mouth. A radiance . . . but he had failed, utterly failed, before all those men. And yet he had loved them, really loved them. That was no pose. Might have many faults . . . might be a little hypocritical at times . . . but did truly love his fellowmen. " I feel real goodwill to everybody always. And I really do care for kindness and courtesy above all things. Lazy, I know . . . ambitious . . . unkind to Amy, and I wish I weren't ; I never want to be unkind to anybody. I'm not wholly selfish ; it's just that I have both in me : self-centredness and love . . . and a real worship of the idea of self-sacrifice. I have the substance of the matter in me, in spite of all."

And again there descended upon him, lying in the cushioned chair, an overwhelming sense of the beauty of holiness and self-sacrifice, and a great desire to be a saint. To cast everything away and give himself to love like one of the historic saints of Christianity : St. Francis of Assisi, St. Francis Xavier, St. Boniface. " I have the substance and the marrow of the matter in me. ' They were stoned, they were sawn asunder, were tempted, were slain with the sword ; they wandered about in sheepskins and goatskins ; of whom the world was not worthy . . . ' " He would like the world not to be worthy of him. St. Humbert . . . St. Humbert Martyr, Hamden Hill . . . Festa di Sant' Umberto. . . . No fame so wide as that. The word " fame " directed his thoughts to a more likely fame than Sant' Umberto's. An archdeacon's. Better a bishop's. And either of these was possible. In the morning—oh, sweet to think of it again !—there might be a paragraph in all the great papers about the little brawl in his church this morning, and his name be published to all as a fearless leader of thought. A bishop. The gaitered clergy were pointed out in street and hotel. They could always, and without criticism, " dress the part ". But stop : this was not sanctity ; it was its opposite ; and the best of him knew that only the saints should be made into bishops. Worldly ecclesiastics and statesmen denied this, declaring that saints were no good in the high places, being too unpractical, too soft, too unworldly. But *he* knew, he knew only too well, that the only truly successful ministers, whether princes of the church or humble priests, were the gentle saints. " I see this because I have spiritual vision. I have all the spiritual vision to have been a saint . . . if only I could really believe all the nonsense. It is no difficulty to me to feel love for my fellow men . . . it comes naturally . . . it pours . . . but . . ."

But this potent, bemusing " but " like a drug, slowly clouded his brain and all his being, and he was asleep.

§

In the morning there was a long and conspicuous report of his sermon in the *Hamden and Hebron News*, which pleased him mightily, but no paragraph in the daily papers about the " scene " in his church—no, not though he sought it diligently

—and this was a disappointment, a considerable fall ; he'd had such hopes of that scene. Never mind : if one door to celebrity closed in his face, there were others, and one or another would yield to his pressure. In the meantime let him be content with this large gift of local fame from the *Hamden and Hebron News*.

On the Tuesday he read that the strike had been settled on exactly the lines he had suggested in his sermon, and he could please himself with wondering, not only in secret but also aloud to Amy, if a rumour of his famous strike sermon had somehow reached the warring headquarters and provided them with an idea. The strike, it appeared, had been settled quite simply, quite easily, and with mutual compliments between the Government and the men's leaders. Yesterday all the talk was of Civil War and Covert Revolution and a Final Parting of the Ways ; today all was mutual congratulation and esteem. It had ended overnight and just when it was at its highest, like the fall, unseen, of a rocket stick.

The air was full of sounds again. From the blue distances above the roofs—so long empty of any railway voices—came whistlings loud or muted, staccato chuffings, clanking of coaches and clashing of buffers, and the long, dwindling rumble of main-line trains. The depôt at the bottom of the hill breathed and sang noisily again ; and through its gates, wide open once more, the drivers and firemen, in their blue overalls and glossy black uniform caps, went to their foot-plates ; the cleaners, steam-raisers, and boiler-washers to their bee-like labours about the great locomotives ; the blacksmiths, coppersmiths, and turners to their various skills in the machine shops ; and the coalmen, sandmen, and ash-fillers to their dusty occupations in the yard.

And the Fields round about the depôt went on their way as the weeks went by ; a tolerably honest way for the most part, but extremely equivocal in the neighbourhood of the Circus ; and, whether honest or dishonest, open or hidden, diurnal or nocturnal, all alike out of touch with the church on the hill-slope, and the Vicarage in its square, walled garden beside it. The Fields had swept up to and touched the gates of the church on that Strike Sunday, but no more ; and now they had fallen again out of the knowledge and sight of the Vicar in his comfortable study or in his pulpit, sanctuary, and chancel stall. They had yet to enter the Vicarage and shake him by the hand.

PART II

CHAPTER ONE

THE Vicar's days, adequately filled with agreeable reading and lazy bustling, narrowed into autumn and into winter. The leaves on his house wall and the trees in his square garden blushed and changed around him, the creepers turning to crimson, the beech-tree to copper, the sycamore to a primrose yellow, and the fine old elm to bronze and gold. A little of this splendour and then the running and snatching winds stripped the branches of their gold, and soon the garden was but a quiet place of dank green grass, naked trunks, and the rusty remnants of leaves.

In the Fields, between the high factories and the long slab-faced terraces, and under the shuddering viaducts, the same dankness lay on pavements and setts in a greasy black mixture of fog-damp and soot. Often the wintry fogs were thicker down here than on the hill-slope and, strangely enough, whether they were yellow as iron-mould or white as a bath towel, they seemed always to throw the same yellow twilight into the rooms. Down in the Fields it was dark at three o'clock on a December day. Oh, depressing places, the wintry Fields, and Canon Welcome who liked the bright and cheerful corners of life, found whatever excuses were available for leaving them alone. Had he gone down that way he might have found them much happier and brighter under a night sky than in the flat, dull greys of a winter daylight. They were bright then with the tawny glow from a thousand unblinded windows, with the reds and greens of the elevated signal lamps on the viaducts and the flame-flushed steam of the engines crossing them ; and perhaps with the garlanded illuminations of a fun-fair in a yard. On an open and cloudless night there would be a blue-green glow about the moon above the silhouettes of roofs and chimney stacks.

The Canon in his easy chair, reading by lamplight, did not know it, but on certain evenings, when the moon was not shining its policeman's lantern on the world, there was a shadowy figure in his garden. The garden was easy of approach by a figure who would keep to the shadows, because of the little priest's gate between the deserted churchyard and the lonely trees on its lawn. And this man lurking against the elm was certainly one who preferred the shadows : they were his own kind, soundless in movement, keeping to cover, lying low beneath bole or wall, and loving not the noonday or any clear and penetrating light.

But supposing, instead, of the moon, a policeman, pounding his beat, had turned into the garden and shone his lantern upon the visitor (which would have been a wise thing to do), he would have created out of the night a face of much interest, since it was a parchment printed with lines, paragraphs, stops, interjection marks, and question marks, all of which had their social significance. A lean and narrow face, it was as crumpled as a dried currant or, if you like, as crinkled as the bark of the elm against which its owner leaned. It was the face of a man not yet sixty but creased and graven like this because his passage through the years had been rough, and his meditations protracted, if not profound. The eyes had retreated under the quickset, thorny eyebrows, where they appeared to be lurking under cover and peeping out at the cops. Wrinkles, radiating from the corners of the eyes like the knotted cords from the handle of a cat-o'-nine-tails (a simile, perhaps in the right mood) or like the seven streets from the Circus (which simile would be to the purpose too) gave a sly humour to the eyes. The left eye was particularly sly because, more often than not, it was half closed and drew its eyebrow down with it, but seemed to be a good deal keener and to be seeing much more than its colleague on the right. The skin, slack as a pulled chicken's, was a canvas which Time, that *pointilliste* artist, had covered with mottles, freckles, blotches and pocks. The mouth was thin and rather crooked, but not so crooked as the career it could tell about, nor so thin as some of the lies it had uttered, when necessary, to policeman or beak. The halo, cast around his head (most inappropriately) by the policeman's lantern would have included a cracked celluloid collar and a slender black tie, marks of respectability which were not justified. The black tie might have been the wear of an undertaker's mute, but the undertakings which it dignified were not those of a funeral director. They were takings, certainly, and underhand ; and soft-footed often, and mute.

The policeman, being local, would have recognized the face at once, because it is the business of the London constabulary (and for this praise be to God) to know all such practitioners in their parish or " manor ". He would have known him as Mr. Frederick Carman, of New Victoria Buildings, Maker Street, and he would have greeted him, very likely, with a " Well, now ! Old Ricky, eh ? Fancy that ! Old Ricky Carman under the spreading chestnut tree " ; for, if it is the business of the police to be smiling and warm-hearted with their clients (so long as they are such as abstain from violence), it is no part of their task to know the difference between a chestnut and an elm.

The conversation, thus amicably begun, would have continued, we may surmise, in the following fashion.

" Now, what precisely would Old Ricky Carman be doing here ? "

" Me ? *Me*, guv ? Now lemme explain——"

" Don't tell me you been to church, Ricky. Not but what a few prayers would do you no harm."

" Now lemme explain. I was jest——"

" You was doing a little gardening for the Reverend Welcome, perhaps. In your spare time, eh ? And after dark."

" No, I wasn't. I never said nothing of the sort. Don't put words in me mouth : that's what you cops always try to do. I was going to explain if only you'd gimme time."

" All right, Ricky. Okey-doke. Just tell me in a couple o' words what you're doing in Reverend Welcome's garden at this time o'night ? "

" Nothing, guv." Mr. Carman always began with this couple of words, unless he was taken red-handed, or, in his own language " caught to rights ". They were words which enabled him to gather time and his wits together before providing the policeman with something a little more convincing. " Lemme explain. To tell the honest truth, I did think of pinching a few bits of wood for firing, see. I'll be absolutely frank about it. There's a lot lying about, see, in the churchyard and this here garden, after them gales. It saves me a copper or two if I can pick up some kindling. That's what I was after, as true as I stand here. That's the whole strength of it, and I'm not lying."

" Don't see none in your hand, Ricky."

" What ? Wossat ? "

" Don't see any of this here kindling in your mitt."

" Well, no, see : I was just looking around ; just prospecting."

" Betcher was."

" I admit it was wrong, strictly ; but I don't suppose the old sky pilot'd mind me gathering up a few sticks. I've had some outa other gardens, if you want to know. I'll be absolutely frank with you, see. Still, I suppose it *is* trespassing, like, relly."

" It sure is, Ricky. And I don't suppose you got the little old aprils with you, have you ? Oh, no ! " It needs no great quickness to perceive why " aprils " in the rhyming slang of Mr. Carman's craft means his tools : his jemmy, his knife, his torch, and his gloves—or, if you will, his stick, his chiv, his glim, and his turtles.

" Course not ! " Mr. Carman is indignant at the suggestion. He is hurt. He can afford to be, since on this occasion, it is grossly untrue. " I give all that up long ago, as you know. You've had nothing on me for more'n three years now. I've turned the lark up, as you know. I been on the straight ever since——"

" Not so sure as I *do* know. Not at all sure."

" You don't b'lieve me ? "

" Well . . . not perhaps all at once, Ricky. No, not as you might say, absolutely."

" Temme I'm a liar, would you ? " Mr. Carman, so deep his hurt, pulls out his pockets, one after another, and throws open his raincoat and his jacket. " There y'are ! Nothing in any sky-rocket. Look for yourself. Rub me down, if you want to. I doh'mind. I got nothing to be ashamed of."

And this is all quite true : he has nothing suspicious there, because the time for his tools is not yet.

" Well you 'op it outa here. And look, Ricky : I ain't seen you in here unless I hear of something missing from the church or the Reverend Welcome's."

" Why the hell should there be anything missing there ? I give all that up long ago, as I tell you."

" Well, that's fine, Ricky. That's fine."

But such a visit must have quashed Mr. Carman's plans in this particular garden. No such policeman, however, disturbed his meditations, and the plans, like good fruit, slowly ripened under the leaves of the trees. They grew plump and pleasant to contemplate. Mr. Carman returned there on several evenings to consider from beneath his thorny eyebrows, and to time, the lighting of the Vicarage windows. Seven o'clock : the light went up in the bedroom on the first floor. The lady was dressing for her supper. He'd heard that the Reverend Welcome insisted on his old woman dressing for supper but made out he was too busy to do much poshing up himself. A light in the dining-room window : the skivvy was laying the supper. Light out in bedroom : lady going down to her supper. Light up in the bedroom again : always the same, night after night : the skiv was turning down the beds. Bloody swank : they couldn't even get into their beds, without a girl opened 'em up for 'em. *He'd* never wanted anyone to open his kip for him, and he'd got in fast enough when there was something good inside. But p'raps that sorta thing was different with a reverend. Now the skiv was opening up the window. *Opening* it ! Thank you, ducks. Ah, but she'd shut down the lower sash. Pity, that. Light in the next window—and out. The old steamer's dressing-room being put to rights. Now only lights on the ground floor : in dining-room and kitchen. All dark on the first floor, and there'd be a safe hour before him in which to play.

Sweetest thing ever. Never a softer drum to screw. Trees all round it ; a wall between it and the road ; and nothing on the bedroom side except an empty church and churchyard. And—would you believe it ?—a jacob all waiting at the back of the church. (Screwsmen of Mr. Carman's persuasion are not as a rule good churchgoers or Bible students : still a " jacob " is a ladder.) He'd seen and worked gaffs in the country as easy as this, but you didn't often get one in London and almost on your doorstep, as you might say. No outside man wanted for this job. No one to divvy up with, on this lark. He could do it on his jack.

On the first nicely dark night.

Three local events in the springtime had directed Mr. Carman's thoughts towards the Vicar and his sheltered garden. The first was his sudden discharge from a store watchman's job. No doubt the usual had happened : the bosses had discovered his past record and promptly blotted him out. This had happened again and again in his three years' effort to go straight ; and it discouraged a self-respecting bloke. The second was the arrival of a fat old sky-pilot, name of Baynes, in a house in his street, not a dozen yards from him. The third was a murmuring among the railway boys against the Vicar at the time of the strike. " It's all very well for him to say that the strike must be broken," they had said in Mr. Carman's hearing at the

Railway Hotel. " He has packets of money. He gets a good screw from his job, which we pay outa our taxes, and he's got wads of money of his own. He lives in proper style, I don't mind telling you. Look at his old woman : diamond rings and a fur coat that didn't cost only sixpence, by any means."

The first had generated a resentment against God ; the second, the arrival of Mr. Baynes in Mrs. Anscombe's front room, had caused him to meditate upon the Ministry ; the third, after generating a justifiable indignation with all parsons as such, had left the lingering thought that while this minister at Mrs. Anscombe's was obviously as poor as a church mouse, his boss up the road had plenty of bees-and-honey and was probably as big a mug as this one.

You may say that these three events happened in the spring-time. That is true, but in the realms of creative art a long period of gestation, with much studious research, and then much hard brainwork, is necessary before you begin to create. It was so with Mr. Carman. He had had to study carefully Mrs. Welcome's fur smother and diamond groins which she'd worn at St. Aidan's bazaar ; he had given time to comparing the Vicarage with other possible gaffs ; he had had to consider all the various methods and times of entry into the Vicarage ; and in the end he had had to wait till the nights were dark at the reverend gentleman's supper-time.

But now gestation was over, and he was in labour of a very bonny infant.

On any nicely dark night.

§

Friday was a nicely dark night ; and Mr. Carman came up the road from the Fields with his mouth on one side and a finger scratching his cheek-stubble, as if his thoughts were far from Hamden Hill—with his old mother, perhaps, who now lived in a Cottage Home for the Aged at Trustham, Essex. You would have had to peer very closely to see that his eyes, and especially his left eye, were not gazing before him, rapt in abstract thought, but furtively scanning all that was visible of the road, up-hill, down-hill, and across. Once he bent down to tie a shoelace tighter, which is an excellent method of looking down the street

66

behind you from between your legs. Satisfied that no one was interested in his movements, he swung into the churchyard with an easy, almost a graceful air, one hand on his hip, the other stroking his chin. He even entertained the churchyard with a muted whistling, to add a verisimilitude to his appearance of ease. His walk through the garden gate of the Vicarage was as direct and brisk as that of a man whose conscience was unworried because his mind was clean. As direct and brisk, but not quite as loud. A few such gentle steps, and he was once again leaning against the elm, with his right elbow resting in his left hand, and the fingers of his right hand pulling thoughtfully at his lips. In this darkness there was no reason why he should bend his head and look up at the house from under the peak of his cap, but old habit caused him to do so.

A light in the bedroom. And in the window of the dressing-room next door. Both lights out. The maid was returning to the kitchen, having left the whole of the first floor in darkness. He drew on his kid gloves, smoothing the fingers home as a lady will who is about to pay a call.

The only lights were now in the dining-room round the corner, and in the kitchen on the far side.

The jacob. Quickly he had the ladder from the back of the church and leaned it against the wall beneath the bedroom window. It was an adjustable ladder, and, his eye being adept at this sort of measurement, he had made it almost exactly the right length, in the darkness behind the church. He waited. No one interested. Silence this side of the house. Was there ever an easier job ? Up the ladder then. His ascent of the ladder, hand over hand, foot over foot, was so animated that you might have called it a trot. He pushed up the lower sash of the window and stepped into the room, which was sweetly carpeted. Drawing from his raincoat pocket the toe-halves of a pair of socks, he slipped them over his shoes and tip-toed to the closed door, torch in left hand, right palm shading it. There was no key in the lock, so he drew a wooden wedge from the same pocket and forced it under the door with his foot. Then to the dressing-table. Any of the right stuff ? Yes, here was a neat leather box, unlocked. The stuff didn't look as though it'd fetch much, sold crooked ; still, into the pockets with it all—brooches, bracelets, trinkets, chains. Only one ring on the bracket. No doubt the fat old mare'd got her diamond groins on. Silver brushes and cut-glass bottles. O.K. : pawnable. The drawers.

67

Any silk stockings or underwear : the only female garments, apart from furs, easy to turn into cash ? Yes . . . but not a very good haul so far. Have to take some lumber and swag it away. Where was a suit case ? Here, alongside the wardrobe : a gent's case ; the old sky-pilot's, no doubt ; what he put his daft petticoat and surplus in. Anything in it now ? No. Open the wardrobe, then. Ah ! The fur smother. And was it a large one ? Not 'ahf. Too big for this case. O.K. find a bigger and better bag in the old barsted's dressing-room.

The dressing-room door was shut, so he turned its handle softly, took the door's whole weight on to his hand and off the hinges, and opened very slowly. The torch peeped and peered. Ah, more silver brushes. But struth ! he was getting forgetful in his old age. There was a door from this dressing-room on to the landing, and he'd left it as a way in. Crikey ! Quickly he kicked another wedge under this door. Any of the right stuff in here ? A stud box. Any red stuff in it ? Yes, pair of gold links and one gold stud. But no pearl tie-pins or diamond shirt studs. These bleedin' parsons wore nothing but a suit and a collar. Any lumber in the cupboard ? Only a bleedin' cassock, and, gawd's love, he'd no use for that. Old Leeman'd never buy a cassock, and he himself could hardly wear it in Maker Street. Right : shut the cupboard and try the chester drawers. Caw, a kettle ; and a nice fat kettle too ; but not going ; stopped at five past three——

Waw'wossat ? ! A creak. The old wardrobe had chosen this moment to give forth, like the statue of Memnon when first touched by the rays of the sun, a sound. A creak only, as if it had only just realized that it had been touched by an alien hand, but to Mr. Carman it sounded like a rifle crack. It shook him. He stood and stared at the wardrobe as if he expected a detective inspector to emerge from it. Truly his nerves were not what they used to be. He felt a strong desire to be back in the other room and nearer the ladder. Gathering up his brushes, and a large suit case, he was bundling with these into the next room when he dropped the awkward clothes brush. Gawd ! . . . Standing as still as any piece of furniture in the room, and even stiller than the wardrobe since he didn't creak, he listened, an ear turned towards the door, his jaw thrust anxiously forward, and his torch out. He waited minutes . . . minutes. . . . No noise of alarm in the house. Good : they'd heard nothing ; why should they ? the dining-room wasn't under this room and the kitchen far away on the other side. Nah, this little job was money for jam.

Pat, patter. Rain. A noise of rain in the trees and on the gravel. So much the better. Everything was helping him. Rain'd keep the people indoors, and its patter in the garden'd overlay any sounds he might make. But best put the old fur wrap in the case. This he attempted in the other room, but found difficult because of the clobber already in the case, and so he decided to do this piece of packing in comfort behind the church, and——

Waw'wossat? A bell, a ting. And steps. Yes, steps crossing the hall downstairs. And the old barsted's voice—talking, talk-ing. . . . What were they chewing the fat about? Him? . . . No, the door shut again. It was jest the maid taking them their afters. But, gawd, if they'd finished their first course, he must'a been here best part of 'ahf an hour. Best be greasing : not a great lot in this job, but it'd been a nice, easy little bust, and he'd no one to divvy up with. Quickly, and by force of habit, he put everything in the room in its right and tidy position, to delay discovery ; then, two cases in one hand, fur coat on the other arm, he went to the window.

Still raining a little, and dark. Well, that was O.K. by him ; in fact couldn't be better. He stepped backwards out of the window, one foot feeling for the top of the ladder. And very carefully, since he was incommoded by the cases and the coat, he went down the ladder, rung by rung, with his back to the spits of rain. Because of his hampered grasp the ladder shook in his hand, and his heart shook with it. Not a doubt that he hadn't the nerves of his youth. Go steadily. Rung by rung. Ladder shaking again, blast its eyes. Damned if he'd put it back if it didn't behave itself. Steady. Nearly there. But just as he was about five feet from the ground he heard a voice say, " All right, laddie, you won't fall. We got hold of it."

He stood where he was on that rung, motionless, as if he must hear that voice again before he could believe in it. Perhaps he was going batchy and had dreamed it. It couldn't be true ; it was too awful ; too like something in a nightmare.

But it spoke again. " Come on, sonny. You don't want to stay there all night. Nor do we. Come to Mother."

Slowly he turned his head and looked down. And there was his old friend Detective Inspector Timmins, tall and plump and pleased, in his dark brown overcoat and Trilby hat, and young

69

Detective Sergeant Corbett, very neat and gentlemanlike in a smart grey mackintosh, and a young flatty in uniform with his cape still folded over his shoulders and his thumbs in his breast pockets, just as if he were meditating quietly at the corner of a street. Inspector Timmins was holding the ladder for him, and stretching up a hand to help him. Sergeant Corbett had one hand on the ladder and the other in his mackintosh pocket, so untroubled he was. And behind these three cops stood the parson in his daft black cassock and with an opened umbrella on his shoulder.

Jesus Christ!

" Let me help you with this one," said the Inspector, offering to take one of the cases. " I think we might have a light now, Geordie. Where's your glim? We want to see who he is."

Death and hell. The thing was a tumble. How the hell had it come unstuck? No chance to lie with these peters in his hands and this smother over his arm ; no chance to box clever ; no chance to say, " Now lemme explain. . . ." He was caught to rights. A sick and desperate disappointment emptied his heart of all but anguish, and laid waste the world. Down the few rungs of the ladder he had come the whole way from a glory to an absolute of misery.

Oh, gawd, gawd.

The young copper's lantern found his face and rested on it.

" Well now ! " Inspector Timmins exclaimed. " It's old Ricky. I thought it was a young one. We know this lad well, sir. Fact, he's one of your parishioners from the Fields."

§

" Oh, ma'am ! Oh, sir ! " The maid had rushed in with these exclamations when the dinner was half-way through. " There's someone upstairs."

" Someone upstairs ? Nonsense ! " All the same her words and her white face had given Canon Welcome one of the pleasantest thrills he had ever known. A thrill of alarm, excitement, and pride. He went quickly from the room into the hall ; pleased to be acting before these women the rôle of a Man, and their Protector, and One without Fear. The pleasure was enhanced by the fact that Amy was terrified. " Oh ! " she cried. " Oh, dear, oh dear. . . ! "

70

" Nothing to be afraid of, even if it *is* someone. Wait. Keep quiet."

In the hall he listened. He tip-toed to the foot of the stairs as softly as Mr. Carman himself, and listened. He crept a little way up the stairs ; and Mr. Carman could not have done it more soundlessly. Yes ; it was so : there was not one throb of fear ; only of delight ; delight in indignation, in the schoolboy game of ensuring a capture, and in his display of calm, prompt action.

" Don't make a sound, or he'll go. We shall lose him."

" I wish he would go," said Amy, trying to be humorous, though afraid.

" Hush. Nonsense. We must catch him now he's come."

" Oh, *sir*. . . ! " breathed the maid, fingering her mouth in doubt and alarm.

" Nothing to be afraid of. No need for ' Oh, *sir* ! ' He's more afraid of us than we are of him. Certainly more afraid than *I* am of him. Keep still. Not a sound."

And he shot into the study, closed its door with precisely the same care that Mr. Carman had used on opening his, and telephoned to the police ; then snatched an umbrella, hurried back into the garden where happy as a child at hide-and-seek, he watched both ladder and door, and ached for the police.

He would not have changed places with anybody. Over and above his excitement in the game there was now acute pleasure in a new thought : what fine publicity this would bring him. In the London papers, this. Almost he hoped the burglar would appear on the ladder before the police appeared at the gate so that the headline might run : " Vicar Captures Burglar Singlehanded."

But here they were, the police. Splendid their promptness ! They must have come in a car, stopped it down the hill, and run to his gate. Three of them : Detective Inspector Timmins, whom he knew fairly well ; a younger man whom he didn't know, probably the Inspector's sergeant ; and a policeman in uniform, whom he couldn't explain at all. Poor show for the lad upstairs.

He smiled and extended a flat, proud, explanatory palm towards the ladder. " And it's my own ladder," he whispered. " From the church. They might at least bring their own equipment with them."

"Sure there's only one, sir?" inquired the Inspector, crisply.

"It sounds like it. Yes, I think so."

"Well, there's no sign of a crow outside. Maybe the crow knew we were coming, and peeled off like a sensible lad, leaving his mate in the collecting box up there. They can *smell* a police car, some of these boys, before it leaves the station. This is Sergeant Corbett, sir. Look, Vernie boy : you go inside in case he comes down that way, and we'll wait for him here. The Vicar'll show you the way, and help you, I'm sure."

But the young detective sergeant had taken only a few steps, and Canon Welcome had only just started to follow him, when a leg of Mr. Carman appeared over the window sill. The leg waved to and fro, twice or three times, like a pendulum in the dark, while it felt for the top of the ladder. It found it, and rested ; and then Mr. Carman's other leg, the rest of his raincoat, his rump, two suit cases, a fur coat, and the upper part of Mr. Carman came clumsily after it.

"Damn!" said the Vicar, forgetting his cassock. "Those are *my* suit cases."

"Probably," whispered the Inspector.

"And that's my wife's fur coat."

"Afraid so, sir. And we shall have to take it along with us to the station. But the lady'll get it back in due course."

"Yes, but meantime he's getting it wet."

And at this he felt in danger of spoiling the silence with a giggle ; and yet more so, as the back parts of Mr. Carman, all unsuspecting, came slowly down the ladder.

"Let me help you with this one," said the Inspector, stretching up a courteous hand to relieve him of a bag.

What a story to tell Amy and Tim and Bettersby and Baynes ! How they would laugh. And what a story for the reporters if all this came out in court. "Let me help you with this one." Laughter in court. This would surely make its way into the London papers—into the evening papers at least. They always had a column dealing with comedy in the courts.

His visitor was now on the ground, staring at his captors. Light from the constable's lantern played on his face : the leathery wrinkled face of an elderly man, with tiny, deep-set, peeking eyes.

"Oh gawd, gawd."

Never were words so full of amazement and despair. The man's mouth squared, his teeth came down on one side of his lips, his eyes held all the misery in the world, and it was easy to see that he was on the brink of passionate tears. " Gawd in His Heaven."

This was such a sigh of despair that an unexpected pity for him stirred in the Canon. And that moment of pity revealed, to him something of what it must mean to have spent a large part of one's life in prison, and to be going back there again. The man stared at the incredible, unspeakable, figure of the Inspector, and said, " Oh, Christ ! " and it sounded like an appeal to Life for mercy.

Inspector Timmins, however, having all the heartiness of a big, plethoric, brown-skinned man, remained cheerful, sportive, and unshaken by too much pity. " This one didn't quite come off, did it, Ricky ? Well now, isn't that just too bad ? And how are you these days ? It's ages since we've seen you. Thought you'd turned the old lark up ? "

" So I had, guv'nor, so I had, and—but hah the bleedin' 'ell did you know I was here ? "

" How the bleeding hell did we know, eh ? Excuse his French, sir. How did we know ? That's our secret. We have our professional secrets, Ricky, same as you."

" There was no one tailing me. That I'll swear."

" I shouldn't be too sure of that."

" And no one grassed me. No one could of, because I never told nobody a word about it. I kep' it absolutely to meself."

" It's wonderful how we get to know things, Ricky."

" Yeah ! Bleedin' wonderful ! " Mr. Carman's little eyes, bewildered, defeated, swung from the Inspector in his brown overcoat to the Sergeant in his neat grey mackintosh ; and if he was not to weep, he must exude the bitterness by spitting reasonless words. " You and your secret police ! " he sneered. " Bloody police state, that's what we're coming to."

" That's it, Ricky. No freedom for honest British workmen like you."

" You get your livin' all right ; why can't you leave me to get mine. I got a wife and children same as you."

" Oh come, Ricky ! You've lost this round, and it's not like you to whine. You never were a whiner."

" Did his Reverence here send for you ? "

" Perhaps, Ricky. Who knows ? Now I wonder ! "

Mr. Carman turned to the Canon. " Did you, your Reverence ? I'd like to know before I go inside. Straight I would."

73

" I don't think I should tell him, sir, if I were you."

" Very good, Inspector. You know best."

" Well, I don't think that's fair," grumbled Mr. Carman. It's just not playing the game, Mr. Timmins. If one's copped, one's entitled to know how. Surely."

" That's what you think, is it ? " laughed the Inspector. " Well, we think rather different, you see. If we've secret weapons, why should we tell you all about them ? "

" Secret ——s." The word was so gross that even Mr. Carman was shocked at its utterance before a parson, and he turned to the Canon. " If your Reverence'll pardon me," he offered.

" Tush, tush, Ricky," chided Inspector Timmins. " I'm surprised at you. Take the two cases, Geordie boy."

" What'll I get for this, guv'nor ? . . . The smother'll go into the large bag, if the lady don't want it to get wet. . . . You know my record, Mr. Timmins ; you know all abaht me ; what'll I get ? "

" Don't know the answer to that one. The old Smudge'll tell you that. Shove the coat in the bag then, Geordie."

" Another lagging, d'you suppose ? "

" Perhaps they won't be too hard on you. But you *can* get up to fourteen years for this, as you know."

" Oh, no ! " pleaded Mr. Carman ; and it was like the plea of a child who begs not to be beaten. " I'm sick and tired of it. I've had all the bird I want. I can't take any more. I tell you I can't take it."

" Well, it rests with you, old boy, when you get a break. When you stop, we stop. That's the answer to that one."

" I did stop, as you know. I did. I swallowed the anchor three yurs ago and I've run straight ever since. But I lost me job, and I was pretty near skint and I thought this was an easy one. Did the guv'nor here send for you ? "

" Perhaps. And again, perhaps not. Perhaps it was just thought-reading on our part. But come on now : I don't know about *you*, but I'm getting wet. Come along."

" Aw'right. Gimme time. I'm comin'. I know when I've bought it. Suppose you've got your old jam-jar there ? "

" Yes, it's waiting down the road, Ricky."

" Aw'right, Mr. Timmins. It's a nick. Lead on, pal."

And between the two detectives, Inspector Timmins and Sergeant Corbett, he went through the gate, not without a dignity, a touch of heroism, in his defeat.

But the Canon's pity for his visitor was not so strong, and therefore not so enduring, as his pleasure in the story he would have for his friends and in the certainty that much valuable publicity was coming to him when the case was heard in court. One's pleasure in an inheritance tends to be more than one's grief for the deceased. Two hours after Mr. Carman's departure he lay back in his copious armchair, smoking a late cigar and as happy, as Mr. Carman, sitting on his bedboard in his cell without a fag and without hope, was in a pit of melancholy.

The hall-door bell sounded. What ? The police back again ? . . .

No ; and it was some disappointment when nobody but old Baynes was introduced into his room.

But, as always with his clergy he showed, and indeed felt, only the heartiest goodwill.

" Baynes ! What's brought *you* through the rainy night ? Come in, old boy. Take your usual chair, and throw off that wet coat—toss it anywhere—it's raining properly now, is it ? You're not the first caller I've had from your district this evening ; but *you* came through the door ; the other came through the window. I've just been burgled." Really Baynes, with his preposterous turned-up nose, and his protruding crumpled paunch, and his trousers short and frayed, showing crumpled grey socks, was almost a figure of fun. And Canon Welcome, because he felt superior to his curate in every way—in education, social position, and ecclesiastical rank, in figure, face, and dress—felt moved to treat him with affectionate banter, as one does with a child. " Remember that old Bettersby said you'd be burgled if you went to live in Maker Street ? Well, he got it wrong. It was me that was burgled."

" So I've heard, Vicar. That's why I came."

" To sympathise ? Well, that's very nice of you. Have a smoke, old chap. The box is beside you. I'm afraid I couldn't offer my previous visitor a cigar. I provided him with a whole squad of police instead. It was really rather funny. I can't help laughing. D'you remember that old Betts said they'd parlour-jump through your front window ? Instead of that it was my bedroom window. He came out of it with poor Amy's fur coat and the police waiting. It was really too funny."

" Yes, I heard something about that too."

" What ! Has it got round to you already ? Heavens, how a story travels in our beloved Fields." Reclining in the deeps of his chair, he was most happy to think that everybody was talking about his burglary. " It's like a tale running its rounds in an Egyptian bazaar."

" It's not quite as simple as that, Vicar." Baynes sat on the front edge of his easy chair, his back upright and his large fat hands splayed over his knees as usual, like twin starfish. He seemed unable to lean back and loll at ease, as Tim or Bettersby would have done, in this fine and comfortable room. He had taken a cigar and lit it, but not as one accustomed to such a luxury ; rather as someone to whom it was a treat. " The man is my neighbour in Maker Street."

" Go on ! "

" Yes, I know him and his wife and his daughter quite well. Very nice people."

" The company you keep, Baynes ! "

" Ah, but he's quite a nice chap. His name's Fred Carman, but in the trade he's known as Ricky, I believe. Well, directly they'd charged him at the police station, they sent an officer round to inform Mrs. Carman. And poor lady, she's distracted. She thought he was going straight, and now they've got him again for Heaven knows how long. She came rushing round to me, wanting to know if I could do anything about it."

" I don't see what we can do about it, Baynes. We can get her some help perhaps. We can certainly get her some help." The idea appealed at once to his kindness, and to his pity. " That's an excellent idea, Baynes. I shall go out of my way to see that she has help."

" I don't think it's that sort of help she needs, Vicar. The people around'll probably look after her. And some of Fred Carman's old cronies and fellow-crooks'll see that she doesn't want."

" You mean they'll give her money ? "

" Good lord, yes ; if she seems to need it. They'll give her a separation allowance." Baynes's eyes suddenly twinkled as he sat there, upright and hands on knees ; but his smile was no more than a half-completed, half-ashamed, thing : a pressing together and a trembling of thin lips, as if he'd shut the laughter within them, as one shuts some secret mischievously within the lips of a purse. " And I'll tell you why they'll do it : because they know she's always been faithful to him and stood by him. They wouldn't give a deener——"

" A what, Baynes ? "

" A bob, a shilling, to a wife who went on the loose when her man was in stir—in prison, I mean. They're very nice people down my way. Very high-principled."

" Are they ? "

" Well, in some ways . . . not quite in all, perhaps." The lips pressed back the smile again. " They'll help old Fred, too. They always stand by a pal who's had a tumble and copped it—that's to say, if he's a good lad and never shopped any of them. They'll have a whip-round and gather enough to pay a good mouthpiece for him and send him a few delicacies in Brixton Prison. And they won't put up pence, either. Some of 'em'll fork out a five-pound note, or even twenty-five pounds. No, probably, not a five-pound note, because the wretched things've got numbers and can be traced. We have to be careful sometimes, down our way. They'll probably pay up in wads of ordinary pound notes."

" Good gracious, Baynes ! "

" Yes, you see, we make good money, now and then ; and when we're in money, we blow it in the most generous style. I think we're extraordinarily nice people—sometimes." The eyes twinkled again, and the lips, tight closed, moved up and down, as he saved them from a full smile. This was the first time the Vicar really noticed this odd, abbreviated smile of old Baynes, and the curious look in his eyes which accompanied it. It was as if both lips and eyes knew, or were thinking of, much more than they cared to say.

" So they send him food, eh ? "

" Why, certainly. Isn't he one of the boys ? Old Fred's told me that he's sometimes had more good grub in one remand week at Brixton than ever before in his life. And I don't suppose he was completely lying."

" Well, good lord ! I never ! I'm learning a lot, Baynes."

" Yes, Fred Carman's not at all a bad old piece, and I think he's had quite enough prison. He doesn't need any more."

" I don't know about that, but, in any case, what can we do about it ? If he *will* go stepping through people's windows and coming out with fur coats. . . . What would *you* do about it ? Try to get his sentence reduced ? "

" No."

" What then ? What's your idea ? "

" That we should get him off."

" Get him *off* ? " This so surprised the Vicar that he rose
from his chair and stood before his fireplace, gazing down at
his visitor.

" Yes."

" Without punishment at all ? "

" Exactly."

Baynes's cigar had already gone out, and he was lighting
it again laboriously. The Vicar couldn't quite control an
impatience with him because he'd let the cigar go out in less
than two minutes. That was a good cigar, and he was ruining
it. Really one should have a supply of less expensive cigars
for chaps like Baynes who'd no idea what they were smoking.
. . . No, Baynes was a good chap. Let him have the best.
But surely he was talking nonsense now.

" But, Baynes, old chap : he can't break into people's houses,
and expect to get away with it, unpunished."

" He can't *expect* to, no ; but it would be rather wonderful
if he did."

" Oh, but really, Baynes ! "

" Why should we send him to prison ? We want to do him
good, don't we, and make him better ? "

" Of course, of course. Naturally. Certainly."

" Well, I'm sure police and prisons are necessary, but I'm
also sure that they never yet made anyone good." And Baynes
blinked at the Vicar, as much as to say, " Challenge that if
you can."

" Maybe not, but they at least made your Mr. Carman fed
up with prison—or ' bird ' as he calls it."

" That's no good. Fear's no good. Fear never made anyone
better. And anyhow, it obviously hasn't had any permanent
effect on him, since he's just come through your window and
gone out with valuables. What he needs is something of an
absolutely different kind. In fact, the exact opposite."

" Such as ? "

" Well, I thought I might go to his trial and offer to help
and look after him if they'd let him off——"

" Let him *off* ? But, Baynes, Baynes, he's got a host of convictions behind him ! He's more likely to get a long spell of
preventive detention than to get off——"

" I know—I know—unless we can move the mountain. . . ."

" We can't."

" I'm not sure. . . . I was thinking we might get him put
on probation—not acquitted, of course—and then I suddenly
saw that *you* were the obvious person to do this. I saw it like
a light, and I just had to rush round here and talk to you about
it. *You* must put in the plea for him."

" Me ? Why ? "

" *Why*, Vicar ? " Baynes lifted his hands from his knees
and spread them before the vicar, as if amazed that he should
not understand. At the same time he dropped the cigar from
his lips on to the carpet, stooped, picked it up, and let it go
out while he held it between his fingers. " Because you're the
one he burgled. You're the one he wronged. If *you* asked for
lenience for him, they might listen. And if they did—if by any
chance they granted you your request—*what* a story ! It would
dramatise the principles of our religion better than all the
sermons we've ever preached."

The Vicar, staring at Baynes, was aware of a new light, a
beautiful light, glimmering, steadying, and slowly enlarging
before him. But first he had, as it were, to clear away some
clouds and scarves of mist that drifted before it. " But Baynes,
old boy, do you mean that if you'd heard a burglar up in your
bedroom, you wouldn't have sent for the police ? "

" I don't think I should have done. No."

" Good God ! Well, what *would* you have done ? Gone up
to him and asked him to come down and have a drink ? "

" Exactly. Precisely." Baynes was delighted with this idea.
The pleasure gleamed in his eyes and trembled on his lips.
He smacked his hands joyfully back on to his knees. " I should
have had a shot at that. I don't suppose it would have been
possible because as soon as I'd have appeared at the door with
my invitation he'd have disappeared through the window with
my silver brushes (if I had any). But supposing he had stayed
for a little chat, I'd have said, ' Come and talk it over, old son.
Leave those things because I'm fond of them, and if you're
really in need, I'll find you something else '."

" Oh, Baynes ! " The Canon said it reprovingly, as if his
curate was talking some rather sentimental nonsense.

" But didn't some prior or other, when he found robbers
in the monastery, greet them as guests of the house and
offer them all they wanted, so that they promptly awoke to

79

a lively sense of their sins, and joined his Order there and then?"

"Yes, but tales, Baynes, tales."

"Tales with all the truth in the world in them."

As Baynes uttered this strange sentence, the truth in them shone before the Vicar like a noonday sun. And he was ashamed and deeply disappointed in himself. He'd prided himself on his spiritual vision, and he hadn't even begun to see this. He's joyfully sent for the police instead of offering Mr. Carman a drink like the saints of old ; and it had needed old Baynes, like the man in the story of Paul, to come and cast the scales from his eyes. "By heavens, Baynes, I believe you're right."

"I know I am. We believe in forgiving our enemies, don't we, and in doing good to those that hurt us ; and that evil can only be overcome by its opposite, which is love."

"Which is love." The Canon was enthusiastic about it. "You're absolutely right, Baynes, old man. My dear chap, I cannot tell you how completely I agree with you. Good God why didn't I see this at first? I, as a priest of the Christian Church, must certainly go and plead for him. Certainly." Let us do justice to Canon Welcome and state that the thought of being benevolent and forgiving to Mr. Carman pleased him far more than the thought that his plea for a prisoner who'd robbed him would be a much grander story for the papers than the mere report of a burglary. But this latter thought was already on the threshold ; nay, it had come a little way indoors. "You put me to shame, Baynes. I thank you—I thank you most humbly for showing me what I ought to do."

"We always say that this is our code," continued Baynes, now very apologetic and explanatory, "but which of us really believes it?"

"I believe it."

"All right then ; but even if we believe in it, which of us really acts upon it?"

"I am going to act upon it. And in the meantime we'll do our part in looking after his wife. We'll race the crooks to that task, Baynes. Splendid. He has children, you say."

"He has one daughter at home."

"Splendid. We'll look after her too."

"Most parsons," began Baynes, pulling at the cigar with difficulty and keeping to his private dream, "pursue those that injure them till they've exacted every penalty. Just as—no, I'm

80

afraid it's gone out again ; where are the matches ?—just as if they'd never heard of Christ."

" They do, Baynes. You're perfectly right. They're generally the last to be converted to the real thing. It's shocking."

Baynes got the cigar gleaming and sparking and smoking again. He threw away the match.

" Let laymen be vindictive if they must," he said, " but not us."

The Canon nodded. " Not us, no. I see."

" And it's not only our business not to be vindictive but to go out and be the opposite."

" Yes, yes ; but, oh lord, Baynes, which of us sees it ? Which of us does it ? "

" Well, this is a chance to do it before all the world. I suppose the case will be reported in the press ? "

" I'm afraid so, Baynes. Yes, I don't see how we can avoid it. But we will use the publicity to good purpose, as you say, as you say. Baynes, I do really thank you for opening my eyes to this opportunity. You've done your priestly task well, converting even your vicar. And now have a drink." He rang the bell behind him. " Yes, of course you must have a drink as your reward. I certainly shan't let you go without one. If anyone deserved a drink, you do. And we'll drink to the success of our battle for the exemplary Mr. Carman."

CHAPTER TWO

" O YEZ, O YEZ, O YEZ, To all manner of persons who have
anything to do at the Adjourned Quarter Sessions of the Peace
for the County of London, draw near and give your attendance.
God save the King."

The old usher, standing on the floor of the court and casting
his eyes upward, bayed this proclamation at the frieze, and then
went and sat by the door. Everyone else sat down too, except
Mr. Carman, who stood between his two prison officers in the
dock and surveyed the familiar place with half-closed, unhappy,
but at the same time quizzical eyes. These sad, wandering
eyes, being professional eyes, when they looked through the
windows beneath the dome of the court, considered a wet slate
roof immediately beyond them and pronounced it a serviceable
means of entry.

Gaw, a gift that'd be ; always supposing there was anything
in this old cowhouse worth pinching. Oh, lord jee, here we are,
boys, in the same old place. Back again after three years.
Same old brown oak ; must have cost a tidy lot, all that carved
oak and red leather ; they treat us handsome so far as this
party is concerned. Same old smell of hard wood and desks :
always brings back that old classroom in Sluke's Church School,
Hebron Town High Road. Same old Lancelot up there on
his throne, though he looks a sight older than when he sentenced
me last—I wonder if he remembers me—they say he doesn't
forget much and dishes out the porridge accordingly ; they say
he's as cute as an old gimlet, even if he does look as though he'd
been six days dead.

Proper crinkled old prune, he is. Oh, law, law, let's get on
with it quickly and hear the worst from him. I'm not what I
was—not what I was—and don't stand up to this sort of waiting
as well as I did. The old heart never used to beat like this and,
to tell the truth, I feel a bit sick. Used to be able to stand it.
Proper comic if I catted over the dock-rail on to one of those
mouthpieces down below.

Old Lancelot don't look the man he was, either.

Lancelot Ellworthy, K.C., was the wigged chairman seated
on his high throne at the opposite side of the court from Mr.

Carman in his high dock. He sat between pillars and pediment of oak, leaning on one arm, like the portrait of a judge in a heavy oak frame. And Mr. Carman scanned his face from under his shabby eyebrows as he had scanned the windows of the Vicarage.

Yeah, the old judge up on high there, and me up on high here, and everyone else below us ; he and I are the important boys here. It's him against me, and me up against him—like tennis, see, on opposite sides of the court. Ha, ha, that's good : opposite sides of the *court*. And what a crowd to see the game : the bogies and bluebottles over there ; a bloomin' regiment of them—the bogies to tell all that's known about us " guilties" and the bluebottles to give evidence against some poor bloke who's swearing to heaven he's innocent. And there are the mouthpieces down there, three packed rows of them, all dolled up in their wigs and bands and hoping like hell for a dock brief. If some of 'em don't get a dock brief soon they'll have to take to crime instead. One or two of 'em young skirts too, with lip-stick and powder and all—might be tarts. Over there the jury, and a lot of silly mugs they look, waiting for us " guilties " to be polished off and put away. Gaw, if I'd pleaded " not guilty " and had had a tip-top mouthpiece, he could have fooled that lot ; he'd 've had 'em convinced, even though I come down the ladder with six fur coats and all the family plate in me 'ands, that I was most crool'ly wronged and misunderstood. He'd 've had 'em in tears before he done.

" Number eight, my lord, Frederick John Carman."

Chrimes, what a bark ! Proper proud of his job, he is, this bloody bald-headed old screw ; bringing us up the stairs and bawling our names at old Lancelot. Oh, Gawd help us, old Lancelot isn't half sticking out his underlip and grunting to himself. One of his bad days, I reckon. Looks as though he didn't love any of us today, cops or counsel or prisoners. Sick of us all. Pity, because it means he'll dish out the porridge in big helpings today. Fat chance I got of getting a light sentence. Not likely he'll listen to old Timmins and Reverend Welcome. More likely they'll put his back up. Oh, well, can't be helped ; luck of the game.

" Frederick John Carman, you are charged on this indictment with breaking and entering the dwelling-house of James Humbert Welcome and stealing therein property to the value of five hundred pounds——"

Law, couldn't 'a got fifty for it, mate. Soft job, the old Clerk
of the Peace's : just has to get up and ask a few questions and
then sit down again and leave the rest of us boys to do the work.
" —are you guilty or not guilty ? "
" Guilty, yer honour—me lord." Jesus, muffed that one !
Calling the old Clerk of the Peace a lord ! Should know better
after all these years. Not used to pleading guilty, that's what it
is. " Guilty, sir."
" I appear for the prosecution, my lord, and my friend, Mr.
Mitchison, is defending the prisoner. My lord, the indictment
to which the prisoner pleaded guilty at the North West London
Magistrate's Court relates to an act of housebreaking, and the
short facts are——"
Mr. Carman sat down, and his prison officers sat too. Why
doesn't the old prosecuting counsel turn his face round once so
that I can see what it's like. Ah, here it comes : Chrimes,
what a map ! Looks as though someone had crowned him and
crushed it all down for him—his forrid, his hooter, his kisser, and
all. And those darned great headlamps that keep slipping down
his hooter whenever he looks at his old brief. Push 'em back,
mate, but get 'em to fit next time.
" The window was closed, but not bolted ; he lifted the sash, and
that, of course, was enough to constitute an act of breaking——"
Ah, showing off ! Turn it up. We all know what breaking
is. Get on with the game. I want to know ; I want to know.
You're the King's Mouthpiece, aren't you ; well, spit it out.
" As between our Sovereign Lord the King and the prisoner at
the bar." O.K. by me. God save the King.
" Fortunately the reverend gentleman heard the prisoner's
movements overhead and was able without disturbing him to
summon the police. The police arrived with admirable prompt-
itude and were waiting at the foot of the ladder when the
prisoner came down somewhat slowly because he was incommoded by two suit cases and a large fur coat——"
That's right : make 'em laugh ; it's a fine laughing matter
for me, isn't it ?
" —and the prisoner could hardly do other than admit the
offence. Those are the short facts, my lord. I'll call the officer."
" I swear by Almighty God that I will true answer make to
all such questions as the court shall demand of me Peter John
Timmins detective inspector S division me Lord——" and
smack went the testament on the ledge.

Not very reverent that. Never mind : old Timmins has promised he'll put in a word for me. Old Reverend Welcome talked him into that. And Reverend Baynes. Out-and-out gent, Reverend Welcome. Would you believe it : screw his drum, and he loves you like a brother ! Don't mind telling you that if there's one house safe in future, it's his. Not a boy'll touch it.

"Inspector Timmins, were you present at the North West London Magistrate's Court when the defendant, Frederick John Carman, pleaded guilty to this charge ?"

"I was, sir."

"And is this the man ? "

"It is, sir."

Fancy that ! They ain't mixed the babies up.

"Well, will you tell my lord what you know about him ? "

Oh my god, here it comes.

"My lord, the accused is a married man, aged fifty-nine, with four children, only one of whom, a daughter aged sixteen, resides at home. The others are sons, grown up and, I understand, in good employment."

Caw, that's a sweet one. If that's all you understand about our Perse—fine. Coo, that's rich. That'll amuse our Perse.

"His parents parted soon after he was born, and his mother died when he was fifteen, so, to a certain extent, my lord, he's had to live by his wits from childhood. After leaving school he worked for a little but, becoming unemployed at seventeen years of age, he got into very bad company and took to petty crime. I should say that from 1916 to 1919 he served in the army as a private in the Army Ordnance Corps and was discharged with his character 'good '."

" ' Good', did you say ? "

"Yes, my lord : ' good '."

That's right : four years without being found out. And if they only knew ! Why, an ordnance depôt's just about the sweetest place on earth for a bright lad.

"There are fourteen previous convictions, my lord."

Not so good.

And out they came, one laid on top of another, in a steadily mounting pile. And the prosecuting counsel stood and stared up at the Inspector as if engrossed, even amazed, almost aghast, at the erection of such a monument. Surely no need to put on an expression like that. And no need to lean back with both his mitts on the desk behind, as if he'd like to sit down while the rest of this recital proceeded. And old Lancelot fidgeting impatiently up there. What's he grunting about? Woss'at? Wossy say?

" Let's have only the last three, inspector. Do they deal with dishonesty? "

" Yes, my lord."

Course they do! What the hell does he think I am? A pouf? A dirty ponce? And what does old Timmins look at his papers for, as if to make sure? He knows I'm a good screwsman. What does he expect to find there? Rape? Incest? Buggery? Just as well we're only taking the last three, though : we're missing out on the Canonbury do, when nine other offences were taken into consideration. That never sounds so good.

" Since his last release from prison more than three years ago, my lord, he has honestly tried to get work with a view to going straight, and until recently he has succeeeded, on the whole, in supporting his wife, who's a very respectable woman——"

That she is! Loyal and true. Yeah, old Timmins is doing the decent now, but I don't see that he need have said, " Come to Mother ' when he pinched me, I don't, really. And just standing there at the foot of the bloody ladder and grinning! Chokey's no joke and he knows it. Gawd knows I like humour in its place, but not to an old lag coming down a ladder with the doings in his hand.

Mr. Carman felt more and more indignant as he considered Mr. Timmins's misplaced humour. " Come to Mother "—at a moment like that! Cheap. Mr. Timmins should know better than that. Very different the way old Timmins talks to a judge. No trying to be funny now. No " Come to Mother " to him. What's he saying?

" —of late, however, or so he tells me, my lord, he's found it impossible to get work. But now, as I understand, some employment could be found for him by his minister, the Reverend Canon Welcome, who's in court."

" *Canon* Welcome, did you say? "

Ah, that's stirred up old Lancelot : a canon ; that shot him up, ha, ha.

" Yes, my lord."

" Very well."

" Thank you, Inspector. That is the case——" began prosecuting counsel.

"Oh no, it isn't," and counsel for defence was up on his feet.

Oh, no, it isn't guv. *My* mouthpiece is up on his plates now and going to do *his* stuff, f'r a change. Going to use *his* clapper now.

"I'm really very sorry." And prosecuting counsel, quite bewildered at having forgotten that the prisoner was defended, made a quick bow to the bench, as if apologizing for having misled it, and another to prisoner's counsel, as if apologizing for having insulted him, and sat down.

"Inspector Timmins . . . one minute. . . ."

What's he looking for on his paper? Gaw lummy, isn't he like his old man, Ernest Mitchison, K.C.? Same long carcase like a clothes-prop with a gown hanging on it and same long face like a table-spoon. Remember his old man prosecuting me in nineteen-o-nine. For receiving. Got me eighteen moon for that. Reckon his family owes me something.

"Inspector Timmins, the prisoner has only once been bound over, I think?"

Think? You can read, can't you?

"Yes, sir. Only after his first offence."

"And that was the last time? In 1907?"

"That is so, sir."

"Never again? Never another occasion?"

"No, sir."

Ah! see what he's up to; but there's not usually one after the last.

"And he's never been found guilty of, or even charged with, any crime of violence?"

"No, sir."

"Apart from these offences of dishonesty, in short, he's a perfectly well-conducted man?"

"Oh, yes, sir. Apart from those."

"And you firmly believe, as you have said, that until this last regrettable lapse he had made every effort to lead an honest life?"

"I do, sir. And if I may add a word, I should like to say that I think he has tried hard against—well, rather difficult odds, sir."

"Thank you, Inspector Timmins. Thank you indeed. My lord, I do most earnestly ask you to bring consideration to bear on one or two points before you come to a decision about this unfortunate man. He is, as you will appreciate, not a man of

87

strong intelligence and he has never been more than the lowest type of petty housebreaker——"

Good gawd ! The dirty stiff !

" The list of previous convictions which the detective in-spector—Inspector—er—Timmins—read out to us did, I confess sound a formidable document, but I would ask you now, with great respect, to consider it in some detail, and then I think—I hope—I shall persuade you that there are aspects of it which support a kinder interpretation. I'm not going to stress the prisoner's exceedingly unhappy and ill-starred childhood, or that he has never had much chance in life, or point out that when for four years he had secure and honourable employment in His Majesty's forces, his character was wholly good—I know these points have already received your lordship's favourable consideration. But I do ask you to direct your attention to the dates of these various convictions. At sixteen he is in trouble for shop-breaking ; at seventeen—yes, at seventeen I'm afraid he's in trouble again—but there is nothing against him, nothing at all, for—let me see—three years. And why is this ? It is because in those years he has taken himself, in hand, pulled him-self together, and is trying to live down a bad start——"

" There may be another interpretation, Mr. Mitchison."

" I'm much obliged, my lord. There may be. Much obliged. But I prefer to accept what——"

" You and I know, Mr. Mitchison, that it is possible by one successful robbery to secure enough to live in comfort and idle-ness for a year or two, before resuming one's profession again."

" Sometimes, my lord, certainly. Much obliged. But not in this case. Not in the case of this man before you. He is but a petty thief whose operations never brought him any large sums——"

And that's a lie.

" I lack your conviction of that, Mr. Mitchison."

" As your lordship pleases. If your lordship pleases. Thank you ; what was I saying ? I was saying, I was saying, much obliged, that I prefer to accept what he tells me and, in view of what happens later, to believe it. He assures me that in each of these long intervals between one conviction and the next he has tried to get honest work, and you have heard from the officer, Inspector Timmins, that the police themselves, who are not easily hoodwinked by these old patrons of theirs (if I may so call them) and who, generally speaking, make it their business to know everything about them, are satisfied that ever since his last discharge from prison he has been trying to lead an honest life. I ask you to believe not him, but them. For some months he earned a very fair living, some seven or eight pounds a week, as a street photographer, registering his business in the proper place as ' Lucky Snaps '——"

" As *what*, Mr. Mitchison ? "

" ' Lucky Snaps ' my lord."

Old Lancelot grins, does he ? What's funny in that ? Still, better the old tea-pot should grin than grouse. Perhaps that's what old Mitchison's up to.

" He prospered for a little, but competition increased in this, you may think, lucrative employment, and he was gradually put out of business by younger men whose appearance and manner were perhaps more attractive and trustworthy than his——"

Blast his soul !

" He then earned some money in other ways, as a potman, a labourer, and in other unskilled fields, but always, he says, his record came up against him and he was—to use his own words—' blotted out ', till at last, being nearly sixty the prospect of finding employment receded altogether. He has a wife and young daughter who has just begun to earn a small living as a finisher in a gown factory and—well, my lord, he succumbs —he succumbs to a sudden temptation——"

Sudden ? That's a hell of a miss. Seven months I give to thinking out that job. Still, carry on with the fanny.

" I would submit, my lord, that if you could see your way to taking a lenient view of this sudden, irrepressible impulse, and could decide not to send him back to prison but rather to put him on probation——"

Probation ? *Probation ?* That's likely, ain't it ? Why, he'll be asking them to take a collection for me next. Probation ! More likely three years.

" —if you could see your way to binding him over in a period of years, there is a chance, a very great chance, that this ageing man will turn for ever from his unhappy courses and become an honest citizen in the evening of his days. I am the more confident in saying this, because I can offer you the very best assurance that he will be looked after and helped in every way. I now have an opportunity, as pleasing as it is strange in this uncharitable world, of calling in support of this appeal no less a person than the reverend gentleman whose dwelling-house he broke into."

Thought so. That's got the reporters going. That's stirred 'em in their sleep. Be all over London in an hour or two, and the missus'll hate it. Still, it's not the first time I been in the papers along with the Prime Minister, and if it'll knock a stretch off me sentence——

" The Reverend Canon Welcome is most anxious to speak on behalf of the prisoner, and he will give an undertaking that work of some sort will be provided for him. With your permission I will call the Reverend Canon Welcome."

There's His Reverence. Gaw blimey, sitting amongst the cops. Hadn't seen him there. Fine-looking old steamer. Kind-looking. But not soft, thank the Lord. He don't look an old sucker, like some of 'em. Lancelot's too old a bird to take any soft stuff, even from a bleedin' archbishop. He don't suck nobody's satin cushions. Perhaps I ought to hang me head here and look kind 'a penitent, but doubt if it'd do any good with Lancelot. He's seen those sort of acts before. Might work with a jury like those boobs over there, but not with our Lancelot : he hasn't a heart. Funny : Reverend Welcome looks real nervous. You'd 'a thought that up in that box he'd feel like he was in his pulpit, and full o' beans. But he's sweatin', and his mitt's trembling. Suppose this is something new to him. Heard that parsons who're terrific in the pulpit, flinging their arms about and shouting the odds, sweat blood on a stage, and that actors who are as happy as turkey-cocks on the stage, showing themselves off, wish they were dead in a pulpit. Can't say *I'd* be much good in a pulpit.

" Canon Welcome, how long have you known this man ? "

" Not long, I'm afraid. Only since—only since he paid a call on me that night."

Laughter. Old Lancelot grinning again. A mutt's question, that. Don't know, though : may be cleverer than I thought. A bloke feels tolerant—kind of affectionate—to someone he's laughed at. Maybe Lancelot's beginning to love me.

" But since that visit have you got to know him ? "

" I have seen him in the police station and in Brixton Prison, and I have visited his home and made many enquiries about him."

" Well, will you tell my lord what is your considered opinion ? "

" My lord, as far as the man himself is concerned, I can only endorse very earnestly everything that his counsel has said. He has given me a solemn promise that he will try hereafter to lead an honest life, and for my part I have no doubt that he will keep this promise. I see a lot of these people, my lord—my parish includes the rather grey and unhappy area in which he lives—and I don't think I am easily deceived by them. I—yes, I will stake my faith in him. And I think I should add that though the district from which he comes has not a good name, there are many decent people keeping decent homes there, and his wife is certainly one of these. She is a most respectable woman, devoted to him——"

That she is ! Loyal and true.

" —and her one desire is to help him in every way to go straight and keep straight. I do most respectfully suggest—and I speak from much experience among these people—that an act of mercy to this man might do more good than harm in an area that presents great difficulties to us all. I would go so far as to suggest that its effects might be greater than any of us can perceive. But I will not labour that point. I will only say, if for one moment I may speak as the representative of the whole parish, that I'm sure that it is worth trying. I think— I feel——"

Why's he stopped ? Has he forgotten what he was going to say next ? He's looking down. Oh, I see : he's got some notes there.

" I personally take the view that there's much good in him. and I'm ready to help him in every possible way. I do most earnestly submit, sir, that, as learned counsel has said, there is here a chance of enabling a fellow creature to redeem himself, and indirectly perhaps to help in the redemption of others, and I should be happy if, thanks to your lenience, I should be able to take some part in that redemption."

" My lord—thank you, Canon—my lord, I will not add another word. With great respect I do ask you to consider all that Canon Welcome, the very man whom he robbed, has submitted to you."

Abruptly Mr. Mitchison bowed and sat down.

And now silence. The chairman twiddling a pen on his desk and scratching his chin. Everyone else sitting still and awaiting his words.

Come on, cock ; come on ; I want to know ; I don't hope

for nothing, so let me know the worst ; I'm not so young as I was and don't stand up to this sort'a waiting so well.

"Frederick John Carman, do you want to say anything to me before I pass sentence on you ? ' "

Sentence, he said. That's finished it. Penal's my guess.

"No, me lord, except that if I can earn enough to support my family, I promise to turn it up and——"

"If ! There are to be no ifs in this matter. No conditions. We don't come to terms with flagrant crime."

Gawd ! Muffed that. "No—what I mean—you see——"

"Yes, yes. I see, I see." He sounds impatient. Weary. Pity I struck one of his tired days, sour old devil. He'll twist his snaky old tongue round me now. "I have listened to all your counsel has said, and he has certainly left nothing unsaid. I have also heard the very eloquent plea from the clergyman you robbed. You are clear, I hope, that I could send you to penal servitude for this. But I do not propose to do that. If I deal more leniently with you——"

Eighteen moon's my guess.

" —you can thank Inspector Timmins and your very good friend, Canon-er-Canon Welcome. One of the few happy experiences that come to us in this court is the constant proof that the police are ever ready, if possible, to save men just out of prison from going back there again——"

If he believes that, he'll believe anything.

" —and as for Canon—Canon Widdycombe—I believe it is not unprecedented for the victim of a crime to plead for the criminal, but it is unique in my experience. I have not his unbounded faith in your reformation, and I'm afraid I find it difficult to believe, as he appears to do, that any mild reformation on your part will have the slightest effect on your neighbours. As a result of that phenomenon I should not expect any material diminution in the number of visitors we receive here from your particular parts. But—well—he may be right, and I think, yes I think on the whole, I'm prepared to take a chance. I bind you over to be of good behaviour and to come up for judgment in a period of three years——"

Jesus ! What did he say ?

"You can go now."

"All right, Ricky," said the big bald-headed warder. "Come on. Don't blub. Anybody'd think he'd sentenced you to be topped instead of settin' you free."

CHAPTER THREE

CANON WELCOME rushed from his place among the police,
and through one door and another, till he came into the large
entrance hall of the Sessions House. He wanted to be there
before Mr. Carman appeared so as to be the first representative of the free world to grasp his hand and welcome him back.
He had to wait by the main doors some minutes while Mr.
Carman, somewhere on the other side of that long east wall,
said good-bye to his prison officers and received the grinning
congratulations of ushers and police. At last Mr. Carman
appeared, walking towards the doors and the daylight, through
the thronging witnesses, the standing policemen, and the hurrying solicitors and counsel. He walked slowly, blinking a little
like a man who has come from half-darkness into a full daylight, but with a cocky assumption of confidence which plainly
he did not feel. Mr. Carman was quite unaccustomed to leaving
the Sessions House, Newington Causeway, by this public, un-
walled, and undirected route.

Canon Welcome rushed forward and, grasping his right hand
in both of his, shook it many times and pressed it warmly. If
Mr. Carman had been happy unto tears at his unexpected libera-
tion, Canon Welcome was almost as moved and happy now.
He loved Mr. Carman because he had so successfully saved
him—loved him as one loves the man one saves from drowning.
The hand which he was pressing so cordially seemed like a prize
he had won after a wavering and exciting contest. Mr. Carman
might have been the horse which had won the Golden Guineas
for him, and which he must now lead in triumph to the un-
saddling enclosure. For a moment he felt like offering him a
cigar, but he could not quite bring himself to this. No, he
would give other things to the good rough fellow, but not one
of his best cigars.

" Splendid ! Splendid, my dear chap ! " he exclaimed, not
letting the hand go. " With all my heart I congratulate you,
Carman. This is fine ! Fine ! And now let me take you
home. I have my little car here."

" Gaw-lummy," said Mr. Carman. " But I reckon you done
enough for me, sir : thank you very much."

" Rubbish. This is a great day. I'm going to take you home to Mrs. Carman. She'll be pleased, I think, don't you ? "

" She'll be knocked silly. She was laying I'd be birded for three yur or more. She wouldn't come to the court because she said she couldn't stand it ; it always upset her so. She's a good woman, she is. A saint, compared to me."

" Come then, let's go and give her the surprise of her life. Great heavens, I'm pleased about this. Come along, old chap."

In the wet courtyard of the grey Sessions House, among the cars of the lawyers, justices, clerks, jurymen and better-to-do witnesses (whether guiltless or sinful) stood the Canon's little blue Standard Ten. He unlocked it (he had decided that it was safer to lock it in these shadowy purlieus where the company was mixed), and he held open the door for Mr. Carman.

" In here? Chrimes ! " said Mr. Carman. He clambered in, and sank into place by the driver's seat. " Gaw, this is a lot better than being carted. Driven off like a gent in one's own jam-jar, as you might say. You could of knocked me block off when old Lancelot said that. Bahn'd over ! Did you ever ? And I hadn't a hope, guv'nor—straight I hadn't—when I went up them stairs. Not a hope in heaven. Blimey, I wasn't sure it wouldn't be penal for life." Excited and confused by the unexpected sentence, Mr. Carman was as garrulous and restless as a kettle on the boil. He talked and talked while the Canon drove out of the courtyard with his prize and into Newington Causeway and along the Borough High Street. " Course I hoped that whatever you was going to say might get me off a year or two ; but you never know. It depends on whether the old judge has digested his breakfast or not, how much gruel he gives you. An' I thought old Lancelot's stomach wasn't doing too well by him. Gaw, it takes some believing. Bahn'd over. I knew that the old Recorder, Sir Ernest Wild, K.C."—Mr. Carman loved titles and letters after names—" was a great one for showing leniency to old lags who'd never had a chahn'st, but I never expected anything like that to come my way. Often Sir Ernest Wild, K.C. 'd put himself about to find the old lag a job of some sort—usually a newspaper pitch or something—but if you come up before him again after that, you were *for* it. You got no mercy. Yeah, a decent sort'a cove, Sir Ernest Wild, K.C. Another was Paul Bennet, V.C., the beak at West London. He'd bind a poor feller over if he could. Bahn'd over ! Can't get over it. And it was your doing, mister. You done it for me. It's you and old Timmins I have to thank. He came it well. Hah much did you pay him to come over with all that bull ? "

" I didn't pay him anything," laughed Canon Welcome, as he drove fast over London Bridge. " I'm not in the habit of bribing the police."

" Oh, I s'pose not. No."

" But I did tell him and Mr. Mitchison one or two things I thought they could say on your behalf." Canon Welcome had decided that he'd like to keep the largest possible credit balance. " That was all."

He wasn't really listening to all of Mr. Carman's prattle. Again and again his mind, exulting in the rare and dramatic victory they'd just won in the court room, turned to the news-story which must even now be hastily dressing for its appearance in the afternoon papers. " Clergyman's Plea Succeeds." " Burgled Vicar Pays for Thief's Defence." " Coals of Fire from the Canon." How much prominence would they give it ? They might even give it headlines right across the page.

" And it was *your* gaff I tried to screw ! Holy Moke, it don't make sense."

" It makes very good sense, Mr. Carman."

" *Mister* Carman. Cut out the ' mister ' and call me Ricky. All my pals do."

Even as he thought with delight of the coming publicity, or longed to tell Amy of his speech in the witness box, knowing that he could make her believe it more remarkable than it was, even as he dwelt thus apart from his passenger at his side, Canon Welcome was touched that Mr. Carman should number him among the " pals ". He felt as if he'd been admitted at last to the freedom of the Fields. " ' Ricky ' by all means. You forget, Ricky, that I'm a parson and we believe in doing good to those that hurt us."

" But why in the name of sense ? "

" Because that's the only way to change their hearts. Revenge never did it yet. It only hardened their hearts. At least that's what we believe."

" And I'm not sure that there ain't something to it. What I mean to say is, I don't mind telling you this : if there's one hah'se in London that's safe from me in the future, it's yourn." His little eyes watered as he uttered this grateful sentiment.

" What I mean is, we don't bite the 'and that feeds us. Nah ! "

" Now Ricky," protested the Canon, with another laugh.
" *Every* house in London is safe from you in the future. You
promised me both in the police station and in Brixton that
you'd done with all that."

" And so I have, guv'nor. I've swallowed the anchor this
time all right. I just forgot it for a moment. Yeah, I give you
my promise, and I keep it. It was time to turn the game up in
any case. I'm not so nippy as I was and, to tell the honest
truth, I don't seem to have the nerve I used to have. Nah . . .
best leave it to younger men."

" But, Ricky, I want you to leave it because you think it
wrong, not because you can't do it any more."

" Wurl . . . yes . . . it's wrong, I s'pose. . . . Cornhill and
Threadneedle Street : they don't 'ahf make the money here
. . . nah, what I really meant was, if anyone else tries to screw
your drum, I'll crown him. I don't bite the 'and that feeds
me. Nor I don't let anyone else."

" But you're not to talk about crowning anyone. Please don't
forget I've entered into recognizances for your future behaviour.
By crowning I suppose you mean hitting them on the head ? "

" That's right, guv'nor. That's correct. Hittin' them so
that they don't know if it's last week or next month."

" Well, we've done with all that from now on."

" Yeah, I suppose we have. Gee, will my Minnie be pleased
to see me back for dinner ? Will it fair knock her block off ? "

" Do you think we'd better let her know we're coming ? "

" Nah ! Rather surprise her. But hah could you let her
know ? "

" I could telephone to my colleague, Mr. Baynes."

" Ah, Mr. Baynes, there's a gent. He don't look one, perhaps, but he is. I don't mean a gen'l'man of your sort, of course,
but the right stuff. My Minnie thinks the world of him. You
seen my missus haven't you, while I been inside ? "

" Several times."

" Well, I don't mind tellin' you there's not a better woman
anywhere. She's loyal and true, she is. I was just palled in
with her at first in a little birch in Endell Street——"

" Birch ? "

" Yeah, birch broom—furnished room," explained Mr. Carman, surprised at the gentleman's ignorance. " 'Ahf a dollar
a week and you couldn't get it for a quid now. She was a

waitress at a caff in Asia Street—it's still there—and she kind'a took to me. But she was always absolutely respectable ; never arst once where I got me money ; always first in the queue on visiting days at the prison ; and never once arst me to marry her till I kind'a felt like it. And I said to meself, I said, ' This woman is loyal and true '. So I married her, and that was the best thing I ever done. I ain't done many good things in me life, but my Minnie was one of 'em." His eyes swam.

" You have—how many children ? "

" Five I've had ; two of 'em dead. Of course they weren't all—what I mean is, they weren't all born, if you'll excuse me mentionin' it, in wedlock. But I've never deserted Minnie or any of 'em. I'm no ponce, making the woman earn the money ; I gone out and got something for 'em. They're all gawn now, except my Phil Janey. You ain't seen my Phil Janey, 'ave you ? She's a real daughter, if you know what I mean ; not a love-child. She's the pride of me heart. . . . Or she used to be, when she was a nipper. Not so sure that I'm so pleased with her now. She's up to gawd-knows-what 'ahf the time."

" Did the children know that you—what your profession was ? "

" The boys did. Not 'ahf ! And proud of it they were."

" And are they—er—following in father's footsteps ? "

Mr. Carman fixed his more cunning and more humorous eye on the Canon's ; his ragged eyebrow was drawn down towards it, but it didn't move or blink ; perhaps one may say that he winked with a dropped eyebrow rather than a dropped lid. " What do I know, guv'nor ? I ain't seen 'em for yurs. Perse has rather more money than he can easily explain, and he sends some of it 'ome to his ma sometimes. Freddy was a plasterer when I last seen 'im—but hah much does that mean ? I always told 'em it wasn't worth it, and Minnie said the same, even when she was being loyal and true to me. Gaw, Canon-bury Road ! I cracked a crib there once. Sweet as pie. See ? Jest dahn there. We'll be in the Fields in no time at this rate. You don't 'ahf know how to drive. Anyone'd think you'd knocked this car off, and the cops were after you. Drive right up to the door in Maker Street, will you ? I'd like Minnie to see us, kind of—and the street too ; they never expected to see me back for donkey's yurs, and some of 'em haven't been talking at all nicely about me. They've said things I didn't care for at all. Let 'em see the car, guv'. And it'll be real comic for Minnie. She expects me back in three yurs' time, and I come back now, three yurs too soon ! "

§

New Victoria Buildings, in Maker Street, were known to all who dwelt in the streets bordering on the Circus, and to all who had their homes in the great hive itself, as " The New ". New it may have been seventy years ago, but it certainly didn't look new today. Outmoded in design, and begrimed by its seventy years, it belonged most clearly to an epoch that was dead. A high bluff of grey brick, relieved by red brick quoins, and six stories high, it overtopped the old blackened Georgian houses in Maker Street by two more rows of tenement windows. Three stone-flagged entries led into this hive. Each entry was open to the weather, and so were the landings above, each landing ending in a " balcony " railing on which you could lean and look down at the pavement below or at the houses opposite, like pigeons out of a cote.

Canon Welcome drove his car up to the middle entry. He got out on to the roadway, and Mr. Carman stumbled out on to the pavement. Mr. Carman stood on the kerb and looked up at the fourth floor. He waited and then addressed a whistle at the windows ; but, for him, not a loud one ; on the contrary, a brief, uneasy, wilting whistle, half cocky and half ashamed. It was not loud enough to achieve anything ; faces appeared at other windows, but none at a window of that fourth floor flat. Mr. Carman looked up the street, and down the street towards the Circus. There were women in doorways and on steps and at windows, and all stopped their work or their talk to gape at him. They called others to gape at him. He stepped further on to the pavement that they might see him well and have no doubt that it was he.

Meanwhile Canon Welcome locked the door of the car ; deciding that if it had been prudent to lock it in the courtyard of the Sessions House, it was doubly wise in a street near the Corners. He dawdled a little over the key because he too wanted to be seen by as many as possible of the local residents. If you do not visit a part of your parish as often as in duty you should, you like to be seen very clearly when for once you are there and doing your duty. Besides he was proud of what he had achieved in the Court and eager to send the rumour of it flying round the streets. Now that he had done something good for his people in these parts, let them tell of it at their shop-counters and street corners, and on the thresholds of their homes.

So Mr. Carman and Canon Welcome tarried a minute on roadway or pavement that they might be recognized by the people ; ·and in this they were a pair.

Then Mr. Carman led the Canon into the entry and up the worn stone treads. Despite the free air from the open landings, and a recent in-washing of rain, the old acid stench of the slums lurked in the recesses of the stone stairways. Perhaps it came from some of the dark numbered doors which stood in pairs, opposite one another, on each landing ; for it was a smell as of old sour sweat and of urinals uncleaned. The walls of these open stairways were of the same grey brick as the façade of the buildings, and since they were outside walls much of the plumbing of the flats came down them in pipes of assorted sizes.

The door of No. 19, on the fourth floor, had no knocker and no bell, so Mr. Carman rattled the letter-box and, leaning down, called through it, "What ho, Min ! Hi, there ! Wottoe, wottoe ! Here's your old man. Min, Min, Min. Come on. Jump to it, girl."

And he came erect again, and awaited results, sucking at his teeth to pass the time.

There was a hurry of steps inside the tenement, and quick shutting of room doors on unpresentable scenes, and then the front door opened.

"There !" said Mr. Carman. "That's Mrs. Carman. And nothing to be ashamed of in that, is there ?"

"I should say not," laughed the Canon.

"Nah ! Best thing I ever done."

Mrs. Carman was a brief, stout woman of fifty, with a pile of henna-dyed hair on the top of her small head. Though it was not yet noonday, and her rooms were not yet to rights, she was tidily and even showily dressed in a blouse of pale blue, trimmed with flounces and lace, and a neat dark-blue skirt, which, however, was so strained over the prominence of her stomach that the fastening had parted. Her legs were in flesh-coloured stockings and high-heeled black shoes. Perhaps she was dressed for the street, but no one out of the Circus would have supposed her an old gaol-bird's wife ; she might have been the wife of a publican, a café proprietor, or a family draper ; but most likely of the publican.

" Fred ! " she cried, staring.

" Hallo, ducks," said Mr. Carman.

" But, Fred . . . ? "

" I've come 'ome. Come 'ome, see."

" But Fred, what's happened ? "

" Yur, you didn't expect to see the old man quite so soon, I'll lay, did-yer ? " The Canon could see that he was a little ashamed of himself and trying to cover it up by speaking heartily and very loud. " It's the Reverend that done it. He done the trick for me. Blame 'im if you didn't want the old man back quite so soon as this."

" Fred . . . you got off ? "

" That's right. That's correct. Well . . . bound over . . . same thing."

" Oh, Fred ! . . ."

" Quite pleased, are you ? Well, give the old man a kiss."

She kissed him and, when the embrace was over, he swung a thumb at Canon Welcome. " It was *he* that done it. Spoke up for me. Said I was one of the best, really."

" We know each other, don't we, Mrs. Carman ? " The Canon took one of her fat, work-scored hands into both of his, just as he had with Mr. Carman's, and pressed it in congratulation and affection. " How are you, my dear ? " He loved her because he had been able to do this for her ; loved her almost to tears. " We got him off for you. It's more than I ever hoped for. I thought there was just a chance of it, but I never said so to you because I didn't want to raise your hopes too high."

" But does this mean . . . ? "

" Yes, it's all over now. And it's never going to happen again. Ricky's promised me that, haven't you, Ricky ? "

Mr. Carman nodded with compressed lips, as if to be done with that item on the agenda as quickly as possible. " Blow me if I don't think she's disappointed. Perhaps you'd rather he'd let well alone, Min ? "

" Don't talk so silly, Fred. Oh, I do thank you, sir. I should'a said so before, but this has quite took my breath away. Won't you step in ? Oh dear, oh dear . . . ! " She rested a hand on a palpitating bosom. " I don't know if I'm on my head or my heels. Do step in and have something."

" Delighted to, Mrs. Carman."

"Yes, come in. Come into the parlour, and I'll get you something."

The dark lobby, small, narrow and close-smelling, suited well enough with the dusty stone stairway without, but directly they entered the "parlour", they seemed to pass from one world to another : from mildew and must to freshness and cleanliness, from slumdom to respectability. Mrs. Carman's pride gleamed from floor and wall and furniture. The sums of money that furnished this room might be crooked and soiled, but everything in it, as if in compensation, was exceedingly straight and clean. The red, patterned floor-cloth was polished till it showed a glaze like fine pottery. It reflected the small mahogany sideboard, and this in its turn reflected a salad bowl and servers, two twin biscuit boxes, and a silver-framed photograph of Mr. Carman looking rigidly respectable in a collar both upright and white. There was perhaps some inappropriateness in the two large engravings on the walls, for one showed a young knight kneeling before an altar and consecrating himself to the service of the Lord, and the other, entitled "Upward and Onward", was a study of Christian with his pilgrim's staff toiling up the Hill Difficulty towards the domes of the Palace Beautiful.

"Well, here we are, sir, in the old 'ome," said Mr. Carman. "Never expected to see it for a yur or more. Lay your titfer wherever you like."

"My what?"

"Your titfer. Your lid."

"Your hat he means, sir. You didn't ought to talk to the reverend gentleman like that. Sit down, sir, won't you?" And unconsciously Mrs. Carman dusted with her hand one of the two imitation-leather arm-chairs before the fireplace.

"Thank you, my dear." The Canon dropped into the chair's embrace, and as he did so, and stretched his legs before him, he noticed the cheap bronze fire-screen and the mantel-piece painted to look like marble. On the mantelpiece was the silver-framed photograph of a young girl.

"I'll nip off and make you a cuppa tea," said Mrs. Carman slipping to the door. "It'll do you good, I'm sure."

"That's right, mother. A nice cuppa char for all of us." And with a sigh Mr. Carman sank himself in the opposite arm-chair.

And now silence stood between them, with its back to the fireplace, so to say, and its face to the quiet room.

The Canon, to dismiss the silence, attempted, " You've got a nice little home here."

" Yes." This remark, like a penny in a mechanical piano, was enough to start Mr. Carman on a rattle of uneasy but unstopping talk. If you don't know what to say it is best to keep talking. " Yes, we got some real nice things, Min and me. And Mrs. Carman likes 'em kep' nice ; it's spit and polish, spit and polish, with her all day. I could afford to buy her nice things : I've handled big money in me time, you see. Yes, I known what it is to have a hundred nicker and more in me 'and at a time ; but, gaw lummy, it was easy come, easy go. Generally I blued it all in no time. Hundred or so in a week or two, and the stuff that fetched it was worth its thah'sand at least ; but one only cops for about a hundred fifty from the buyer. He don't give you more than fifty for a smother worth a thah'sand. I shouldn't 'a got a quid for your missus's."

" Wouldn't you, really ? "

" Nah ! Not likely. But I tell you it's not easy to run straight after you've held your hundreds in your hand. And it's not only the money you miss. I tell you, guv'nor, you get so as you don't know what to do next. Turn the game up for a month or two, and there's an awful temptation to get out and hustle. It was that as much as anything, which started me piping off your plant."

" Please," begged the Canon with a smile. " Would you translate, *please* ? "

" Wurl . . . piping off . . . weighing up the gaff . . . watching the hah'se to get a line on the habits of the people in it and to know when it'd be convenient for you to nip in. I can tell you all about your habits at the Vicarage."

" But that didn't help you much in the end," laughed the Canon. And for greater comfort he slipped a little deeper into his chair and, bringing his hands together before his breast, enclosed a fist within a palm. He was happy in this chair with Mr. Carman before him. As a man of the world he was proud to be in the den of a burglar, learning about life ; and as a priest he was proud to have descended into the darker parts of his parish and to be really helping and loving the people there, even the worst. Such had been the way of the saints. But it was as a man seeking curious information rather than as a priest seeking a soul, that he said, "You must tell me all about your—er, activities one day. I should find them deeply interesting."

"Tell you? I'll tell you all you want to know. Nothing about a good screwsman's life that I can't tell you. We can talk properly now, you and me. I couldn't tell you anything really before that sergeant in the copperhouse or those ruddy twirls in Brixton. Not anything really interesting. One can't talk properly in front of coppers and warders. It's just silly to think you can."

"How did you begin?" the Canon intervened, wanting to keep him to the point. And he watched him, and listened, like a spectator at a theatre.

"Begin? I began at ten and at the bottom. Got in with a bunch of little hoisters who'd lift anything that was arstin' for it on a chemist's counter or a stationer's or in front of the ironmonger's. We'd grease home with it like lightning to one of the kid's fathers, and he'd dispose of it where he knew how. He'd give us a corner out of it, and usually a rotten cheating corner too. But that game was nothing." Mr. Carman brushed it to one side with the back of a hand as something unworthy of a clergyman's interest. "I soon done better'n that. I got in with a wizz mob, a gang of dips, if you understand——"

"I don't."

"—a gang of pickpockets, and we'd stand about at the old Corners there, and wait for a chahn'st of some shoot-fly; that's to say, when some cove come along with a belly like a balloon, and a chain hung acrost it that you wouldn't put on a dog, one of us'd snatch it and grease, while all the others got in the old mutt's way and perhaps accidentally tripped him up when he started to run after his watch and chain. By the time we'd helped him up from the pavement his old kettle and chain wasn't in the same parish any longer, guv'nor; it was somewhere in Smatthews Highbury. Sometimes we'd buzz off and work the West End at the big bus stops. One of us was the tool and the others the stalls who had to create a little diversion while the tool got to work, see. The stalls'd work up a real crush round some well-dressed gent and shove and push and dig him in the back, and as he turned round to see what was hittin' him, the tool's fingers were in his breast pocket, and the fish was landed. Simple as pie. But I soon learned that there was no big money, working with a mob like that. If you row in with a lot of others, you got to share out with 'em. There was just not enough *to* it : we'd had a good day if we cut up at a nicker apiece. I decided to work on me own ; I've always preferred that ; so I took to a sort of moll-buzzing. Jer like to know what moll-buzzin' is ? I'll tell you, old boy."

Canon Welcome was somewhat shaken at being called " old boy ", but, perceiving that Mr. Carman in his enthusiasm for his subject, and for himself as a learned expert in it, had forgotten who his visitor was, even to the point of leaning forward and tapping him on the knee, he accepted the friendly apostrophe in good humour and abandoned himself to a very real interest in what moll-buzzing might be.

Mr. Carman defined it very quickly and with an admirable clarity. " It's opening ladies' handbags in a bus or train. It's quite simple ; you could do it yourself, old boy, any day. You sit yourself next to some sleepy old geezer who's got her bag on her knee. You sit yourself as close as possible to her because of the crush and read your paper—the *Times*, if you're sensible, because nobody can imagine anything crooked going on behind the *Times*. You turn sideways towards her, to get the light on your paper, see, and as you read down a column, see, the paper droops over and over your two 'ands till it's nicely hiding the old lady's bag. You open the bag with one hand, read another 'ahf column till you're sure she's noticed nothing, and then dip your 'and in and land all the salmon you want. You close the till like a gent—always leave things tidy—and decide that this is where you change your bus. But law, there was no big money in that, neither. Only bits and pieces, like. And I wanted to get a bit higher in me profession. I was always ambitious like what no dah't you are."

" I see. There's a kind of hierarchy, in your profession, is there ? "

" A kind of what, guv ? "

" A hierarchy. A——"

" Well, some ranks higher than others, yes. I should say a con man was top of the profession like what your archbishop is."

" And an ordinary burglar, where does he come ? "

The more knowing of Mr. Carman's two little eyes was now very knowing indeed : its eyebrow lay very low over it, like a cover that has been lifted half an inch from a secret and is about to hide it again. " A good screwsman ? Well, he's about level with a vicar or a canon. He can look down his nose at the mere drummers like what I was when I started. And the drummers are a sight better'n the dirty little sneak-thieves. They're——" But Mr. Carman's flat hand waved them away as if they were beneath his contempt, even though he'd been one himself in his humbler days. " A good grafter takes a risk, you see. He goes in for the heavy work where there's a heavy penalty if he's claimed. I wouldn't have anything to do with sneak-thieves any more than I would with ponces or narks. I got me reputation to consider," he added almost sulkily, as though someone had tried to decry it.

" You began by being a drummer, you say. What's that ? "

" A housebreaker what goes about weighing up drums to see if they're empty and letting 'em be if they aren't. I got me first con at that lark. Found a big hah'se that was obviously empty, and went in by a back window. Gaw, I could take what I liked ! And I filled up a cuppla suit cases with silver and what-not and was just going to walk out of the front door as honest as you like when it opened, and a young working-class lad steps in. And there we were, face to face. He sees me two bags and says, ' Ooer you ? ' My brain worked quicker in them days, and I says, ' I'm a porter at the hotel where the gen'l'man's staying, and he's sent me for these bags.' And in case he didn't seem satisfied with that, I says, ' But ooer you ? That's what I'd like to know,' as if I thought it highly suspicious, his coming in with a key like that. He says, ' I've come to feed the canary.' *That* was one I wasn't expecting. But, blimey, that was all he had come for, and I always say that that bleedin' canary got me my first spell of bird. Before I could inquire further about the canary, he suddenly sees that all the doors of the hah'se were wide open instead of properly shut and swings round and yells ' Pleece ! Pleece ! ' I saw this was a tumble if I didn't do something quick, so I give him a straight left in the Newington Butts, flings him into the hah'se and says, ' Don't you trouble about the pleece, old boy. I'll get them for you.' And I slams the door on him and runs. But he was out in a sec. and racing after me, shouting the odds to the street and soon I had a string of busybodies after me. He came up with me round the first corner, so I turned and grabbed him and yelled to the people, ' Here, cop him, the dirty thief.' But it didn't work. They knew which was the chaser and which was being chased. Nine months in the Scrubbs that day's work cost me, and as I served it with the old hands, being a year too old for a juvenile adult, I completed my education there. I learned all that was to be learned from the boys in there. Law, I never knew how ignorant I was till I got to College like that."

At this point the room door was kicked open by a foot, and Mrs. Carman entered, bringing a tray on which was her best crochet-work cloth, her best, very flowery, tea-set, and a plate of sweet biscuits.

" I'm sure you must be wanting something," she said.

" I been telling the gen'l'man about my first tumble, Minnie. You know : time I was knocked out by a canary."

" Oh, really Fred ! He won't want to hear that stuff. Besides . . ."

Canon Welcome, trying to interpret that ' besides ', wondered if she was ashamed of his record, or would only pretend to be, in front of the Church. Mr. Carman's next words partly answered his question.

" Well, don't let us embarrass yer, Min. 'Op it, while we talk. Thanks for the char. . . . Funny things, women," he said, when she had gone with smiles. " They don't seem to mind what you do, once they've taken to you. But most of 'em'd as soon you went straight. There's bigger money now and then in the crooked line, but too many ups and downs. They find it unsettling."

" Yes, of course ; now about this going straight."

" Yepp. It's not going to be easy." Mr. Carman, scenting an offer, began to work up the price. " Your only chance is if you're your own master. Try to work for someone else, and he learns your record sooner or later, and out into the street you go."

" Well, my idea is that you *should* be your own master in a small way. You really are prepared to go straight ? "

" Reckon I got to now, or they'll mix it for me properly."

Within himself Canon Welcome both sighed and smiled. Outwardly he only smiled. " But I hope that's not going to be your only motive. I want you to do it because you want to do it. Now, how are we going to set about it ? "

" Well, I'll tell you one thing, guv'nor. I got lots of pals, and often after I've come out, they've had a whip-round to set me up again. They respect me, you see. Well, they'll be tickled that I got off so nicely, and if I don't exactly say that

106

I'm through with 'em, they'll put up quite a little to start me in something. But not enough, of course. Nothing like enough."

"But, Ricky, that wouldn't be straight, would it? And we shouldn't quite know where they got their money. If we're going to start straight, it must be with clean money."

Mr. Carman lifted his shoulders, as if defeated by these barriers in the path of honesty. He frowned and pursed his lips, as he pondered the objection. "I should'a thought it'd be puttin' the money to good use, helping an old lag to go straight," he submitted.

"No, we can't begin by taking their money. I'll tell you my idea. I've been making enquiries, and I think the best thing'd be this : I find enough money to set you up as a hawker of perishable goods—we'll buy a load of stuff at Covent Garden——"

"Yes, I got pals who are costers, and they'd show me how to buy."

"And we'd hire a barrow, and get you a board and scales——"

"Yes "—Mr. Carman joined in with some fervour—" I got pals who got pitches, and I'm sure they'd say, ' 'Ere, boy, poke in 'ere with the old bow-and-arrer '."

"But I understand that if you're a hawker without a licence, you can't stand still. You have to keep moving."

"Wurl . . . they *say* so," nodded Mr. Carman, "but . . ." and he shrugged his shoulders in some contempt for this ordinance.

"Right, then, Ricky. Shall we try this? I believe if you work well at it, you can make quite a fair living."

"Fair? You can make ten or twenty pound a week," said Mr. Carman, as sanguine about this as about any of his previous jobs.

"Yes ; and listen to this : I've heard of one man who because he had a reputation among all the women of selling only good stuff at fair prices, made enough to hire and run several other barrows, and to retire at seventy."

"Then he must'a been the only honest coster that ever was. Why, I know a boy with a pitch near Victoria Station, and he tells me he makes his twenty pound a week extra givin' short change."

"Oh, but, Ricky, you're not to do that."

"No . . . no . . . his is a floatin' population, see. He treats his reg'lar customers right. Naturally."

"Well, there's going to be one other honest coster now," declared the Canon with a laugh, but with imperfect confidence.

Mr. Carman said nothing : perhaps he too lacked the complete confidence.

And the Canon, in conclusion, said " Good ". He said it for something to say, but in an unrelieved doubt as to whether the word was a perfect fit.

§

He rose to look at the silver-framed photograph on the mantelpiece. It was the photograph of a little, thin-faced fifteen-year-old girl with a wide brow and a pointed chin. The nose was brief and tipped-upward, and as rounded at the end as the chin was pointed. The eyes were beautiful—wide and widely spaced. You could see as you looked into them that she was striving to put on a most pleasing expression before the camera ; you could deduce from the expression that she could be perky and angry and self-conscious and vain ; and yet—and yet they were sad eyes ; too sad for their childishness ; let them cease from smiling or posing or listening and they would lapse back into this wistful melancholy, like the eyes of some animals which, having no understanding, seem to carry in their depths the unexplained sadness of the world.

An instant pity and affection ran from the heart of Canon Welcome to the thin little face in the frame.

" That's my Phil Janey," said Mr. Carman, watching him.

" Very sweet," said the Canon, as one does to a parent. " Charming."

" H'm . . . don't know about that. She used to be. Used to be the pride of me heart." And he pushed a hand into his inner breast pocket and brought out a pocket-case, from which he extracted a collection of browning, rotting and dirtied papers, probably his ticket of discharge from the Army and sundry testimonies to character given to him by employers before they'd learned of his past. From between these broken tributes he drew a glossy but cracked photograph and handed it to his visitor.

" That's what she was," he said proudly.

" Delightful." The Canon said this justly, for he was looking at the face of a twelve-year-old child, when her cheeks were full and round and her eyes only laughing and friendly and innocent.

" She was the pride of me heart then, my Phil Janey."

" But not now ? "

" Nah. At least not so much. She's rude. She don't seem
to care what she says to me. She says awful things sometimes.
Shocking. You'd think she'd show a bit'a respect for her old
man ; but does she ? Not a trace. Nor love, neither."

" Does she know—forgive me—the truth about the times
when you've been in prison and—and so on ? "

" She didn't at first. Her ma kep' it from her all right. But
she knows now, of course. She's sixteen, and there's no keepin'
nothin' from a woman once she's gone twelve."

" And what, may I ask, does she feel about it ? "

" I dunno. Our Phil Janey never says nothin' these days ;
she's a close one, these days. We don't know what she gets
up to. Just at present she's dancin' mad like all the rest of
'em. Out every night. I don't know where she gets the money
from, or who it is gives it her. I only hope it's all right."

" I'm sure it is," comforted the Canon, though he didn't
feel at all sure, but rather much interested in what she might
be up to, this child of a burglar with her tipped up nose and
her eyes at once impudent and sad.

" I dunno how to make her tell me anything—or behave,"
sighed her father. " I can't very well give her a bashing on
the arse like I used to, not now that she's gone sixteen. It
wouldn't be proper. Besides, if I did, it's my belief she'd pack
up and go. Kids are disappointing things, if you arst me."

" You love her a lot, I see."

" Course I do. Isn't she me own child ? And the only gurl
I got ? Isn't she what I mean, the child of me old age ? "

" Oh come, Ricky. You're only sixty still."

Mr. Carman closed his ears to this objection, not wanting to
cool the blast of his pathos. " If she was to go it'd just about
kill Minnie. And if Minnie dies, wurl—I make a hole in the
water. See ? I don't know if you could talk to the gurl some
time. That's what she needs : a talking to."

" You want her to grow up a good girl, eh ? " asked the
Canon, raillery in his eyes. " Law-abiding—what ? No running off the rails for Phil Janey ? "

" Wurl . . ." Mr. Carman hesitated, lest there were a trap
here. " I don't want her going wrong, if you see what I mean."

" Do I see ? I don't think I do."

" Well—law lummy—I don't want her bringing home a
blasted baby."

" Why not ? "

" Gaws heavens, *you* to arst me that ! Because it's—well it's wrong."

" Why wrong ? "

" Well . . . I dunno . . . everybody knows it's wrong. You're not going to say it isn't ? "

" Is it any more wrong than—stealing ? "

" Oh, *yurse*," affirmed Mr. Carman with conviction.

" Then you wouldn't mind so much if she only took to crime ? "

" Pardon ? " An apology to gain time.

Canon Welcome repeated his question, and Mr. Carman pursed up his lips in some doubt and uncertainty. Canon Welcome, eyes fixed on him, perceived his dilemma. An itching remnant of parental care made him want to save Phil Janey from the paths he had trod, but he couldn't very well say so aloud because it would imply that he disapproved of his actions in the past. And he was half ashamed of his desertion to the Enemy at this point. In a word, he wanted to save Janey and was ashamed of wanting to.

" I don't particularly want her to get up to them larks, no," he temporized.

" But why ? "

" Well, it'd break her mother's heart," he said, suddenly, grasping his wife as a buoy in these difficult waters. " You see what Mrs. Carman is."

" Then, if your wife were not there, you wouldn't really mind what she did ? "

" Pardon ? " Gain time again.

Mercilessly the Canon repeated his question. " You, apart, from Mrs. Carman, wouldn't mind what she did ? "

" I wouldn't say that." Mr. Carman knitted his brows, and sewed up his lips, over the problem. He inserted a thumb-nail between the lips and scraped the interstices of his bottom teeth, one after another, till he'd contrived an answer. " I'm not altogether ashamed of what I done," he said, pulling out his thumb-nail to see if there were any trophy on it, " but it's not for gurls. I don't know but what you mightn't put that to her. She won't take anything from me, but she might take it from you, especially after all you done for her old dad. She has a heart—or she used to have."

CHAPTER FOUR

HIGHER up the hill from the Vicarage the home of Dr. Bettersby and Clara his wife, which they had inherited from old Colonel Hanover, stood in a square of rusty garden, a tall grey house with three sharply-pointed gables which faced towards the sprawl of London, east, west, and south. Of date 1871, its sitting-rooms were long and large and lofty, and so was the kitchen along the passage, because in the days when the house was still young many hands and much labour and a profound seriousness went to the preparation of meals. Dr. Bettersby, the present owner, was well worthy of this fine, long, lofty kitchen, and of those old dead cooks and kitchen maids, for never had the house enclosed a master who devoted more love, care, and scholarly knowledge to the substances which he ate and drank. If he was a classical scholar of high pretensions (1st Class, Classical Mods. and 1st Class, Lit. Hum.) he was also a high savant, a learned doctor and master of arts, on all branches of gastronomy and viticulture, and in his later days a more enthusiastic student in these fields. He would confess that, while his memories of the Greek dramatists and the Latin poets were somewhat abating, he could rehearse in every detail the more exquisitely dramatic menus produced by the Masters (such as Monsieur Emile Malley and Monsieur Louis Diat) and enumerate, with chapter, verse, and exegesis, all the noble poems, the choice and lovely lyrics, composed in the Châteaux of the Médoc.

And on a certain April evening, at about seven o'clock, you might have seen him standing before his gas-cooker with a woman's bibbed white apron taped over the shoulders and round the waist of his black clerical jacket. One hand was stirring the contents of a saucepan, and the other enlarging and diminishing the supply of gas through the pipe as tenderly and delicately as ever the Abbé Vogler controlled the swell of his organ music. His long, thin, peeking nose seemed red to-night, not with frost, but with the steam rising like an incense from his pot. You might perhaps have likened him to a priest before an altar with an apron for chasuble, and he would have accepted the simile as just. A stove is indeed an altar, since a man should praise the Lord in all His gifts, and not least in the glorious fruits of the earth, and the great skills which He had implanted in His children, for their blending, seasoning, and concoction.

As he turned off the gas under the saucepan, and carried the saucepan to the hot-plate of the kitchen range, which was also aglow with bright life and labouring hard, the halldoor-bell on the wall above him jarred and rattled the steamy air. He laid his long wooden spoon on the hot-plate and looked impatiently up at the bell, as if to ask what it meant by this disgusting interruption.

" In the name of God," he exclaimed to Elsa, his middle-aged cook-general who, under his tuition, and in a saucepan on the range, was cooking butter, diced pork and small onions, " and likewise in the name of all the patron saints of good eating and good drinking, who, think you, is that ? Elsa, who can it be ? It is only seven o'clock, and we invited them for dinner at eight. Who is this fool who has come too soon ? I cannot—I will not—leave my cooking for anyone. Mix well, my dear : we shall be ready to add the peas in a minute ; let their bed be ready for them and their reception kind. Are the onions a golden brown ? Good ; then put them to one side and run and see who this intruder is. Doesn't he understand that cooking is a solemn and sacred art, not to be lightly disturbed ? We shall need absolute silence while we are preparing the Potatoes Lorette. But see—see who it is."

The woman returned saying, " It's the Reverend Clay."

" What, Tim already ? "

" Yes, sir, Mr. Timothy. I've put him in the drawing-room and asked him to wait as the mistress isn't near ready. He was very sorry for coming all this early."

" Tim ! And an hour too soon ! But, of course—I forgot—he's in love again—in love with the Who-dyer-call-it girl—and his wits have dissolved. They are as vapour in the wind. But *he* doesn't matter ; Tim doesn't matter ; we'll have him in to help." He went to the door, wooden spoon erect like the sword of a commanding officer when Majesty comes to review his troops, and shouted along the passage, " Tim. Tim, don't sit there and do nothing. Come and help cook. Clara won't be dressed for another half-hour, and, what's more important, neither will the Salade Carltonia."

Tim came, apologizing all the way from drawing-room to

kitchen, "I say, I'm awfully sorry, sir. I couldn't remember if you said seven or eight, so I thought I'd better be on the safe side. I'm quite ready to go away and come back again."

"No, for heaven's sake don't do that. Don't do that or you'll forget to come back. Or you'll be an hour late, and the meal will be ruined, and all my and Elsa's very fine efforts will have been rendered nugatory. Elsa, give him an apron. I see you've dressed, Tim, and I'm glad." Tim's broad chest was covered with a black silk waistcoat as high as his clerical collar, but, for the rest, his evening dress was his dinner-jacket suit of undergraduate days. "I take it as a courtesy, not so much to the women, though they like it, and it justifies their frou-frous and fripperies, but to the wine I propose to give you. That is the real guest of honour. Do you know what it is? Château Lafite, my boy, 1871. Are you impressed? I say it again : Château Lafite, 1871."

"What's that?"

"My god ! *Mon dieu !* A wine that's taken its place in history among the immortals, and he asks, what's that? Tie his tapes for him, Elsa. I am not a sentimental man, Tim, I am not given to wild and unreasoning exaggerations, so I will allow that once in history there has been—perhaps—a greater wine, the 1864. But this 1871 has a charm, a sunniness, a winsomeness——" he brought two fingers and a thumb to his lips and blew a kiss into the air, as to some sweet and price-less memory. "She is a lass unparalleled. Extraordinary that in 1871, when the foul and unspeakable Huns were in Paris, a wine of France should have blushed into such beauty. It is of the same vintage as this mansion and, come to that, of our bishop, but as beautiful in its serene maturity as they are out-of-date and, may we say, somewhat unlovely. I do hope—I do sincerely hope you realize what manner of wine it is you are going to meet tonight—in a minute we will decant it. At present it is breathing, slowly and peacefully, in the dining-room."

"I'll try to be worthy of it, sir."

"I fear you will not be. The Vicar will be worthy of it, but only just—he has a feeling for good wine, but is deplorably ignorant of the deeper truths. It will not be wasted on Mrs. Buxton—who's Lilian Eadie to all of us now, and I hope to you. Odd to find a woman who can distinguish one wine from another, but, as I think I told you before, the late Buxton educated her. I am educating Clara, but it's a long and arduous task. I still believe her enthusiasm for a fine wine to be wifely rather than sincere, because I have known her talk—not to say, cackle—about other things when she was drinking it. Of Amy Welcome I can only despair. Fortunately she doesn't drink much, but it is sacrilege to give it to her at all—sacrilege. Look, Tim : slice the beetroot, the cucumber, and the tomatoes for the Salade Carltonia with which we shall trifle between the duckling and the Coupe Beatrice. Arrange the slices on each of the lettuce hearts in a pleasing sequence, and put a sprig of water-cress on each rosette. Hold !—heck !—how is my lovely Madrilène faring ? ''

He ran to his saucepan on the hot-plate and peeped at its contents with the anxious eye of a lover at his bride asleep.

" Is it O.K. ? " asked Tim, who'd been suddenly alarmed.

" It is O.K. It is more than O.K. ; it is perfect. Soon we will cool her down and strain her. I suppose I should be considered profane if I said she was like the Magdalen inasmuch as we cool her down and cast out all impurities. Yes, I think it would be profane. Would you like to know what the menu is, Tim : the menu of which your crude and uneducated palate is quite unworthy ? It is all, of course, but a background, a setting for the Château Lafite. First there is a crab cocktail—we must crush the ice, soon, Elsa—then the Consommé Madrilène——" and here Dr. Bettersby lifted his eyes to heaven and closed them in an ecstasy of contemplation. " An Amontillado Pasado will accompany the Madrilène with, I trust, a perfectly bred grace and courtesy. Then there will be an innocent spring duckling with new peas Bonne Femme and Potatoes Lorette."

" And apple sauce ? " asked Tim unwisely.

Dr. Bettersby laid down his spoon. A kitchen chair was handy, and he sat upon it to recover. In some such fashion did Prospero break his staff, and Orpheus put by his lute. He sighed as one who despairs and will welcome death and release. " Tim. Tim," he rebuked, looking at him with the forgiveness of a man on his death-bed. " Did I not tell you that I am going to give you one of the greatest wines of all history. Would you have me kill it with apple sauce ? "

" Sorry, sir," said Tim, perceiving he had erred. And he fell to the safer business of slicing the cucumber.

" I suppose it is because you are in love," said Dr. Bettersby, rising from his chair, and deciding to live again. " As I understand it, you are now in love with the Who-dyer-call-it girl. My boy, tonight I will introduce you to something worth falling in love with. First you will meet the Amontillado. But that is nothing. It is good, but compared with what follows— nothing. It is as Rosaline to Juliet. Then the Lafite—ah, my boy, my boy . . . let us pause here. The Lafite 1871. Let us keep silence for a space while we meditate on the goodness of God. . . . With the salad, nothing. Then with the Coupe a Cockburn 1912, and with the demitasse a Biscuit Debouché. You appreciate the sequence—— My God, what's the time? Let us decant. We should have decanted earlier. Oh, my God! Come. Follow me." And he and Tim, each in a bibbed white apron, priest and acolyte, went in procession to another altar, the one which might be called the High Altar, the sideboard in the dining-room.

§

The magnum of Château Lafite stood upon the sideboard, deliberately placed as far as possible from a light spring-time fire that was chattering and sniggering in the grate.

" Ah ! " At the sight of it Dr. Bettersby raised both palms to shoulder height, somewhat in the manner of a priest who is about to celebrate a mass. " There she is. I have left her, Tim, in this chambered solitude since early this afternoon that she may adjust herself to the temperature and the mood of the room. The cork, you observe, I removed about an hour ago that she might breathe for a little. Some schools hold that a wine should be allowed to breathe only after decanting, but I have never been convinced. The decanter over there, please, Tim. Thank you."

" Can I do it, sir ? "

" No. Oh, no, Tim. This is not a light matter for the reckless hands of youth. Youth is an age of slapdashery at best. You might shake it. You would certainly shake it. One should do nothing to disturb its serenity, its—may I say ?—its rapt stillness and peace, as of Plotinus or Jacob Boehme in contemplation of the Absolute. Besides you're in love. Just put on that wall light there that I may see when the crust moves." Having cleaned the neck of the bottle with scrupulous fingers, and held the bottle for a second between him and the light, he tilted the decanter sideways and poured the wine so that it slipped down the decanter's side instead of falling on to its base. " Steady. Steady now. Slowly and sweet. The wine should slide into its new home like love into the heart of a middle-aged man. Slowly. Did you ever see a colour of such quiet courtesy, such extreme good breeding ? Ah, stop. Stop. The lees move. Some schools would have you strain it through a fine muslin lest the second half of the bottle should be less unspotted and innocent than the first—as, my dear boy, is certainly the case with some old men like myself. But we will not insult this great lady with any such rude apprehensions. We will just leave a glassful to rest undisturbed on the bottom, like the memory of our sins. Come. I do not know but what Elsa is poisoning the crab cocktail with a drop too many of the Tobasco sauce."

§

The crab cocktail and the Consommé Madrilène had come to the sacrifice and perished amid praises, and the spring duckling was on the table before the hostess.

Clara Bettersby was a fine broad-bowed battleship of a woman, as broad across bows and beam as her husband, Dr. Bettersby, was lank and peaked and lean. Indeed it would not be intolerably unfair to say that Clara, seated at her end of the table in a broad-shouldered and flouncy dress of dark blue silk, was a big, blue cube, whereas Dr. Bettersby rising to visit the sideboard, was a long, black line. A loud, laughing, intolerant, thrusting woman, with a voice nearly as masculine as her square shoulders, Clara Bettersby spent most of her noisy and joyous tattle on these occasions, disagreeing with her husband. Did he state a case for railwaymen strikers, she would cry, " Stuff and fiddlesticks. I'm a soldier's daughter and believe in discipline for everybody," and suppose she was being clever. Did he expound to the table his Liberalism in politics she would crown the argument with the snort, " I know nothing about that. I only know I'm a good Conservative like my father before me, and always shall be." Did he expound his Liberalism in Theology and Biblical Criticism, she, who'd heard nothing of the great German and English critics, and their long-accepted overthrow of Verbal Inspiration, and didn't want to hear anything about them, would retort in some heat, " I've no patience with it. Either we believe in the Bible or we don't. My old vicar, Archdeacon Jayes, believed in the Old Testament as simply as any saint, and what was good enough for him is good enough for me. As a clergyman's wife I prefer to believe in the Bible." It was remarkable that this masculine, square-shouldered, hectoring woman always thought of herself, and spoke of herself, as ancillary to a man—her father, her old vicar, or her husband. Had she had a son, and he grown up, she would have snubbed him with allusions to her father, her old vicar, or *his* father, and yet thought of herself as ancillary to him.

On Dr. Bettersby's right sat Amy Welcome, fat and simple and agreeing with everybody, in a dress of quiet and sober grey; and opposite her, on the host's left, sat Lilian Eadie, brilliantly vested in honour of the Château Lafite. She wore a dress of some colour between scarlet and orange, and the palest sunburn tint, but no other, on her too pale, hollowed face, and a deep red on her lips, which was matched by deep red earrings, moulded into rosettes, on the lobes of her ears. With her black hair severely strained from the central parting, and her large, long-gazing tragedienne's eyes, she was as certainly the most striking feature at the table, as a flame on a smouldering hearth.

Dr. Bettersby, walking to the sideboard, was annoyed that these women should be talking noisily, their tongues loosed by the Amontillado, as if indifferent to the grandeur, the unique and inimitable importance of this moment. " Tut, tut," he muttered to himself, as their entangling voices clacked on. " Wine shouldn't be wasted on women. They prefer talk. How different the Vicar, who is watching me now, and properly salivating, I hope. Like a good and cultivated man, he's far more interested in the wine than the women. And Tim too ; though I fear he's only watching, because he's too shy to interrupt the gabble, or to offer any observations with his boss sitting opposite him." Taking the decanter from the sideboard, he went first, as the conventions demanded, to Amy Welcome, but his heart was low within him to think that he was giving the first glass to one who would have been equally content with a glass of unspeakable cider. At her side he announced his wine, partly in irritation with this ignorant and unpalated woman, and partly in imitation of the sommeliers of Bordeaux.

" Château Lafite, 1871."

" Thank you, Dr Bettersby, I agree with you, Clara, I said the same thing only the other day to Humbert, it's ridiculous for him to set up his opinion against a man of Humbert's education, or Dr. Bettersby's ; after all, he was only at a Theological College."

" Damn the woman," stuttered Dr. Bettersby behind set lips ; there being occasions when a clergyman is justified in a commination. And he could bring himself to pour only a small quanity into her glass ; a punishment which she did not observe, for she was listening to Clara.

" I know I ought to have asked him really," Clara was saying, " but really I could not. He's so gauche. I felt he'd spoil our little party ; to say nothing of being one man too many."

" And he's so ugly ! " Lilian reminded them, lest they forgot this important reason. " Oh, dear, very unprepossessing."

" I don't mind that—don't mind that at all," snorted Clara. " What I mind is that he's not a gentleman. The Vicar's been exceedingly naughty. I said to him—didn't I, Vicar ?— I said, ' If you're getting us a curate, by all means let him be a good man, but let him be a gentleman too ; and if you can't get both, well, it's terribly important to have a gentleman.' And he went and got us *this* ! "

" It's of no importance that he isn't a gentleman," denied her husband, now at Lilian Eadie's side. " What's of importance is that he's an ignoramus. Château Lafite."

But Lilian too was listening to Clara. And Clara was answering her husband, " I disagree with you entirely, dear. The Vicar thought he'd be the right man for Little Bread Street because he's more or less working-class himself ; but I don't agree ; my father always used to say that the men of the regiment liked to have a gentleman for an officer, and that the officers who'd risen from the ranks were never much good."

" Château Lafite, Lilian ? "

" He was here the other night, Lilian, talking the most dangerous Socialist stuff. I had no patience with him, and in the end I got up and walked away. He tried to make out that all the gangsterism and crime down there where he chooses to live were, at bottom, a matter of money."

" That isn't quite what he said, dear," interrupted Dr. Bettersby, impatiently beating his foot as he waited, in manners, to serve Lilian.

" That's exactly what he said ; and he got quite hot about it ; almost rude. He said that if the people down there had lovely surroundings instead of a world-without-end of dingy streets, and if they'd enough money to be as well educated as my husband, the boys wouldn't go searching for happiness in crime and gambling and fighting, and the girls in dancing and sex. Such nonsense ! Arrant nonsense."

" Of course it is," agreed Lilian, like a good and well-dressed guest. "As my husband always used to say—and *he* employed them —' Give them more money, and they'll only spend it on drink'."

" Château Lafite, lady." Declining to wait any longer, and deeply disappointed, he filled her glass.

" So this is it ! " cried Lilian Eadie, holding up the glass like a connoisseur to see the colour and state of the wine. " Ah ! " And she passed the glass under delicately opening nostrils. " How Chesney would have appreciated this ! My husband was something of a connoisseur, Clara, but not, of course, anything like Dr. Bettersby."

Better.

And he passed on with his decanter to Clara, his wife. But now she was talking about crime. She was asking the Vicar how his dreadful Mr. Carman was getting on with his barrow, and Lilian Eadie was exclaiming as she clasped her hands in an ecstasy, " Oh, but I think that was so wonderful of the Vicar ! A dreadful man comes and burgles him, and he first pays for the man's defence and then sets him up in business ! "

" Very noble, no doubt," laughed Clara, haw-hawing like a man. " But I hope he doesn't make a habit of it. An incorrigible old rogue handsomely rewarded—why, it's putting a premium on crime."

" I suppose it is, really," Lilia Eadie promptly agreed.

Now, the Vicar, recently enlightened by his curate, Baynes, was not worrying, like his host, about the lack in women of all real appreciation of wine but about the dimness and crudity of their spiritual vision. He was irritated by their attack on Baynes. And though he had no more desire to give the credit to Baynes for having shown him what to do with a burglar than a man who has just scored with a witticism is anxious to explain that he heard it last week at the Club, yet, in an uprush of affection for old Baynes, and in loyalty to him, he overcame his desire to keep the credit and flung it to his curate. " You may laugh at old Baynes," he said ; " you may call him gauche and an ignoramus, but he happens to be worth all of us put together, Bettersby and Tim and me. He is my master, and I sit at his feet."

" Oh no, Vicar. Oh, *no* ! " chimed Lilian. " Oh really ! Come ! "

" Château Lafite, Clara." Bettersby's nose began to look exceedingly frost-bitten.

" I daresay he's all right for those people down there," Clara allowed, " because, after all, he's one of them. You see——"

" He's all right for them, certainly," submitted the Vicar. " Not, however, because he's one of them, but because he's the opposite of them."

" What . . . on earth . . . do you mean ? " enunciated Lilian. " Do tell me. " I know I'm terribly silly, but I don't know *what* you're talking about."

" It was old Baynes who showed me what as a priest of God I ought to do when a burglar comes through my window."

" And what did he tell you to do ? "

" Well—roughly—that I must meet him not with a bevy of policemen, but with love and help."

" Oh, what a wonderful idea ! Oh, how beautiful ! " Lilian flung up her hands in adoration of the picture. " The lovely man ! I must really get to know him better. Love and help ! Of course ! "

" Sentimental nonsense," scoffed Clara. " Why, no clergyman's house is safe now. My husband says he's expecting burglars through the window any day. The right thing for that old scoundrel was a longer dose of prison than he's ever had in his life. Let him be kept there, and let us live in peace. I'm sorry, but I'm a soldier's daughter and believe in discipline. My brothers and I got the cane, and I think it's a pity they don't use it more in prison. The only place those people feel anything is in their bodies."

" Oh, Château Lafite, woman." Patience exhausted, he poured it splashingly into her glass.

§

Having filled all his guest's glasses, he went back, somewhat sulkily to his seat, and there, determined to stop this profane cackle, he raised his glass, savoured the bouquet, and sipped from it. "Well, all of you, how do you like it?" he snapped.

"It's lovely, I'm sure," said Amy Welcome, and the words were nothing more than politeness; she would have said the same about a corked Sauterne or a mildewed Burgundy.

Lilian Eadie knew her part better. She sipped, shut her eyes, spread her hands as one bewildered, and asked in a voice as low as the dusk of evening, "Who are you, mysterious man, that you can produce a wine like this?"

"You like it?"

"*Like* it! I don't *like* it. Why, it's one of the great experiences of my life."

Abruptly the Vicar looked up from his glass. "My heavens!" he exclaimed. "That's just what she said about one of my sermons."

"Did I? Oh, dear me! Oh dear, oh dear! But you know I really meant it when I spoke of your sermon. Which one was it?"

"Never you mind. We won't speak of it again."

"Oh, but I did mean it, Vicar; I did. And I mean it now—but in a different way, of course. Oh lord, I'm getting so mixed up; I'm saying dreadful things."

"There is no need to apologize, dear lady," assured her host, greatly pleased. "The Vicar will think any parallel between his sermons and this wine the summit of praise. That is so, isn't it, Vicar?"

"Certainly. Extravagant praise."

"H'm . . . doesn't sound as though he meant it. Still, he should have done. I doubt if six sermons in the course of history have equalled a bottle of wine in producing brotherly love. I ask you, do we all feel a love for our neighbours swelling within us and warming out hearts as we slowly imbibe a sermon of the Vicar's——"

"Oh yes, *yes*," affirmed Lilian.

"Do we slowly accept without further question or desire for controversy all the beatitudes? I trow not. I certainly make no such claim for any sermon of mine. But wine, whenever and wherever it's been allowed to carry its mission and its message has produced peace on earth and goodwill among men. Drink, all of you."

"It has also produced a good deal of quarrelling and hate, hasn't it, sir?" inquired Tim, anxious to break his shy silence.

"No more than our holy religion when taken in too great

quantities, Tim. *Corruptio optimi pessima.* But the truth of God is in both. I pray you, drink deep and perceive it."

Canon Welcome drank, and drank again. " Yum, yum, yes," he said. " Delicious."

" *C'est merveilleux,*" Lilian Eadie breathed above her glass.

" You'll get no such wine at the Anti-Duellers next month, Vicar. There'll be a longer procession of gracious and gifted wines, and a finer series of dishes as a background to the distinguished procession, but they will not give you the peer of my Lafite. No, no. It has no peer—except the '64."

" But what is this ? " demanded Lilian. " Anti-Duellers ? What are they ? "

" The Anti-Duellers, Lilian dear, are a very select club of somewhat senior citizens, but men of great public spirit, who are banded together to prevent the barbarous practice of duelling."

" But what nonsense ! No one fights duels now."

" Very well, then. Our little club exists to prevent them beginning again."

" Fiddlesticks ! "

" Not at all, dear. We can't have duelling any more in this country. We dine about it four times a year, and next month the Vicar is coming with me as my guest. I am our chaplain."

" What in mercy do they need a chaplain for ? "

" Because we are a very religious club. We renew at the beginning of every meal our vow never to accept a challenge, and then the chaplain reads a passage before we sit down."

" What passage ? "

" Leviticus, dear ; the nineteenth chapter. Go home and read it. ' Thou shalt not hate thy brother in thine heart. Thou shalt not avenge, nor bear any grudge against the children of thy people.' A noble scripture, I think."

" Oh, Amy dear, aren't men silly ? They're really too absurd. What women would get up to such games ? Do you invite women to your dinners ? "

" Certainly not, Lilian. Women have no palates."

" Is that so ? And you dine four times a year, you say ? "

" Four times, lady. So far that has been enough to prevent any recrudescence of the unworthy practice of duelling."

The Coupe was now being served : a raspberry ice with sliced peaches and whipped cream. Dr. Bettersby went to the sideboard for the port. He handed the decanter to Lilian that it might begin its round, and resumed his seat. Lilian, having finished her ice took a cigarette absent-mindedly from her golden vanity bag and lit it. Dr. Bettersby looked at her, groaned, cast martyred eyes at the ceiling, looked at Canon Welcome as at one who would sympathize, and at last, unable to sustain the fret any more, said, " Put that out at once, woman."

Lilian let out an actress's scream. " Oh, I have done something wrong, have I ? I've done something dreadful." She stubbed out the cigarette on her plate. " Yes, of course. I remember Chesney used to say we mustn't smoke till the first glass of port, at least, had gone round."

" Your husband was a civilized man," said Dr. Bettersby, waving away the smoke of her cigarette with a hand like a fin. " I have opened a very fine port for the Vicar ; and he and I, if no one else, desire to appraise its flavour."

" Oh, don't be angry with me, please, please," she begged. " It's living alone that gets one into these careless habits."

" Do we forgive her, Vicar ? "

" This once."

" Very good then."

" You must," she endorsed. " Oh dear, oh dear. Oh, my heart. It's so difficult to eat and drink with those who understand. One is always in danger of getting one's lines or one's business wrong."

CHAPTER FIVE

HALF-PAST ten in the morning after the Bettersby's dinner party, and the Canon lay back in his study chair with a warm sleepiness in his eyes and a dry, yellow, sandpaper taste in his mouth. They had followed the Cockburn 1912 with a Biscuit Debouché 1825, and towards midnight quenched a real but slightly unreasonable thirst with whiskies and soda. It had been one o'clock before Canon Welcome was abed, and now, in his chair, he felt equal to nothing but a semi-recumbent position and a dilatory trifling with the *Times* crossword puzzle. One clue, however, teased his wits so much that he laid down the paper, took a cigarette, and lit it ; he could do this now with an easy conscience, and without fear of being seen by Amy, because the infernal nuisance of Lent was over. The cigarette comfortably smoking, and the match laid aside, he returned to the paper and the teasing clue. It engaged his wits so completely that he did not hear the front-door bell.

His study door opened. Amy !

" Are you busy, Humbert dear ? Could you see—— ? "

Amy ! Amy once again disturbing him at ten-thirty in the morning ! Amy repeating the offence, in spite of twenty years of protest ! Amy coming in and——

He threw the paper on the carpet. He rose. He flung out his arms and dropped them like dead limbs. " In the name of God . . . oh, it's impossible ! Let me die. Have I ever said—will nobody ever believe me when I say that I'm not to be disturbed in the morning, my most important time for work ? Neither by asking, beseeching, explaining, shouting, can I induce anyone to take the statement seriously. Supposing I'd just been pulling a tooth ? Because I'm sitting in a chair it doesn't mean that I'm not working. If I'm reading it doesn't mean that I'm not working. Anyone who has to mould public opinion has to read a large number of journals, study all sides of current controversies, and keep abreast of the March of Thought." One could erect this kind of screen in front of Amy without fear ; Amy would never see through its embroidery of fine embossed phrases. " Besides, I quite often think out my sermons sitting down. How can I study, how can I write sermons, how can I do *anything* if I'm interrupted? "

" But, dear——"

" How can I even earn a living for us all if I'm not allowed to work? We shall just starve if I'm not allowed to work. When I say that an interruption scatters my imagination into a thousand pieces, and it may be an hour before I can really concentrate again, I happen to be speaking the simple truth. But will anyone ever understand? No. Not in this world. Not though one raises one's voice like the bull of Bashan and roars to heaven." He began to roar. " Do *you* understand? No. It is morning. It is ten o'clock. It is the time sacred to my work——"

" But this is Mr. Baynes."

" Baynes? "

" Yes, isn't Mr. Baynes business? "

" Baynes? No." He said it sharply, since one must justify oneself; but he had to give a second or so to considering why Baynes wasn't business. " No, not necessarily. Not at all. By no means. Not unless it's something extremely urgent. And I can't imagine that there's anything so urgent that it can't wait till this evening."

" Hush, dear. He'll hear you."

" Where is he? "

" He's in the hall."

" Oh well, if he's there, I'll see him, I suppose. Tut-tut. *Tst-tst.* . . . Dear, dear, dear, dear. . . . *Come* in, Baynes, old boy; come along. How's things with you? This is fine. No, don't apologize. Delighted to see you. What are you doing? Visiting a sinner who chances to live in the Vicarage? You couldn't employ your time better. Sit." Almost in his geniality he was going to offer him a cigar, but he thought better of it, remembering Baynes's distressing treatment of those expensive luxuries. " Have a cigarette, my dear fellow. Lent's over now."

" Thank you, Vicar." As usual Baynes had sat himself on the front of the low chair so that his knees pointed upward at an acute angle; and when he had lit a cigarette and seemed to be pulling at it no better than at a cigar, he splayed his fat hands over the knees in his own peculiar version of a seated Buddha.

" Well, what can I do for you, Baynes? " asked the Canon,

smiling affectionately at the comic figure. " If it's anything in my power, command me."

" Well, quite frankly, Vicar. I want you to come and preach at Little Bread Street. You never come. D'you know, you've not come once since I've been there."

" I know I haven't. It's shameful of me. But you know how it is. Tim is only just priested, Bettersby can't help very often, and I feel my congregation expects me here. But I really will come some day ; I really will." A safe promise, committing him to nothing.

" Yes, but when, Vicar ? I want to tell the people you're coming."

" When ? You're not going to fix me to a date, are you ? "

" Oh yes, I am. And I'm not going till I've got a date from you." The eyes, if not the mouth, smiled. " That's why I came in person this morning. I'm waiting no longer. We want you, you see."

" Oh, dear." It was a bit much, thought the Canon, before he could stop the thought, to ask him to come and preach in a little mission church to about twenty people—and they the poorest, the least educated, and the least influential. He'd provided a parson for them—and a devoted one too in old Baynes—surely that was all they could expect. Such was the instant thought, but he was too genial, too soft-hearted, to be able to refuse Baynes.

(Or indeed to refuse anyone. Sometimes a man with a persuasive tongue would get past Amy's or the maid's barricade and, on presentation in the study, turn out to be a man with a hard-luck story and a request for a benefaction. Such a successful trespass would infuriate the Vicar at first, but usually before the trespasser had sidled from the study Canon Welcome had given him a half-crown, both because he liked to be liked and spoken well of in the streets, and because he could never snub or wound anyone who stood before him. And always after he'd slipped such an alms into the man's hand and said his " Good luck, old chap, and God bless you," he would feel happy and think, " I'm not altogether a hypocrite, really ; I have the substance and the marrow of the matter in me.")

So today : he couldn't disappoint Baynes and he wanted to be liked by him. And . . . well . . . any old sermon would do. Just twenty half-illiterate people from the Fields. Some sermon that he knew by heart. . . . " O.K., Baynes. You're absolutely right : I must do my duty. When do you suggest ? "

" I suppose Sunday fortnight wouldn't be possible ? At Evensong ? "

" Three weeks' time ? " He took his engagement diary from a pocket in his waistcoat, where it always looked an extraordinarily small book to issue from so ample a mound. " Yes, there's nothing that week—nothing at all—nothing till old Bett's Anti-duellers on the following Monday." Three weeks seemed a long way off, as he lay back again in his chair. Needn't worry about a sermon for a long time yet. " Yes, of course, Baynes. All right. Sunday fortnight. I shall look forward to that. I ought to have come long ago. Shameful."

" I'll tell the people you're coming, and try to get all I can. I'll go round everywhere and tell them. But I'm afraid there won't be very many. They don't mind me coming into their houses, but I can't get them to come into mine. At least, only a few."

" You needn't worry about that, Baynes. You know me. You know I don't mind if it's twenty or two thousand people. Good, Baynes. Sunday fortnight." Pleased with his conquest over himself, he was really happy to be going down to the Fields again, like a conscientious and hard-working vicar. " I shall look forward to this. There : I told you you'd come to visit a sinner who was neglecting his duties ! Excellent. Excellent, old boy. That's what you're for."

§

The Vicar went down the hill and turned into the Fields. He wore his cassock and priest's cloak in the clear evening light, because it was as well for a vicar, who was too often an absentee, to publish his appearance in these parts. A solid, well-rounded Giottoesque figure in the long cloak, he passed under the viaducts into the grey canyon of Feldgate Street. From the railway depôt came its acrid smell of old smoke and cinders and the short, untroubled whistlings or quick asthmatic breathings of engines full of steam. From farther away came the clatter of shunted waggons and the brisk coughs of some huge locomotive heaving its train out of the Terminus on its way to the North.

He turned eastward along Sloe Lane towards Maker Street. All the little shops, the hairdressers, newsagents, fish friers, "dress agencies", and bagwash laundries were shuttered and blinded in the Sabbath evening; the roadways were empty except for an occasional bus; but the pavements were almost as full and noisy as on a weekday because the factories, breweries, and metal works had emptied their young men and girls into the May sunlight. The only business houses that were brightly alight were the cinemas with their coloured neon signs. Dribbles of patrons, in couples or in families, were passing through their doors and as he came upon the flood-lit vestibule of one of the largest, he read the title of the film that was to be shown that night. It was " Gentlemen, the Killer ".

Now he was in Maker Street, where Mr. Carman's New Victoria Buildings towered above the eighteenth-century terraces; and the memory of Mr. Carman came towards him to rebuke and upbraid. All too soon he had wearied of well-doing with Mr. Carman, and it was four months since he had seen or heard of him. As, somewhat ashamed, he passed the entry of the Buildings he started guiltily, for some people were coming out into the street; but it was only a pick-up band of three negroes carrying their instruments towards a dance hall. The last turning but two before the Circus was Little Bread Street, and Canon Welcome turned into it. It led nowhere, for its end was closed by a black arcade of coal-bays and behind this arcade the railway lines ran towards the Gospel Road Coal and Goods Station. Its left side was a row of small uniform houses pressed against the pavement, and the right-hand side was the same, except for a low, brick ark with pointed windows, which was the Little Bread Street Mission.

Canon Welcome had hoped that his coming to preach might have seemed an event of importance in these streets; that Baynes's going to and fro with the news might have interested the people; and that he would see them approaching the chapel in twos and threes, somewhat as they had dribbled towards the cinema doors. But there was no one in the street. Canon Humbert Welcome was of no significance to them. He felt disappointed and a little angry that when he, a preacher of distinction, condescended to come to a back-street conventicle, it should mean nothing to the neighbourhood at all.

He pushed open the chapel door, hoping against hope to see a fair congregation within; but no : there were six persons in the seats : four of them lonely old women, and the other two, a mother and a restless child. Ah well, it was still only a quarter past six and perhaps early for the people of the Fields. He walked up the nave towards the chancel.

"Nave" and "chancel", let it be allowed, are words too big for this dun, bare, dusty mission hall. Give a square barn with an open-timber roof, two rows of imitation lancet windows, several rows of hard chairs, and a wooden dais with prayer-desks, lectern, and altar, and you have the Little Bread Street Mission Church in Hebron Fields.

Canon Welcome glanced around him. The leaded windows begrimed with the drifting coal-smoke, let in a brown light ; and, quite astonishingly, because Baynes's services were of the simplest and without ceremonial, there was a smell as of old incense in the blank and silent room. Perhaps it was something to do with the smoke from above the coal-bays and the varnish of the pitch-pine dado. Fresh from the sunlight he did not at first discern a dark figure kneeling on the step of the dais. Then he saw it, a hunched figure in a frayed cassock—solid, round, and robed. It was Baynes : his hands were clasped and his head bent, and either he hadn't heard the Vicar's steps or he imagined they belonged to one of the congregation, for he continued in prayer, only unclasping his fingers at intervals to scratch his head. The soles of his black shoes presented themselves to the people from under his cassock. Often the Vicar had noticed these worn-down soles and heels protruding from under a white alb when Baynes was celebrating at the altar in St. Boniface's, and always they reminded him that an elevated priest in alb and chasuble had only the feet of a man-in-the-street.

He stopped, not wanting to break into anyone's prayer. He waited till Baynes should rise from his knees, and he could go forward and greet him. But Baynes did not rise ; instead he turned back his head as if to send his prayer through the rafters and force upon the attention of God the needs of his people and their service tonight.

It was Canon Welcome who now bent his head. He bent it in some shame, wishing that he was as devoted a priest as his curate ; and very quietly he sank himself on to the nearest chair. And he not only sat but, obeying an irrepressible impulse, knelt down too and asked God to forgive, if He could, all his sins and hypocrisies and use him as an instrument however soiled and unworthy, for the aiding and strengthening of these few poor people tonight.

And he was pleased that the example of Baynes should have so moved him that for a little while he too was being good and saying a prayer that was sincere. He was proud to be on his knees and for a moment wanted Baynes to see him there ; but he quickly perceived that this was a whisper from the old Adam, and instead, and in stern self-discipline, he sat back abruptly when he saw that Baynes was about to rise.

Baynes, still unaware that his vicar was in the church, went quickly to the bell-rope by the side of the dais and pulled and pulled it like a man in a dream. Its tongue gonged unevenly above the roof, now loudly and quickly ; now slowly and absent-mindedly ; and anon quick and *fortissimo* again. No one entered in response to its summons except one old man who leaned heavily, at each step, on a rubber-ferruled stick. Baynes, hearing this lame, iambic tread, looked up from the floor, saw the emptiness of his church, and pulled with a new energy and resolution.

But, as he did so, it broke upon his abstracted eyes, like a vision of Truth, that the dark figure seated yonder was the Vicar. Instantly he let the bell-rope go so that it took a leap towards the rafters. The bell above the roof rang once and again on its own, as if indignant at this cavalier treatment ; then stated its indignation with one expletive and stopped.

Baynes came hurrying towards his vicar. " There's not much of a congregation yet, Vicar, but more'll come. I've told 'em all you're coming—how are you, Mrs. Faroe ? And you, Cissie ?—come to church with Mummy, have you ? Good. I'm sure some'll come along, Vicar. They hardly ever come till they've heard my bell, and some are probably waiting out there with their last fags till the clock strikes—ah, here's somebody you know. But how unexpected, how nice ! "

It was Lilian Eadie : Lilian Eadie, tastefully but soberly dressed in black for these unfashionable and possibly dangerous parts. She must have heard from Bettersby or Tim that the Vicar was preaching in Little Bread Street tonight ; she came to every service or meeting at which he was billed to speak, no matter how remote the district or how dismal and murky the streets.

" Lilian ! " the Vicar exclaimed. " Good gracious, what are you doing here ? "

"Tsh . . ." she whispered. "I've come to hear you, of course, but oh dear, oh dear, what dreadful parts ! How does anyone live in places like these ? I'm terrified, darling. I feel like Livingstone in Africa. Shall I be murdered ? How do you do ? " Baynes had automatically put forth his hand in welcome, and she shook it fervently. " Is it all right, Mr. Baynes ? I've left all my valuables at home as I understand your parishioners are wonderful at snatching, but how brave of you to work down here, how wonderful."

Baynes, put out of countenance by flattery and rendered dumb, only smiled, shook his head, muttered, " They're very nice people," and pointed to a seat. As she sat gravely and gracefully, he cried with enthusiasm, looking towards the doors, " Ah, here *is* Somebody, Vicar ! Now this really is an honour. This has never happened before. I thought you'd draw the people. I said they'd come if you came."

" People " was a generous word for the two persons who had entered the chapel and were coming, one behind the other, up the gangway between the chairs. The first was Mr. Carman, a rather uncomfortable and embarrassed Mr. Carman, in a new, ready-made but uneasy Sunday suit, and holding a bowler hat somewhere near the seam of his trousers. Apparently he was prospering with his barrow (whether by giving fair prices or short change) because the suit was not only shop-new but, being of a lively grey and a merry pattern, might have been styled a joyful suit. The bowler hat, down by his thigh, had a sheen of newness too ; and it seemed possible that it had been bought especially for this rare and perplexing visit to divine service. Though doubtless pleased with his well-dressed appearance, he was palpably nervous as he walked up this unfamiliar avenue. He screwed up his little eyes as he looked around ; he knitted up his thin lips as he reconnoitred the position ; he fingered his chin as he weighed alternative schemes, and, withal, swaggered slightly, lest anyone supposed these were symptoms of nervousness.

The little figure behind him was certainly none other than Phil Janey, his daughter. Canon Welcome identified her at once with the photograph in the silver frame. There was the same unlovely little face with the beautiful, wide-spaced eyes, the tipped-up nose, the wide mouth, and the pointed chin. The only thing for which he was not prepared was her exceeding smallness. A daughter of the Maker Street tenement, who'd known hunger when Mr. Carman was out of money or " inside ", she combined the slightness of a thirteen-year-old child with the maturities, at breast and hip, of her sixteen or seventeen years. This evening the wide mouth was not smiling perkily as in the photograph. It was set rather sullenly as she followed behind her father like a dog ; and the big eyes, as he had noticed in the photograph, held something like a dog's acceptance of the unexplained sadness in the world.

Turning towards her, Mr. Carman, either in his nervousness or in his ignorance of ecclesiastical customs, spoke much too loud, and with a deliberate, self-conscious ribaldry. " Where the hell do we sit, Phil Janey ? You know something about it : where do we park our bottoms, eh, ducks ? Suppose we can sit anywhere, can't we ? It's not dearer in front, like what it is at the Hippo ? It might be, you know. Blimey, it's forty years since I done anything like this, and you never know what games they get up to——"

But at this point the Vicar had reached them, and his sudden greeting—" Well, Ricky, this is fine ! " halted Mr. Carman like a thug's gun pointed at him.

" Christ, you give me a start ! " he declared. " Yuss, I come along—good evening, Rural Dean—often I thought I would, because your Mr. Baynes is a real gentlemen, but I been waiting till you come along. And when Reverend Baynes stopped me in the street and told me you was coming and arst me to come too, I said to him, I said, ' Why not, I don't mind if I do.' And I made Phil Janey come too. She's always wanted to meet you since what you did for her old dad. Law, we've never got over that ! And I've all along wanted her to know you, because—well, because I thought you might do her some good. She does a sight too much dancing and messing about with the boys. Don't seem right to me, not at sixteen. It don't, I *must* say. Come on, Phil Janey. This here is Rural Dean Welcome."

The girl put her head to one side, shyly. " Pleased to have met you," she said. But her eyes, instead of smiling with pleasure or gaiety, looked up at him a little frightened ; and she had nothing else to say.

The heart of Canon Welcome, because of her childishness and her timidity, and because she was a young girl, rushed out to her. He, for his part, smiled upon her affectionately. " How are you, my dear ? " The benignity was easy and natural, because he truly felt it. "I've heard about you, and it's good to meet you at last."

"Quite well, thank you," she said, in a voice that could hardly be heard.

"She talks a sight louder than that at home," explained Mr. Carman. "Especially when she's saucing her mother. Blimey to hell, you'd think she'd never sauced anyone in her life. She's sauced her old dad sometimes till he's given her a bash to show that he's had enough of it. Packet of impudence, that's what she is sometimes. You'd never think."

Phil Janey tossed her head in some anger at this description and looked away.

The Vicar picked up her hand. "We're very, very pleased to see you," he said, and all his heart was in the words.

"I'm very pleased to come, thank you," she answered like a well-instructed child at a party. He almost expected her to curtsy.

"We're going to get to know each other better. And I'm sure, Ricky, a little dancing doesn't do her any harm."

"*I'm* not so blamed sure of it. There's dancing and dancing."

"The Church doesn't want to spoil your happiness in any way, my child. It only wants to increase it."

The girl smiled, but not yet with the gaiety of the photograph; rather with the smile of a child at a party who is just losing her shyness.

"*I'd* spoil some of it if I had half a chahn'st," said Mr. Carman. "Where do we sit, Rural Dean?" He had apparently been instructed by Mrs. Carman that this was the correct way to address his benefactor. "Anywhere we like?"

"Why, of course. Come up in front. Come, Phil Janey."

They followed him, Mr. Carman remembering the advice of Mrs. Carman and saying, "Thank you, Rural Dean."

"No need to call me that, Ricky. 'Vicar' 'll do. You have—er—you have a Prayer Book?" he inquired doubtingly.

"No, I haven't, but Phil Janey has. Her teacher give her one some time ago when she was all set on getting her to go to church. She did go for a bit and I wish she'd kep' it up, meself. It's better than dancing, anyway. She knows her way around a Prayer Book, and she'll show her old man. There's not much she don't know about it," he added proudly.

Canon Welcome suspected that there might be quite a good deal, but he only smiled fondly upon her, and directed them into a row of chairs near the front.

" Go on, Phil Janey," ordered her father pushing her forward to a seat. And determined to be lively, and unabashed by these religious surroundings, he whispered, " Sink your buttocks there, my dear, and let the old man have the corner seat where he can look out of the window " ; and plumped himself on an end chair, his back very straight and his little eyes gazing around him. Canon Welcome, turning towards the vestry, couldn't help wondering whether those eyes, being professional eyes, weren't noticing the chances of a " knock off " : those brass candlesticks on the altar, for instance, those vases, those surplices in the vestry. . . .

§

The vestry was fifteen square feet on the right of the dais, curtained off from the rest of the hall. The curtains, dimmed and dusty, were no more inclined to meet than the curtains on an amateur stage, and the congregation had always one or more glimpses of Mr. Baynes bending down to plunge into his surplice or flinging his black-stuff hood over his head. For the same reason Canon Welcome today had a view of the incoming people as he pulled on his surplice and reached for his hood and his scarf in his bag.

A few were coming in now in response to Baynes's bell. For the most part they were old women, tired and waddling, or old men such as one sees sitting along in public gardens and smoking in the sun. But there were also a few who were young : perhaps ten or a dozen girls dressed in cheap and flouncy dresses and three or four youths in ready-made suits light enough and bright enough to be the younger brothers of Mr. Carman's. These few girls and these shy and self-conscious young men represented, no doubt, Baynes's little harvest after twelve months' labour in Hebron Fields.

And as he watched them taking their places, the Canon's hand suddenly let fall his handsome M.A. hood of black and white silk, because his heart had run out to them. It had gone through the curtains to the old men and women because they were weary and resigned ; to the youths because they were young and fresh and sanguine ; and to the girls because they were feminine creatures, and their dresses were cheap but brave proclamations, none the less, of their unbounded aspirations and dreams. It was a really overwhelming sense of love that went out from him, and he let the hood remain in the bag where it lay. He left also his black silk scarf with the medal ribbons in the same dark privacy. Usually he was proud of these robes and liked to parade them before the people as proof of his academic and military distinctions, but tonight he felt that they might hang as a barrier—a barrier of class and money—between him and these people. And they might contrast him to his advantage with old Baynes. For Baynes had only the black stuff hood with the purple piping which his Theological College had given him, and his cassock was too short so that it showed the hem of his trousers, and the hem of his trousers was too high so that it showed his coarse grey socks. Moreover, completely indifferent to his appearance, he invariably allowed his surplice to fall to one shoulder and the hood to loop over the other. Canon Welcome tonight accepted this indifference as a better thing than his own ostentation and left his fine robes in the bag. He might be a canon, a rural dean, a candidate for gaitered rank, but tonight he would stand before them in the simplicity of a surplice, no better vested than a choirboy.

And when he and Baynes walked out of the vestry to the chancel he deliberately walked in front of his curate, though his seniority in this his own church entitled him to walk last. And while Baynes sang the service in a voice too strident for the building and too loud for the small company, he watched the congregation singing its best with him or saying their part of the prayers, and his heart continued, almost with pain, to embrace them all. Here only a few feet from him was Phil Janey, a burglar's daughter, and he could hear her singing. Her voice was curiously like her eyes in that while it was beautiful and young and could be happy, it was also very wistful and seemed to hold in its depths some of the long sadness of God's world. Its wistful tones made an immense attack upon his pity. What chance, he thought, had she ever had ? Was it not natural that she should try to escape into dancing or into cinemas or into sex—this last the only door of escape that stayed open always and everywhere for all ? Just now she was escaping into this happy singing alongside of others.

135

Only just behind her stood Lilian Eadie, singing or saying the responses in her well-trained voice ; and he was ever afterwards to remember this first conjunction of these two, Lilian slim and neat in her black, silk frock, and Phil Janey singing heartily in a tight little hat with a tall quill feather.

Baynes, constantly pulling the straying hood back on to his shoulder, read and sang the service in a manner as hurried and expressionless as that of the most insincere professional priest who cares little for his task and much that it should be quickly done. His voice changed only into something natural and kind when it turned from the set formulæ and following his eyes, addressed the audience with some such words as, " Now look, all of you : we're going to sing a children's hymn but one that's good enough for us, however old and clever we think we are. Three three two. ' There is a green hill far away.' Yes, three three two."

The people sang it in young, fresh voices or old and creaky ones, and the hand of their vicar, as he listened, went down into his cassock pocket. Here was the old sermon which he'd preached a hundred times and judged to be good enough for these insignificant people—a sermon packed with pleasant parables and clever conceits—but it seemed now a poor, insincere and shameful thing to a heart as moved as his. What was this to offer to that child seeking life and happiness, old Carman's daughter ? He felt it in his pocket and left it there. He left it there, as he'd left his hood and his medal ribbons in his bag. He would make no use of it at all. Tonight, for once in a way, he would speak only out of the fulness of his heart. Surely his heart would give him something to say.

It was now the last verse of the " hymn before the sermon ", and he must go to the preaching place. This was no pulpit, for the little mission church didn't possess such a thing ; it was merely the chancel step—if we may continue to call a wooden platform by the grand name of " chancel ". The people sang him to this place, and clearest of all were Phil Janey's sweet liquid tones laced with unconscious tears.

Thy touch has still its ancient power ;
No word from Thee can fruitless fall ;
Hear in this solemn evening hour,
And in Thy mercy heal us all.

The singing ceased, and he stood before them, with neither manuscript nor notes, nor yet an idea, in his head. Thirty years he had been in the ministry, and this was the first time that he'd dared to wait on God for words—or, in simpler speech, to wait on the love in his heart.

The silence had lasted long enough—he had no desire to-night to hold it for dramatic effect—and he must speak.

"My dear people," he began, "I am not going to preach to you this evening. I am your Vicar and, as I look at you, I wonder if the best sermon I could preach would not be to ask your forgiveness that I have come so seldom among you. But may I now speak a word or two about an affection which I really do feel for you? It is all I have to speak about. As I've sat among you tonight, I've learned a great deal from it; I've learned more clearly than ever what I believe, and what I want you to believe. Like many of you, I dare say, I find some difficulty with this or that article of our creed, but I find none whatever—absolutely none—in believing, in knowing as well as I know anything on this earth, that God is love and that I am—or, rather, I ought to be—a channel through which this love tries to reach the world. I am your priest and as I stand here, even though terribly conscious of unworthiness, I seem to feel this—this *something*—forcing its way through me to you. When it is really forcing a way through a man it is not wholly a pleasant feeling—no, it burns and punishes him because his selfishness has left it so narrow a channel. And it is just the same with you. Listen : you too feel this love breaking down and burning away your selfishness as you look upon your children, or upon someone old who is sick and dying or even upon a dog in the street who has been hurt and limps in pain.

"I simply tell you that this is God and that, whether you know it or not, you worship it. Why, you go to your cinemas to worship it. You go to see the hero or heroine doing kind, loving, self-sacrificing actions, and when you see their love in operation, your heart is stirred in its depths and your eyes smart. Because, you see, you have come into this world provided with something which tells you, ' That is Truth. That is Goodness. That is Beauty.' Say only also ' That is God, and It is in me,' and you have the best part of all that we want to teach you."

Very simply, the words coming easily, he showed them how this love, if they encouraged it at all, must slowly widen its

137

channel by wearing away their self-centredness and, if anyone were to give it room enough as the saints had done, it must in the end diminish the self almost to nothing. Did not something tell them, when they were loving properly, that the self was conceding too small a channel and that some of it must give way if the love was to get through ? It was all so obvious, so simple, he said. They must choose either this spreading love which would force open the channel more and more or the congealing, hardening, constrictive self which, if they left it alone, might narrow and narrow the channel till there was no opening at all.

Pausing here, while he wondered what else he could say to drive home this truth, which tonight seemed so simple and clear, he perceived that every eye was on him and that every heart, for a brief moment, was his. For a moment, in this room like a cemetery chapel or a mortuary, life was stirring. Smiling down on them while he waited for words, he looked towards Mr. Carman and Phil Janey. Phil Janey was staring up at him as at a revelation, with one thumb at her teeth like a child absorbed.

The words came ; they seemed to come for her sake, as if she were the representative of them all ; as if a child were leading them. " Is there one of you here who has not sometimes felt this love and pity struggling through ? Not one. Not even the worst of you ; not even the youngest of you ; no, no matter what selfishness or sins you may have on your mind. Well, if sometimes you feel you can't believe in God, say instead, ' I believe in this struggling love in me ' ; and, though you know it not, you will still be saying, ' I believe in God ' ; because, though all the dogmas about God may die, this thing will never die. It never has, and it never can. It is everlasting, you see, and it strives everlastingly for good."

He went on to argue—and it was the whole truth for him tonight—that if this thing existed everlastingly it must be a person. How could love be other than a person ?

" I believe in it, and I worship it, no matter how grave my sins. You do too. Come here then, as well as to your cinemas, to worship it. Come to praise God because He is this love, and therefore you can't help worshipping Him. I think, if you try to keep this belief of yours in your homes only, you will gradually lose your hold on it. That is what nearly always happens. So come often here—as your vicar I ask you to—

come to Mr. Baynes who will be here to welcome and help you. Come to witness to the world your belief in Love as God, and to show it to one another, and to strengthen one another, in this belief. Come to find perhaps thirty other people in this little church, and to know that there are thirty people whom you love, and thirty who love you. Come when your supply of love seems to be shortening, to get more and to take it away with you. Take some of it, much of it, away with you now, and don't forget this : come back, always come back for more."

§

In the vestry Baynes came forward with an outstretched hand. "Vicar, you were wonderful. So simple, so real. I wish I could talk like that. I know you got right into their hearts." And Canon Welcome could not answer, for he knew that he had done so, and felt humbled and ashamed.

There were things to do in the vestry : the preacher's book to be signed, his robes to re-pack in his bag, his priest's cloak (which now seemed a guilty garment) to be slung round his shoulders and clasped ; and the mission room was empty as he walked down it to the door. He stepped out of the door into a street that was filled with the last bright light of a May evening. An unclouded sun had just gone down behind the roofs and stained the air with rose.

The little blunt street was empty except for one figure linger-ing on the pavement half way to Maker Street. By the tall quill feather in its hat he knew it for Phil Janey's. He knew too why she loitered there ; and a happiness, almost like the glow in the evening air, filled his heart. It was not Lilian Eadie this time who wanted to tell him that she'd liked his sermon, but old Carman's daughter, Phil Janey. He went towards her with a friendly little grin, and as he came nearer she took a step to meet him, with her hands clutching nervously behind her back. "Oh, sir," she began, and her eyes were alight with something he'd lit there, "excuse me, I did so want to say I did so enjoy what you said. It was wonderful, like."

CHAPTER SIX

On that occasion in the mission room Canon Welcome had not only convinced his small congregation, but he had most powerfully convinced himself. Walking home that night he had thought, " I believe that it was the only really good sermon I've ever preached, because, all the time, I was caring nothing about myself or my glory but only about the people before me." And as he climbed up his hill he had determined to *try* to live by the light of all he'd seen and told to the people. To try, but without much hope of success. It was too late now. Too late at fifty. Too often before he had begun to be good, but never had he been able to sustain the effort. His habits and his self-centred ambitions were the masters of his home now and could not easily or long be evicted. Too late. Too late at fifty.

Nevertheless he did sustain the effort for some days. The old masters remained evicted. The new tenants stayed in occupation with the doors securely shut. He prayed night and morning to that God whose name he'd given to the people ; and in the strength of that name he tried to love and help everyone he met. He forced himself to be very gentle with Amy ; he was careful to give her from every dish the slice that he would have liked for himself ; he even kept his temper when once, in spite of all, she interrupted his morning's work to beg for some notepaper ; he controlled himself then though a reverberating explosion was utterly desirable ; he lifted himself again and again out of his cushioned chair and forced himself to work ; he was patient with fools in the street, suffering them, if not gladly, at least with a continuing smile ; and he stayed his hand on cigar box and wine bottle that he might learn to love himself less and others more.

There were six days of this, and he was very happy in it ; he could not remember an occasion when he'd been sweet and self-denying so long. He was able to say to his conscience, " Say what you like ; I have the substance and the marrow of the matter in me." The sweetness sat on his face, and he had a task not to feel it there and be glad about it. It would be all wrong if the sweet smile began to take on the character of the priest's cloak.

But the old masters came close to his house door when Bettersby announced, in the vestry of St. Boniface, that among the distinguished guests of the Anti-Duellers on the morrow would be a member of the Government. Canon Welcome no sooner heard the member's name than a warm flame of hope sprang up in his heart. This minister, a prominent Churchman, was known to be one of the Prime Minister's confidants and counsellors whenever he had to advise the King on the appointment of a dean or a canon of Westminster or . . . yes, a bishop. The name of this statesman was an Open Sesame to the doors of Canon Welcome's newly cleansed and whitewashed heart. The doors unlocked themselved and opened a little way. It would be absurd not to get into talk with this man of power and leave the best possible impression upon him. "The Very Reverend the Dean of . . ." "Canon of Westminster . . ." a real canon, and not just one of those prebendaries who called themselves canons. "The Right Reverend the Lord Bishop of . . ." One by one the old masters stepped indoors again, and the new tenants, who'd so enjoyed their sojourn, slipped silently and not unsadly away.

§

The Trimestrial Dinner of the Anti-Duellers was held, by courtesy of the Worshipful Company of Sutlers, in their sixteenth-century Court Chamber. This celebrated room, one of the few such guild rooms to escape the Great Fire of London, had all the flamboyant but joyous elaboration of carving and moulding that its Tudor craftsmen could give it, but four hundred years had so ripened and encrusted this extravagant floreation that the room was now as mellow and gracious as the wines that were drunk within its walls. The panelling of these walls was carved and chamfered and black with the years ; the white ceiling, much moulded, dropped in ornate pendants as if the plaster had begun to melt once but had been arrested and solidified as it fell ; and the oak tables, spread for this feast, stood beneath these pendants, arranged in an E—principally so that the top table might entertain as many distinguished persons as possible, but you might think the formation exactly suited to an ancient Elizabethan room. They were fifty years older than the room itself ; long tables with six or eight legs, and all those legs swollen into bulbous ovoids as round and sleek as some of the bellies which brushed against the boards above. The chairs were oak too, with carved patterns on their backs and carved crests on their tops. The Master's Chair, which the President of the Anti-Duellers was privileged to occupy, stood like a king among courtiers in the centre of the top table and, fittingly enough, had a crown carved on its apex to commemorate the happy restoration of King Charles the Merry.

The company walked in from the ante-room, Canon Welcome and Dr. Bettersby among them. Canon Welcome walked with satisfaction to the top table and stood behind his chair : he had been well pleased to see on his programme that the Anti-Duellers, like all good men with purses and palates, had a reverence for the Church and would not put their chaplain anywhere but at the top table, nor his guest anywhere but at his side. Thus Canon Welcome would be quite close to the member of the Government and might exchange some good talk with him, such as would leave an impression. This guest of honour was now standing at his place, on the President's right. He was a little stout, self-satisfied man with kindly, commonplace features, and Canon Welcome thought he looked more like a grocer of good heart or a butler of moderate intelligence than a minister of the Crown and a privy councillor. He, the Canon, could think of a man in that room whose face and form and bearing would have suited this high position much better ; and that man was standing behind his own chair.

" Now what do we have ? " asked Dr. Bettersby, consulting his menu. " Caviare, Clear Turtle, Salmon Trout à la Christiana, Saddles of Southdown Lamb, Roast Surrey capons, Salad, Asparagus, Sauce Divine, Soufflé Groiselle Glacé, Genoise Pastry, Dessert. That should do."

Canon Welcome had likewise his menu in his hand. " They don't state the wines," he said.

" The wines will come," answered Dr. Bettersby with confidence ; and just as he said this, the President tapped the table with his gavel, enforcing silence. " I'll ask our worthy chaplain to read the passage and say grace."

Promptly Dr. Bettersby recited the passage from Leviticus and with hardly a pause continued, " For these and all thy mercies given, We bless and praise thy name, O Lord. May we receive them with thanksgiving Ever trusting in thy word, To thee alone be honour, glory, now, henceforth, for ever more. *Laudi Spirituali,* 1545," he explained to his guest, as if he were identifying a bottle of wine ; and he and all the company sat down.

Canon Welcome discovered with much satisfaction that his neighbour on the other side was no less a person than Sir Eyre Storm, the famous foreign correspondent of *The Times*. A newspaper man always seemed to him a valuable " contact " ; and for much of the meal he worked steadily and skilfully with the burin of his tongue to grave an impression on Sir Eyre. Learning that he was a Freemason, he declaimed, " Oh, I became a mason more years ago that I care to count. I thought it would be an excellent thing for a parson to do as it would bring me into contact with all types of men, most of whom would probably be—if I may say so—of an idealistic and thoughtful kind and perhaps able to help me in my work with their advice and experience." Sir Eyre agreed that the step had been sage, and sipped his sherry.

The wines were dancing by in a lively procession : golden and smiling ; golden and sparkling ; rich red and portly ; old gold and mellow and wise. A Birch's Punch had marched ahead of them all ; then came a sherry, Domecq Oloroso ; and a dry Graves, Château du Roi ; and a pair of Champagnes, Veuve Cliquot and Cordon Rouge ; and an old port ; and Brandy or Benedictine at the procession's tail.

Canon Welcome declined none of them. There is a need in popularity-loving parsons to demonstrate their virility before the laity, since so many of the laity have denied it ; and Canon Welcome, though as masculine a figure as any seated at that table, was not free of this need ; and since all these other virile diners were drinking well and deep, he drank dutifully, and with an increasing pleasure at their side. At one stage, but the Canon was never quite sure which stage, a loving cup went round, and when Dr. Bettersby stood to drink with his neighbour on the far side, Canon Welcome stood behind him to see that no one stabbed him in the back. This, as he knew, was the custom when the loving cup passed from guest to guest, but it occurred to him, as he waited his turn to drink with Bettersby, that this precautionary measure was a little inappropriate to an Anti-Duellers Club ; and he said so to

Bettersby after he had sipped and bowed and handed the cup to Sir Eyre (who'd protected *him* from a stab in the back). His head was in a high condition now for such lucid commentary, and it stayed so until the liqueur brandy and the Benedictine were in possession of the tables. Then, suddenly and with some dismay, he noticed that the elaborately-carved patterns on the oak panelling were losing their precision. They were even retiring at times into some insubstantial dreamland. He blinked and stared at them sternly ; and they came hurrying back. They stood still, but only that all their vertical lines might vibrate and fade like harp-strings plucked. And in something of the same way the sentiments which he was expressing to Bettersby and Sir Eyre—sentiments witty and profound, as he thought them at their start—not only needed an effort if they were to be kept stable and precise, but had a tendency to drift sideways, or fall forwards, so that he had to snatch and hold them sternly if he were to lead them to a right conclusion.

The natural thing to do if one is visited by a faint dismay is to sip one's drink in the belief, or the hope, that it will clear the head and straighten out the entangling cerebration. The Canon accordingly sipped. But so quick-footed had been the dancing of the wines that besides the brandy in his liqueur glass there was yet some port, and some champagne, and even a little Graves, in the assortment of glasses about his plate ; and Canon Welcome, lacking, as we have said, a perfect mastery of thought and clarity of vision, found himself sipping port or champagne—or Graves—when he intended brandy. None of them tasted well, taken in this alternation, nor did they serve to marshal the undisciplined thoughts and get them into smart, straight ranks again. However, he continued to sit there hoping that the wine he had taken would lose its potency in time. It did not ; on the contrary, it seemed to be maturing in cask. He now felt as soft and sweet as a sleepy pear. Likewise he continued to sip, hoping that his hand, which was now largely autonomous, would choose the brandy. Often it did, but not four times out of ten. Meanwhile he pulled at an enormous cigar which, desiring to appear as masculine as Sir Bettersby and Dr. Eyre—no, as Sir Eyre and Dr. Bettersby— he had selected from the waiter's tray. The cigar was little help ; rather did it abet the mischievous wines in the public damage they were working. The dizziness increased, and a new dismay sat, or danced, in the Canon's head as he took another sip and another pull : would he be able when he rose from his chair to walk as correctly as a prebendary should ? The anxiety was not lessened when his throat, which was now in as loose control as his fingers, needed an adjustment and made it without reference to him. Fortunately it was not a very audible eructation, and the din from the diners, which outdid the gabble in a monkey-house, drowned it, but how if another such discharge, free of all control, should be a massive one, like a gun at noon, and cause a silence in the company ? He took another sip and closed his lips like prison doors.

But Bettersby, old Betts, a dear fellow, was speaking to him. Had he been speaking some time ? The Canon rather thought so.

" A curious thing, Vicar, that this kind of dining club is always a masculine affair."

" Mmm, mmm . . ." conceded the Canon through locked lips, wishing to be safe rather than sorry.

" Has anyone ever heard of a club of women gourmets ? "

" Club of what ? " asked the Canon quickly, barely parting the lips.

" Women gourmets."

" I certainly haven't," ventured the Canon, and closed the sally-port tight again.

" Shall I tell you why ? "

" Why ? " A safe small syllable.

" For a perfectly simple reason. The Lord God hasn't thought fit to equip them with palates."

" No, no, certainly not, ha, ha."

That comparatively long sentence, and that " ha, ha " marked a change in his condition, an advance. The last sip of brandy—or was it port ?—had thrust him over the frontier of anxiety into a country of charming insouciance. A land of freedom and sunshine, this. He symbolized the new freedom by slipping his fingers under his black-silk waistcoat and un-doing the top button of his trousers. Better. Free. The wind in his stomach, so suddenly unconstricted, escaped, but not this time by an oral eructation. This alternative egress was not so disturbing because, unless it was distinctly audible, one could disclaim by one's manner and by one's continuing talk any responsibility for it. In this blessed freedom the Vicar of St. Boniface became a youth again, an undergraduate, and felt a surging desire for some wild " rag ". He even, though he wouldn't have told this to Bettersby or anybody else in the world,

145

felt a desire to visit Piccadilly by moonlight. Not that he would really accept the invitation of any coy beckoning eye there— no, he had both too much loyalty to his cloth and too much fear of the consequences. One's thoughts, however, need not be published as one draws at one's cigar or sips one's liqueur, and the Canon, a warm-blooded and unsatisfied man, indulged himself in a few pleasant imaginings. Clearly the wines had temporarily unfrocked him, lifting off the prebendary and the rural dean and leaving only an ordinary sensual man. But not sensual only (he demurred) no, no, because he really loved and pitied those poor girls on the streets, those dear girls, and was so far deeply Christian. He had the substance of the matter in him.

"One must have love," he said to Bettersby who a moment ago, as he seemed to remember, had been getting argumentative about the Johannine authorship of the Apocalypse, and making much play with the name of one Papias, Bishop of Hierapolis. "One must have love. 'Fuve got that, you've got ev'thing."

"Exactly." Bettersby nodded many times, his eyes moist and glassy. "What does it matter who wrote it? I mean: it's there, and there it is. Papias might have known John the Presbyter who, if we can trust Epiphanius, died in one one seven ; I mean to say——"

"One must have love," continued Canon Welcome. "I'm perfectly sure of that."

"Naturally. That is the ultimate essence—no one's arguing that—but what I mean is, how could John the Presbyter possibly be John the son of Zebedee? It's impossible ; it's rubbish ; unmitigated rubbish. I will maintain, and, if necessary, under persecution, that the whole thing's impossible ; why, I mean——"

"One must have faith," said the Canon to the glasses and cutlery before him. "I mean love. Faith in love . . . that is, we seem to be going now."

"Yes, we're going into the other room now. Come on."

"Chrimes ! " muttered the Canon, an expression he must have learned from Mr. Carman. His moment of trial had come.

He planted his feet firmly on the floor, and his hands on the table. Humour overcame his doubts, and he said, " One must have faith " ; then carefully rose. The legs he found were in fair control. "Splendid," he proclaimed to no one at all, expect to the glasses which had so nearly undone him. Walking forward, he erupted again and said, " Beggar pardon " to the inattentive air, while he brought a hand to his mouth. No one answered him : only Bettersby turned and said, " Come and meet the Minister."

" Oh yes, yes. Rather ! Every time ! Why not ? " he agreed merrily ; and he thought, " Now must make good impression." His voice sounding rather thick, he cleared his throat so as to be able to deliver the good impression. But his eyes and heart were merry, and the ambition to leave a good impression was difficult to hold in this reckless mood. He felt it slipping from its seat and joviality succeeding it, as in a game of Musical Chairs.

Bettersby led him up to the fat little Minister who was talking and laughing rather noisily in the midst of a circle of admirers. Always these tedious, pushing sycophants round a guest of honour. Bettersby worked his way through them and when his opportunity came, said, " This is my guest, Canon Humbert Welcome. He also happens to be my Vicar."

" Canon Welcome ? " repeated the Minister. " Well, welcome, Canon, ha, ha." And all the circle laughed with loud flattery.

" How do you do ? " said the Canon, smiling into a pink swede of a face whose features were capriciously mutable but apparently pleasant when they stood still. Pleased with them, and with the discipline in his legs, he felt on the summit of the world, and the equal and pal of any privy councillor.

" Canon *what* Welcome, was it ? " inquired the Minister.

" Hump't," explained the Canon. " Hump't Welcome."

" *Hunt* Welcome ? Sorry. I didn't quite catch." Obviously the Minister's perceptivity, like his own, was fumbling a little in its grasp.

" No, no ; ha, ha. No, no, not Hunt. Hunt the slipper. *Humpert*, my dear sir. Can Humpert Welcome."

" I'm sorry—I'm a fool—how is it spelt ? "

The Canon grinned, and brought a hand to his mouth to prevent an undesirable extrusion. " How's pelt ? "

" Yes."

" Oh, with or without an H."

A loud laugh from many, and titters from more, proclaimed that he had scored a success. He had hardly thought the joke worthy of this fine reception, but he now perceived that it was excellent. Really prodigiously funny. Ha, ha, ha. Someone had winked across the circle. Another was demanding, " Woddy say ? " and on being told " With or without an H," he roared with laughter. Ha, ha ; ha, ha, ha. It was a triumph, and the Canon smiled amiable acknowledgments upon them all.

§

A triumph? Not the next morning when he turned in his bed and woke. Not then ; then shame stood at his bedside like a policeman waiting to charge him. And shame was succeeded by despair. He had disgraced himself. Disgraced himself before a crowd of important and influential men. " With or without an H." Awful ! And this piece of comedy back-chat uttered in the thick cloudy voice of a parson who'd drunk too well ! They had laughed, but was it not the laugh with which they greeted the absurdities of their pals when drunk? The Minister had laughed as loudly as any and would probably repeat the words to the Premier this morning. " There was a padre there who was clearly well oiled. A Canon Humbert Welcome——" he'd have to remember the name in order to tell the story. " He couldn't pronounce his name very clearly, and when I asked him how it was spelt, he explained with a radiant smile, ' With or without an H '."

Oh, God. . . .

The Prime Minister would remember the name, and re-member it as a subject for laughter, not as a name to submit to the King. No, there was no evading the truth ; face it ; face it ; last night instead of advancing his chances with those who had the gaiters in their giving, he'd likely enough expunged them for ever. Bettersby also had been plainly a little too ripe, his lean face too rosy and rich with wine. To state it plainly, he had been as ripe and oozy as a wasp-bitten plum. Very wrong of Bettersby to indulge himself in this way and thereby underline the over-ripeness of his Vicar.

" There were two padres there, and both had glorified God by partaking liberally of his gifts."

Canon Welcome turned over in his bed and groaned.

" A learned doctor and a canon, and their hearts were merry with wine."

" They had certainly poured out their libations before the Lord."

" They'd obeyed the charge of St. Paul enthusiastically, and used more than a little wine for their stomach's sake."

Oh, God. . . .

" With or without an H."

This shame and despair he took into his study after a silent breakfast with Amy. Nothing else could he think about. He shut the door on a harried and miserable man. In disgrace what else can one think about except one's disgrace ? With head drooped forward, he walked up and down the soft, mocking carpet, wondering what to do about it. Wearying of the fruitless walk, he stood with his back to the marble fireplace, his hands clasped behind him, and his head raised as he stared into a future which now looked like a desert.

When one is disgraced before the world—or when one thinks one is, for it is likely that the Minister and all the other diners, being *bons vivants* and tolerant men, if they remembered the Canon's rich condition at all, accorded it only a laughing forgiveness and liked him the better for this lapse—when, I say, one believes one's fame irreparably overthrown, there are but two roads into healing and peace ; and one is suicide, and the other sanctity. Suicide, by ending the self, ends all shame and pain ; sanctity, by overthrowing the self, cares no more about past shame and is utterly happy doing good in the present. Canon Welcome considered the possibility of blowing out his brains, and then dwelt upon the joy, the sweet peace, of a life centred in God. He leaned his weary heart long upon this imagined peace (having always had an inclination that way). " Casting all your care upon him, for he careth for you." " Oh, rest in the Lord. . . ." " Take my yoke upon you, and learn of me, and ye shall find rest for your souls. . . ." How wonderful it would be.

" With or without an H."

Damn !

Where was the sense in attempting sanctity again ? Always it was the same. Always he could see, but never, or never for long, could he live the things that he saw. Old Ovid spoke the perfect words for him : *video meliora proboque : deteriora sequor.* He could see like a fine artist, but he couldn't create what he saw.

What could he do to rehabilitate himself in the eyes of the world—oh, but look, here he was, back in the prison of egotism again. Could he not do some grand thing in public that would win him more praise than last night's misbehaviour had lost him—some resounding thing that instead of emptying his credit balance would swell it. The pain eased—for a moment it turned into pleasure—as he contemplated the swelling of his credit balance. It must be something that would get into the papers. Into the local press and if possible into the London press. How could he hit the whole of North London so hard that the papers would have to take note of it ? He mused on the dates ahead and on his engagements. Wait—stay—yes, why not ? A month ahead was his Patronal Festival, the feast of St. Boniface Martyr. A procession. A Procession of Witness through all the streets of his parish, and especially through the grey and lawless streets of Hebron Fields. A procession led by the Hamden Prize Silver Band—no, led by a processional cross, and then by the band. Young Tim, a big, handsome lad, and a good advertisement for manly Christianity, to carry the cross. All the eighteen parishes of this rural deanery to be invited to take part. Their clergy would come : they loved robing and walking in procession, whether round a church or along a street (he loved it himself). Some of their choir boys and choir men would come (all boys and men being alike in their love of a parade), and each parish would muster a contingent of the laity. Mass the choristers into three surpliced choirs with contingents of laity between them ; then a splendid and multi-coloured phalanx of clergy in their academic hoods ; and last—last of all, naturally, and maybe in a cope—the Rural Dean. Four stations, and at each a hymn, a brief talk, and a blessing. One station in the Circus itself at one of the Corners. The Church at the Devil's corner. General Humbert Welcome directing his forces like an arrow at that strongpoint of sin. Headlines : " The Vicar Marches out to Battle with the Spiv." Editorial comment : " Next month the Church in our neigh-bourhood will be concerning itself, not so much with those who have never heard of Christianity, in the dark places of Africa, but with those who, having heard of it, disregard and despise it, in the darkest places of North London. The spearhead of this gallant effort is Canon Humbert Welcome— " with or without an H . . . oh, God !—" the indefatigable Vicar of St. Boniface. . . ."

A return to St. Boniface and a Festival Anthem sung by the combined choirs—no, something more original than that. The close and climax of the procession, and the anthem too, to be on and about the steps of the Little Bread Street Mission. Everything to be of help to poor old Baynes. Crowd the street : the police would certainly allow a great assembly in that blinded lane. Draw all the people of the Fields, like the children of the Pied Piper, to Baynes's very door.

The mixture of motives in Canon Welcome now was as remarkable as the mixture of wines which had driven him on such a different course last night. A desire for rehabilitation and personal glory was alternating and blending with a genial desire to help dear old Baynes, and a real penitence, and a real love for the people in his parish, whether sinners or saints, but especially for the sinners.

There was no turning away from this idea now. It gleamed before him like the light of a new dawn. Hurrying to his telephone, he summoned Bettersby and Tim to an " extraordinary " staff meeting—and Bettersby didn't sound at all pleased. Having summoned them, he rang up, one by one, the eighteen incumbents of his deanery. " Is that you, Jack? . . That you, Hemans? . . . That you, Cecil, old boy? . . . D'you know my Circus? I'm appalled at its godlessness ; it's the worst spot in all our deanery. I was preaching there the other Sunday "—as well to publish this—" and there weren't thirty people in the church, and that in spite of the fact that my curate-in-charge is one of the best fellows ever. I am determined to do something, and you've got to help. This is a voice from Macedon, old boy : ' Come over and help us.' You will ? Good ! I knew you would. What did you say : ' Like heck you will ! ' ? That's the spirit, old boy, if not quite the language."

§

The procession formed up on the hill slope outside the gates of St. Boniface, its head down the hill. The Canon's staff work had been tirelessly creative—was he not enthusiastic about his rehabilitation and therefore fertile in ideas ? His vicarage for the last three weeks had been a Brigade Headquarters alive with work, and here was the outcome : a column of choirs and people stretching from his gate almost to the foot of the hill.

First, and far away, was Tim with his brass cross ; then the Silver Band ; then his own choir boys and a few of the choir men, for the June evening, after some cloud and distressing rain, had broken into sunlight, and they were happy, work hours over, to march and sing. Behind his choir, in files of three, were some two hundred of his congregation, one hundred and eighty of whom were women. Among these, of course, and in

151

the front file, was Lilian Eadie who'd declared, " But most certainly I'll come, darling ; I think it's a beautiful idea, darling, and I shan't be the least afraid to go down into those dreadful streets in procession. They can't murder me with all you enormous men around me." In another file stood Clara Bettersby who'd proclaimed to him and to the world, " Of course I'll come. I'm a soldier's daughter and always ready for this sort of thing." Portions of other choirs and congregations had come in answer to his invitation : enough to blend into two more choirs and two more contingents of laity. One of these contingents, like his own, was headed by churchwardens with their wands. Behind the adult laity came the children : Sunday School children, Bands of Hope, Scouts with their cubs, and Guides with their brownies. All the banners were out among the people : the banners of the Mothers' Union, the Girls' Friendly Society, the Guild of St. Boniface and the Company of Altar Servers.

Twenty-three banners in all floated above the column and fronted the way to the Fields.

A procession is an art form, and any competent craftsman knows that he must keep his grandest moment to the end. The robed clergy, twenty-eight of them, came at the end : a goodly muster of vicars, curates, and honorary assistant clergy. Canon Welcome had been right in his guess that they would parade in some strength : the saintly and gentle men because they were always ready to march humbly to the glory of God ; the less saintly because they enjoyed dressing up and wearing bright robes in the sunlight ; and the quite unsaintly and slothful because they liked this publication and exhibition of themselves, and had nothing to do on a week day. The crimson hoods of Oxford, the white of Cambridge, the brown of London, the blue of Dublin, and the shyer and narrower colours of the Theological Colleges made these ranks of clergy into a fine bed of flowers, some of which were well-blown blooms, others mere pink buds, and a few in the dry and faded leaf. Here stood Bettersby and Baynes, side by side, Bettersby in the lustrous scarlet silk of his doctor's hood, Baynes in the humble black stuff of Frentham Theological College. Bettersby's nose looked extremely frost-bitten at this exercise, but there it was, bringing him along behind it, in loyalty to his Church and in loyalty to his vicar. Occasionally it tweaked.

And last of all came the Rural Dean in his rich red cope. He

had been in some doubt about induing this handsome cope, and
to judge by their eyes and their nostrils, some of the other and less
generous clergy had been in doubt about it too ; but he'd been
quite unable to resist the temptation. "Every man," Lilian
Eadie had said, "looks a heavenly creature in a cope." He
knew he looked splendid in it, with his silver, waving hair ; and
he watched with interest and hope the steps of a press photographer.

Two sidesmen had been detailed to marshal the ranks and
determine the pace of the procession ; and they were as pleased
with their duties as two boys playing at being sergeant-majors.
One of them, when all were arrayed, and his wrist-watch said
six-thirty, gave a nod to Tim : Tim lifted his cross on high ;
the big drummer struck his drum ; the band blared out the
first hymn, the drum beat time, and the long, singing procession,
representing the whole deanery marched downward to the Fields,
with its choirs and banners and clergy, because the Rural Dean
had erred at a public dinner and was vexed by the memory.

§

Rank behind rank, marching and singing, they all supposed
that it was a Festival Procession : only the Rural Dean in the
rear knew that it was a Penitential Procession. It had been
advertised well on shop-doors and hoardings, and he was
pleased to see, as they passed under the viaducts, that some
broken threads of people stood along the kerbs, waiting for
the show. Behind them were women in gossiping groups, men
lingering at public-house doors, loafers lounging at corners,
and youths and girls strolling along with their fingers linked ;
for the benign evening had brought many into the streets. All
these people were drawn by the music and stepped closer to
see the passing show : the women silent for a while, the men
lipping their fags, the lads still holding their girls ; all interested
by the spectacle, and all unmoved. Canon Welcome realized
with some despair that they would no more mix with this
intruding thing which he had inserted among them than water
would mix with a rod dipped into it and withdrawn.

Only the children came running along at the procession's side.

Things improved, however, at the first station because the
Canon, after his two-minute talk, invited them to come along
as far as Little Bread Street where the combined choirs would

sing for them a Festival Hymn ; and quite a few came along the pavement, slowly, to hear the hymn.

Plotting the route in his study, he had sent it down Maker Street to the Circus, as at the heart of the enemy's force ; and now they were at the beginning of Maker Street, and he could see, high and frowning darkly above the old terraces, the block of New Victoria Buildings. The column was moving rather slowly now, because Tim, who in his ardour and youth had been leading them much too fast for the fatter ecclesiastics in the rear, had just been cautioned by a marshal ; so the Canon was able to look about him and scan everything on the pavements or up in the house windows. Among the people watching on the pavements were faces from many parts of the world : Jewish faces from Eastern Europe ; swart, fat, smiling faces from Italy ; black, flat grinning faces from Africa ; and small, slight, beautiful countenances from India. Strange migrants on his Fields, all these, and what did he know of them ? What did he know, if it came to that, of all these people walking along by the fringes of the procession : weary-faced, middle-aged women ; young back-street madonnas with their babies in their arms ; grey-haired and work-worn men ; girls abreast and hand-in-hand ; and of course the children running and skipping along gutter and kerb ? Sometimes, glancing up at a house-front, he saw the face of some old unwanted and unheeded woman looking down from the window of her last, cluttered room. And the procession passed on and left her there.

Choirs and people were now singing, by a bold choice of his own, " The Sower went forth sowing ", and the sweet moving air brought all the tenants of New Victoria Buildings to their entries, window-sills, and landing-rails, so that the huge block really did look like a dove-cote with all the doves looking out. There at their fourth-floor window were Mr. Carman and Mrs. Carman and Phil Janey, side by side and smiling.

> One day the heavenly Sower
> Shall reap where He has sown.

Just as the tail of the procession came near the main entry, the band and the voices fetched Phil Janey running down from her high floor, and she walked along almost at the side of the red-coped Rural Dean—escaping as usual from a constricted and dreary life into something that offered colour and excitement and beauty. Not five seconds later Mr. Carman, who must have run down the stairs too, came out but with dignity and nonchalance and his lips deliberately puckered into indifference. He too followed, but some way behind, and sucking an irreligious pipe so that no one might suppose he was as curious as his daughter or in any danger of getting religion. His manner suggested that he was as innocent tonight of churchgoing as on previous evenings he had been innocent of any desire to weigh up a gentleman's home or to visit it via a window.

The heart of Canon Welcome, as he looked at Phil Janey and all these other poor and possibly dissolute or criminal people, was moved once again. It expanded with affection for them, and he wished, as he'd wished in Baynes's church, that he could have given his life to their service because they were tired and astray, or young and in danger, and therefore dear to the heart of God. He would have liked, in the manner of the saints, to have made himself of no reputation, and taken upon him the form of a servant, seeking no reward except to bring goodness and comfort to the poor. " Of no reputation " —and all this exhibition had sprung from his need of reputation !

Unhappy now because of his weaknesses, but drawn along like a red and gold tassel behind the procession he came into the Circus. Young men loafed and leaned at the famous Corners, and he wondered how many of them, like Mr. Carman's companions in his youth, were " wide boys ", expert in dipping and dragging and shoot-fly. Some of them, with their hats tilted sideways or caps tipped back, and cigarettes languishing at moist, open lips, looked peculiarly cocky and loathsome louts, but he tried to love them.

The procession, having threaded round the Maker Street Corner into Graeme Street, halted on the marshal's order as soon as the Rural Dean was in the Circus, so that he could deliver his talk at this most important station of all. He mounted the little street-corner rostrum, which two exceedingly happy boy-scouts had been carrying far ahead of the column, erecting it at each station, and then standing severely on guard over it. He looked out over the large gaping crowd that was around him now, here in the very axle and nave of his more scandalous streets ; and he longed to be able to speak to them in love. There in front of them all, just under his rostrum, was Phil Janey, hatless and with hands clutching behind her back, like a street child waiting for the drama of Punch and Judy to begin. There among the camp-followers at the back, was Mr. Carman, smoking. Mrs. Carman, having doubtless turned down her stove, and tidied her dress, had joined him and was standing at his side. Canon Welcome longed to feel all that love and power which he had felt in Baynes's church, but though some of it was in him today, it seemed diluted. He could not forget that this procession had been designed far more for his own interest than for his people's. The heavy red cope about his shoulders hampered him because he knew it to be the very gesture of self-aggrandizement.

Still, he tried. He tried to speak sincerely.

He tried to say again what he had said in the Little Bread Street chapel, about the natural love that was in all of them, but he knew that he was saying it with less potency, because of that heavy cope about his shoulders. Some began to move away.

"Don't go away. That is all I'm saying for the present. Think it over. And come a little further with us. Come as far as our little chapel in your midst, and there we will sing you a hymn, and perhaps you will let me give you my blessing, for what it may be worth to you."

He stepped down ; the marshals signalled to the band ; and the procession moved on, singing, "The royal banners forward go". By turning into a side street, it completed a circuit like a noose and twisted its way into Little Bread Street. Here all the choirs disposed themselves about the chapel steps ; the laity stood on either side of the choirs ; the people whom the procession's dragnet had captured stood in a crowd before them ; and all, choirs and laity and crowd, conducted by the choirmaster of St. Boniface, sang (the Vicar had deliberately, chosen this hymn because they would know it from their childhood) : "Once in royal David's city".

There were tears, genuine tears, in the throat of the Vicar, as he listened to the massed voices of the old women, the young women, and the boys singing this communal song in a backwater street, while the light above the roofs lapsed into the first bright hue of evening. What a fine, full, glorious flower to have sprung from the seed of his penitence.

As the last words died into the golden air, he closed his eyes tight, because he really wanted to pray, and lifting his hand, gave them his blessing. They waited reverently till he had done, a few bowing their heads ; then the robed clergy and choirs went into the chapel as into a sacristy, and the people slowly dispersed.

CHAPTER SEVEN

It was the Tuesday after the procession, the morning when both the *Hamden and Hebron News* and the *Hamden Gazette* dropped on the Vicarage doormat, and the Canon, behind the well-closed door of his study, stood beside his writing table, resting his weight upon his palms and studying the two papers spread open before him. They were open at the pictures of the procession : three pictures in the *News*, two in the *Gazette*. He returned again and again, as a man or a woman will, to the photographs which included himself. One showed him following behind the other clergy with his hands issuing from the cope and pressed together before his breast. The other showed him on the rostrum and spreading those hands before the people at the Circus corner. The pictures pleased him with their publicity value but displeased him because he had supposed he was younger-looking, yes, and better looking, than this rather squat and bulky priest. There was a picture of Tim leading with his cross, but this did not draw the Vicar's eye a second time.

He was still studying his own portraits when, if it is to be believed, someone opened the door at ten in the morning and broke upon his studies.

As a bell rings when you tread upon a shop mat, as certain retiring rooms come alight when you open the door, so the Vicar sprang erect from his bent posture as the door-handle turned ; sprang erect and faced the interrupter whom he could only imagine was his wife.

" In the name of God. . . . Have I ever said I'm not to be . . . oh, let me lie down and——" But, alas, it was not Amy ; it was Norah, the young maid, and his sword was blunted, his flame damped. You cannot speak to a servant as to a wife, especially if it's a young and rosy-cheeked maid for whom you could feel, did you encourage it, a notable tenderness. He spoke now rather with long-suffering than in wrath.

" Oh, Norah, have you never heard . . . ? Ah, well, it is useless, useless. Not in this world shall I ever make it clear to anyone that I mean it if I say I'm not to be disturbed in the morning when I have difficult work to do." He hoped his body stood well between Norah and the pictures. "It is morning, Norah. It is ten o'clock. It's the hour which is sacred to my work."

"I'm sorry, sir. But it's a gentleman and a——"

But Amy was in the doorway, having hurriedly arrived like a first-aid party or a police-car upon the scene of a collision.

"It's Mr. Carman, dear, and he's all dressed up. Couldn't you possibly see him?"

At Amy one could discharge the balked gun. "To blazes with Mr. Carman! If he has nothing to do, I have. He's retired from his recent profession. I can't think of retiring for years yet. I have to work—work like a city clerk—or I should never get the mass of business done. Just because he doesn't choose to push his barrow out this morning——"

"But he's brought his daughter with him. And they have both so obviously put on their best to come and see you. Oh, you must see them if you can."

"His daughter?" Immediately at the mention of Phil Janey, as at the sight of Norah, a tenderness began to play upon his fires and extinguish them. "What does she want?"

"He said it was about her being confirmed."

"Confirmed?"

"Yes. Confirmation is business, isn't it? I think Norah thought it was business."

"I wouldn't say it was business. There's a proper time for making application. Still——"

"They must have given up their morning's work and put on their nicest clothes to come and see you, poor dears."

"Old Carman wants his daugher confirmed? Well! This is indeed a triumph. Well, in that case"—it is never easy, immediately after you've raised your voice in condemnation of an action, to allow that it was right, and Canon Welcome did not do so now—"in that case, you can show them in, I suppose."

Amy withdrew to collect them, and Canon Welcome promptly folded up the newspapers.

Old Carman bringing Phil Janey for confirmation! How did they know that the Confirmation Classes were about to begin? And how strange it all was: if the massed singing in Little Bread Street had been the fine flower of his procession, was Phil Janey the one fruit of it? And was it she who had taken this step because she was now seized by the desire to

158

escape into love and good works ; or had Mr. Carman urged her to be godly ; or, equally conceivable, was Mr. Carman offering up his daughter, like Agamemnon or Jephthah, to keep the fount of benefits sweet ?

Whether it had one of these roots or, quite possibly, all of them, the Vicar was pleased with the offering. He was always glad of a new confirmation candidate because he liked to collect a large number and impress the bishop. Each time he enlisted a new girl or boy for confirmation he felt rather like an actor-manager who has just sold another ticket for his benefit performance.

Mr. Carman and Phil Janey came in, Amy throwing wide the door for them. " 'Morning, Canon," Mr. Carman saluted. " I hope it's all right coming along to see you like this when you ain't busy. And look what I've brought in on me boots— and on to your nice carpet ; it's our Phil Janey."

" And how welcome, how very welcome you both are." The Canon's smile enfolded them both as he went forward to meet them.

Mr. Carman was in the same rather horsey grey suit with which he'd honoured the mission service. Phil Janey was un-mistakably dressed for an important social call ; she wore a neat blue frock, probably home-made, a white coat more showy than expensive, and a hat that was something between a cap and a casque, with a white feather curled about it. Her hollow face and snub nose were powdered and her wide lips scarlet with lipstick ; no taller than a child of thirteen, she wore the clothes (making them at home) and carried the air of a society woman of thirty.

" Come in, my child. Delighted to see you." Canon Wel-come stretched out both hands to greet her. He took her narrow hand in both of his ; and all the contents of his heart flowed down into his palms. " Sit down." He led her to the deep, cushioned chair opposite his own ; and she dropped to the edge of it, drawing her legs to the side of her at an awkward angle. She might wear the clothes, but she knew nothing about the deportment of a lady in society. " And you, Mr. Carman—Ricky, I mean—sit you there and be comfortable." He pointed to his own deep chair, while he, as usual, stood before the fire-place. " It'll be good to see you in my chair."

Like his daughter Mr. Carman sat on the front edge of it, placing his bowler hat upon his knees. His little eyes, under their quickset eyebrows, swept the large room ; skilled, professional eyes, they carefully refrained from resting upon, but apprehended with expert interest as they passed by, the silver inkstand on the writing table, the silver candlesticks on the mantelpiece and the silver goblets, spoons, and cups in the glass-fronted bureau. They caught the Vicar's eyes watching them with amusement, and they twinkled—or, rather, one of them did, very slyly.

" I ain't been in this room before, guv'nor. Nor in your hall, now I come to think of it. I only been upstairs."

" Yes, yes," laughed the Canon, " but forget that. We know you called on us once before. Very pleased to see you again."

" They're nice rooms upstairs, Canon." Further instructed by Mrs. Carman, he now understood that " Canon " and not " Rural Dean " was the way to address the Reverend. " So's this one. I'll say it is. It fair asks to be turned over some time when you're taking divine service. Yupp, I come to the front door this time, Canon, and rung the bell. Not last time. Didn't ring no bells then. Nah, hush-hush all the way that evening lest I disturbed your supper. I still don't know how you come to hear me and get the cops in time. And I don't mind telling you it give me quite a turn this morning when I come into the garden with our Phil Janey here and remember those blood—those blinking cops at the bottom of the ladder."

" I daresay it did, but forget all about it and have a cigarette."

" Don't know that I've ever had a nastier knock in me life. Three of 'em, old Timmins trying to be funny, old Sarge Corbett, and a blue-bag, and you standing there in them same black skirts, and with your umbrella up. Gaw' strike me—it was some tumble, that ! And ' Come to Mother ' old Timmins said."

Phil Janey sat extremely upright, fingering her handbag uncomfortably and averting her eyes from both of them. These reminiscences of what seemed, in this refined room, to be exceedingly low life, matched but ill with her dress, her manner, and the ladylike plume in her hat.

" Which reminds me," continued Mr. Carman, irrepressible : " I never had time to put the ladder back. I meant to do, honest I did, Canon, but gaw ! the slops marched me off, leaving it sticking up there."

"Never you mind, Ricky. I'll take the thought for the deed. It was nice of you to want to put it back."

"Not so much nice as using some sense. We always leave things nice so's no one'll notice nothing till we're twenty miles away. It's just common sense, I mean."

"You mean ' we *used* to leave things nice '. That's all over and done with now, isn't it ? "

"Yeah, of course it is. Why, lummy, I go to church now— or as near as makes no difference. I been once to Mr. Baynes's when you were there and I went along and heard you at the Circus the other day, and I quite enjoyed it. I don't mind saying I did."

"Yes, I saw you there. And Phil Janey." He turned and smiled on her, and she smiled nervously back, while one hand scratched her leg below the knee.

"Yeah, and our Phil Janey was a lot taken by all you said —about love, wasn't it, ducky ?—same as she was the time before in Mr. Baynes's church. She went along again on Sunday as you arst them to—I'm afraid I didn't—and Mr. Baynes spoke about this Confirmation business. Well, now, strike me, she wants to be done. And being as it's her week off, I lef' the little old bow-and-arrer in its shed and come along with her."

"Splendid, Ricky."

"Yes, I brought her along. Her mother wants her done too, and by you, if possible. You're the cat's whiskers with my Min. She thinks you're just fine. That's so, isn't it, ducky ? "

Phil Janey nodded, brought her hand back from her stocking to her bag, and rested it there alongside her other hand. Small, narrow hands they were, but red and roughened, and in places puffy. She had worked with creams and paints upon her face, but had given no thought to her hands. Her face was, or tried to be, that of a sophisticated society lady ; her hands were the raw hands of a schoolgirl.

For a few seconds all three kept silence, while Canon Welcome considered the proposal. He couldn't doubt that, whatever other motives Mr. Carman might have, he was highly pleased to be offering his daughter to the Church. The Church had been a useful source of financial help in the past, and it would be good business to keep it sweet by a gift so easily come by as this. So, directly Phil Janey had put the idea into his head, by showing a readiness to be offered, he had acted quickly, wasting no time, and very proud of what he was doing.

"So you'd like to be confirmed?" said the Canon at last to Phil Janey. "You really would?"

"Yes, please," she said, but almost soundlessly.

"Well now, that's great. Tell me how you came to think of it."

"Oh, I don't know. I thought when you said——"

"It was what you said about love." Mr. Carman trusted nobody but himself to explain such a difficult situation. "You said a whole mouthful about it, if you remember. You said we'd all got it and could make it better if we tried, and if we come back to church sometimes to get a spot more. I was quite impressed myself, I don't mind saying, and our Phil Janey fair got the idea of it. She's all for going to church now and getting bags of it. She never goes slow on nothing, she doesn't. Get an idea into her nut, and there's no stopping her. But I'm glad meself, and so's her ma. I may've gone on the crooked game, as we all know, but "—he pursed his lips and shook his head—" it's no job for gurls. And I've never, as you know, liked her going about with the clever boys—not, being a gurl, I mean. I know too much about 'em; she don't understand. Why, I wouldn't put it past some of 'em to be knifing her, even if they aren't already getting up to something worse. I'd much rather she took up with you."

"So would I," suggested Canon Welcome. "On the whole, I think, yes." And as he said this, laughingly, he glanced at her to see how she had taken this reference to "something worse". Her eyes had turned away, exasperation or shame was wet in them, and her underlip was defiant. He was stirred to a yet larger affection—and to a less admirable curiosity.

"Yes, I would, straight," averred her father. "And that's the truth. I would, even if I hadn't turned the lark up. There! I've said it, Canon." He seemed to think he'd said something so remarkable as to be almost shocking.

"We shall be delighted to have her as a candidate. We shall do everything possible to help you, my dear."

"Thank you, sir," breathed Phil Janey. "I would like it, if you don't mind."

"Yes, she's properly cottoned on to you, my little gurl has," said Mr. Carman, promptly taking over all explanation. "More

162

so than Mr. Baynes, though I like Mr. Baynes. She said she'd be done if you done it. She likes you a lot, you see."

Canon Welcome smiled down upon her. "May I say it's a mutual liking? I am very happy that you're coming to us like this."

"Yes, I thought if she was going to do it at all, she'd better come at once, like. And I say if she's to be done at all, it's to be by the C. of E. *That's* settled and certain. What I mean is, I'd rather see her dead than a Roman Catholic. I'd rather see her in her grave. Put it that way."

"She belongs to us, certainly, Ricky."

"Yes. . . . Yes," agreed Mr. Carman, after some doubtful examination of this statement. "Yes. That's right. So I bring her along meself. I knew the way, you see. I knew the way up this hill and into your garden." And he winked.

"And I'm very glad you've trodden that path again, Ricky. The Girls' Confirmation Classes are here in this room, my dear. There'll be a dozen or so other girls, much of your age. At six o'clock. Can you manage that?"

"I think so, sir."

"Yes, she can manage that all right. She has a cuppa tea where she works, and if she's late back her mother'll keep her tea for her. And look here, Phil Janey: when you come here, just you come by the front door and not by the window upstairs, see, like what your old dad done. Is there anything to pay, Canon?"

"Good gracious, no!"

"Oh—I see—not but what I'd'a been ready to put down something for my little gurl's sake. If I was in your place, I'd charge something. What I say is, if people are ready to come to a do, they're ready to cough up a fair price."

"Well, you needn't cough up anything for her. You can spend it all on a nice white dress."

"Chrimes, is that what I got to do? She ain't getting married."

"Certainly you've got to. What are fathers for? Isn't that right, Phil Janey? You give her the material, and she'll make it up for herself, I know. Won't you, my dear?"

"Yes, I——" but a nervous giggle in the presence of a social superior, like a gurgling spring, washed the rest of the sentence away.

"Oh, yes, she can make anything she likes when she wants

to," assured Mr. Carman. "There's nothing she can't make. She's for ever making clothes for her Troxy Dance Hall and her Lyceum Palace and her Pallay de Dawce." His pride in his pronunciation of this last name was only surpassed by the dead weight of contempt he poured on to its final syllable. "Pallay de *Dawce* fr'a kid hardly sixteen and a working man's daughter ! It'd be comic, if it wasn't so daft. Now she's got something worth making a nice frock for ; something I can approve of. Blimey, for two pins I'd screw a draper's and knock off some nice white silk ; but I suppose that wouldn't quite do in this case."

"It certainly wouldn't, Ricky. You go out and buy some."

"All right, Canon. Okeydoke. Nothing more to do, is there ? Bon. Well, if that's all, kiddy, I suppose we'd better be hopping it. Come on, Phil Janey." He rose to go, and Phil Janey rose with him, holding her bag with both hands below her stomach. "No, you needn't come too, guv'nor. You stay here and get on with the holy work. I shan't knock off anything as I go out, I promise you."

But Canon Welcome escorted them as honoured friends to the door, and then returned to his study. And, standing by the table, where the papers with the pictures of the procession lay folded up, he thought again, "So it produced one fruit, a very unripe one : Phil Janey, a burglar's daughter." And he was not happy as he stood there, beating his fingers on the table-top, because with all his heart he wished not to fail her, but he knew himself and knew that he would.

CHAPTER EIGHT

HE drove through the late evening light to Chelsea, and the trembling glow in his heart seemed to partner well with the lambent effulgence in the midsummer sky. The sun was going down before him, above the end of the long road. And he drove towards it, sitting behind his steering wheel in a holiday suit of grey and a bow tie, brightly blue, because he had put off the parson for tonight. In the same fashion his thoughts had thrust the parson from memory—no, not from memory because that black-robed figure was still there to frighten him— but into a corner. These exceedingly secular thoughts troubled the blood and made the heart to tremble. He was driving out to—what? To an experiment. An experiment that excited him, and frightened him. Excited the man ; frightened the clergyman.

He was not wholly happy as he drove on. Not as happy as he would wish to be, because he couldn't forget those clerical clothes which he'd left behind, and he couldn't forget Amy whom he'd left behind. Amy with her simple faith in him. Sometimes when, instead of the glamour in the sky, he saw Amy sitting at home, he muttered, " She must never know. I don't want to hurt her. I never want to hurt Amy. I love Amy. I love her whatever I'm doing now. She comes first. She's always first—no question about that." But he drove on.

Perhaps the experiment would end in failure, and nothing really wrong come of it. He half hoped it would. Perhaps he wasn't even right in thinking he'd been invited to the experiment. Go back and think over the past. Sit back and think. Absurd—sham modesty—to deny that Lilian Eadie was more than a little in love with him. And like many leisured and lonely women, unable to indulge their love for a married priest, she had asked some months ago if she could come and speak to him about all her sins. This spiritual intimacy was always permissible. And in his study, on a most interesting evening, she had rehearsed them all, expressing a proper remorse and sadness, but enjoying the performance. She had told him, her large eyes staring into his, and her voice and hands using, perhaps without full awareness, every trick at an actress's command, of more than one infidelity to the late Mr. Buxton, alas, and of not a few covert and questionable transactions with his money. In short, of adulteries and fraudulent conversions. And he had listened, wearing all the compassion and understanding of a good priest, and been thrilled by the performance.

Such a scene, remembered by both, had inevitably produced a new closeness between them. That was what she desired. And this closeness, like an invisible aura, had strengthened its influence on both till one evening (he being then a man only and not a priest) he had told her of *his* sins—but only of such as were amiable. And she had been most understanding and discussed them in a low, stage voice and with unlimited forgiveness.

They both knew that they were sinners now, and weak. But amiably weak, of course. And last Tuesday, after the Finance Committee, she and he had dealt with the Stage Life of twenty-five years ago—how this had burgeoned out of Finance he couldn't quite remember—and in the end she had gushed, " Oh, but you must come to my little flat one evening, darling —one evening after all your wonderful work is done—and see all my old programmes, and my old letters from Pinero and Barrie and Henry Arthur Jones—*such* wonderful letters !—and my old photographs of me with Hawtrey and du Maurier, yes, and one with Forbes Robertson, the dearest soul. A really lovely man. But just you alone, darling. No one else would appreciate them like you would. I'd be afraid of boring anyone else, but you're so *really* interested. You're an artist yourself, in a way, and you can understand what it all means to me. Just you alone, and I'll have a nice little something for you to drink."

They had named tonight for the visit, and here he was, driving out to see her old programmes, but with the suspicion that she had a far older programme in mind.

Think not that he was picturing, as the car sped on, the final dereliction. No, he was promising himself he'd never do that. He set his lips upon the certainty. He'd too much decency, too much sense of his cloth, and of Amy—and too much fear. No, all that he wanted, and wanted so terribly, was to hold a beautiful woman in his arms once again and kiss her. He would be content with that. It was as far as a parson could go. But what was he saying ? A parson really shouldn't go as far as that.

Still, so far would he go, and no further ; no further certainly
—he hoped.

Long thoughts as long as the road. And many of them
excuses. Here was he, a lonely and unsatisfied man—unsatisfied
because he'd always perforce behaved himself—and a man
(one couldn't deny it) attractive to women, who might have—
might have had as fine a time as any other man—as those
Clever Boys, for example, of whom old Carman had spoken ;
surely he was entitled to a little more romance, a little more
sweetness—before he was too old. He was not asking much.
And Amy, poor, dear Amy, could never give it to him. Amy,
with her ruddy, unpainted face and her uninspiring clothes—
" why couldn't she make herself attractive like other wives ? "
But how could she when her body, unclothed, was a shapeless
pulp (one uses harsh terms when chafed and resentful), a mass
of slack, sagging protuberances. Amy had grown very in-
prepossessing, bless her. Could a hearty and hungry man of
fifty, vicar though he might be, help it if he studied rather
too long the pictures in a magazine of the girls at the swimming
pool, or thought natural thoughts as he watched the shapely
thighs of the *corps de ballet*, or sometimes crossed the road to
get a closer view of sweet girlish features ? Was it not natural
that he should pursue researches, not only in the *Sunday Times*,
but also in the *News of the World* and tell Amy that he did so because a vicar could not know too much about human nature ?
The thoughts that he encouraged at such times were not such as
he would wish his congregation to know or suspect—though it
was possible that Major Partridge and Sir Layton Eaves and
some of his sidesmen had similar thoughts. Very possible.

To understand all is to forgive all, saith the proverb, but
he couldn't quite forgive himself as he saw the immense brick
mountain of Whitehorse Mansions, Chelsea, and ran his little
car *rallentando* into the private parking place at its foot.

§

Whitehorse Court, Chelsea, held far more flats than New
Victoria Buildings in Hebron Fields and many of them were
smaller flats, but the corridors to them had golden walls and
golden squash carpets and were lit with hidden lights instead of
being bare and dark and open to the weather. There was a
lift in a golden cage ; and at a touch its magic carpet raised

you high above the murmur of the world. It raised Canon Welcome almost to the top of this big rock candy mountain, ascending smoothly and with a purr ; unlike the Canon's heart which went up with a knocking and a pinking and a missing of its stroke. All the way up his nervous mind kept repeating the anthem, " Get thee up, get thee up, into the high mountain."

On the sixth floor, where it magically stopped for him, and where he left it, he saw Lilian's door slightly open like the lips of a patient woman and a light shining through it like her pondering smile. Hearing him enter, she swept out to meet him, her movements as skilled and elegant as ever : " Oh, darling, this is wonderful " ; and she picked up his fingers like a child's and led him into her illuminated and expectant sitting-room. This was a tasteful, if theatrical, chamber, with a mushroom grey carpet, cool blue walls, rose-covered sofa and chairs, and frequent cushions of grey. June it might be, but it was also evening ; and twin electric bars flung an orange glow within the fireplace wall. The voice of the city was but a vague thing up here ; you were high above the old chimneys and you could almost fancy yourself above the steeples of the churches.

They sat on the sofa side by side that they might with the more convenience study, under the aureole of a tall shaded lamp, the programmes and photographs and letters ; but it was remarkable how quickly this speciality of the evening, this *plat du jour*, was served up and cleared away. Lilian withdrew to a stool at his feet and held a graceful hand towards the orange glow ; he lounged cross-legged on the sofa, smoking one of the cigars she's laid out for him. Her long frail fingers with the diamond-and-sapphire rings recalled to him the little red, scorched hand of Phil Janey.

And he talked of Phil Janey because he was postponing the opening of the experiment. Smooth as a broad river the surface of his talk ; nothing about it to show, as he glanced at her slender limbs, the undertow of desire and doubt. Sometimes he observed a ruching around her dark eyes, a tightening at the corners of her mouth, and beneath her chin a dropped skin that was a young sister of Amy's disappointing dewlap ; but he contrived to lose sight of these things lest they flawed the evening's glamour.

But, really, Phil Janey was not the subject he'd come to talk about, and the experiment must begin.

" Sapphires are your colour," he said.

"Why?" Her pleased eyes gleamed at him like the jewels themselves. "Oh, but why?"

"Don't say 'why' when you know quite well." He felt that, for one of so little experience, he was opening with an admirable skill.

"I'm not at all sure that I know what you mean, darling. Is it something nice or not? Is it something nice and poetic?"

"No, something completely literal. Isn't your hair a blue-black and skin pale enough to have a hint of blue and your eyes a sapphire blue? Of course they are."

"That sounds nice. Oh, but I'm ugly. I hardly dare look into my glass I'm so ugly now. So haggard. So old. Oh, I think it's dreadful growing old. Why are we subjected to this atrocious cruelty. I think it's a shocking arrangement, and I don't know why I believe in God."

"Don't talk about growing old. It's I who am growing old."

"Ah, but it doesn't matter for a man. It improves a man. Look at you. I'm sure you're handsomer now than ever you were. For a woman it's the end. It's death, darling, death; and if we antique creatures had any sense, we'd creep away somewhere and die. Instead we dive into creams and oils and varnish—and hopeless hope."

"My dear child, you're talking considerable trash. Have you never observed that some women are more beautiful in their forties than in their twenties?"

"No. I most certainly have not."

"Well, they are——"

"Nasty haggard creatures. Or fat. Revoltingly fat. Oh, my God, darling, but it's awful! It's wicked of God. Like any other man He has no feeling for us poor women at all."

"Lilian, cease! You are a singularly beautiful woman and you——"

"Any woman could have shown Him how to arrange things with a *little* more sense."

"——and you always will be——"

"Creams and oils and varnish, darling."

"Your difficulty, my dear, is that your canons of beauty are still completely materialist and infantile; and may I add, in parenthesis, you have a completely beautiful hand?"

"Have I? Have I really?" Her hands at that moment were interlocked around a knee, and she undid one of them to examine it, as if in a light entirely new. " Yes, perhaps my hands are not too bad. Not too truly awful."

He picked up the hand with both of his, since it was the object in debate, and as if his two hands were the brackets of the parenthesis. He considered it so as to arrive at a true verdict. " It's beautifully modelled—I think the most beautiful I've ever seen."

" Oh, but how nice of you to think that. Oh, but I'm happy again." She sighed like a purring cat, and her voice resumed its low and level tranquillity. " Ah well, ah well, it's some small comfort, darling, that even if one's face gets awful one's body stays young."

Ware now, Canon Welcome ! A hand on the brake.

Because afraid, he was silent, and she softly slipped the hand away from his. " Have a whisky and soda, darling. You don't want any more of that dreadful liqueur. It tastes like aniseed balls. Have a nice whisky."

" I will." Tense and masculine and unperturbed, that " I will ".

" Darling, it's over there." The hand under discussion waved in a beautiful gesture towards a distant table. " Oh ! " she shrieked, and the hand rushed to her lips. " I forgot to put out any glasses. I must be mad. It was excitement at your coming. I'll get them, a glass for each of us." And she shot up from her stool as gracefully as Venus from her scalloped sea-shell, and went singing from the room.

He could not doubt that the singing was intended to demonstrate her voice and not unrelated to the song which the sirens sang.

When the glasses were filled and she had lit herself a cigarette at the end of a long holder, she sank to the stool again, blew forth the first whiff of smoke, and commanded, " Now go on talking. I like to hear a man talk. Talk about yourself, not me. I enjoy hearing a man talk about himself."

" Then your opportunities of enjoyment are innumerable," he said. " You shouldn't encourage us. We're all too ready to expand in the warm glow of a sympathetic woman."

Nevertheless, within a minute, he was launched upon a discussion of himself. He was out in the deep sea, out of sight of land, tossed and heaving with reminiscences ; while she sat and gazed up at him, her fingers linked about her knee. He told her of his mismanagement in childhood by parents and

teachers, and of his sufferings then because the misunderstand-
ings pierced so deep ; leaving her to suppose he had been a
most attractive child and that anything could have been done
with him if he'd been handled right. She stated that such
was her impression. " Oh, you must have been adorable ! "
she said in her most silken and stroking voice. " A heart-
rending little boy." He told her of his early loves and of the
sufferings which they had caused him because, with his over-
sensitive nature, they too had cut very deep. He implied that
one of them had left its scars and, like an old wound, could
ache even yet ; and she breathed low, " Oh, I understand !
How I understand ! But fancy a girl turning you down." And
he hastened to explain, not quite liking this interpretation, " It
wasn't quite like that. It was rather a case of obstacles too
many and a love so searing that it flies from itself—if you understand." And she assured him that she could understand.
Perfectly. Perfectly.

She intruded here a few reminiscences of her own, chiefly
unsatisfactory reminiscences of the late Mr. Buxton. And he,
partly listening, marvelled that women, on the least encouragement, and even at a first meeting, were ready to talk against
their husbands. How much more conscientious were men.
Never, never did he say a word against Amy—except to his
best friend, old Marcus Brumley. On the contrary he now—
so soon as she let him talk about himself again—said fine things
about Amy, because they enabled him to imply fine things
about himself. " She was very beautiful. I wish you could
have seen her at twenty-one. She was known all over Cambridge as ' The Beautiful Amy Edgcumbe '," he said, implying
that she might have had any man in Cambridge but much
preferred him. " You may believe it or not, Lilian, but she
was quite lovely." And Lilian : " I'm sure she was. She's
so good and sweet."

This excursion into Cambridge justified a mention of the
distinctions he had collected at the university. He explained
that his Lusus Greek Testament Prize was, if he was to tell
the truth, an honour greatly coveted, and he gave an exact
and convincing analysis of why he'd only just failed to get a
First in the Classical Tripos. And when she begged, " Oh, do
explain what a Tripos is. I always thought it was a stool," he
described a tripos in detail—in resounding detail, mentioning
all the Classical authors it was necessary to have read, and the

searching and exhausting nature of these Final Honours examinations. A Second Class in the Classical Tripos, he gave her to understand, was something not to be sniffed at—nay, rather it was a pretty hot achievement. Many bishops had less.

This let her right in. "Oh, but you'll be a bishop one day, I know," she declared in a voice like the low light of evening. "I'm *absolutely* sure of it." And he: "No, no, most unlikely"; but he would like, let him confess, a rather larger sphere of activity than St. Boniface's, because he could not but feel he had certain administrative gifts and—to put it frankly—a fecundity of ideas that was quite unusual. Look at his procession the other day. It had brought the confirmation candidates rolling in from the Fields. The staff work he'd put into that procession! She'd never believe! A little drunk with her interest and sympathy, he opined that he had a genius for administration. And she: "Oh, but you've got to be a bishop and nothing less. I insist. Anyone who looks like you should be a bishop."

This stirred a memory. "You've said something like that before."

"No!" she delicately screamed, and very archly. "I've never said it before. I've thought it a thousand times, of course. I've thought it every time I looked at you. But I've never said it until this moment."

"What you said was, No one with a power like yours should be less than a bishop."

"Did I? But how true!"

"No, woman: what flattery; what indecent flattery. Yesterday it was my power; today it is only my appearance."

"No, no, it is both. Both things I said are absolutely true. And fancy you remembering them. My dear, I look every time through the Honours List to see if they've made you a bishop."

"But, heavens above, dear lady, bishops are not made through the Honours List."

"Aren't they? Well, then, you ought to have some other honour in the Honours List. All the silly people that appear in it! People no one's ever heard of. Couldn't one write to the King or the Prime Minister about it? You see, I'm madly jealous for you, darling."

At this he gathered up one of her hands. "You're very, very sweet," he said.

"Ah, no . . ." she sighed, as it might be, Bernhardt or Rachel in the rôle of Iphigènie. "I'm not sweet. Only to those I love."

He drew her by the hand. "Come and sit here by me."

"Very well." And, smiling, she came, but he did not release her hand.

"Oh, I wish . . ." he began.

"You wish what, darling?"

"I wish—oh, never mind."

"Ah, but you must tell me now what you were going to say."

"I wish I were everything that I ought to be. But I'm not. I'm as weak as any other man."

"Oh, well . . ." she spread outwards her one free hand, as much as to say, Why worry about that? "A few weaknesses are quite attractive, my pet. I shouldn't like anyone who was *too* much of a saint."

"I am weak . . . weak. . . ."

"Why do you say that? Why do you harp on it?" She was most eager to know.

"Why? Can't you *see*? Can't you *feel*?"

"No."

"I so long to take you in my arms and kiss you."

She brought her other hand over to his hand and gently grasped it. Surely consent? So he took her into his arms. And for a long time he kissed and caressed her, listening the while to the muffled voice of the city below. And when he had taken enough he gently put her away and said, "No, I must not." And he felt brave, and easier in conscience because he'd stopped at the point where he'd told himself a parson must stop. And because he'd been so far loyal to Amy. When they rose from the sofa, since he must go, Lilian said only, "Darling, I'm not bad, really. I don't want to do anything to injure you." Here she took both his hands. "May I say one thing? If ever I can do anything in any way to help you, you will let me know, won't you? That's all I ask."

And on this they kissed, gently, and pressed hands strongly, like two old friends.

CHAPTER NINE

CANON WELCOME always assured the parents that he took the Girls' Confirmation Class himself. And sometimes he added with a smile, " It would hardly do to entrust a parcel of schoolgirls and young women to a curate of twenty-five." This he said, just as if there were any difference between twenty-five and fifty, when neither is sanctified. The Canon, having a heart as soft as a down cushion, couldn't help feeling a great and wholly admirable affection for his girl candidates, sitting there in their freshness and bloom, and looking up to him and loving him, but, this notwithstanding, there was no difference between his hidden enjoyment of the intimate and private talks that he must have with them and the hidden, unavoidable interest that might be Timothy Clay's, since neither he nor Tim was sanctified. Thwarted by his calling, by his natural decency, and by the fret of Amy's disappointing unsightliness, his heart and feelings must soften and melt at the sight of any charming feminine shape ; and nothing but sanctity could have corrected this ; indeed, if some of the hagiographer's tales are true, not even sanctity is a sure prophylactic against that devil's upholstery, the cheeks, breast, and limbs of a woman. And Canon Welcome, having never once since his ordination, no matter where his thoughts might stray, sought those assignations and assuagements that laymen might allow themselves, considered those words about " committing adultery in your heart " if you even look after a woman with some stir of desire " a bit hard ". He never preached on this text.

Not to strain this matter too far, Canon Welcome's prurience was as active as any other man's, and he enjoyed preparing young girls for confirmation because he loved them and because his instruction would arrive in due time at the seventh commandment and involve him in a private talk with each of them about their temptations and sins under this head.

There were fourteen girls this year for Confirmation, and they gathered in the Vicar's study one evening. Their ages ran from thirteen to seventeen. Six were children from the congregation : that is to say, daughters of people more or less gentlefolk who attended his " Children's Church " on Sunday afternoons ; seven came from Hamden High School, sent by Miss Ethel Hardwick, the Principal and one of his most faithful worshippers, and he was very grateful to her for presenting him with this cluster of seven, since it doubled the handsomeness of his bouquet for the bishop. Without them the bouquet would have been embarrassingly small. These thirteen children sat in a semicircle of chairs, most of them in their school uniforms of navy-blue gym tunics, white shirts, and beribboned straw hats ; as fresh a garland of flowers as you could wish, though by no means all the choicest blooms. A little elongated, some of them ; a little florid and shiny, others ; be-spectacled or be-spotted, a few. At the heart of the semicircle stood the Vicar in his cassock and cincture and with a love for them all, and especially the beautiful, in his heart. He was troubled now and then at having to teach them much which he could no longer believe, but happy to be teaching these dear young things to be good.

The fourteenth candidate was Phil Janey, sole ambassadress from the Fields.

Having furthest to come, she was the last to arrive, and she entered upon the company, dressed as for a visit in high-life circles. The others were schoolgirls ; Phil Janey, though of like age, and smaller than many of them, was a lady—a lady from the tenements, with scarlet on her lips, varnish on her nails, a most potent cheap scent (" Springtime in Paris ") all over her. On her head squatted the tight little hat with the tall quill feather. Conscious that she'd have to sit among " a lot of stuck-up things ", she'd plied her powder puff, lipstick and varnish most carefully, determined to hold her own. And the tall quill feather was her standard of equality with them all. It was a lance upraised in challenge to all comers—nevertheless, when she saw the semicircle of stuck up things, and their high-school hats, and the Vicar in his cassock and sash, she went pale beneath the rouge ; and she giggled nervously as the Vicar called out in his heartiest voice, " *Come* in, Phil Janey. This is Phillis Jane Carman, whom everyone for some reason or other calls Phil Janey. Sit down, my dear. We love to have you."

The schoolgirls suppressed their giggles. The new visitor's scent was irradiating them all ; and it was as the fragrance of a gardenia gone mad. They suppressed their "phews ! ". Had any one of them added to her allure by an application of scents,

Miss Hardwick, or one of her sisters in the scholastic cloisters, would have sent her out into the playground to air herself and at the same time pronounced her unfit as yet for confirmation.

The Vicar, smelling the springtime in Paris too, said, " Yes . . . well . . . sit down, my dear. We're delighted to have you."

She sat down ; but, afraid for herself, and therefore quick with sensitiveness, she had observed the inchoate giggles and the unuttered but enacted " phews ! ", and she flushed a red so deep that it outshone the rouge on her cheeks. She sat on the last chair of all, and as shyly and awkwardly as an under-housemaid compelled to sit with the mistress and her guests at Family Prayers.

§

The class lasted an hour, and all the time as the Vicar paced up and down before the girls expounding the Catechism and the Commandments, and how they must renounce the pomps and vanities of the world and believe all the articles of the Christian Faith, she sat with her hands on her lap, her brow furrowed, and her eyes strained ; little comprehending. She had come to hear about love and being loved " like what he'd said before ", and instead he was " going on " about being vain and overdressed, and setting up oneself as a graven image ; and about idolatry, which was loving anyone more than God ; and about profanity, which was swearing and using words like " Good God " and " Christ ". Even " Gosh " and " Crikey ", it seemed, were undesirable in girls after they had been confirmed.

His way of talking was merry enough, and all the other girls laughed at his jokes, but she couldn't bring herself to laugh with them, somehow. Now he was telling them that they must believe every clause in the Creed. She tried to believe them all, frowning with the effort, but so far everything seemed unreal to her. Did he believe it all ? Conceived by the Holy Ghost . . . born of a virgin . . . rose from the dead . . . ascended into heaven—what, up and up and up, far above the aeroplanes ? Where did he stop ? Where did he sit down on the right hand of his dad ? And how would he come again ? Down and down and down ; a spot among the clouds getting larger and larger till everybody, looking up, saw that it was a man in the sky ? Did anyone believe it ? Presumably all these staring girls did. They were just listening, quite unworried.

At last she was listening no more, but looking round the room at all the pleasing objects in it. Those deep, leather chairs : must'a cost pounds. And this here writing table : pounds and pounds. And all them books. Suppose he must be right in all he says, if he's read all them books. Lovely garden. Gaw, love to have a garden like that. Lovely lupins and delphiniums and anemones—and the cherry tree ripening, and the birds hopping about the trees. What was that bird with the curving beak ? Hadn't there been a picture of it on the wall-chart at school. Alongside the chart of Favourite Garden Flowers. Oh, she'd love to live among flowers and birds. Fancy a little cottage with a nice patch of garden, all sweet williams, red and pink, and marigolds and campanulas and roses, roses, roses, like those in New Victoria Park. Give her that, and anybody could keep old Hebron Fields. *Real* country she wanted, not make-believe places, messy with people and the muck they left about, like Epping Forest and Hampstead Heath. Real country miles from anywhere and anybody. There'd be lovely walks along leafy lanes, and climbs on to high hills, the higher the better, like those you sometimes saw in the films. " I'd like to climb mountains, I would. . . ."

" That'll be all for today. . . ."

Coo ! She woke up and listened to what he was saying. Seemed the class was over.

" Now do remember, dears, that you have taken a great step and offered yourselves finally to God. That means that you must show before all your friends a Christian demeanour. They know you're going to be confirmed and you must let them see some difference in you. Now what should be the demeanour of young girls who've decided they want to be Christians in earnest ? Gentle and considerate with all, I think ; kind wherever possible ; scrupulously honest in word and deed ; and absolutely modest in language and manner, keeping their tongues well under control. You will try to be like that, won't you ? Good. Shall we . . . ? "

His familiars, knowing what he meant by these two syllables and by the folding of his hands before his breast, immediately stood up to show that they knew ; and the rest stood up, copying them ; and Phil Janey stood up last of all, taken by surprise. All bent their heads and folded their hands ; Phil Janey, not to be different, did the same ; and the Vicar prayed.

Then he said, " Good-bye, my children. Next Thursday at six ; and bless you all."

Phil Janey's chair was nearest the door but, unable to over-come her sense of their social superiority she let them all pass out before her, just as a housemaid suffers the guests to precede her after Family Prayers. She had accorded them this precedence before she could force herself not to. And the Vicar, seeing her hesitating there, came out of his way to say a special good-bye.

" This is very nice—very nice to see you in my Confirma-tion Class, Phil Janey."

" I rather like it," she said, hardly knowing what to say. " Yes, I quite like it."

" Good. That's fine. We must make you like it more and more. You'll be here next time ? "

" Yes. That's right."

" And you really want to become a good little church-woman ? "

" Yes. That's right."

" How really splendid." He put out his hand. " Well, good-bye for today, Phil Janey."

" Good-bye, sir." And she took his hand, adding in her blind nervousness. " Pleased to have met you."

The other children had gone dancing and laughing into the garden, and when she came out, last of all, they were all standing in a bevy on the drive and chattering at the tops of their voices.

Curiosity silenced them as she passed. One of them mumbled, " Gosh . . . lipstick " ; one of the oldest, liveliest, and least reverent said quite loudly, careless if she was heard or not, " Not lipstick only, my sweet, but half the contents of the chemist's shop " ; one of the youngest giggled. It was a giggle that happened in her nose, and more resonantly than she'd intended.

Instantly the wine of indignation, which had been warmed in the study by their muffled giggles on her entry, boiled up inside Phil Janey and burst its bottle. She stopped and faced them—on almost exactly the spot where her father had once stood and faced the police. Standing quite still on the gravel, she glared at them. And they stared back ; and some giggled again.

It was not cruelty, nor even snobbishness, which made them separate themselves from her like this ; it was just that Hebron Fields had moulded her so differently from them, and it was not in children of their age to do other than herd together and apart. And to giggle at a situation that was uncomfortable.

" What you staring at ? " she demanded.

" I'm not staring," said one turning away.

" Oh, yes, you are. I should think you'd know me again next time you see me."

" Gosh ! " The older, irreverent girl chose to ridicule this outburst of temper. Another made a grimace, as if to say " What a spitfire ! " The very small girl giggled again. Another caught the infection of the giggle, but stopped it with a hand at her mouth.

Phil Janey's face flushed as red as one of the splendid dahlias nodding by the house wall. Her lips came together ; she surveyed the girls with opening nostrils as if weighing their worth and accounting it small ; she tossed up her head, lit up her eyes, and said, " Silly bitches."

" Oh ! " they cried in shock ; and " Gee ! " in amazement ; and one well-brought up child, from a most genteel home, was so acutely embarrassed that she turned from this shattering word as she would have turned from a horse relieving itself with a plash in the gutter.

Phil Janey realized that her flaming wrath had burned up her sense and that she had " demeaned herself " before them. This made her want to cry, so she did what any child would have done—projected her exasperation with herself on to them, and plunged even further. Throwing her closed lips forward, she made the sound—the dreadful sound—of wind escaping through a tight orifice ; she gave them, in fact, what today men call a " raspberry " ; then walked out of the garden and down the hill with her quill feather high. The feather went vibrating ahead of them, like the plume on the crest of King Henry of Navarre.

§

At first her mood was " never to go near the class again ". Thinking of those girls in her bed, at her trestle table in the gown factory, and on the pavements as she clicked along them on her high heels, she would mutter to herself, either behind her lips or aloud, " They weren't civil to me. . . . Cocky things. . . . They overstepped. You can't get away from it : they overstepped. Giggling and half sneering. . . . I don't like it, and there's no pretending I do. . . . Who do they think they are, anyway ? Lot of silly schoolgirls. I've a good mind to be done with them all, I have, relly."

But her social timidity stopped her from taking at once this irreparable step. Her position was something like that of a girl who half desires to break her betrothal and daren't do it yet. She'd told so many people in the street that she was going to be confirmed. She'd almost, as you might say, boasted about it. And she'd actually started on the white dress, which she still wanted to wear in church like a bride. And, over and above these weaknesses, she still hoped she might find some of that complete happiness in loving and helping others of which Reverend Welcome had spoken. So she called the whole bundle of motives Pride and announced, " I'll give them another chah'nst. If they laugh at me again, or if they take any liberties, or if they make too free in any way, I'm through with them all. I am, straight. They can keep their old Confirmation. If it weren't for Reverend Welcome, who's niceness itself, I *must* say, I'd call it all off now. It's relly only for his sake that I go. I shouldn't care to disappoint him, like ; it wouldn't be right, relly."

To her father and mother, when they asked how she enjoyed the class and what the other girls were like, she said much the same. " Don't fancy them somehow. They're inclined to overstep. Reverend Welcome's all right. He's ever so nice. But the girls are a pain in the neck. How do I mean ? Well, they kind'a laugh at you because you're dressed in something different from their soppy school uniforms ; and I don't like it, I *must* say. But I'm not taking any liberties from them, you can be sure of that."

And Mr. Carman was emphatic in his parental encouragement, " Don't you, ducky. What the hell ! Bloody little runts." And Mrs. Carman soothed her, and silenced Mr. Carman, and tried to keep her in the path she had chosen.

For the rest of the classes she was inclined to cling to Reverend Welcome as to a support in rather deep water, and he justified all her faith in him. Always kind and fatherly, he would lay his hand on her shoulder affectionately as he welcomed her, or keep her hand in one of his, and pat it with the other, as he said good-bye. And she loved him.

The waters were easier than they had been, because the other girls, used to the sight of her there, had quite ceased to stare and giggle. None spoke to her because they were shy of her ; but she didn't mind that : she'd have been " put about " and strained if they'd spoken to her. But, while socially more at ease, intellectually she was in a wonderful fog. So little that Reverend Welcome taught them dovetailed with life and its possibilities, as she knew them. She glanced at the other girls. None of them seemed the least worried by this remoteness from reality ; they just sat there " like a lot of silly cows ", drinking it all in with open mouths and thinking him sweet.

" I suppose that in their Ladies' High Schools and what-have-you they've never known any real life at all. Not what you might call _real_ life." And she felt rather proud to think that for the last two years she'd been out in the streets, shaking hands with it every day. Silly great cows.

Two examples of this lifeless unreality particularly troubled her : one, he taught them that any jokes or stories which were even faintly profane must be avoided by them henceforth and for ever ; and, two, that money and worldly possessions were vain things, not worth the pursuit, and that it was a sin to be jealous of other people who possessed them and to covet them for oneself. Now Phil Janey had the shrewdness of the street and, in respect of the first of these injunctions she wondered what worth-while humour was left if the least spice of irreverence was a sin : and, in respect of the second, she looked round the handsome room as Reverend Welcome trod up and down his fine carpet, with his palms thrust into the sash of his cassock. A doubt, or at least a wonder, about his sincerity, stirred for a second, but, longing to believe in him and to love him, she didn't let the doubt pierce above ground.

One of his doctrines did most seriously put her about and alarm her. He assured them, and on the undoubted authority of One Corinthians Eleven Twenty-Nine, that if after Confirmation they approached the Sacrament unworthily, they would " eat and drink damnation to themselves ". This so affrighted her that when one evening it was her turn to go alone to the Vicarage for the " private talk ", she decided that she'd better tell him all those things that would certainly shock him, lest she ate and drank damnation ; and she walked up the hill, free that night of all powder and paint, and as apprehensive and ashamed as a child who must confess an infraction to the Head Teacher in the room with the cane.

She was trembling, and felt a moisture on her brow. The evening wind chilled the moisture. She bunched her handkerchief into a ball and dabbed it on her forehead and neck ; then clutched and clutched it convulsively. Oh, she could never tell him. . . . Not a clergymen like him. . . . But " eat and drink damnation " ? The Bible said it. And she couldn't back away from Communion now, any more than she could back out of Confirmation. As her lips parted in dismay, her teeth chattered with a rhythm of their own. But she walked on, because she couldn't see anything else to do.

Here was the Vicarage garden. Oh, dear. . . . Her heart stamped and hammered in protest as she rang the bell. It stumbled and nearly died when she entered the study and saw the Vicar in his black cassock, the uniform of the servants of a wrathful God Who had damnation as well as love in His hands. She was a little relieved, however, when he came towards her and took her hand in both of his. " Come along in, my dear. Now sit down. Let's have all these books off this comfortable chair. There. Sit there." But she wiped her brow again as he went to the door and shut it on them both.

" This is a great occasion for you, Phil Janey." He had returned and was standing before her as she sat perched on the brink of the low, deep chair. " Have you enjoyed your Confirmation classes ? "

" Oh, yes, sir."

" And understood all that I've tried to teach you ? "

" I think so, sir."

" I think so too. You're thoroughly intelligent, and I don't think I could have made it simpler." Pulling forward the revolving chair from his big desk, he sat himself beside her. His seat being higher than hers, he rested his elbows on his knees and leaned towards her. " And you're completely satisfied that you want to be confirmed ? "

" Well . . . no, sir . . . it's all according, see."

" All according ? "

" Yes ; all according to a lot of things . . . you see."

" Oh, dear, dear ! Difficulties have arisen, have they ? Now what are they ? "

" Well . . ." but she could only look up at him, unable as yet to speak.

" Come, we'll talk it all over together. What is troubling you ? Are there any things you want to tell me ? "

Still her tongue wouldn't talk. Her eyes dropped to the carpet.

" Is it some temptation you find difficult to conquer ? You'll be much easier in heart and mind if you confess it. You can be perfectly open with me ; and quite certain that no one else will ever know anything at all of what you've told me."

She was becoming vaguely conscious of the carpet's pattern —arabesques of blue and beige and green on a rich red ground.

" Come. Don't be afraid, my dear."

She looked up at him again. " I suppose I ought to tell you one or two things, relly."

" Yes, dear ? What things ? "

Red and blue and beige and green . . . wonder what it cost. And the curtains match it in a way. . . . Shouldn't care for so large a room myself. Like something cosy. . . .

" What things ? " pursued the voice above her. " Don't be afraid to speak."

" I'm afraid you'll think I'm awful, sir."

" Oh no, we're used to hearing all sorts of things—far worse, I'm sure, than anything a little girl like you can tell me. You'd be surprised at some of the things I hear." And he lifted up one of her hands to encourage her.

" Well," she began, now looking at the window and at the trees fluttering above the flowers in a gentle wind, " once or twice I been taken a liberty with."

" Taken a liberty with ? What do you mean ? "

Oh, drat the nervousness which had caused her to giggle ! An idiotic little giggle, and it had sent the blood rushing up to her face. She fingered the clasp of the handbag on her knees.

" Well, sir, there was a time when Dad give me a bashing because I come home late from a dance, and I was so mad at him that I just walked out of the Buildings, half inclined never to come home again. And——"

" Yes ? "

" And I met some of the boys I'd been dancing with, and I didn't seem to care what happened, so I let them come it with me a bit."

" Come it ? You mean ? "

She told him what she meant as delicately as she could, and added that it was only one of them that went off with her and " took the whole liberty, if you see what I mean."

" But, my dear child, why in heaven's name did you ever allow such a thing to happen ? "

" Oh, I dunno. I relly don't know. I wasn't all that struck on him, either. I was just wild with Dad—furious, like. I just didn't care much what the feller did. I just felt kind of ' Please yourself. I don't care.' "

" Has this kind of thing happened often ? "

" Once or twice. Yes, once or twice. I thought I'd better tell you."

" By ' once or twice ' you mean ? "

" Well . . . a good many times, I suppose. On the whole, yes. A good many times, sir."

His expression was amazed. Dazed. That of a man who'd expected a friendly talk and received instead a blow between the eyes. Clearly she'd confused him. Almost it was as if he was now the learner, and she the teacher, telling him things that he'd never really grasped. Things that he might have heard about, and talked about, but never really believed till now, when they sat in his room and his chair. Oh, she was ashamed. . . .

He seemed unable to speak.

" I know it sounds dreadful to you," she appealed, " but it's different our way."

" It shouldn't be different," he countered, weakly. " It shouldn't be different anywhere."

" I know. No, of course it shouldn't. Not relly."

" Several times, you say ? Several times this has happened ? "

" Yes. That's right. To be absolutely frank, yes."

" But, my child, where ? "

It was not in Phil Janey to perceive that this was an unnecessary question ; merely a most interesting one. " Oh, in an entry, sir. Or a basement, like . . ."

" Good gracious. Good gracious." He gaped—defeated. " My dear . . . my dear. . . ."

" Never relly in bed, like," she added, because this made it sound a little better."

" You will never, never, never do this sort of thing again, will you, my child ? Never in any circumstances whatever. When did it begin ? "

" Well, the first time, sir——" and she told him how, when she was thirteen a man quite old, getting on for fifty at least, had lured her into an empty house and taken a liberty with her, not as bad as some, of course, but still, definitely a liberty.

He nodded, understanding, and inquired about later cases, asking detail after detail, so deep his shock—and his interest. She told him of all, fearful of leaving anything out lest she ate and drank damnation. She answered every question, no matter how the details shamed her.

And after he'd heard her to the end, he lowered his head in thought and said, " Phil Janey, my dear, I'm quite certain that all of these things haven't been your fault, and quite, quite certain that God will forgive you them all. But it must never, never happen again. Not till you're safely and, I hope, very happily married." That was all that he could think of to say.

" Yes, I know. That's right."

" You must just keep away from youths and men who you feel are likely to try and take such advantages of you," he added, struggling to be equal to the need.

" Yes, I know. I won't go with them any more. To tell the truth, I never cared for their taking liberties with me. Sometimes it absolutely gave me the spike. I used to tell 'em I wasn't that type of girl, but you know what boys are."

" It gave you—what did you say ? "

Surprised that he shouldn't understand her commonplace word, she translated, " I mean, it just aggravated me beyond words. And I would tell 'em so."

" I'm very glad to hear it, Phil Janey. So we're agreed : all these things are for ever at an end. Is that so ? "

" Oh, yes, I think so, sir. Yes. That's right. I been thinking about it a lot, and I see just what I got to do."

" And what's that ? "

" I must pick up with some nice feller regular, and go about with him."

He nodded and smiled, hoping that perhaps she'd provided a solution. " Yes ; perhaps that's best. I hope you'll find someone you can love as God wants you to love, and who'll love you in the same way. Then everything will come right, I'm sure."

So Phillis Jane Carman, one week-day afternoon, sat in the heart of St. Boniface's, Hamden Hill, dressed in a white frock and a long white veil, and with neither powder on her nose nor hint of irreligious scarlet on her mouth. She sat in a square block of sixty similar white veils, for other parishes had sent their musters of candidates to this, the largest church of the neighbourhood. On the other side of the nave a drove of boys sat impounded in another square pen, but this block was smaller, male animals being notoriously more difficult to herd into church than females. They made almost as black a patch as the girls made a white one, since each boy who had a dark suit had cleaned and donned it for this solemnity. The rest of the church was bespattered with the families and friends of the candidates ; and among these, some way towards the back, sat Mr. and Mrs. Carman, also clad in dark garments for a solemnity.

Mr. Carman sat at the open end of a pew so that by inclining his head outwards he could gaze up the nave and see all that was going on. He was often at a loss to know what was going on, but he stood up when all the others stood up—usually a second or so late because taken by surprise—and he sat down when—again unexpectedly—they all sat down. When they knelt, he leaned forward with his elbows on his knees. He felt bashful about praying himself, because he remembered certain triumphs of salesmanship at his barrow's side, and now and then a margin of profit such as the Reverend Welcome could hardly approve ; but he did mumble once or twice when his head was dropped towards his clasped hands, " Gawd forgive me all me sins and bless our Phil Janey."

" Do ye here in the presence of God and of this congregation . . ."

It was the little old bishop's voice, and Mr. Carman saw his Phil Janey, the smallest in her pew of older girls, leaning sideways to get a glimpse, through all them white veils, of the the little old barsted where he stood on the steps before his big arm-chair. Blimey, a crumpled red face like a smiling raspberry, and looking all the redder for all them red things he'd got on. They did doll themselves up, these bishops. More like a telephone box on the prowl than anything else.

" . . . acknowledging yourselves bound to believe and to do all those things which your godfathers and godmothers then undertook for you ? "

" I do."

All the kids had said it in one big murmur. Kind'a got you. Gave you a lump in the throat. Didn't hear our Phil Janey, but suppose she'd said it all right. Anyhow too late now because the old bish had just said something—" Our help is in the name of the Lord "—and all the kids were answering something and—" Oh, gawd help us !—they're all kneeling down again."

Mr. Carman leaned forward and put a hand before his eyes. But one of his eyes, the acuter one, continued to study the proceedings over the top of his hand.

Ah, now was the time. Now the kids were filing out of their pews like lags being marched out for exercise. Mr. Carman sat back again and watched, leaning out into the nave. Reverend Welcome was forming them up in pairs so that two could kneel side by side in front of the old bishop's chair. See, they were kneeling there, and the old tomato was putting his mitts on their heads. There was Phil Janey, coupled up with an enormous long girl like a blooming great hollyhock rather the worse for wear. If that girl was the same age as Phil Janey, she was twice her height, and they didn't half look a pair walking up towards the bishop. Mr. Carman, leaning outwards to see his Phil Janey done, turned and grimaced at Mrs. Carman. " Crikey ! " he whispered. " Look at our Phil Janey and her mate. The long and the short of it, not 'ahf. Kind'a Mutt and Jeff."

Mrs. Carman hissed, " *Tsh !* " rebukingly, but leaned over, herself, to see better.

Now Phil Janey and the maypole were kneeling before the bishop, and he'd got a hand on each of their nuts, so that one hand was rather high and the other rather low like the hands of that there organist when he was fair blowing out the tune.

" Defend, O Lord, this thy child—and this thy child—with thy heavenly grace that they may continue thine for ever. . . ."

Mr. Carman, having heard other people say the Amen to this constantly repeated prayer, said it himself now that it was his daughter that was being done, but he said it rather too loud and too late so that Mrs. Carman laid an anxious hand on his knee, chiding him for speaking out of his turn. But he only grimaced triumphantly at her as if he'd just publicly distinguished himself, and winked. After all, why shouldn't he pray for Phil Janey? He wanted their Phil Janey to be good even if *he* wasn't. It was best, all said and done, for a girl.

And here was little Phil Janey coming back to her place with her head down, properly blessed by the old bishop, and presumably good now. And on the whole he was glad ; real glad ; and that was a fact. He'd tell the Reverend Welcome so after the service ; he'd say, " I'm glad I gave my little gurl to you ", both because it was the truth and because it sounded well and would please a gentleman who was always friendly and sometimes useful.

What, another hymn? Mr. Carman struggled to his feet with the rest and, recognizing the hymn as a lively one which he'd sung often enough out of sheer boredom after the sergeants had marched him muttering to Church Parade, or after the screws had shepherded him, still muttering, into the chapel at the Moor, he reaffirmed his right to pray by singing it with a lustihood that turned a few heads in his direction, and bent Mrs. Carman's in doubt and embarrassment. He let it go with a will, quite pleased with the quality of his voice, and winking now and then at the reproachful Mrs. Carman :

> Soldiers of Christ, arise,
> And put your armour on.

§

For a little while after the Confirmation Phil Janey tried to believe all she'd been told to believe and to do all she'd been told to do. For a little while she tried to say prayers each morning and evening. For a little while she left her nose unpowdered and her lips unpainted, and suffered proportionately every time she looked in the glass. She made her First Communion in St. Boniface's, and thereafter came up the hill to the church on the first Sunday of each month. She came to St. Boniface's rather than to Little Bread Street because she'd persuaded herself that it was the Reverend Welcome whom she loved. But it was not only towards him that she came up the hill through the cold and empty loveliness of Sabbath mornings ; she was also climbing towards the God who loved her and whom she loved (or tried to love). The low pale sun-light, touching the chimneys and the tops of the trees in the Vicarage garden, and the tower of St. Boniface's, seemed like the radiance of His love ; and she felt one with all His elect people of a thousand upon a thousand years.

Each night before Communion she " did her self-examination ", kneeling by her bed with the little manual Reverend Welcome had given her. She addressed to her conscience all the intimate questions which the manual provided and said the prayers which it recommended as each frailty disclosed itself. Some of the questions seemed fair enough to ask of a girl who wanted to be religious, but others—well, others, though at first she struggled against the idea, seemed to demand of her quite impossible things. In her own words, or, rather, in the words she longed to say, " They're just impossible, ridiculous. They don't make sense." Have I forgotten to put God first every hour of the day ? Have I offended against perfect purity in thought ? Have I been vain and given too much thought to my appearance and dress ? Have I been discontented with my lot, envying others their worldly possessions and being covetous of money ? Since the answer to all these was undoubtedly Yes, she said the penitential prayers provided, with her face buried in her hands.

For a little while, and then suddenly, one evening, kneeling at her bed and asking grace to renounce all covetous desires, she let the truth of her heart fly out like a bird breaking prison. Leaping up, even with the manual between her fingers, she said, " It's all bloody nonsense. It don't make sense. I'm *not* contented with my lot, and I don't intend to be. I want to look nice and be loved like anyone else, and to do that I got to put on lipstick, and I'm going to. I want happiness and money to get it. I want fun and adventure and excitement and to get out of this blasted Hebron Fields ; I want to get somewhere where there are trees and flowers and hills and mountains ; and for that I need money. Am I covetous for money ? Like hell I am. Do I envy those who got it ? Ask me again."

The absurdity, the shame, of telling her to be content. She strode about her room in her exasperation with the absurdity. Reckon the boy who wrote that didn't live in Hebron Fields. Or know much about it either. All right to be content if you'd got a lovely house and lovely garden like Reverend Welcome's—

189

yes, wouldn't envy nobody much then, especially if you could shift the house a hundred miles further from the Fields—into real fields with buttercups, and cows munching, and old sheep sitting down with their lambs beside them. Like in the pictures sometimes. P'raps Reverend Welcome could believe it all. Or, again, p'raps he couldn't. How could anyone really believe that one must renounce all desire for worldly possessions ? How could a girl really give up wanting to make the best of her appearance ?

It didn't make sense, and that was all she'd got to say about it. She jumped into bed, happy and relieved, because she was now swinging true to herself. Tomorrow, instead of getting up early to go to Early Service, she'd get up nice and late and put on her powder and paint again and go in search of happiness along the ways she really believed in. She'd have to keep out of Reverend Welcome's sight, of course. And this grieved her a little, even wounded her, when she remembered how he'd held her hand and patted it or smiled so fondly on her, or laid a palm upon her shoulder and guided her into his room ; she'd felt a real love enfolding her then—but, oh, the whole business was too confusing, and this attraction by Reverend Welcome did not counter-balance her desire to be done with the things he'd taught her. That which had been so pleasant in him was a little less wonderful now, and it didn't seem worth the price she must pay for it. And that price, quite simply, was no longer within her purse.

§

So Phillis Jane Carman had been given to Canon Welcome for a little while, and then slipped out of his hands. Not for weeks did he notice that she was coming to church no more in the early mornings ; and when he did observe it, he told himself that she must be going to Baynes at Little Bread Street ; or, more accurately, that he *hoped* she was going there. One day he must ask Baynes about her. But he had other interests, not all parochial ; and the weeks and the months came in like a tide over the head of Phil Janey, and sunk her from his sight. The weeks and months, swift in conquest and unforgiving, made up a year, and it was Confirmation time again, under the summer sun. Then he remembered Phil Janey and determined, with prickings of remorse, that something must be done about her. Down the hill he went, determined to be a good priest and visit the Carmans in the very heart of the Fields. He ought to have gone long ago, but he so disliked parish visiting and especially in those haggard and forbidding streets. Here was Maker Street—really it wasn't as bad as one had thought. Not when the sunlight was bathing its old grey faces and its long grey floor on this balmy July afternoon. He climbed the stone stairs to Mr. Carman's door ; he was welcomed by Mrs. Carman and shown into her clean little kitchen ; and there, to his surprise for he'd supposed that there was brisk business to be done in the streets under this encouraging sun, he saw Mr. Carman reclining in an easy chair in shirt sleeves, and smoking a pipe over the afternoon paper.

"Ah, come in, Canon," he said. "Come in. Sit down. Yurse"—quickly explanatory—"I been out all the morning with the old barrow but I got this pain in me back and had to give it up and come home, not above ten minutes, or p'raps a quarter of an hour ago. It's standing s'long on me feet that does it. Gaw, it gets something crool sometimes, right acrost the small of me back."

"You continue to flourish ? " inquired the Canon, sitting down.

"Wurl . . . not too bad. Mustn't grumble, I suppose."

"He's doing very nicely," said Mrs. Carman, who'd also sat down, so as to do honour to the visitor. And Canon Welcome suspected that he might be doing more nicely than she knew. These were good days for the boys with the barrows.

"I came to inquire about our Phil Janey," he said. "We never seem to see anything of her now."

"She's gawn," said Mr. Carman. He announced it with an obvious relish in the statement's drama, but hoping that his face showed only bereavement, sorrow, and a lasting wound.

"Gone ? " echoed the Canon.

Mr. Carman nodded with lips bitterly compressed ; and Mrs. Carman agreed, "Yes," sadly.

"Yepp," repeated her husband. "That's the truth, Canon. Gawn. The missus says it's all my fault, but I can't see it. Straight I can't. I couldn't stop the gurl. She give up going to church, though I done my best to keep her at it, and Minnie tried her best too—didn't you, love ?—but she only sauced us whenever we opened our mouths, and went back to her dancing and carrying on. I wish to Gawd she'd stuck to you. I talked to her—it was me duty as a father, wasn't it?—and she told me to my face to mind my own bloody business."

" *Ts-sh!* Don't use words like that, Dad. Not before the minister."

" Well, that was what she said, wasn't it? Those were her exact words. Them and a lot more. She riled me—I don't mind admitting it—she riled me more than I could stand, saucy monkey, and I bashed her one."

" Bashed ? "

" That's right. I mean, what else can you do with the little tart? I gave her what-for. I wouldn't say but what I'd got a few hops in at the time. I admit that. I'm not perfect."

" You give her a very nasty blow," submitted Mrs. Carman. " I shouldn't have cared for it meself at all."

" Gahn, mother, turn it up ! Give it a rest. She only got what she arst for, the rotten little tart."

" Tsh, Dad ! Please ! "

" Well, Canon knows what I mean. Not p'raps a tart yet, but going the right way about it, and it's her dad's business to stop her. I admit I got me rag out, but she was screaming offensive words at me—very offensive. She yells out, ' Call me a bad gurl, and be done with it ', and when I says, ' That's just what I *am* calling you, and for your own good ', she starts in about—well, things I done in the past, and the times I been in—well, inside—and I just lost me temper and gave her one to be going on with. She flounced out of the room, packed up her things, and said ' Good-bye, Mum. I shall stay tonight with Doreenie Someone-or-other ', and to me with the dirtiest look, ' I ain't never coming back, Dad, and don't you think so '— this, after all I done for her. She's got a temper like a powder barrel. Her ma begged her to stop, and begged me to arst her to stop, but I didn't see my way to saying anything just then. No. Flinging herself out like that just because I landed her one ! I didn't at all see why she should be all that touchy."

" No girl likes being knocked about, Dad."

" Gaw, it wasn't a hard one, lovey. If I'd given her one of me best she'd'a been in no condition to go anywhere that night. Nor the next night, either. It's my belief she'd got somewhere to go to, and only wanted an excuse to be off. Anyhow, off she goes. And she'll never come back now ; no, she'll never come back now. Poor Minnie here was nearly off her chump with worrying about her, till the gurl writes and says she's all right and not to worry. Not to worry, mind you, when her Mum was blubbing half the day, and snivelling all the night, and she'd given her old father the biggest sorrow of his life. And no address, no address, mind you. We don't know her address, but we mean to find out. It's somewhere not so far off, because she's been seen. Yes, she's been seen," he reaffirmed, perceiving that this was a good dramatic line.

" Don't they know at her place of work where she's living ? "

" Law love you, she's left that lot. She's cute, our Phil Janey, and she peeled out of that place the same week, knowing, I suppose, that she'd get another job easy enough, because there's precious little she can't do with her machine and her needle. Safe for a good job anywhere, our Phil Janey."

" Could you set the police to look for her ? I mean, you're still her legal guardian."

" The cops ? Gaw, that's a hot one ! Not likely, Canon. They might find out too much. She might be—you never know—up to some caper or other, and, anyhow, they'd have a down on her as her old dad's daughter."

" Phil Janey'd never do anything really wrong," interposed Mrs. Carman. " You know she wouldn't."

" No, but she might get mixed up with something that the cops aren't so keen on. Put it that way. F'rinstance, Canon, she might'a gone to her brother, our Perse, and to tell the honest truth, I don't rightly know what he's up to. Nah, I'm not putting the police on to Phil Janey, never mind what she's said to me, never mind if she's broken her old father's heart. The less me and my family have to do with those crooks, the better. Besides if the police were to start looking for all the gurls round here who grease at seventeen, they'd have no time to keep their eyes on, well, shall we say, all the old burglars about." He winked ; and then remembered that he was bereaved. " No, if we find her at all, we'll find her ourselves ; and that's that. But she'll never come back now. She's gawn, and gawn for ever. Yes."

§

Canon Welcome asked them to let him hear if they learned anything, and, taking a cordial leave of them, went back up his hill. She was gone. And he knew with some shame that he felt relieved. Now he need feel no compulsion to go looking for her because she was failing in her attendance at church. Should Mr. Carman send word of her present lodging, he would write to her new vicar and commend her to his fatherly care— if he remembered to do so. Apart from this there was nothing he could do or need do now.

But he received no word from Mr. Carman, who liked an additional task no better than his vicar. And it seemed at last that Phil Janey had been one of those persons who would be familiar faces in a congregation for a few weeks and then be seen no more. An unusual catch, this singular little fish had quickly slipped the net and swum home to the cover of its rocks. And that appeared to be the whole story.

But not seldom in the next few years he would remember her with her feather and her scent and her lipstick, and with all the sadness of mankind, unbeknown to her, in the music of her voice ; and he would wonder what had become of her.

PART III

CHAPTER ONE

" I WONDER, my dear people, if you've any idea what I'm going to talk to you about this evening." Baynes, standing on the top chancel step, smiled down upon the congregation in his little dim church. As usual, his surplice had swung to his left shoulder, and the black hood kept straying over his right, so that he must constantly put up a hand to draw it back into the place where it should be. His cassock, four years older than when we saw it last, had faded into tinges of green and, as often comes about with the erosions of years and the onset of senility, had shrunk and shortened. Like a theatre curtain which has gone up a little way and then stuck, it now revealed his worn black shoes, his crumpled grey socks, the frayed hem of his trousers, and some inches of the trousers up towards the calf. But if his cassock had shortened in both length and value, his congregation had increased in quantity and quality, though it was not yet, by any means, a large congregation. It didn't fill the chapel to the walls ; but it was as forty to ten compared with the attendance that Sunday evening when the Vicar, Canon Welcome, preached here.

Too large a proportion of it, now as then, were old, weary women, seeking some comfort, interest, and companionship ; but there were also a few buxom and merry wives from the streets near-by, and a gratifying few of the thousands of young girls who on weekdays worked in the factories, laundries, and shops. Tonight there was also a number and an unusually large number of young men, middle-aged men, and lads. Most of these sat huddled together for mutual support in shame-faced companies at the back—much as the railwaymen had done in St. Boniface Martyr's on the Sunday of the Great Railway Strike.

A few were lads whom Mr. Baynes had prepared for Con-firmation and watched grow up into tall men ; others were youths and men who always gave him a friendly smile as he passed in the street but forbore to come to church. He had worried and barked them into his cattle-pound tonight by going round the whole of his district on his bicycle, approaching every young or youngish man he knew (and he knew many after five years of restless parish visiting) and begging them to come along, if only for once, because he'd got something extra-ordinarily important to say to them. " It's about this ' Out Aliens ' business," he explained. And because they liked him, and because the Anti-aliens business was the excitement and news of the moment, they had come in some strength, both " to please a decent little guy " and to satisfy their curiosity as to what he was going to say. Tossing their fags away, after his bell had lost its first high vitality and stammered and died, they had straightened their ties or their hair, or both and, sidling bash-fully through his chapel door, had sat themselves with much humility at the back of this sacred place, conscious of their secularity and their sins.

" You all know the story of the Good Samaritan ; at least, I hope you do : the story of how the Samaritan came to the help of him who fell among thieves. I always wish myself that it was called ' The Good Neighbour '. That was what Our Lord called it—practically, at any rate. Yes, The Good Neighbour."

Baynes's locution was that of a stuttering chairman who takes refuge in an expansive smile while he fumbles for words. If he had to wait for them too long he would occupy the time, rather than waste it, by pulling the transitory hood back over its shoulder before it travelled too great a distance.

" Let me tell you a more up-to-date story tonight. It's much the same tale, really—or at least I want it to be. It happened not ten days ago, and not a hundred yards from here. You all know that certain shameful things have been done in our streets in the last few weeks : gangs of silly and dangerous youths, inflamed by a succession of mob-orators at Gladwin's Corner, have been rushing about those parts of North London where so many shop-keepers have foreign or Jewish names and smashing their windows for them, or wrecking their shops, or even beating up the poor people in their homes—after provoking a quarrel—which is easy to do, as we know, because they tend to be more excitable, these foreign guests of ours, than we are ourselves. As the foreign area of North London overlaps our Hebron Fields, we've had our share of these disgraceful incidents.

All right. All right. That's what I want to talk to you about."

He pulled home the erring hood, and automatically consulted his wrist watch, as if it carried some helpful sermon notes on its face.

"These raids and assaults have been accompanied, as you may or may not know, but I expect you do, by blackmail—and a savage form of blackmail too. Gangs of youths, calling themselves 'protection gangs'—whether or not the same silly and misguided lads as the raiders and wreckers I don't know—are forcing these foreign shopkeepers to pay them a weekly tribute as the price of protection. If the wretched people refuse, they know what to expect. Their shops are solemnly marked with the idiotic sign 'Out Aliens' and that evening or the next a lot of young savages bear down upon the place and break it up. Why can't the police stop it, you say. But you know the answer. No one dare complain to the police. If he did, if he squealed, if he undertook to prosecute and give evidence, he'd have a visitor in his shop before many hours had passed, and his face slashed with a razor blade."

Baynes sighed. He looked down at his broad black shoes, whose toes turned upward as if in response to his glance. He turned back the sleeves of his surplice as if for work ; and looked at the people again.

The silence of the people, showing that they were held by his words, encouraged him to go on.

"The other day—this is the story I promised you—a very good Jewish friend of mine, a man nearing seventy, with whom I've often sat in pleasant talk, was brutally attacked by a tall young man with a razor blade. He was sitting at his shop counter, totting up some figures, when this lanky young man, this overgrown child, came into his shop and demanded 'protection money.' He said, 'They're after you, these lads, but my mates will protect you if you make it worth our while.' He said 'Fork out a quid, and we'll see that nothing happens to you.' Well, my dear old Jewish friend is not the sort that parts easily with a pound "—here there was a titter over the congregation, and Baynes, though smiling, added, " any more than any of us would do. He said, 'No, no. I'll look after myself.' His visitor held a fist in his face and ordered him, 'You pay, you old skunk, or you'll be sorry.' But my old friend shook his head resolutely and refused to part with a penny ; and the young

man went on with a menacing, ' All right, cock. Just wait and
see.'   Next evening, as my friend came out to put up his shutters,
he walked right into a group of youths who were loitering there
and as he lifted up the first shutter "—Baynes illustrated the
movement, uplifting both arms—" one of them slashed his face
from ear to chin.   A decent man, coming along the pavement,
saw the attack and began to chase after the assailant—there
are as many good men, boys, in our parts, as many good
neighbours, as bad—but the other lads managed to get in
his way and hamper him, so that the offender has never been
identified.

" That's the story, boys.   What I'm asking you is : are we
going to have this sort of thing ?   Are we ? "   He waited, as if
waiting for their answer ; but they only stared at him without
speaking ; so he went on :   " These Jews and foreigners are our
neighbours, boys.   I want to be a good neighbour to them.   So
do you.   So do the best of you.

" It is Sunday evening, and a fine Sunday.   Even as I speak
to you, someone else, down there at the Corners, is probably
speaking to a crowd of young imbeciles and inflaming them to
similar brave deeds.   It's always on a Sunday evening that this
thing is done—that this offence is committed against these little
ones, these silly lads, causing them to stumble so badly—always
on a day that God meant for our peace and renewal in love.
' Which, think you, was neighbour to him that fell among
thieves who wounded him and departed, leaving him half dead ?
And he said, He that shewed mercy on him.   Then said Jesus,
Go and do thou likewise.'

" Last Thursday I came into this little church of ours and
shut the door.   I said my evening office to myself—as all we
parsons are supposed to do, you know, each day—and then I
went and knelt at this step where I'm standing now.   And I
asked God to show me how I could ' go and do likewise.'   And
it seemed to come upon me, all of a sudden, what I might do—
oddly enough the idea was given to me by the young man himself with his talk about his protection gang.   I thought I would
ask all the best of you boys to come and join me in protecting
the homes of our good neighbours, especially when they are
strangers in our midst.   I seemed to see that you could always
overcome evil with good, and that it would be a grand thing to
show everybody that, as Christians, we look upon every man as
our brother, no matter what his country or his faith.   I thought

of those lads loafing outside my good old friend's door with evil in their hearts, and I had a vision of you and I "—yes, Baynes's grammar was no securer than this—" a vision of you and I loafing there too, but to protect instead of to hurt. God's loafers, eh? God's protection gang. If these stupid, undeveloped, and probably cowardly boys knew that we were loafing around, and plenty of us, all sworn to defend our brothers and to identify the offenders to the police, no matter what the consequences to ourselves, then I think they might not be so ready to act. But wait a minute ; please, please understand that I'm not preaching vengeance, I'm not asking you to give them their own medicine—you can never, though the world will never, never see it—overcome evil with its like—you just *can't*—I am suggesting that we just put our bodies, and the strength of our arms—and our indifference to what happens to us—between our foreign brothers and those who would hurt them. We will use all the force that is necessary and no more—I hope," he added doubtfully.

" That's my idea. We may get hurt too, because we for certain will carry no weapons, but, well, there it is. D'you know : I thought as I knelt there, I thought, As long as the world's full of evil like this, I doubt if I as a priest can be doing my job till I'm half afraid to venture out into the street. Perhaps a true priest is bound to be loved by a few—I believe I have the love and loyalty of some of you—but hated by many. All right : it can't be helped. Can't be helped. And this, in a smaller way, should go for all of you as Christian people. Now which of you young men will join me in this? I want a really big protection gang. I tell you what : I should like a few of you to come forward now—only a few, because I mustn't jump you into this—you must think it over—you may get hurt—but just one or two of you, please, as an example to the rest, and as an earnest of many more to come. Yes, one or two of you to dedicate yourselves to this truly Christian and manly job—one or two of you who will not be ashamed to be known as doing this job. The rest needn't be known. They can join you in secret—all boys, and men too like to join a secret society—and it will be an excellent thing if these foolish louts do not know which of the lads loafing in the street, or in the next street, or at the corner, are on their side and which are sworn to stop them by force, report them, and if necessary, give evidence against them. Yes, an excellent idea. Now, would any of you like to come forward and—er—just stand in a row here. I offer you a likelihood of abuse and threats and wounds, I know, but there it is. Who will come ? "

He stopped, and there was not a sound in the church. Not a sound of any one moving. Only from without came the voices of children playing in the street and the clatter of a freight train being shunted into a siding of the Goods and Coal Station. The moments passed, and no one moved or even fidgeted, for very awkwardness and self-consciousness. He smiled upon them up there in his loneliness ; and, when the silence continued, added " Remember : which of them was neighbour to him that fell among thieves ? He that showed mercy on him."

And at this a tall young man from near the back, pushed past the knees and toes of his friends, his lips set defiantly, and came up the nave between the chairs, slouching a little in his shame. Immediately another followed with a sheepish grin ; and another, hanging his head, came from a side wall and along by the windows ; then a big full-faced man with a paunch, feeling that he could do anything these boys could do, and probably a good deal more, came rosily and importantly forward, with no nonsense about self-embarrassment ; and soon there was a danger of them all coming up because they were ashamed to stay in their seats, so Baynes, who'd bitten his lips as he saw the young men approaching, cried out " Stop ! No more ! That's enough. That's great. I only want a few—just a few to encourage the others and to represent them now when we all kneel and ask God to help them in this work. If you lads will kneel there, see. . . ." Obeying his finger like children they knelt on the chancel step, and he, turning his back on them, went up to his altar and knelt, and all the congregation, copying him, knelt too.

Silence possessed the church again ; the people seemed to be waiting to see what he would say. He too, kneeling there, waited to see what he would say ; and the silence became prolonged. At last, in his too loud voice, gabbling the words, he prayed, " O Lord, we beseech thee mercifully to receive the prayers of thy people which call upon thee, and grant that they may both perceive and know what things they ought to do and also may have grace and power faithfully to fulfil the same."

Then, having no sense of what was trite or obvious but only of what seemed to him simple and right, he rose and said, " Well, now let's all sing together Hymn 540, ' Fight the good fight.' "

The congregation, and especially the men, roared it very cheerfully, but none quite so loudly, since he was leading the hymn, none in quite such overwhelming voice as Mr. Baynes.

§

This was a thing done in a corner. Half England had heard of the " Out Aliens " rioting, but no one had heard of Baynes and his mission church round a corner from Friar's Circus. Not even the people worshipping in the mother church on the hill knew anything of Baynes's Volunteers, because the Vicar had once again lost all touch with this distant, depressing, and unprofitable part of his parish, resting his conscience on that comfortable pillow, the knowledge that Baynes was a good, devoted, and hardworking chap. And Baynes, not thinking his action of any great importance, or anything more than a routine job, didn't trouble to mention it to his vicar or Bettersby or Tim. Why should he talk about it : it was nothing more than himself and a number of lads (keep the number quiet) loafing along the streets past the shops of the foreigners, or idling un- recognized at the Corners whenever the orators of the Enemy, ringed around by a bodyguard of toughs, were haranguing a crowd at the Circus.

Hebron Fields knew all about it, of course ; the street tele- graph and the bar-parlour network saw to that. But not quite all about it : they knew that Reverend Baynes had turned some of his boys into " a blooming protection gang to help protect the homes of the Yids," but they did not know, and only pre- tended to know, how many boys and men were members of the reverend gentleman's mob. They knew and published the names of those who, on that Sunday evening in Little Bread Street, had stepped forward and volunteered to help, but not the names of many others. Baynes had been right in saying that all who joined them in this effort, whether they were sixteen years old or sixty, would rejoice in secrecy and in being sworn to divulge neither their own membership nor anyone else's. So, quite uninformed as to the exact number of this comic army, the Fields placed the figure at great heights ; there were " hundreds of 'em," they said, " thah'sands of 'em," and they even hinted, in the right company, that they themselves were members but mustn't disclose the fact. They whispered, hinting that they

were in a position to know, that there were now " over a thah'-
sand Yiddisher lads among the Reverend Baynes's Boys : all the
Yids joined up, you bet " ; and one wit commented, and all the
rest, when he was not around, reproduced his wisecrack as their
own, that for once the Jews and Christians loved one another,
and it was to be hoped that this didn't mean the end of the world.

There were no such numbers, of course, in Baynes's private
army, but the rumours of their multitude, running through these
naïve and romantic-hearted streets supported and advanced their
purpose like fighter-cover aeroplanes in the sky ; the number of
attacks on Jews and aliens dropped abruptly ; they ceased for a
while almost entirely, the xenophobic and the blackmailing gangs
(whether or not the same) being ever in two minds as to who
those boys were, and what they were up to, strolling along the
street towards them. And meantime Baynes's boys, whether
sixteen or sixty, were enjoying their job ; they were getting much
more fun out of it than the gangsters ; they patrolled streets,
stood at corners, cycled around, made secret signs, and imagined
themselves C.I.D. inspectors, guards of an occupying army,
despatch riders, American G men, special agents, and members
of an Underground Resistance. One clash only developed between them and a gang outside an Italian *pasta* shop in Jason
Road, and it was a fine affray enjoyed by them immoderately,
though they lapsed rather heavily, in the course of it, from the
Christian principles which their padre had enjoined.

On the whole the Fields approved of what Reverend Baynes
was trying to do. The law-abiding citizens, who, even in the
Fields, made up the majority, were full of praise for him. They
had been shocked at the brutalities in their streets, and all the
more indignant because the perpetrators seemed to be people
from outside their own parish. What right had these hooligans
to come from all over London and create trouble in their streets ?
They called all such violent behaviour un-English and were
harshly critical of the police for being unable, or unwilling (as
the more knowing suggested) to stop it. And the more they
reprehended the police, the more they commended Mr. Baynes.

Most of the bad lads were on his side too, though they did
nothing to help him. They did not purpose to do more than
watch at the ringside, if there was a tournament between the
parson's boys and the visitors, and perhaps give an occasional
cheer to the home team. Themselves might be burglars, brothel-
keepers, cardsharpers, or anything from petty shop-draggers to

highly esteemed con men, but they had small sympathy with crimes of violence. As sheep-like as any others, no matter how Wide they thought themselves, they accepted the canons of their community and reiterated, as in duty bound, that only amateurs and idiots resorted to violence when " on a job ". Some of them, not wishing to appear soft, would explain that the game just wasn't worth it since it laid you open to one hell of a lagging, five or ten stretch or more ; but most of them believed that while a little violence was justified in the home, and the more the better in a fair fight, it was unsporting and un-English to inflict it on defenceless people. It is quite possible to be a good screwsman and have, in addition to light fingers, a tender heart. Mr. Carman, of New Victoria Buildings, for instance, was entirely on Mr. Baynes's side. He agreed heartily with all his old chinas who were still in practice that the bashing of of Yids and Eye-ties was un-English, and gave their neighbourhood a bad name.

A brothel-keeper in Graeme Street, who had been vexed with Mr. Baynes for having converted one of the nicest and most profitable of his young ladies and persuaded her to leave the game and take to the praying lark, did yet admit that in this business of the man-handling of aliens the old barsted was only doing his job. And other casehouse keepers, who took it as a liberty that sometimes on a Saturday night the minister would walk up and down before their doors and try to stop the drunks from coming in for their bit of crumpet, stated almost with enthusiasm that he had all their support in his effort to suppress this dirty bullying, because it was essentially un-English. Lee Montieth, who ran the Paradise Club in Sleeve Street, where all the laws and bye-laws against drinking, betting, soliciting and importuning were nightly broken, had a grievance against him for having turned his smartest and widest barman into a hymn-singing softy who now earned as a kitchen porter in a hotel up West about a tenth of what he used to pick up at the Paradise ; but he too, after calling the Reverend a " bloody little inter-ferer " declared to his customers that, so long as that there Baynes didn't poke his snout (and what a snout !) into *his* business, he could interfere with the lousy Jew-baiters as much as he liked. Some of Lee's best customers were Jews.

But there were those in the Fields and beyond who, so far from approving, took no little umbrage at this interference of a " bucking little back-street parson ". What business was it of his if they had a mind to teach the dirty, thieving Jews, and the foreigners who were taking the bread out of the mouths of Britishers, a thing or two ? Did he really think that he and his few sammies were going to stop them ? Time he too had a lesson. Time someone showed him where he got off and sent him back to his bible-house in Little Bread Street.

§

Baynes would often take his supper at Albert's Café Restaurant in Jason Road. Jason Road was another, and the broadest, of the seven streets that met and joined their hands at the Seven Corners and the Circus. It was the broadest because it was the main channel for traffic, pedestrian and vehicular, across the Circus ; and Albert's Restaurant was nicely placed in the last shop but three from the corner. The name on the facia might be Albert, but the name on the rent book of the proprietor was Fred. He was Fred Lanark, and one of Baynes's good friends, even though he'd only been inside a church once since his wedding twenty-seven years ago, and that was for his daughter's wedding twenty-one years later. He would explain that he never had no time to get to church because his restaurant was open seven days a week. A signboard, hanging over the pavement, proclaimed that the restaurant was open from 8.0 a.m. to 12.0 p.m., but in point of fact, at about half-past ten, if no one else looked like strolling in to one of his marble-topped tables, or up to his marble-topped counter, Fred switched off his window lights and shut and bolted his shop door. Often Baynes was his last patron. He would come in at ten o'clock or later, having spent the evening with the Boy Scouts or the Men's Club or the Girls' Social in the old discarded Church Army hall. By this time he was usually very hungry and, having no views on asceticism, would lap up with relish and speed a soup, a dish, and a sweet from Fred's menu. The dish would be Something and Chips—and the Something might be roast lamb, escalope of veal, fillet of cod, sausages, bacon, or rabbit, but always it was married to chips because Baynes liked his chips at the end of the day. As he ate he either read his evening paper for the first time or his Prayer Book if he'd not yet said his evening office. It was no uncommon thing for him to have behind his lips both the Magnificat and fried veal and chips.

Or it might be that Fred, confident that Mr. Baynes was his

last customer, would give a last wipe to his marble counter, hang the wet cloth on a handle of his tall, shining, steaming urn, mix himself a cup of sweet, weak tea, and come and sit sideways in a chair opposite the Reverend Baynes, his legs crossed under his apron and his shirt-sleeved elbow on the table. He enjoyed a crack with the Reverend about one thing and the next ; and he sat thus sideways for the talk, because he was a big, heavy-limbed man who did not fit easily under his own tables.

One such night, at about half-past ten, Baynes, seated there alone, was eating a liberal plateful of fried bacon and chips, taking sips of tea between mouthfuls, and reading his Late Night Final all the time. The last of the other customers had left, and Fred, after sitting awhile with his guest, had just passed through a door in the side wall that led to the narrow passage and steep stairs of the old eighteenth-century house. He had hurried out because his daughter's children, who ought to have been asleep hours before, were squalling in a bedroom above, and it was enough to drive a man off his rocker. Baynes, sitting and chewing with face towards the open door, occasionally lifted his eyes from his paper and gazed absent-mindedly into the street. The naked electric lights in the cream-painted restaurant, and along its shop window, caused the darkness of the street to seem a deep blue-green, a dark but luminous colour almost as theatrical as the blue night-glow beyond the windows of a stage-set. Because of the broadness of the highway this blue-green darkness was neither changed nor brightened by the lamps of vans, cars, and lorries as at ever larger intervals they went drumming or rattling by. Fewer and fewer, as Fred's big wall-clock crept towards eleven, were the figures on the pavement, passing the open door. Featureless shadows now, they passed like grey dream figures ; and more often than not they were a youth with a girl in the bend of his arm.

Fred, having returned from his impatient and disciplinary raid upstairs, prepared to close his shop as soon as the Reverend Baynes should have finished. He replaced his tea-cup on the counter and, fetching a broom from behind a cupboard door, began to sweep the crumbs from the worn and cracked linoleum and from the bared floor-boards where the linoleum was torn away.

" Rose's got no more control of those two brats than I have of the King and his sister," he said. " She won't give 'em a hiding like she ought. Slap 'em, yes, but they don't mind that ;

she's afraid to do it so as it'll really hurt. They yell blue murder when she's done it, of course, but it's my belief they rather like it. They get bored in bed, you see, and want something to happen, and a slap on your face or your arse is definitely something that happens."

"I shan't be a minute or two, Fred, if you're wanting to pack up."

"Don't you worry, Mr. Baynes. Lord, I'd sooner be here talking with you than upstairs listening to those brats. Mind you, they don't stop yelling if they been slapped; they go on till they get what they want, knowing she'll give in to them, if only to get some peace. Cute as ten devils, they are. And what *do* they want?" Fred paused before Baynes with his broom and with this capital question.

"I don't know," laughed Baynes. "What do they want at this time of night?"

"They'll say they want anything, the little scabs! And the girl's the worst of them. All they really want is someone to come and have a crack with them and break the montony, like. They'll say it's their potty they want, but when Mrs. Lanark puts 'em on it, they can't do a thing. They just sit. It's all a barney and I don't know why she listens to 'em; I mean, why should they both have a call at the same time? It's not natural."

"I suppose such a situation could occur, Fred," grinned Baynes, his mouth full.

"Not at eleven o'clock at night. No, it's a put-up job, brother; more often than not the girl after she's sat on the potty ten minutes, gives over trying and starts to giggle instead, and then he starts to giggle too. They egg each other on. You can thank your stars you aren't married and can't have kids or grandchildren. It's wearing Mrs. Lanark out, but what can one do? You can't see your own daughter homeless. If ever I find that husband of hers I won't answer for what I do to him. As like as not there'll be a job for you at the cemetery."

"No, please not, Fred. Very busy just now."

"Well, I'll try to hold my hand in; perhaps I'll only coat him and give him a couple 'a kicks up the bottle, instead of finishing him off properly; but what I say is: best not to have any daughters at all; though it's a bit late for me and Mrs. Lanark to be coming to that conclusion. Boys you can turf out and tell 'em to fend for themselves, but a girl with two nippers,

206

I mean, you just got to do something for her. But, blimey, Mr. Baynes, I'd give a quid any day to be rid of those two brats. One wants a little quiet at my and Mrs. Lanark's time of life. But what are you to do? There's no place anywhere these days for a girl with two young kids."

He had just picked up the dustpan and was about to gather his sweepings into it, when one of the children above started crying again.

" Oh, to hell ! Do I love those two children ? You bet I do. Let me go and kiss 'em, my little sweethearts." Leaving the pan on the floor, and chucking the broom into a corner he stormed through the side door. Baynes heard his footsteps, quick and purposive, on the stairs.

Alone again, he turned the page of his newspaper in search of further interest.

He glanced up. Were more persons coming in for a meal, as late as this ? He heard the voices of several in the darkness beyond the shop window, and the slithered steps of people standing there ; once the window shook as if a figure had been laughingly pushed against it. Inclining his head sideways, to see better beyond a pyramid of soft-drink bottles, he made out the silhouette of a man leaning back comfortably against the plate glass. By the shadow's slimness and slackness he got the impression that it was a tall youth with hands bedded in his pockets.

Louts pottering there in hope of mischief ; in hope of a girl, or girls, perhaps. He sank his eyes in his paper again.

But he had not read ten lines before he was conscious of a step on the threshold. A step into the shop, and towards him. A step less quick but as purposive as Fred's on the stairs. He looked up to see a lanky youth slouching out of the blue darkness into the light of the room ; a young man of about twenty with a finger and thumb in his waistcoat pocket. His grey plaid suit must have been a flash suit once, the coat lapels being wide and pointed, the waistcoat cut low and double-breasted, and the trousers half as full as a clown's, but it was faded, stained, and mis-shapen now. His brown felt hat, thrust to the back of his head, had its brim turned down so that if he pulled the hat forward again, this brim would fall in a dandy's style over one eye.

Baynes knew him by sight and by name. He had often noticed him on the skirt of the crowd at an Anti-aliens street-meeting, where he would stand, both his fingers and thumbs in his waistcoat pockets, and argue hotly with anyone who dared heckle the speakers. One felt then that he would be at blows with any opponent, if the police were not standing around, apparently listless and incurious, but with their eyes open and their hands ready. He would shoot shifty glances at these officers, both at the constables in uniform and at the detectives in mufti, with their notebooks and pencils in their hands.

This boy particularly had caught Baynes's eye because his figure was so tall and well-made and his features were worthy of it. Figure and face should have been those of a most attractive youth, if it hadn't been for the slouching of his port and gait, the extreme selfish hardness in his blue eyes, and the thin irascibility of his mouth. What might he not have been, Baynes would think, if his college had been other than these grey, infected and excitable streets. Len Farrow was his name, but he was known to his mates as Fenton Len, because he'd been put away for three years at the Fenton Hill Borstal Institution for burglary, housebreaking, and breach of recognizances.

Quickly, guiltily, his eyes swung to counter and side door before he sat himself in front of Baynes on the chair pulled out by Fred Lanark. He sat there without a word, leaving his long legs in the gangway and keeping finger and thumb of his right hand in the waistcoat pocket. But he sat thus for a few seconds only and then, undecided, stood up again and bent forward over Baynes, his left elbow drawn back as if the fist were ready to strike—the other finger and thumb still hiding in the pocket.

" You think you're Somebody, don't you ? " he demanded, his voice quick, low, and grating like a file on a nail-head.

" How ? " Baynes had fastened his eyes on the youth's eyes, as one does on an animal's that may leap and tear.

" You and your Good Neighbours ! Who are you to butt in ? What do you think you are ? The Chief of Police ? "

" I don't think I'm anyone," said Baynes, confused.

" Got any idea of stopping your bucking interference ? "

" No," said Baynes, and as his anger grew, together with his fear, he repeated, " No. Certainly not."

" Oh ? " The youth now put his free hand on his hip in what was meant to be a sarcastic stance ; the other finger and thumb remained where they were—ambushed in the pocket. " You haven't, eh ? "

" No, Len," repeated Baynes.

The boy looked startled at this deliberate use of his name.

" Oh, you know my name, do you ?   Or you think you do ? "

" Yes.   Len.   Len Farrow, and you live in Borrett Street, or you used to."

" Oh, so that's my name, is it ?   And I live in Borrett Street ? Well, you've just got all that wrong."

" 13a, Borrett Street, Len."

" Gahn, you're thinking of someone else.   It's yurs since I even lived in these parts.   You're mistaking me for someone else."

" Oh no, I'm not, my boy.   Len Farrow, or Fenton Len, as they sometimes call you."

" I tell you you're guessing," declared the young man angrily. Shaken by this statement of his name, he turned once in his indecision and looked back towards the dark street.   But apparently he saw that—or those—out there that forced him to go on. More frightened of whatever was out there than of anything this little parson could do to him, he reiterated, " You're not going to stop your bucking interference.   Is that right ? "

" That's right.   Yes.   Yes, most certainly."   Baynes said it impatiently, even though he was much afraid, heart beating fast, elbow raised from the table and ready to ward off a blow, head poised to swing back.   " Don't waste your time, Len.   I'm not stopping anything because you don't like it."

" Oh ? "   The lad hesitated, as if he were being forced into something he didn't altogether want to do.   " Not if . . ." and he let his eyes suggest what his lips couldn't say.

" Not if anything, Len."

" Cut out that ' Len.'   I'm not Len Farrow, and I've never seen you in my life before.   Don't know where you got that idea from.   You're mixing me up with someone else."

" Oh no, Len."

" Stop it, I say ! "   His eyes flared like a furious child's. " Are you or are you not calling off your interference ? "

" Of course not.   For you ?   *No.*   I don't take my orders from you, lad.   I happen to think what I'm doing is right, you see."

" And that's all, is it ?   That's the lot you got to say ? "

" Naturally."

" Well, *we* don't think it's right, you see.   We don't fancy it." And his right hand flew from the pocket to Baynes's face ; Baynes's fascinated eyes had just time to see something white, something little bigger than a postage stamp, between the finger and thumb ; he had just time to wonder what it was, when a thin, deep pain lanced from his ear to his chin, and a warm moisture gushed and streamed down his cheek. He knew then that it had been a razor blade wrapped in tissue paper with a corner protruding.

He clapped his hand to the draining and dripping moisture, and the warm blood laved it.

Len Farrow was running through the shop door. Voices and steps outside showed that his chums had been waiting there. Baynes heard him say to them, " He knew me, the old stiff." Then all were running.

" Christ ! " Fred Lanark, who had come down at the sound of Len's voice, supposing him to be a customer, was standing by the side door, gaping at Baynes's blood-washed cheek, blood-stained celluloid collar, and blood-drenched clerical stock. " Mother, come quick. They've attacked the Reverend Baynes. Come and help him quick. Oh God, what are we going to do now ? We don't want trouble."

CHAPTER TWO

BAYNES walked home from the casualty ward of the hospital with eight stitches in his cheek and a white bandage round his face like the wimple of a nun. Next day he went about his work with his black velour hat sitting high and insecurely on the two tops of the white bandage. Every eye in the Fields turned towards him, and not so much because this perching of the hat was ridiculous as because the street telegraph, set in operation by Mr. and Mrs. Lanark and by Baynes's landlady, had shot the news of last night's attack into every quarter of the Fields. People stopped him in the street to commiserate with him and to tell him that he " didn't look too good and ought to be resting " ; but he mumbled, half afraid to move the jaw, " A nice clean cut. Nice clean cut. It's not all that serious." Many asked him who it was who'd done it, and he, turning his eyes from them shiftily, and looking at some invisible thing in the distance, answered, " I don't know. I really don't know. It was all over so quickly." They asked, did he think it was someone from the Fields or from outside, and he shook a bewildered and unhelpful head. " But how can I say ? I was eating and reading and looked up—and that was that. He was gone before I realized what had happened."

One who stopped him was Mr. Carman. Mr. Carman, seeing Mr. Baynes and his bandage, left his barrow standing on the roadway and rushed towards him, driven by a decent compassion, certainly, but by a high curiosity too. " Tell me what he was like, Canon," he begged, forgetting for the moment that " Canon " was only proper to Reverend Welcome up the hill. " I know all the boys around here and if he comes from the Circus I can identify him for you. And I'll tell the cops too. I'd never grass on a good screwsman, but on a sod like that, I'd split tomorrow, and I don't care who knows it. *I'm* not afraid of their razors. You didn't properly see him ?—well, that's a pity. I hope they get him and put him away for life. He could get penal for life for this ; I know enough to know that." Mr. Carman always prided himself on his knowledge of Law ; after all, he'd attended enough *viva* examinations, performed enough experiments, heard enough lectures from the country's experts and spent enough terms in residence, to be worth at least a pass degree in certain aspects of the Law. " Yes. Grievous Bodily Harm. Offences against the Persons Act, Eighteen Sixty One. And the maximum's life. Penal for life."

Baynes returned home in the afternoon and learned from his landlady, Mrs. Anscombe, who at the sound of his key, came hurrying from her kitchen, wiping her hands on a dish-cloth, that a couple of detectives were sitting in her parlour. " Yes, Inspector Timmins—*you* know him—and a sergeant. I put them in there, seeing as how your room—well, anyhow there's more room in there, and it's nice and tidy. And quieter too." Mrs. Anscombe, flurried and pleased, was a round little woman with a heart as matronly as her figure, and as warm as her face at this moment when she'd just left her cooker. " I told 'em you'd sure to be in to your tea. I told them also that in my view you'd no business to be out at all, and if I had my way, you'd be having a nice lay in bed. I told them you looked just awful when you come from the hospital last night. And I wouldn't say as you're looking too good just now. I've taken 'em in a cup of tea."

Mrs. Anscombe's parlour was the room behind Baynes's on the ground floor. Once it had been a drawing-room over-looking a small garden ; now it overlooked a back-yard impregnated with a stale-water smell and littered with a disused hen-house, a cast-out mangle, two dustbins, some slung washing, and some rugs of worn grass. But it was as lovingly curtained, furnished, and polished, and as little used, as Mrs. Carman's parlour in the Buildings down the street.

As Baynes entered, the two policemen rose from the two Rexine chairs of the three-piece suite. The Inspector laid his tea-cup on the imitation-marble mantelpiece, the Sergeant walked with his to the cheap little sideboard of fumed oak.

In five years Inspector Timmins had grown even bigger and broader and, if possible, merrier than he had been when he stood at the bottom of Mr. Carman's ladder in the Vicar's garden. He was in a capacious blue suit—it needed to be of a large and generous habit ; an old-fashioned gold watch-chain danced across the comfortable slopes of his paunch ; an assort-ment of pencils and fountain pens peeped above an upper vest pocket ; and he looked, in brief, the large and solid em-bodiment of competence, self-assurance, and good nature.

The sergeant with him was not Sergeant Corbett, who'd

recently been promoted and was now an inspector in a neighbouring division, but an entirely new one : Sergeant Wayne. A much slighter man with a lean almost ascetic face, he was dressed in a well-cut suit of a very dark grey. Baynes had never seen him before, and the hundredth part of a grin twitched his mouth as he thought, " If ever Detective Sergeant Wayne needs a disguise, he's only got to put on a clerical collar, and he'd pass anywhere as a clergyman of a very scholarly type. Not to say, of a saintly type. He could even call himself a Canon."

The Inspector introduced him. " Good afternoon, sir. This is Detective Sergeant Wayne who's working with me now. Shan't keep him long, I'm afraid. Too smart. Be an inspector before we know where we are, like Corbett. You remember Vernie Corbett, don't you ? Well, he's going ahead like a house on fire ; he'll be Chief Constable one day, and I'll be taking orders from him. Well, sir, how are we now ? You don't look too good."

" Not too bad, Inspector. But do let's all sit down."

" What about your tea, Mr. Baynes ? The lady gave us some."

" That'll wait. I'm most interested to know why you've come. Why on earth should you want to come to me ? Can't imagine."

" You find it none too easy to speak, I see, with those bandages. And all stitched up like a mail-bag. Well, I never ! You won't want to talk too much, I dare say ? "

" We'll see." And Baynes grinned. " Perhaps it'll be all right. Carry on, Inspector."

Inspector Timmins had flung himself back into his chair ; Sergeant Wayne had returned more quietly to his ; Baynes was now on the settee ; and so all were seated round an exceedingly clean and empty fireplace, which had a fan made of newspaper screening the grate. Perhaps that clean, empty, screened fireplace was a picture of Baynes's mouth just now.

The Inspector thrust a thumb into a waistcoat armhole and looked again at Baynes's bandage, which was now somewhat wrinkled and soiled. " So they carved you up, sir. All right. We propose to make rather a mess of them. That's the order of the day at the moment."

" It certainly is," said the Sergeant, either because he wanted to assert himself and say something or because he was very new and must shine. " The devils ! We're going to turn the heat on them now, sir. We'll get this lad and make an example of him ; you can be sure of that."

" I don't mind so much if they razor each other," continued Inspector Timmins. " One can turn a blind eye to that, and even wish 'em a little more success at it. But when they turn their attentions to innocent people, and to a gentleman like you who everybody respects, we move. Yes, sir. We get busy. That's the line, I think, Clemmie ? "

" Absolutely, sir. It doesn't matter to me which gang is massacred, or if both are. But we can't have reverend gentlemen massacred."

" No. Very well, sir. Who was it ? Have you any idea ? "

The Sergeant drew a fawn notebook from his left breast-pocket, and extracted the pencil attached to it.

" Who was it ? " echoed Baynes.

" Yes, sir."

" Oh, some lad or other."

" That much we know, sir," smiled the Inspector. " We don't think it was a lady. They very seldom use razors—they use their tongues instead, which are twice as sharp. 'Pon my soul, I wish at times some of them'd try the other thing. Then we could put them away to cool, eh, Clemmie ? A lad, was he ? "

" Yes . . . though he might have been any age, I suppose . . . any age from—say, eighteen to forty."

" That's a wide margin. Tall or short ? "

" I didn't rightly notice."

" Didn't notice ! " exclaimed the Inspector. " Well, would you know if he was dark or fair ? "

" No, I wouldn't know if he was dark or fair."

" Fat or thin ? "

" Neither, exactly—I should say."

" Helpful, Clemmie, isn't he ? Can you tell us anything, sir ? "

" I don't really think I can. Not anything really helpful."

" You wouldn't know, for example, if his eyes were blue or brown."

" No, no. I certainly wouldn't know that."

" I thought not."

" You see, Timmins, I was reading and eating when all of a sudden he was leaning over me and asking me if I had any ideas about stopping my so-called interference. I said, None, because that was the truth, and I couldn't think of anything else to say——"

" Oh, sir, but you'd never say anything but the truth, I imagine. Or would you—ever ? "

" There might be occasions. I can imagine a few rare occasions. Yes."

" This isn't one, by any chance ? "

" And the next thing I knew, Inspector, was this slash in the face. I shut my eyes with the pain of it—that was natural, wasn't it ?—and when I opened them he was just disappearing into the dark."

The Inspector, after a pause, looked him in the eyes and asked, " Mr. Baynes, are you trying to shield this boy, youth, man—centenarian ? "

Baynes raised his eyebrows in an assumption of surprise. " Shield ? What in heaven makes you think that ? "

" Well, we think you not only saw him clearly but also know his name."

" Yes, we have reason for thinking that," put in the Sergeant, feeling it was time he spoke again.

" Really ? Goodness me ! You'll be telling me next that I know where he lives."

" Yes, sir : we're suggesting that too."

" You do a lot of guessing, don't you ? But why should you suggest any such thing ? "

" Because Fred Lanark more or less told us so. He, of course, declares that he didn't see anything. He says that he'd gone from the caff into his back parts because the children were squalling and he only came back in time to see the man disappearing through the door. I don't believe him any more than I—we don't believe him, do we, Clemmie ? "

" We most surely do not, sir. He used far too many words explaining himself. I thought he'd never stop talking."

" Yes, and we know that sort of talk backwards. They all say it : they say, ' I'd tell you like a shot, Inspector, if I seen anything more than his back.' They never do see anything more than a back. Think it's safer not to, or they may have to give evidence, and then they'll get carved up in their turn. But he did say he thought you might care to tell us something because he'd heard the fellow say to his mates outside, ' The old stiff '—if you'll pardon the word, sir—' knew me '."

" The old stiff ? Is that me ? "

" 'Fraid so, sir."

" Gracious ! How rude."

" Very rude. Unforgivable. So would you let us have his name and number, sir. We can't have our padre talked about like that. His name, please, and his address too, if you really have it. Come on, Mr. Baynes. We all know you well enough to know that you'd never refuse to talk just to save your skin."

" No, I certainly shouldn't do it for that reason."

" No, you've shown the whole of Hebron Fields that you aren't afraid of—oh, but you would do it for *some* reason, would you ? "

" I can imagine such a situation, yes."

" And this is it, is it ? "

" This ? Oh, no, Inspector !—but it's just that these stitches are beginning to hurt quite a lot. I don't think I'd better talk much more."

" We'd be quite pleased for you to write it down. Come along, sir. You must want us to get our hands on this lad."

" That might be arguable, Inspector, but I've told you all I can. A lad . . . neither fat nor thin. . . ."

" You mean you can't, or won't, give us the fellow's name ? "

" I cannot."

" You don't know it ? "

Pause.

" No."

" You bring no charge against anyone. Is that it ? "

" That's it."

" All right then." The Inspector shrugged in disappoint-ment. The Sergeant thrust back his pencil into the notebook, and the notebook into his pocket.

Inspector Timmins tried once more. " But, hell—forgive me, sir—I thought the whole point of your boys was that they should report the criminals and be ready to give evidence."

" Yes, that was rather the idea, Timmins."

" But then you're failing them ! And you their leader ! Tut, tut, sir. For shame ! "

" Oh no, I'm not. I don't think I am. My idea was rather that we should report those that attacked others, not so much those that attacked us. I'm told he might get life."

" Oh, my God ! " The Inspector was baffled, undone, con-founded. " I can't understand you padres. I remember your

chief, Canon Welcome, wanting to reward old Carman handsomely for breaking into his house, and making me swear in
the box that, given half a chance, he'd be as honest as the day
was long—when, to tell the truth, I was a lot doubtful about
it. Pretty well making me perjure myself at the Sessions House !
And what's the old boy up to now ? He's selling bunches of
' lovely vi'lets ', but, let me tell you, the irresistible smell he
holds out to women is on his fingers."

" On his *fingers* ? "

" Yes. It's ' Parma Violet' from Timothy White's the
chemists. Last time I shook hands with the old boy my hands
smelt of violets for a week."

" Ah well, Inspector, don't many highly respectable advertising firms do much the same ? I mean, isn't the excellence often
in the advertising rather than in the thing sold ? "

The Inspector thought over this. " All right then. I'll give
you old Carman. You may have done him some good, between you. Not much, but some. But I can't get it in this
case. Refusing to prosecute a lad who's sliced you up ! I can't
get it. Still, it's for you to say."

The two men rose and moved towards the door. Baynes
followed them guiltily into the hall. " I'm so sorry, Mr. Timmins. I quite see your point of view and I wish I could help
you more."

" Do you, sir ? I wonder. Would you say he did, Clemmie ? "

" But I do, really," protested Baynes, holding open the street
door. " It must be maddening for you if people won't speak.
I don't see how they can expect you to do your job. Good-bye
and thank you so much for coming along."

§

Inspector and Sergeant had hardly gone from the house
and round the corner of Maker Street when there came a
single knock on the front door. Baynes, now in his own room,
sitting on his bed and removing his shoes, heard Mrs. Anscombe
running in a new excitement to the door and young men talking
loudly. A laughing voice said, " That's all right. You needn't
be afraid of us, Ma. We ain't come to slash anyone ; that's
not our game. We're on the old teapot's side." Mrs. Anscombe

argued, and another voice averred, " But we don't want all to come in, Ma. Just one or two of us."

" Oh well, boys, I'll see. But he ought'a be left alone a bit, if you ask me. He's not well. He ought'a be resting."

Mrs. Anscombe knocked at his door and looked in. She shut the door mysteriously. " There's three young men want to see you, sir. I think they're all right. I don't think they mean no harm. Shall I let 'em in ? "

" Of course."

" They don't *look* the kind that'd be up to any violent stuff."

" Neither did my friend last night. On the whole, a nice-looking boy."

" Oh, you *did* see him then ? I couldn't help hearing you tell Mr. Timmins that you hadn't an idea who he was. If you know who he was, I should tell Mr. Timmins, I should really. Shall I let these lads in or make 'em understand you're wore out ? "

" Bring them in."

Mrs. Anscombe went back to the street door, which she'd left agape, and pulling it open, said, " Here you are, lads. This way. He'll see you " ; and the three young men walked in, pulling off caps or hats.

Baynes knew two of them by sight and reputation. Both came from these streets and had served terms of imprisonment. The oldest, and apparently the leader of the three, George Rother, was a long, stringy, but powerful hobbledehoy with wiry reddish hair and a small furry red moustache so soft that you knew he'd never shaved it but nursed it from the time he was sixteen. He was known in the Wide Circles as Pop Rother, the " Pop " being all that was left of " Ginger Pop ".

" Come in, boys." Baynes welcomed them. " Sit down where you can. I object to ' teapot ', though."

" Christ, did you hear that ? "

" Of course I did. Really wide boys like you ought to know when to keep your voices down. There you are, Pop, sit on that trunk."

" Pop ! D'you know all our names ? "

" Some of them, Pop."

" Well, who's this here ? " Pop, seated on the trunk, pointed with his thumb to a thick, bandy lad who'd seated himself on a chair. " Who's he ? "

" James Lang ; or, if you like, Brewer Jim. Of eight—or nine, I forget which—Glasgow Street."

" Strike me ! "

" Yes, you used to work at Mart's Brewery, didn't you, Jim ? "

" That's right," said the bandy lad. " That's correct. S'time ago."

" And this cove ? " asked Pop, of the know-all, pointing to a tall boy now leaning against the chimney-piece with his hands in his pockets.

" No. I don't know him, Pop. Introduce me."

" Shall I ? No. P'raps it'd be just as well if you didn't know too much—not that you're the sort that'd grass anybody. Oh, then—what the hell !—he's Puncher Collins, a very good lad, though the bogies don't seem to think so. They pinched him for a ' sus ' a little while ago when, honest to God, he hadn't a tool of any kind on him."

" Wicked. Really wicked, Pop."

" Yuss, they were just a couple of young cops wanting a case, and they done the usual : they swore they'd kep' him under observation and seen him kick at a door and then go on from one shop to another, laying his arse against the doors to see if they give."

" No ? Never, Pop ? Disgraceful ! "

" Yuss, and they got him a carpet for it. And there was nothing in it at all, was there Punchy ? "

" Absolutely nothing. They just wanted a case. They just got a down on me."

" A down ? Then they'd had dealings with you before, I take it, Mr. Collins ? " suggested Baynes, the tenth of a twinkle in his eyes.

" Oh, well . . ." The leaner against the mantelpiece shrugged. " Yes. . . ."

" Yuss, well, leave that," recommended Pop. " Now, see here, mister : this is what we come about. We know you been razored, and we want to say we're sorry, see."

" Thank you very much."

" But we're not going to stop at being sorry, see. We intend to find this feller and his mates and give them such a lamming that they'll think three times before they try anything like that again."

" In short, you're looking forward to a real good fight."

" Not 'ahf we ain't. There's some things we don't intend to let go by. We know that this bloke and his gang must come from somewhere round here, because Mr. Lanark told us, on the strict, that there's not much *you* don't know about him. Now who is he, guv ; and which mob was it ? "

" Which mob ? "

" Yes," said Puncher from the mantelpiece. " Just give us the whole office and you can leave the works to us."

" Which mob ? I wonder. Now that's something I don't know."

" Well, tell us anything you do know, see."

" His name and address are all we want," explained Brewer Jim from his chair. " We'll do all the rest."

Baynes turned and smiled at Brewer Jim ; and then, with the same tight grin, as if his bandage constricted it, looked back at Pop. " Listen, boys : if I tell you something, you won't shop me to the police, will you ? "

" Is it likely, guv'nor ? We're not grasses. We don't split on anybody. Ever. Not even on the dirty buyers, though they cheat us every time. That's right, isn't it, Brewer ? "

" Right enough, Pop."

" Of course you don't split on fences," agreed Baynes, most approvingly ; and added, " If you did, nobody'd buy anything from you again."

" Gaw, he's too clever, Punchy. Knows too much by half."

" Thank you, Pop."

" But tell us what you wanted to tell us. We shan't use it in any way if you arst us not to. It's as safe with us as an ugly old girl's—it's quite safe with us."

" O.K., boys. I do know who he was and what his name is and where he lives."

" Fair enough ! "

" And I fancy I can guess the gang to which he belongs."

" Fine ! "

" And I'm not going to tell you or the police or anyone anything about any of them."

" But why—to Christ why, guv ? We'll protect you from 'em all right."

" It's not that, Pop. I'm not afraid of that. They won't try slashing me a second time."

" No, that's right."

"Right enough," said Brewer. "Not twice they won't carve him. That's correct."

"So listen : you wanted to do something for me. That was nice of you. Well, will you do something else instead ? " He looked round inquiringly upon them all."

"Like hell we will," consented Pop.

"Course we will," encouraged Puncher, who was now prodding between his teeth with his thumb nail, as Mr. Carman was wont to do. "Yepp " was all that Brewer Jim said.

"All right. Now you've no jobs on Sunday evening, have you ? "

"Jobs, guv'nor ? " Pop Rother looked completely innocent and bewildered. What could Reverend Baynes mean by "jobs " ?

Puncher sniggered at the innuendo and examined the thumb nail.

"Yes, jobs." Baynes made it clear that this was the word he'd used. "Nothing in line for Sunday ? "

"No. Though I can't imagine what you mean——"

"Never mind that. You've asked me why I won't tell anything I know to the cops or you or anyone else. Well, for once in a way, Pop and Brewer and Puncher, will you come along to my church next Sunday evening and I'll tell you why."

"To *church* ? "

"Yes, just for once. And bring all the boys you can. I'd like to tell them all why."

"What, go to church and sing hymns ? We'd get our heads ragged off."

"Not if you all come. Not if a crowd comes. And you needn't sing if you don't want to ; but just come and hear what I've got to say. I want to tell you all something."

"I'll come," said Brewer.

"Yeah . . ." Puncher had removed his thumb nail from his teeth, and was now screwing his little finger in his ear. He withdrew the finger and looked at its tip to see if any *trouvaille* were there. "So will I," he said.

"And you, Pop ? "

"Suppose so. Suppose I got to ; yuss."

"Yes, you've got to. And don't you, any of you, let me down. I'm trusting you to bring everybody you can."

"Wurl . . ."

" Yes ; you've promised, and you're not the sort that lets anyone down."

On this he showed them to the front door, and there shook hands with each, like a minister at the end of Evening Service. Several of their mates, shy boys, who hadn't wished to come in, were waiting on the pavement, and Baynes, as he shut his door, heard Pop say to them, " Gaw, Jesus, all we got out of him is that we got to go to church next Sunday."

§

The story did not travel up the hill to the Vicarage till evening. Then, on the lips of the man from the wine shop, who was bringing the Vicar's ale, it reached Norah, the maid. She carried it at a run into the Vicar's study, her mistress being out to tea. It was evening, and she need not fear to run into him. This was not the hour sacred to work : he was probably resting now after the labours of the day.

" Oh, sir ! " she began, having opened the door. " Sir ! " The Vicar *was* resting. He was reclining in his chair behind his evening paper.

" Hullo, Norah dear."

" Oh, sir, they've slashed Mr. Baynes with a razor."

" *What ?* " He dropped the paper to the floor and sat up abruptly. " A razor ? "

" Yes. Mr. Orford's just told me."

" Orford ? "

" Yes, the man from the wine shop. Someone rushed in when he was eating his supper and slashed at his face with a razor blade. Oh, did you ever hear anything like it ? "

" Good heavens, Norah dear ! But who did it ? Do they know ? "

" Mr. Orford said it was one of them gangster boys."

" Is Mr. Baynes in hospital ? "

" No, they took him to hospital but they let him come away after they'd put a whole lot of stitches in him. Mr. Orford says his face is all bound round, like."

The Vicar stood up. " I must go and see him at once —at once. But why—why did this man attack Mr. Baynes ? "

" Because he's been trying to stop them attacking the foreigners."

222

" Have they got the man ? "

" Oh, I don't know that. Mr. Orford never told me that."

" I sincerely hope they have. I hope they get him and teach him a lesson he won't easily forget."

" So do I, sir. Men like that ought to be hung."

" Well, I don't know about that, Norah. But he deserves the severest punishment." And, even as he said the word, he remembered how Baynes had rushed up to the Vicarage to persuade him that the best way to treat Mr. Carman was to give him no punishment. Oh, but that generous idea couldn't apply in this case. Not even Baynes could believe that this brute should go unpunished. So sure did the Vicar feel of this that he said it aloud. " Even the kindly Mr. Baynes, Norah, would agree to that. Criminals like this have got to be put under lock and key and left for a year or two to think things over."

He hurried into the hall, and, the house being silent, felt annoyed with Amy for being out gossiping when he wanted to tell her that Baynes had been slashed with a razor. He was still in his Russell cord cassock, the easy robe which he loved, so he took down his wide-brimmed shovel-hat which he usually wore (if he wore any) with a cassock. And out into the street he went, and down the hill, his thoughts a simmering mixture of compassion and pleasure, with the pleasure undoubtedly predominating. The compassion was strong and full, but the pleasure lay in many other things : in the very overflowing of this sympathy, in the thought that he was hurrying nobly to someone's help, in the sense that, as Vicar of the parish, he was of importance in this affair, and in the satisfaction that something as exciting as this had broken the dullness of the day.

But as the tilting road began to flatten out and he passed under the viaducts, he smelt the cindery smell from the railway depôt, and saw on the pavements and setts the deposit of oil and soot like printers' ink ; he glanced up at the gaunt and seedy terraces whose sooted houses were but the clinkers of what they had once been : and he had a sudden vision, almost like a revelation, of a whole helot city couched down here, and heaving in half-conscious hurt and resentment. A little encouragement, an overspill of provocation, and the universal human appetite for damage and destruction could rise up from these sluttish streets and raven abroad. Was it wholly un- natural that their crudest elements, their jungle cubs, had

razors for claws ? Here, near a lamp-post, were a parcel of
youths who might well be gangsters loafing, waiting ; there,
farther along, some idle and sour-faced men propped up a
corner wall, and watched his black cassock and hat without
affection, as he went by. Women, their heads bound in scarves,
standing at gossip with their shopping nets or baskets filled,
stayed their chatter to consider him as he came near ; and
their inimical eyes followed him. Children sniggered at his
strange costume, and one boy shouted to his fellows, " Guess
what it is, and you can have it."

And now, unexpected, the idea leapt upon him that, if he
put himself at Baynes's side and deliberately associated himself
with those actions of his curate which had provoked this attack,
some savage hand might slash him too. His heart stopped and
faltered and beat faster. Not only did he dread the pain of a
razor slash ; even more he dreaded lest his face should be
scarred for life. (" Nobody who looks like you should be less
than a bishop.")

Nevertheless he did not halt in his walk towards Baynes ;
he did not slacken his pace. He might feel this sweat on his
brow, he might hope that his heart would quieten soon, but
it was not within the compass of his thoughts that he should
fail his curate now. And he was pleased to perceive that this
was so. " The captain should be in the forefront of the battle
. . . the captain should go down with his ship. . . ." " Whatever fate our souls await, Let me be there, Let me be there.
. . . I shall be there, I shall be there, With you. . . ." And the
more he saw a merit—even, as some people might think, a
splendour—in this facing of danger at his curate's side, the
more he determined to do it as openly as possible. Why, this
attack on Baynes might be featured in the press ! There might
be a big noise about it in the London papers, and he must be
associated with the noise. " Curate slashed. . . . Vicar Stands
at Curate's Side. . . . Vicar Arrests Dangerous Hooligan
Single-handed. . . . The Fighting Vicar. . . ."

Thus in the head of Canon Welcome, as he came into Maker
Street and into sight of Baynes's door, new emotions were
added into the brew simmering there. They had fallen like
herbs into a pot as he hurried along : an established readiness
to be hurt if the situation demanded it (a readiness, however,
which had no element of eagerness about it) ; a real pleasure
in this pluck ; and a considerable interest in the advantages

that might accrue to him from this shocking and exciting event, the assault upon Baynes.

The Maker Street people looked on him from window, doorstep, and open staircase as he hurried by, and he hoped they took note that he knocked on Baynes's door.

No one answered the knock, so he pushed open the door and walked in. He went straight into Baynes's room and saw him seated on his bed, leaning forward to pull off his shoes, with his head bound about like a fifteenth-century matron's in a chin-band. Baynes started up as his vicar entered.

" Hallo, Vicar. Nothing but visitors ! First the police. Then the opposition——"

" What do you mean : opposition ? "

" Well, the boys on the opposite bench from the police—decent-hearted lads, though terribly crude. And now the Church ; and I don't quite know which side that's on."

" My dear chap ! " Canon Welcome was staring at the pale, dead, flaccid skin above the wound. Deep pity drove all ignobler motives from his head. " My dear *fellow* ! I've only just heard. No, don't get up ; you must rest. Tell me all about it. Or perhaps you're tired and would rather not ? "

" No, no ; it's not bad now. Sit down here." Baynes cleared his slippers off the chair on which Brewer Jim had sat, and returned to his seat on the bed.

" Do you know who did it, Baynes ? "

" Yes. Stupid lad."

" Stupid ? Brutal and degraded, I should say. Inhuman. If you know who he is, we can surely get him."

" I know him well enough, but please don't tell anyone I do, Vicar, or I shall be arrested, or something. I fancy I've just committed perjury, or something. Or else I'm an accessory after the fact. Can one be an accessory after the fact to one's own wounding ? A nice point."

Canon Welcome scanned his curate's eyes, not sure that Baynes's wits weren't a little shaken by shock. " But, my dear chap, if you know the man's name, you must say so. We've got to find him—obviously. We've got to put him away. Not even you could deny that. Personally I find it very difficult to remember why he shouldn't have a dozen strokes of the cat. I'm fighting a very hearty wish, Baynes, that he should be made to suffer and squeal, because you told me I mustn't wish it, but nothing'll persuade me that we mustn't catch this lad and give him a lesson. Personally I think he should be put on the hot plate for a year or two and left to stew."

" I'm all for giving him a lesson."

" Quite so. I thought you must be. I suppose you'd say that a dose of the cat would only harden him. But how can you harden anyone who deliberately slashes a completely un-offending person—and one of the best, too, as everyone knows ? He's iron-hard already."

" It might not harden him any more, Vicar, but it certainly wouldn't soften him."

" Soften ! Will anything soften a thing like that ? "

" One ought to hope so. One can hope. And . . . yes . . . I do." He got up and walked to the window. " Oh, I don't know," he said, looking out. " I only know one thing : the police can't make anyone good."

" Oh, but, Baynes, that's a bit sweeping."

" Well, they may help a little when they're doing the opposite of what they're paid for."

" How do you mean ? "

" Well, giving a bob or two, and a spot of advice, to some lad they could legally arrest ; as Inspector Timmins did to young Garson only the other day. He thinks I don't know."

" Does all this mean you're not going to tell the police ? "

Baynes, looking out at Maker Street through the white port-hole of his bandage, seemed hardly to have heard this. He went on : " The police are there to do *us* good, but not the boy him-self. Prison won't do him any good, either. Still less, the cat."

" But Baynes, old chap, what are you going to do about it, then ? You must do something."

No answer from Baynes at the window.

" Do you mean you're going to do nothing ? "

" Yes."

" *Nothing ?* "

" Yes. Nothing except tell the necessary lies to the cops."

" But, Baynes, *you* tell lies. *You ?* "

" Afraid so. Don't see what else there is to do."

" Why ? To save this awful young brute from the conse-quences of his crime ? "

" I suppose that's about it."

" But——"

" Didn't you do something like that with old Rick Carman, and didn't it work ? "

"Up to a point, yes—but only up to a rather small point."

"Oh, well, old Ricky's getting old and rather set in his habits. This boy is young. He is still young."

"But, Baynes——" Canon Welcome, however, did not continue. He sat silent. Something in the words, "He's still young" touched his heart, and the veils shook between him and the things his curate was seeing. It was as if Baynes, putting a finger on the veils, had parted them an inch and showed him a glory beyond. But they fell to again, and Canon Welcome was left frowning, with strained eyes, at the point where they had opened. He must fight a little longer against the too-bright things beyond the curtain.

"I'm sure that's all very noble," he objected, "but ninety people out of a hundred would say it was carrying things a bit too far."

"Most certainly they would ; and you underestimate the number—ninety-nine out of a hundred would say so—but, even so—even then, Vicar—it's not carrying them as far as our Lord carried them."

Baynes, screwing and unscrewing the acorn on the blind cord, held his eyes away from the room, as if ashamed to speak thus before his superior.

"Yes, but, Baynes—yes, of course, but——" but the vicar couldn't see what he wanted to say, because the bright glimpse beyond the veils had momentarily dazzled his eyes and shimmered all things out of focus. He added weakly, "I see all that, but one—one has to be reasonably practical in this world."

"Exactly, and, unless I am entirely wrong, this is the only practical way. I can't explain it all now—I'm a bit tired—but I can't help feeling this is a chance to do something really practical, and that I may not have such a chance again. This silly lad by opening up my cheek has handed the game to me, I think. It's created quite a sensation round here, believe it or not, Vicar, and I've a fancy I can use the excitement to good purpose. I told those boys just now that I was going to say a few things on Sunday evening, and if I know them they'll tell everyone else. It's a shot in the dark, but I believe quite a few will come. Quite a lot, in fact. They may not come for the best reasons, but when I've got them, I can tell them something. It may do no good but you never know. A seed here and there . . . it may not germinate for years . . . but you never know."

All through this speech the vicar had been telling himself, " You're dimly seeing something, Canon Welcome. Be loyal to it " ; and now he answered, " Look here, Baynes, old man ; will you let me be there ? I want to be there. I want to hear what you're going to say—I suspect I need it as much as any— but, above all, I want to associate myself with you in everything. I want to show them that I'm with you."

" My dear Vicar," said Baynes, swinging round from the window, " it's for you to say if you'll come into one of your own churches. But if you will, I'm sure it'll be of help to us all."

" I shall be there. And Baynes "—he looked again at the dead, white cheek—" I am terribly sorry this has happened. I never imagined that anything like this would be done to you when I sent you down here."

" Don't you worry about me, Vicar," answered Baynes, laughing now. " It didn't hurt at the time half as much as you'd think, and it hardly hurts at all now. Waste no sympathy on me. Probably it's a sin but, to tell the truth, I'm finding the whole thing rather jolly. These are my people, and I'm glad to be sharing something with them."

CHAPTER THREE

Canon Welcome, robing in the curtained vestry, whose shrunk and faded curtains, like tetchy old ladies, declined to meet and kiss, watched through the aperture the people of the Fields pouring in. Not yet twenty past six ; the night threatening rain ; Baynes not yet at his bell-rope ; and the little church was nearly full. Baynes had been right : the attack on their parson had been local sensation enough to draw the people even through the doors of a church. Pop Rother and his friends had told their tale to everyone they met ; and everyone they met had passed it on ; and here they all were, pouring in. Probably most thought Baynes a little mad in declining to strike back at his assailant and hit him hard ; a few may have admired the madness ; many, for sure, were completely impatient with it ; but all were disposed to come and hear his explanation. Some came with a show of ease ; others half ashamed ; a few with grins or giggles and a sense of mischief and fun. For the first time within memory the Little Bread Street chapel was going to be crowded.

Baynes in the old black cassock, his cheek now patched with a gauze dressing and bands of adhesive tape, was dodging and weaving among the people as he delighted to welcome them. He was sending boys and young men to the Church Army Hall for chairs and benches ; he was distributing tattered hymn-books and prayer books to the unprovided (who were many) ; he was taking the books back again from those who had two and could do with one ; at one stage he left the people, to go and pull his bell-rope ; he pulled it for thirty seconds, and then left the bell to tut-tut indignantly and the rope to swing at a loose end ; for he had realized all at once that there was no sense in summoning more to the feast.

The boys and men, all equally pleased to be allowed to fuss with chairs and benches, and to show the strength of their arms, came carrying the chairs high above the heads of the waiting new-comers or driving the benches between their legs, a bearer at each end and both controlling their merriment in this sacred venue. Baynes fussed with them, directing the benches where to go and the people where to sit, and saying " Nonsense, my dear " to large, heavy women who maintained that they were quite able to stand by the wall ; that they weren't a hundred yet, Mr. Baynes ; and that there was no need for young Dave or Mr. Gowers to get up and give them their seats. " Nonsense, woman. Come along. Do what you're told." And young Dave and Mr. Gowers got up, accepting the fact that Reverend Baynes was in command of this parade ; and Baynes, as happy as a barker on a fairground whose booth was filling fast, guided and pushed the ladies to the vacated chairs. Soon, as a result of all his rearrangements and transpositions there was something like a separation of the sexes in the church, the men and boys leaning against the walls, sitting on the window sills, or standing three deep at the back ; and the women seated in a mass between them.

Canon Welcome, standing within the parted curtains, felt a lone stranger, an odd-man-out, in this sacred jamboree.

At length the church was so full that no more could be packed in. Voices, coming through an opened window, showed that there was still a throng of people in the street, unwilling to go home ; and an excited fringe of children wondering what was toward and shouting thrilling lies about it.

And yet it was still a thing done in a corner ; there were no reporters there.

With the last sightseers within, and the doors closed, the congregation sank into silence. Impossible to have a church, a hall, or a theatre packed to its furthest wall without a high expectancy catching everyone by the arm ; and so it was into a charged, waiting, and staring silence that Canon Welcome and Mr. Baynes, robed for the service, walked from the vestry. Once again the vicar deliberately walked in front of his curate, leaving him in the place of honour behind. And he read and sang the service for him (his voice management and oral delivery as near perfect as Baynes's were far from it) leaving him only the lessons and the sermon. The singing of this congregation was weak in responses, canticles, and psalms but powerful, and at times, uproarious, in the hymns. Hardly a man against the wall but had been in the army and (like Mr. Carman, who, by the way, was there at the back) relieved the tedium of a compulsory church parade by roaring these hymns to impress or entertain his neighbours ; and they roared them now. They rejoiced to make a merry noise, but not in all cases (it is to be feared) before the Lord. This fine volume from the basses encouraged the women to offer their best, and some of them to compete, but even so the united volume wasn't enough to submerge the terrific roar of Baynes, who clearly felt it incumbent on him to keep this mob in the strait and narrow way of the tune. His voice, like the nose of a sea-lion in an ocean, was well above the waves all the time, but even then he didn't quite achieve his purpose of leading his people in Truth, for many at the back of the church were stragglers, loping along in the rear of the tune.

Canon Welcome, listening to the roughened voices of the men, the shrill or quavering voices of the women, and the sweet or wistful voices of the girls, some of them holding without knowledge (as Phil Janey's had done and some negroes' voices do) the tremulant music of our long human trouble, felt rising in him that old love for them all, even the ugliest and the wickedest, and a great wish that he were a better man, giving himself to them instead of shutting himself in the cell of his own desires. He could wish that it was he who had been wounded, fighting in the front of their battle—and not any more for the sake of publicity but because it would draw all these dear sinners towards him. He looked at Baynes bawling " Hail him, ye heirs of David's line," regardless of the soiled dressing and tapes on his face ; he looked at the little unlovely meeting-house, packed for the first time in fifty years with old and young, men and matrons, lads and maids ; and into the heart of his self-reproach came the words, " I if I be lifted up will draw all men unto me."

Now they were singing the hymn before the sermon, and Baynes was on his knees with his face in his large coarse hands, asking a blessing on his words. Canon Welcome, left to lead the singing people in the paths of Truth, deserted this command for a moment, while he too, standing in his stall, sent up a prayer that Baynes might have help in all that he desired to do.

Baynes walked to the middle of the chancel step, yelling joyously, " Death will come one day to me," and he stood there with his surplice falling as usual to one side, his black hood looping over his left shoulder, and a postcard of sermon notes resting on his hymn book. At these notes he glanced for a last time even as he yelled the final words of the hymn and the Amen.

§

The hymn was over. Canon Welcome sat himself down, crossed his legs, folded his arms, and leaned back in comfort.

And he fixed his eyes, as did everyone else in the church, upon the preacher.

Baynes, looking down upon the postcard, read out his text. He read it rapidly and with no effort to give expression or drama to the words.

" Suffer ye thus far."

Shutting the hymn-book and holding it against his armpit, he said, " Now wait—wait a minute . . ." which seemed strange since nobody in the church had started to do anything, but all were sitting completely still. " First I must tell you the story from which these words come. You may have forgotten it " ; a euphemism which caused him to grin at them. " This is it, everyone."

And with some stuttering, some scratching of his head as he worried for words, and no art, he yet told with a strange effectiveness, partly because the church was so crowded and silent and all were waiting for something, the story of the young man in the dark valley garden with a few friends about him, and of the approach through the night—down the steep hillside from the old city walls, across the valley bottom, and up again to the garden—of a big crowd, a mob, a loud rabble of excited men and violent youths armed with sticks and swords—" as it might be razor blades " he interjected with a smile—and of how one of his friends, an impetuous chap called Peter, did actually let fly with a sword at one of the foremost of the mob, almost hacking off his ear. Baynes made an extraordinary vivid picture of it— the congregation were no longer in a bare, brown room in Hebron Fields but in the dark garden above the brook Kedron and under eastern stars ; and he translated them thus, because it was all so vivid to him and because he had such a throbbing, vibrant feeling for the beauty of the tale. " And the young man, Jesus, told him to put up his sword again because those that take the sword always perish by it in the end ; and, stepping forward to this wounded man who had been in the forefront of his assailants, he just said ' Suffer ye thus far,' and touching the wound, healed it."

And what happened then, asked Baynes. Eh, what happened then ? The congregation didn't know, so waited for him to say. And he told them. " His friends and followers, when they saw he was going to adopt this absurd, this mad, this impossible method of refusing to meet the savagery of others with a like violence, ran away. They forsook him as a hopelessly unpractical person who would land them all in disaster, and fled. And it has always seemed to me," said Baynes, suddenly laying the hymn-book down upon the floor as if it were a nuisance, and action were now about to begin, " that his followers have done the same thing ever since."

He rubbed his freed hands together, interlocked the fingers, and, smiling on all the people, pronounced with a slow deliberate emphasis, with whatever is the vocal equivalent of italics : " The followers of Christ accept parts of his teaching, but practically all of them fly from his first, his topmost, his Number One doctrine, namely, that you can't overthrow the evil in a man's heart by doing what he has done to you, but only by doing the opposite."

And he paused for quite a while to let that sink in.

" Was he right in that idea ? " asked Baynes, when the interval was over. " Well, let me ask you this : what happened to that violent young man whom Christ wouldn't allow to be hurt ? You don't know, do you ? Neither do I. Nor does anyone, because not another word is told to us about him in the Bible. But I will venture this belief : he was not made perfect by that courteous touch of the man he wanted to lynch—far from it—but, unless human nature was wholly different then from what it is now, he was never quite the same again.

" I think that touch troubled him all his life, don't you ?

" Why, of course it did."

Much more he said to them in this kind, and then at last, with unconscious art, came to the part they all wanted to hear. He looked down at the hymn-book on the floor, as if surprised to see it there ; he tried to shake his hood off his left arm and on to its proper place but, finding that this couldn't be done, he pulled it into place with one hand ; he looked up at the wooden roof, pleating his eyebrows as if straining to see something there ; then brought his eyes back to the waiting people. The secret, uncompleted smile troubled his lips.

" Now you know perfectly well why I'm talking about these things. You know what I'm getting at. But before I come to this point, let me just remind you what I am. Why am I dressed like this in a white surplice "—he glanced down at the surplice —" it might be whiter, I'm afraid—and in a black scarf, and this thing ? " and he tweaked at the hood. " Because I am now a minister of that young man in the garden. Because with a rash self-assurance I have taken upon myself the responsibility of explaining his way of life to you and persuading you that it is the best way—in fact, the only way that does any good in the end. And because of this it's my business to follow him as far as I can—which isn't very far, I'm afraid—not very far. But I must keep on trying because, if I'm to persuade you that his teaching is right, I shall do it best—and indeed *only*—by example. I have dared to place myself beside him in the garden, and, oh my dear people, I don't want to be among those who, when the crisis comes, forsake him and fly. And I don't refuse to do this just out of loyalty to him, saying ' My Master, right or wrong,' but because I know him to be right ; absolutely right, finally right.

" You see me standing before you with my face patched up and looking like nothing on earth, and you know that a silly and violent lad slashed at me the other day. Any man is silly when he's violent. I am. Children and schoolboys, of course, can't be expected to see this ; but it is the essence of a full-grown man to see it. I doubt, alas—I doubt very much—if many of you see it yet—I fear that your creed is ' A blow for a blow, and, if possible, two blows for one '—yes, I see that some of you thrill to that as if it were a fine creed, instead of a poor and savage and childish one—but I hope you will see the grown-up thing one day.

" Now some of you think I know the name of this so silly and violent youth "—and here he lifted his eyebrows as a comedian does, as much as to say " Upon my soul you may be right " ; and then went on, " And you want me to explain why, if that's the case, I do nothing about it. Well, I hope the answer's beginning to become clear to you. The police, as their duty was, have come to me declaring their readiness to take the sword against my young attacker ; some of you chaps—good-hearted lads—have shown not only a readiness but an eagerness to take the sword against him ; but there it is : I am under the orders of a different captain. And, as I have said, I firmly and finally believe his orders to be right. It is vengefulness that hangs the world. This is very difficult to see at first ; only a few have managed to see it in two thousand years ; indeed it is only by practising it that you gradually see it. But here it is as I begin to see it : the more violent your assailant, the more violent must be the opposite way in which you treat him. If he stabs you, the best thing to do is to stab him with forgiveness, and it is possible—I think it even likely—that he will stab no more.

" Now, my very good friends, I know our neighbourhood well enough to know that with a crowd like this in our little church (and bless you all) the words I say will reach the ears of the youth who attacked me. I therefore send this message to him : I forgive him with all my heart ; I pray for his happiness in the future ; and I ask that my blood may be the last he sheds."

And with that he went back to his place.

§

It fell to Canon Welcome to give out the hymn, and he rose to do so, but before announcing it, he said very simply, " Some of you may not know who I am. It is a long time since I have been able to—it is a long time since I have come among you. I am your vicar, and I came along tonight because I wanted to show you that I was at Mr. Baynes's side in everything he has done. And now I want to add that I agree with every word he has just said to you. At first like many of you, I was full of vindictiveness against this man who had so cruelly injured my good friend ; I wanted him given a dose of his own sharp medicine ; but Mr. Baynes is right. He has shown me what my duty is as a priest ; and he shows us all a better way."

And after the service, in the vestry, he just said to Baynes, " Thank you, Baynes. I think you made a great impression on them all."

But Baynes shook his head. " A seed here . . . a seed there . . . perhaps. One never knows. A seed in a silly boy's heart, perhaps . . . and perhaps not . . . but I like to think yes. . . ."

One seed, anyhow, had fallen into the soft, quick soil of Canon Welcome's heart. He walked slowly up the hill towards his home—slowly because he was turning over in his mind the possibility of being, even now, a saintly type like Baynes. He would so like to be. Sometimes he walked so slowly, that his movement was little more than a halt on the pavement. Then his head went down and his hands closed behind his back. He so wanted to be. Had there been others on the hill they must have turned to watch this irregular, tarrying, halting pace. Some might have wondered if he had partaken of wine too old, too potent.

And indeed he had drunk of the strongest wine on earth. He had visited the world's most destructive fire, and his outer garment was alight. " Always when I see the real thing, the nobility which is asked of us, and of which we are so plainly capable, I fall down and worship it. Always I am completely convinced by it. I catch alight at it. That must mean that there is something in me *like* it ; it is only like that answers to like." By now, climbing the hill, he had almost decided that he was really what might be called "a spoiled saint". And he was asking himself, Was it possible that he could yet shake himself free of the fetters of fifty years and give himself at last to the thing that he could see. He was not hopeful. It was the doubt in the heart of his hope which shook his head and slowed his step. " One can try again, I suppose."

And he longed to try again—so wonderful, so full of light, was the prospect he saw before him, somewhere at the top of the hill : a prospect of daily holiness, and of the gaunt happiness of a priest worn out in the service of others, and of a death too soon because the candle had spent itself lighting the paths of the straying and lost. Of a death surrounded with the love of all. Of a great name left behind to ring through the ages—but no ; this was self-seeking again. Put it aside. It was the evil thing. It was Satan himself. " I will try. I will try yet once more." But he said it with little hope. " From this moment I will try. I want to. I want to very, very deeply."

And having come to this decision, he stepped a little faster, eager to walk into the new happiness. By this decision he was become—even as he walked—good, holy, selfless ; and the thought was more than wine in his veins. This exhilaration, was it conversion ? Had that miraculous experience come to him at last ? Almost he could hope it had. There yonder was his vicarage, wrapped about with its coronal of trees. A big house for a saint ; somewhat pretentiously furnished for a St. Antony of the Thebaid or a St. Aidan of Iona ; but he would live very simply in it and use it not only for himself but for all his people whom he so truly loved. Turn the drawing-room into a club room . . . turn no mendicant from the back door . . . treat him as an honoured guest, yea, as the Master Himself in hunger and need. . . .

He let himself into the Vicarage as into a new life.

CHAPTER FOUR

AND in the ensuing days he tried to be unselfish and holy. Amy, though she said nothing, was astonished at his new patience and at his daily, smiling sweetness. Norah, the maid, observed no difference, because of his habitual tenderness with her. And Timothy Clay and the people of the parish remarked nothing, because of his habitual *bonhomie* with them. Only Amy. And the Vicar himself, who was much encouraged, as the days multiplied and he sustained the unselfishness.

But then there fell the Diocesan Conference ; it fell on the last day of June. There were more than a thousand clergy in the North London diocese ; lay representatives would attend ; and no hall was big enough to hold the massive business except the old Lincoln Theatre and Palace of Varieties. This had seats for seven hundred, and some such number might be expected to attend. There would be, in the more usual and secular idiom of the old theatre, a capacity house.

The old Lincoln Theatre stood among the shops in Hebron Town High Street, a furlong to the south of Friars Circus, and in the parish of St. Stephen's, Hebron. Built in 1868, it had been named at first the Lincoln Opera House, though no one quite knew why. Nobody, not even the oldest, could remember any operas having been sung there, though in the seventies there was a brief golden age when Hebron Town held the homes of gentry and merchants, and when their ladies, doubtless, had the time and money for culture. People not yet seventy could remember it as a Music Hall with " the Smartest Varieties in North London," and would speak of the artists who sang and danced before the gas footlights, which occasionally sang and danced too. An old copy of the *Hamden and Hebron News*, dated 1893, states, " The stars in the heavens are dimmed by the radiance of the stars that appear these days at our Lincoln Palace " ; and if you consult the advertisements of this and other copies to learn who, pray, were these transplendent stars, you will read of Chirgwin, the white-eyed Kaffir, Professor Wynne the juggler and shadowgraphist, Professor Duncan and his College Dogs, the Sisters Caselli, Champion High Kickers, Dora Nelson's Combination in the Dramatic Sketch, " The Bailiff's

Daughter," and the Espaliers in their remarkable slide from Gallery to Stage.

In its paint and decoration the theatre on this June day was just the same as when it enshrined these old acts, except that the few remaining gas brackets in pit and gallery were as dead as the old artistes before whom they once lowered their heads and humbled themselves to nothing. Redecorated in 1895, it had kept the same colour-scheme ever since : cream and golden walls, now tarnished with smoke ; crimson hangings to boxes and proscenium, now shot with dust ; and crimson upholstery to the seats in stalls and circles, now faded and stained and worn. Pit and gallery had only benches ; and their walls were tiled shoulder high, against the activities of patrons who had paid but ninepence for the " area " seats, and threepence for the gallery.

From oval cartouches in the high ceiling the great dramatists of England looked down : Shakespeare, Dryden, Congreve, and Sheridan. Probably they were better pleased with the Varieties than with the essays in their own art when the theatre, at the turn of the century, became a home of melodrama. Then from their golden Valhalla up in the ceiling, where each had a private window, they could watch—if they didn't shut their eyes —such moving pieces as *The Lights of London, Sins of the Night, A World Against Her*, and *The Poor of the Streets of London*. This last drama introduced on to the stage a real fire-engine with steam up and horses champing and pawing—and occasionally, in their enforced idleness, doing more than champ and paw.

Nowadays, as a rule, the great dramatists looked down upon " revues " and " musicals," some of whose patter must have made even Congreve blush and Dryden raise an Augustan eyebrow, up there in the privacy of his cartouche. Today, however, and at ten in the morning, of all untheatrical hours, they looked down upon a scene that was yet more calculated to raise their eyebrows ; a scene as sober as the others were ribald and reprehensible ; almost one might say it was the very opposite of last night's scene, because it came from the other end of the moral driftway. All the seven hundred seats were filled by persons in sober garments, of whom an immeasurable proportion were clergymen ; clergymen, old, young ; portly, slight ; expanded, shrunk ; plum-coloured or pale or pink ; and all in their sable or subfusc livery. Out of all the boxes, and there were three tiers of them, peered sleek ecclesiastical faces, like blackbirds or black falcons in an aviary, peeping from high cages. Certainly the curtain was up, revealing a drop-scene of Hyde Park Corner, because it would have been impossible, it would have provoked unseemly smiles, to have rung up the curtain on the bishop with his suffragans and archdeacons seated in a bashful line on either side of him, like the Kentucky Minstrels on either side of Mr. Interlocutor.

In the fourth row of the stalls, side by side, sat Canon Welcome, Dr. Bettersby, and Timothy Clay ; and it was Bettersby who, putting up his glasses on his long, thin, frost-bitten nose and staring at the painted black cloth of the Ionic Screen to the green levels of Hyde Park, pointed out that when the bishop took his place at the table he would be sitting in the high road somewhere between the park gates and St. George's Hospital. " And the gentlemen on the extreme left of his holiness will be sitting in Piccadilly, and those on the extreme right in Knightsbridge opposite the Lavatories."

" Hush, Betts," chided his Vicar. " Remember Tim."

" Ah, yes," he assented. " *Maxima debetur* . . . certainly . . . *siquid turpe paras—*"

" Tsh ! And don't display your learning."

The show—or, rather, the day's business—was about to begin. The Platform walked on to the stage : first the Bishop ; then the Bishop of Dunstable, who was to open a discussion ; then the two suffragans, the three Archdeacons, the Honorary Clerical Secretary of the Conference, the Honorary Lay Secretary, and Sir Herbert Miller, the Chairman of the Diocesan Board of Finance. These gentlemen took their seats, the two diocesans in the centre, and the lesser gaiters to left and right of them, and the lay trousers at the extreme ends.

The Bishop, with his purple cassock, white bands, and pectoral cross, was the only colourful figure in the parade. Canon Welcome, who liked to be distinctive in his dress and even (without vulgarity) spectacular, thought how much he'd like to wear a purple cassock and a gold cross. The Bishop was a very little man, and Canon Welcome could not but feel that his own figure and face were much better suited to that central chair.

As the Bishop arranged his papers before rising for Prayers, Bettersby, scanning through his spectacles the rank of blacksuits, where it stretched from wing to wing, inquired softly, " Do they give us an opening chorus ? "

" *Tsh !* " warned his vicar again, for now all were rising for prayers.

239

The Bishop prayed, and the audience, bending its thousand heads, prayed with him, to the astonishment, one may fancy, of the dramatists up in the ceiling. After the Bishop had finished his prayers, all remained standing with heads drooped for a few more seconds, presumably adding their private petitions; then one and all, and at practically the same moment, dropped back into their seats. Bettersby, turning to push down his tip-up stall, whispered, " Even the audience this morning is part of the show. It is at once performers and audience. We act the holy men before each other, and most of us know we're doing it; but we keep it up ; the show must go on."

" Oh, come, Betts ! " This had seemed unjust to Canon Welcome who for some weeks had struggled after holiness— though not without a sense of strain in the latter days. " Have a little mercy. Some of us try to be genuine."

" Five in a hundred," suggested Bettersby.

" Oh, no, no. Twenty, Betts. Twenty in a hundred."

" I doubt it. I doubt it exceedingly. But do I blame them too severely ? I trow not. Who but a saint could keep in touch with reality under the strain of perpetual and perennial iteration ? But even if we're not feeling real, we must keep up the show of it ; and so the virus of hypocrisy enters the blood. To every trade its exceptional disease, and hypocrisy is inevitably ours ; all but our saints are martyrs to it ; and oblige me, vicar, on this admirable occasion, when you have the whole diocese before you, by pointing out the saints."

This was not impossible, but not easy, so Bettersby, expecting no response, put up his spectacles to examine the Bishop of Dunstable. And having possessed him in detail, he mumbled to Tim from between hardly opened lips, " Wotsy goin talkabout ? "

" ' The Obligations and Duties of Church Membership ' " supplied Tim.

" Obligations ? Duties ? " Bettersby's long, thin nose looked more frost-bitten than ever. " Mean the same thing. Tautological. Still, let sound, as always, have precedence over sense."

" Is he a good speaker ? " asked the youth.

" Dunstable ? My dear boy, I know no more than you. All I know, after a lifetime of desolating experiences, is that in a bishop the capacity to speak intelligently cannot with any confidence be assumed."

" In fact, *Infandum, regina* . . ." quoted Canon Welcome, not to be outdone in scholarship by Bettersby.

" Precisely . . . *jubes renovare dolorem*," completed Bettersby, lest Tim should think he hadn't recognized the quotation. " Virgil, Aenid, Book Two, Line Three."

First came the Bishop's presidential address ; his " Report on the State of the Union " as Bettersby called it, sinking into his seat in anticipation of a long period of desolation ; wherein he was not disappointed. Next the Bishop of Dunstable rose to speak, and it was learned at once that he had a good voice and the technique of an experienced platform orator. His pleasing manner made acceptable to most, if not to Bettersby, who had closed his eyes and clasped his hands over his stomach, the absence of anything new or original in the matter. All were feeling at ease, and applauding occasionally, and tittering occasionally, when of a sudden the theatre's loud-speaker system, which from the first had been reluctant to work at ten in the morning and out of stage hours, lost all self-control and, like a bad-tempered child, gave the adults, urging it on, more than they asked for. It bawled.

Bettersby woke up. " Oh my God ! " he complained. " What was that ? " And he started up from the almost recumbent position into which he had sunk. " Lord help us."

The Bishop continued his speech with a smile ; the loud-speakers neighed and brayed and barked.

" My God ! " repeated Bettersby. " Was there any need of this ? I trow not. His words are hardly worthy of enlargement. A mistake—definitely a mistake to amplify them. Such triteness as is in them—and there is much, you will allow—is stressed beyond endurance if it's shouted at you. It's the same with a man's face : it may be acceptable till you magnify it, and then when its flaws and coarseness and animal pelt are seen, Lord, who shall bear it ? I think it was a clergyman, Dean Swift, who first pointed this out for our confusion." And he sighed.

The amplifying system, after a few more moments of sullen non-compliance or insolent ululation, consented at length to play its part and, indeed, decided to deliver the episcopal observations itself, rather than trust the Bishop to do so. Only occasionally it remembered its wrongs and relapsed into sulkiness and disobedience.

The main fault of the Bishop's allocution, as of so many that come from our Fathers and Chief Ministers, whether in ecclesiastical synod or civil parliament, was, in Bettersby's phrase, its indefatigable continuance. Twenty minutes of it, and Bettersby shrugged his shoulders, turned a sad eye towards his vicar, spread despairing hands, and slid further down into his seat. Here he abandoned himself to boredom, but not in complete passivity ; he sought relief by intermittent demonstration of his condition, of those beside him. He examined his finger nails this way up and that way down ; he compared those of his right hand with those of his left ; now with the hands wide open, now with them turned about and half closed ; he sighed ; he dredged for an old envelope in his pocket and having pencilled a comment on it, passed it to Tim, who spluttered over it ; he withdrew it from Tim and transferred it to his vicar, who smiled.

For a space he listened with open eyes and then, not encouraged to continue, shut them again and put forth the appearances of sleep. Once, sleep being unattainable, he opened a single eye and, perceiving a stain on the lapel of his coat, scratched at it with his index finger and then brushed it with a handkerchief moistened at his lips. This done, he pulled the lapel forward and squinted sideways at it, to see if it were now cleansed and in its right mind. Then dropped the lapel, and settled into comfort again.

Did the Bishop attempt a pleasantry, and the non-episcopal audience dutifully laugh, he preserved a marble incomprehension and when the last rumble of laughter had faded away, sighed.

When at length the Bishop concluded and sat down he changed abruptly from his slumped position into a more erect one and quoted, " Lo, I have borne my burden ". The audience were applauding faithfully, so Bettersby, out of courtesy, made a show of copying them, but his applause, the tapping of four fingers on a palm, seemed rather an indication of resigned acceptance than of approval.

Now the Bishop of the diocese announced that he was going to adopt an unusual course. " Among the obligations and duties of Church membership," he said, " is the financial support of our church fabrics, our schools, our many undertakings and activities and, not least, our clergy. Well, we have Sir Herbert Miller here, with his report on the diocesan budget and its present unhealthy condition, and even if it is not strictly in order, I think it will be eminently suitable to ask him to give it to us now while we are all inspired by the Bishop of Dubstable's eloquent words, instead of at a later stage when half of us may

have left the place, and some of the remainder be asleep."
Laughter, very loud, since this was the Bishop's joke. " Sir
Herbert has much to say to us of the highest importance."

Sir Herbert rose from his platform seat. Bettersby looked at
him and at his thick sheaf of notes ; he sighed yet more heavily
than hitherto, murmured, " *In manus tuas commendo spiritum
meum*," and, shutting his eyes, slid into recumbence again. His
eyes remained shut, even though, on Sir Herbert's announcing
an unconditional bequest of a thousand pounds, he felt moved
to tap his fingers on his palm in approval of such proper behaviour.

§

At this point in this financial recitation Canon Welcome, no
more interested in it than Bettersby, cast his eyes upon Archdeacon Stockhill. The electrician, at a request of the Secretary,
had just heightened the lights above the stage, and Canon
Welcome for the first time really looked at Archdeacon Stockhill
sitting three seats to the left of the Bishop. Good heavens. . . !

Archdeacon Stockhill was seventy-four but he seemed to have
aged thirty years since Canon Welcome last saw him. He
looked a centenarian. Always he'd had the face of a scholar
hermit, chiselled deep as if by long austerities among desert
rocks, but now its eyeholes and cheeks were more cavernous
than ever and its vellum skin was nearly as grey as his long hair.
Had this old theatre stage required a ghost for its current drama,
or the gaunt figure of Death for a character in the play, Archdeacon Stockhill could have walked on under the lights without
make-up of any kind, so ashy, so carven his face, so long and
shrunken his limbs. But then Death would have been a distinguished figure and saint, for Archdeacon Stockhill's face had
the ascetic beauty of a saint's, and the beauty did not lie : when
Bettersby said " Show me the saints," the Canon might well
have pointed to the Archdeacon ; and Bettersby could only
have bowed in acknowledgment.

Much whispering was abuzz in the house as Sir Herbert re-
tailed his dreary arithmetic, and Canon Welcome took advantage
of this general conversazione to mutter, " Old Stockhill looks
dreadfully ill."

Bettersby's nearer eye, which had been closed, opened. " He
goes into hospital on Monday. Told me so in the foyer."

" Why, Betts ?   What's the matter ?   What for ? "

" A colostomy.   Operation on Tuesday."

" Dangerous ? "

" Most certainly."

" Good heavens !   Good heavens ! "

" Old man's quite resigned.   ' God's will be done ' sort of thing."

" Dear, dear ! "

" Says he ought to have gone into hospital last week."

" Why didn't he ? "

" Because he wanted to be with us today in case it was the last time."

" Dear, dear !   Oh, dear, oh dear ! . . . Thinks he's going to die then ? "

" Yes.   And ready, and perhaps more than ready, to go."

At these words Canon Welcome's effort at holiness, which had been wilting for days past, took its last blow and left the fight.   If old Stockhill died, the archdeaconry of Hamden would be vacant.   And was not he, as Vicar of St. Boniface, Hamden, the natural candidate for the succession?   Was he not a rural dean, one of the Bishop's inner college from among whom he would choose ;   and, moreover, Rural Dean of Hamden itself?   Why, the appointment was almost a certainty !   He didn't want dear old Stockhill to die—exactly—there wasn't a better man anywhere—but—but no, were he to face the truth, he must say he longed for him to die.   Ashamed by this truth, he looked again at the Archdeacon sitting there with his thin gaitered legs crossed and his lean ivory fingers on his lap.   How abominable to kill him in imagination, but there it was :   the heart of man seeks its own, and the heart of Canon Welcome was bounding with hope.   His finer vision, always independent of his egotism, suggested to him that it would be a shocking exchange, the saintly Stockhill for the (to state it brutally) hypocritical and now homicidal Welcome ;   but his heart continued to leap and dance with hope.   Yes, in truth he must state that he wanted this issue more than anything.

What must he do ?   He must show himself to the Bishop today, and to those senior clergy whose advice the Bishop might seek.   To be in sight was to be in mind.   If the opportunity offered, he must mount that platform and speak—speak to impress them all.

Sir Herbert had finished.   The discussion on Obligations and

Duties was now open. Canon Welcome trembled with the desire to speak. But no chance as yet. No ideas had come into his head ; and no break was occuring in the chain of speakers advancing to the stage. One after another, confound them, they took themselves to the side of the Bishop's table and the microphone, some earnest, others mere self-thrusting busybodies. None of them had said anything that was new, anything that was provocative in content. All professed the whole faith and the whole morality ; and waking no opposition, raised no excitement.

Excitement only breathed through the house when it was seen that Tuppy Williams was standing by the pass door that led to the stage. All heads moved to see him there. Then Tuppy Williams was going to speak ! Before he had said a word, before he had gone through the door, parsons all over the house, and of all schools, felt excited and entertained for the first time. Canon Tulse P. Williams, F.R.S., D.D., D.Litt., B.Sc., known to them all as Tuppy Williams, Canon Residentiary, Chancellor and Examining Chaplain, was the scintillant nucleus of controversy in the diocese. In the eyes of the orthodox among his brother clergy, that is to say, in the eyes of ninety per cent. of them, he was the Master Heretic—though the orthodoxy of some of these was rather a professional garment than the true vesture of their souls. Long a leader among the modernizing clergy, a regular and acid contributor to the *Modern Churchman*, author of a book, *The Twentieth Century Creed* which, two years since, had provoked a correspondence in the *Times*, a six weeks' storm in the *Church Times*, and a somewhat ambiguous but on the whole regretful rebuke from the Archbishop, he had just emptied a drum of petrol on to these old embers by another book called *Messiah without Miracle*, which bluntly argued that the miracles attendant on Jesus's birth and death, and those attributed to him during his ministry, so far from helping the modern world to believe in him, were intellectually offensive and spiritually a stumbling block.

No one looked less like a scholar, less like an acetose fighter whose tongue was an adder, than Tuppy Williams. He was a small, round, rosy man, absurdly young in appearance for his high position in the Chapter, and the soubriquet Tuppy sat on his plump, boyish figure far better than the string of academic degrees which flew after his name like a kite-tail. Nevertheless his brain was the quickest and sharpest in the diocese, and out of his mouth proceeded two-edged swords.

There was a fine silence as he walked from the wings on to the stage ; a tribute of ice. Bettersby unlidded an eye to interpret the silence and murmured, " Oh, my God, vicar—Tuppy Williams—don't say he's going to worry us all with the bothering bases of the Creed." But Canon Welcome was not bothered at at all ; he sat forward, waiting to hear, and with an idea at gestation in his breast. Nor was Tim other than pleased and alert, for he had a boy's deep respect for any man who had achieved celebrity. He had it in mind, before the day was over, to waylay Canon Williams in the foyer and ask for his auto-graph—for his sister.

" My lord." Tuppy Williams glanced once and in obeisance at the Bishop and then turned to face the great audience, casting his eyes up at boxes and gallery. " Ladies and gentlemen, I know it is seldom the custom to discuss doctrinal matters in our Diocesan Conference, but I do want to make one point so as to bring this debate nearer the world of reality in which we happen to be sitting. Only one point, and it is this : before we discuss the obligations and duties of our membership we must be sure that we can retain any membership worth having."

A murmur of disapproval from parterre, circle and balcony (which knew what was coming) went wafting towards him, like the lift of an easterly wind ; and he nodded and smiled at it in friendly recognition. " The first obligation I feel is to make this point in season and out of season. Look you ; we can count on keeping the simple and uncritical, so long as there are any left, and we can hold, as long as it pays them, the hypocrites. Yes, hypocrites, ladies and gentlemen : I regret the word but shall use no other ; because, even if some of us were sincere in our youth, we grow older and wiser, and if the Church persists in imposing impossible beliefs upon us, we slide into a slough of complacent hypocrisy."

" The man speaks sense," mumbled Bettersby. " I regret to admit it, but this is sense. The first today."

" A Church which can win no adherents from the finest minds of its age, and daily loses the critical young, had best, I submit, look to the terms of its membership before it studies the obligations and duties thereof. Because, you see, it might find itself left with the obligations and duties but without, alas, the members."

A few laughed ; not many.

" The simple and uncritical, I say, will believe and do all

that we tell them ; they will take from our hands the dogmas and duties ; but the scholarly and critical will do no such thing ; them we have to win, and in days like these by a great effort of spirit and mind. And thus, in my view, this discussion has so far wasted your time, gentlemen. Not until you recognize the compelling, the imperious, need to think out our creed afresh and re-interpret it in a way that is not only acceptable but convincing to modern intellects, can you feel that you will retain any significant place or power in the world."

And while they murmured, while some in the resentment ostentatiously rose and walked out, he asserted that the modern intelligence, after three hundred years of shaping and tempering by science, was finally certain that miracles, in the sense of capricious interferences with natural law, did not happen. It was futile to describe the miracles of Christ as faith-healing, because this was to concede the point that miracles in the old-fashioned sense did not happen, and therefore to deny possi-bility to the two major miracles which were all that some of them were concerned to defend, the Virgin Birth and the Bodily Resurrection of Our Lord. In his view there was no course open but to accept, however deep our first recoil from it, the fact that the birth stories and the bodily resurrection stories were not history but edifying legend. The legend of the Virgin Birth was probably an accretion, ripened in a warm pagan climate which could believe that Plato was the son of Apollo by a human mother, and that the Emperor Augustus was conceived by his mother during a visit to a temple of the same God. "Ah yes, you may resist and spurn this, you may run from listening to it ; but gentlemen, there is no real need for this scamper. To any clear mind and profound spiritual vision these doctrines of the Virgin Birth and the Physical Resurrection must gradually become unacceptable—wait, wait, and I will show you why : their whole conception is too materialist to be acceptable. Spiritual things are spiritually discerned and not by tricky demonstrations in the realm of matter——"

But Canon Welcome had ceased to listen. His idea was now full-born, and his mind, like a mother, was wholly given to it. He must mount that stage before anyone else, and reply to Tuppy Williams in a fervent defence of orthodoxy. Who-ever answered Tuppy first would reap the harvest of cheers. "I shall defend the faith with fire and passion." He had wanted to show himself to the Bishop and the powerful clergy, and what a way was this ! See, the reporters from the local press were sharing that bottom box with a harp—the orchestra for the current revue having overflowed from its pit. Other reporters, London reporters, were in the opposite box. And all awake to the possibility of " scenes ", because fanaticism, as they could feel, was smouldering and might soon be afire in the theatre. *He* would capture the publicity their pencils held.

Nervousness possessed him like a devil. A tiny sweat bedewed his brow and palms. But he must not fail. He must not stutter or stammer or dry up in his part. To fail, so far from advancing his career, might damage it. He must put everything he'd got into this performance on that stage. His brain raced as he snatched a pencil from a pocket and wrote notes on the folded newspaper in his hand : notes of points and pithy repartees that he'd often used in argument, or heard others use in argument and thought worth delivering as his own. Not since his first sermons as a deacon had his hand shaken with nervousness like this—but he would not, he would *not*, be defeated by fear.

This desire to shine before the Bishop and a great audience, this determination to crush down his fears, generated all the steam-energy to drive him on his course. It whirled the wheels of his brain so that he remembered note after note to jot on his paper. It bent him forward in his stall so that he could spring to his feet and catch the Bishop's eye the moment Tuppy Williams ceased.

Tuppy Williams ceased ; he gave a quick truncated bow to the Bishop, and went from the stage. Bettersby opened his eyes and said, " I see that all things come to an end, but his commandment was exceeding broad." Tim suppressed a giggle. But Canon Welcome, hearing neither, was on his feet and holding high the rolled-up newspaper like the torch in the hand of the Statue of Liberty. The Bishop saw this white scroll before anything else.

" Prebendary Welcome," he called. " Hamden Deanery."

And the energy drove Prebendary Welcome at speed on to the stage. No applause greeted his appearance. Disappointing this : a reminder that, though well liked by many, he was not one of the most popular diocesan figures. All right ; they should hear from him now. This gramme of disappointment only heightened the fermentation of energy and resolve.

"My lord." Exactly as Tuppy had done, he gave one glance at the Bishop and then turned and faced the audience. "Canon Williams has very rightly said that we don't as a rule discuss doctrinal matters at our Diocesan Conference ; since saying which, he has done nothing else." Laughter and "Hear, hears" greeted this, because it sounded funny ; and all nervousness fell from him : he was stripped for battle—battle for his career. "Do not imagine that I am going to do the same thing. Do not imagine that I am about to debate with him the articles of our Faith, one by one. It is just that I hold it to be of cardinal importance that the attitude to our Creed which he has expounded this morning should meet with an immediate disclaimer." Loud applause, and it spurred him to a yet livelier canter. "We are discussing the duties of Church membership, and his contention, as I understand it, is that we shall have no membership worth speaking of unless we abandon the Gospel stories of our Lord's birth and resurrection. If this is so—and I don't believe it is—then, in God's name, in the name of our Master and Founder, let us have no membership worth speaking of." Applause stormed towards him, rising to cheers ; and he waited for it to sink. "Let us have the simple and the foolish and the babes, to whom, perhaps, the Father will have revealed those things which he has hid from the wise and prudent—*and*, ladies and gentlemen "— here he used the rolled-up newspaper as a lifted baton to emphasize his point—"hid, perhaps, from the scientists and the mathematicians and the physicists in whose theories and affirmations Canon Williams apparently places so much more faith than in the distilled experience of twenty centuries of saints. All the wisdom of Canon Williams and of his infallible scientists may yet, I believe, be shown—nay, may already be known in the hearts of some of us—to be foolishness with God. It is not necessary to remind this gathering of the words (a favourite text of mine), 'The wisdom of this world is foolishness with God.' *Ladies and gentlemen ; the first duty of Church members is to accept the faith and charter of our Church.*"

During the fervent applause for this he let the rolled newspaper fall to his side ; then raised it again and held it in both hands before his breast, in readiness to stress his own points and wave away Tuppy's. "A Church without dogma is dead. The few dogmas which we regard as *de fide* are not ossifications, as Canon Williams implies, but the very vertebrae, developed and grown throughout the years, without which our Christianity would be a spineless thing. What I want to ask Canon Williams is this : does he believe in the Incarnation ? If so—and I'm sure he does—can he not see that all smaller and subordinate miracles are as nothing in the dazzling light of that staggering, beautiful, formidable, terrifying Fact. If we believe in this well-nigh incredible thing—and if we don't, let us fold up our Church and put it away—if we believe that Jesus, the young carpenter and joiner, was He who carved all the suns and the stars out of nothing, then any miracles which happened at his entry into this poor world and during his lifetime on it, and at his going out of it, did not happen to prove to us that he was God but simply because he *was* God."

Immense applause again while the orator, waiting for it to stop, thought, " Yes, that was an inspired sentence," and wondered what it meant.

" Canon Williams thinks he's in the van of modern thought. I suggest he's lagging and limping a long way behind. He thinks he's ever so far ahead of you and me and all of us. I feel he's only just caught up with the materialists of the last century. I feel he's just padding by the side of Darwin and Huxley. He's made it so very clear to us, you see, that he has none of the humility of our latter-day scientists. Still, he's young, and the modesty may come with the years. The *enfant terrible* may yet become the staid father gently moderating the extravagances of perfervid, rebellious, iconoclastic youth. I desire to ask him, my lord : does he not know, has he not so much as heard, that many scientists have lately admitted that after certain experiments in extra-sensory perception "—he was proud of this learned term—" they can now lay no final limit to the powers of the human mind. Their experiments appear to have proved—*proved*, ladies and gentlemen !—that even to our poor, undeveloped intelligences prevision is possible, and the transmission of thought regardless of distance, and even the actual moving of solid objects, near or far, by some power of thought alone. There are also published cases, apparently perfectly well substantiated, of levitation, bodily irradiation, stigmatisation, post-mortem incorruption, and other super-normal phenomena——"

" Good God ! " muttered Bettersby to Tim. " This is Christian Science, I infer."

" Hush ! " warned Tim. " It's nothing of the kind."

" If it is, it is neither Christian nor scientific."

" Hush, *please*, sir ! "

" It is then like the *cor anglais*, which is neither English nor a horn. It is usually the same with a gentleman farmer " ; and Bettersby shut his eyes to sleep again.

Meanwhile Canon Welcome was declaiming with baton outstretched : " In their modesty they admit, gentlemen, that they know hardly anything about the nature, the reach, and the powers of the human mind. And this is the moment when our Canon Williams, our young materialist in a hurry, would urge us to jettison any and every dogma which the outmoded scientists of the last century would not accept. I respectfully suggest that he does great harm by these public statements of his old-fashioned and reactionary materialism. They get reported. I watched my friend of the *Hamden News*, down there with the harp, getting it all down for publication in his next issue. And then what happens ? Some ancient wiseacre who reads his local paper with his pint asks me, when I go to preach in my slums——"

Dr. Bettersby woke up. " When does he preach in his slums ? " he murmured out of the side of his mouth to Tim.

" I've known him do it," said Tim. " Twice."

" Hush, don't talk, boy. Listen."

" I am no fundamentalist, ladies and gentlemen. I fully agree that in each generation, as knowledge increases, there is a compelling need, a duty laid upon us all, to think out our dogmas afresh. We have to mediate between the old simplicity and the modern sophistication. Always we are confronted with this intellectual task——"

" When does he begin on it ? " asked Bettersby of the floor.

" Tsssh, sir ! " admonished Tim. " This is great. I'm enjoying it. Up St. Boniface Martyr's ! "

" —but to abandon them, no. If our Church is anything at all, if it is a body which exists to declare a Revelation from on high and not a parliament to refute and cancel it, then I say it is not a democracy with power of repeal, but a Kingdom, a Monarchy ; and in a Monarchy some things are best left to the King."

So loud were the applause and the cheers at this sentence that Canon Welcome, though not at all sure what it meant, and though he had other things in mind to say, decided to quit the platform while the going was so good. The applause and the cheers accompanied him the whole length of the stage, and as he walked along the gangway to his seat. It was the triumph, beyond question, of the morning ; and he hoped, almost with anguish, that no other speaker in the course of the day would win a like acclamation. This was improbable, he knew, because it was only over doctrinal fisticuffs that such fervour could be aroused, and he'd stolen the punches of all who might succeed him. The popular award of the day was almost certainly his.

As he clambered back towards his stall, the cheers still following him, Timothy was applauding vigorously in honour of Canon Welcome, the local boy from St. Boniface Martyr's who'd made good. " Hurray ! " he cried to Bettersby loudly and laughingly because no one further away was likely to hear him. " Tuppy Williams hit hard but the old man hit harder. We won ! Up St. Boniface Martyr's ! "

Bettersby did not clap but listened with lifting nostrils to the clamour. " I see no cause for these hosannas," he said. " I was edified by neither performance. Each gentleman assumes that he alone is Jehovah's Witness, but I feel no confidence that either assumption would survive a moment's real experience of God."

" You don't, sir ? But why ? "

" Because that shocking experience would immediately empty them of their combativeness. Still, who am I ? Who, my dear Timothy, am I ? A most distressingly combative type. And you ? Manifestly blind too, as all that schoolboy percussion shows. Thank God that in twenty-three minutes we can go to lunch. I have listened to two episcopal allocutions and a dozen displays of clerical egotism, and so wasted a morning. And now I am subjected to this deafening manifestation of ecclesiastical fanaticism. Still, I am glad if our brother is made happy by it."

CHAPTER FIVE

HERE at all events was something which was *not* done in a corner. A squabble in a Church synod ; a concomitant hubbub ; the doctrines of the Church in the seethe of the pot—these made a " story " that flew to the headlines like birds to telegraph wires ; hardly a newspaper next morning but reported the scene with some prominence and in some detail. Canon Welcome, pleasure effervescing in him like soda in a bottle, spent two of his sacred post-breakfast working hours in the newspaper room of the Public Library, drinking up the accounts in the papers and searching in hope, but without success, for editorial comment. The editorial comment came later. This news did not quickly go cold in these quiet midsummer days, and two mornings later Canon Welcome, with a leap of gladness, perceived in his *Times* a long letter from Bishop Foyle, one of the most learned and revered figures in the church, under the heading " Faith of the Church of England ". And the great bishop supported Canon Welcome though he was very gentle and understanding with Canon Williams. Bishop Foyle having spoken, the debate was on the table. His letter was but the first of many in the *Times, Church Times,* and *Church of England Newspaper* ; and some of these letters (but far too few) mentioned Canon Welcome by name. By a single speech he had become —or in more precise statement, he had some justification for imagining himself—News.

In any stage drama, Lilian Eadie used to tell him, the protagonist must play opposite someone or something ; and in the days after the Diocesan Conference Canon Welcome played opposite two columns of the *Times.* For the first few days he played opposite the Correspondence Column, but when this ceased to mention him by name, he played with more feeling and power opposite the Obituary Column. It became his first interest, because he was awaiting the issue of Archdeacon Stockhill's operation with—with hope.

Often he was ashamed of this hope ; often he forced himself to look at other pages of the *Times* before coming upon the Obituary Column ; often before looking at it he deliberately sent aloft an ejaculatory prayer, " O God, make him get well and live long " ; but it was useless ; who can grub out, or who by a miracle change, the stout old tree of ambition which has fifty years' root in the soil ?

And so he continued, day after day, to greet with interest and affection the Obituary Column. They were pleasant days, aglow with a faint exhilaration because this hope, now shining bright, now clouded, now out and shining again, was warming them like a pale young April sun.

The column having no answer for him, no, not in fourteen days, he made occasional, unemphatic inquiries among his brother clergy, saying, " By the bye, how is old Stockhill ? ", but they didn't know, not having his interest in the reversion. And at last he found himself at his telephone in the hall, ringing up, not without remorse, the hospital.

" Canon Welcome speaking. . . . Oh, could you tell me, how is my dear old friend, Archdeacon Stockhill ? "

A low pleasant contralto voice, sweet with youth, a voice one could easily fall in love with, answered, " The operation was quite successful. The Archdeacon is very comfortable."

" He is going on very well, is he ? "

" Yes. We've been very pleased with his response."

Oh ! . . .

" Oh, I'm so glad. We have all been very anxious, but I didn't like to disturb you before. This means—I hope—that he will get perfectly well again."

" The doctor is here, Canon. Perhaps I'd better ask him to answer you."

" That's most kind of you, Sister." No harm in calling her Sister, however young her voice. " Sister " pleased them. " Oh, doctor . . . good morning. . . . I was just inquiring if we could hope that Archdeacon Stockhill will get quite well and join us all again."

" The Archdeacon—oh, he's responded splendidly. I think he should have now some years of comparative comfort. With a little care it's quite possible for a patient who's had a colostomy to carry on his work more or less normally."

Oh . . . Ah, well. . . .

" That's grand. I'm most grateful to you, doctor. It's an immense relief to us all."

Ah, well. . . .

After that he inquired of the Obituary Column no more. The hope had been pleasant to handle and examine, but one face of it had always been doubt, and it was no great disappointment to lay it aside. Soon he forgot all about Archdeacon Stockhill and the little bud of hope which his deathly grey face had ripened like a sun. But one Friday morning, in that sacred time between breakfast and midday which must never be interrupted, he lay back in his chair with his feet on the stool and the entertaining pages of the *Church Times* in his hands ; and after reading on the first page an article about the Holy Places, and on subsequent pages the Political Summary, a review of *Christianity or Chaos*, by Bishop Walton, and a leading article on *The Catholic Mission Field*, he came suddenly upon two small headlines, " In Memoriam. Henry Leigh Stockhill, Priest."

And he read, " The Ven. H. L. Stockhill, eleven years the devoted Vicar of St. Mary-at Entham and seven years Archdeacon of Hamden died last week at St. Luke's Hospital from an embolism following an operation. He was seventy-four——"

And Canon Welcome, seeing this, was elated and ashamed.

The hope was back in his house ; and it is pleasant to live with hope. The days were full of interest again. Every knock of the postman, every ring of his telephone, every fall of a letter on his hall-door mat, was a pleasant excitation. He walked his study with the hope, he took it out with him into the streets, he sat with it at committee meetings while other men talked, and he stood or knelt with it in church services while the people prayed.

But the days filed by, each properly vested in its sacred attire, like surpliced choirmen in single file ; and never on to the mat dropped the letter he looked for. The sweet mistaken hope, like an irritant condition, healed and dispersed. And again its loss was no great grief because the site of the lesion had always been partly anæsthetized by doubt.

§

But :

ARCHDEACON OF HAMDEN

Canon Tulse P. Williams Appointed

This was a blow between the eyes. This started him up in his chair one Friday morning when he saw it in the *Church*

255

Times. So much so that he had to look at it a second time. *Tuppy!* Tuppy Williams! That boy! That boy who didn't even believe anything. It was an insult to the whole diocese. It was an insult to him personally, after his fiery reprobation of Tuppy's heresies before the whole Diocesan Conference. Oh, what it was to be an examining chaplain and a canon residentiary, and in the Bishop's eye! It was the same in all careers : you must be a staff officer and have the eye of the General if you wanted promotion and honours and mentions in despatches. In the Church as in the Army you got little enough if you were out in the front line, working yourself to death among the poor in the slums. Tuppy Williams, nearly twenty years younger than he! Ordained nearly twenty years after him—and he had overtaken him and shot thus far ahead. Canon residentiary yesterday, archdeacon now, bishop one day.

Canon Welcome's heart sank down in a bog of disappointment. His anger smouldered like a scrub-fire above its grave. The resentment was so high that he decided there and then, thrusting out his lower lip, to defend the old dogmas no more. Infinitely easier to be a " modern churchman " when you could enjoy the emoluments of your benefice without believing anything. And a lot more likely, it appeared, to get you preferment. His heart was so mastered by his ambition to achieve gaitered rank, so held like a gyroscope car to this monorail, that it cried aloud, before he consented to the words, " I'm not going to be beaten. I swear I'm not going to be beaten. Nobody's going to beat me. I never give in."

He had failed to capture the interest of the Bishop ; possibly, it seemed now, because the old man was a scholar himself and hadn't at all liked the outburst of fanatical approval for his censure of Tuppy Williams. That speech, belike, instead of advancing his interests with the Bishop, had retracted it. All right. All right. Not all preferment was in the hands of the Bishop. It was the Prime Minister who recommended the appointments of bishops and deans. He would aim higher than a mere archdeaconry. And his campaign would begin at once. How did one arrest the eye of the Prime Minister? How? The Prime Minister must surely have heard his name, after that correspondence in the *Times.* Why, the King must have heard of it. Get your name known, get into the spotlight whenever possible, and half the difficult terrain was conquered between you and the episcopal palace or the deanery. But prime ministers, like bishops, no matter how they might attempt impartiality, tended to prefer men of their own colour. This present Prime Minister was a conservative—yes, but who would be prime minister in the next parliament? The results of all the recent by-elections had been astonishing, alarming. Socialist gain after socialist gain. Canon Welcome had been not lightly shocked to see that even people of education and rank were declaring themselves socialists, even officers in the services, even knights and peers and their ladies. Had Marcus Brumley been right? Many a splendid tip, yielding its hundreds of profit unassessable to income tax, had old Marcus given him, for there was none shrewder than he. Indeed Canon Welcome, though loving his friend, would often wonder (like his Master before him) how old Marcus could in one part be so devout a churchman and in the other part so successful a stock exchange tipster. Were his political tips as safe? As long as five years ago, at the time of his famous sermon on the Railway Strike, Marcus had said, " It's silly to attack strikers, old man. You're backing the wrong horse. Labour'll be in power within five years, and may stay in for ten." And he, in astonishment at this prophecy, and in no small alarm, had replied, " Oh, no, I can't believe that, Marcus, old boy ! Not in England. England will never go Socialist." But it looked as if the old boy was right. And if so. . . if so . . . .

He went to his bookshelves. He took down a book. It bore the title, *The Inevitability of Socialism*. His nephew, Alec Welcome, a fanatical young Socialist with whom he would argue till he lost all patience and politeness, had sent it to him as an impudent gift for Christmas. He went to his deep chair with the book. And all that morning and afternoon he read it. And when at six in the evening he finished it and laid it on the table beside him, he announced to the empty room, " I am converted. He has convinced me. I feel sure of it."

He thought of the Circus, the Corners, and the career of Mr. Carman. He saw again New Victoria Buildings and the Little Bread Street Mission. He saw Baynes with his bound face, and all the dear, poor people, good and bad, for whom he had really felt such a stirring of love. And he told himself, " It is my work in the slums that has convinced me. But I think I must have always had the seed of Socialism in me. Why, did I not say five years ago, in that magnificent close to my Strike Sermon : ' The old harsh order is passing, and a new and more Christian one is born, an age in which all working men will be given an economic status, higher and happier and juster than heretofore ; an age of social sanity that will bring a new benediction to mankind ' ? Phrasing in the grand manner. Eloquence. Obviously I have always been a Socialist in heart. Socialism was my inevitable haven in the end because, all said and done, it is simply practical Christianity and, whatever my faults and failures of belief, I have always worshipped that."

He lay dreaming. " Prominent Canon a Convert to Social-ism." Headlines about a sermon in the Cathedral where, as a prebendary he must preach once a year. " Canon Denounces Apathy of National Church. A Challenge." A trumpet-call, in fact. An epoch-making sermon like the Assize Sermon of John Keble in 1833. Stories, to shock the congregation (and incite Fleet Street) of the North London brothels and drinking clubs and gaming houses. Stories of such as Rick Carman, Len Farrow, the razor boys, and Phil Janey. . . .

By the way, what had become of Phil Janey ? Phil Janey who had come to him for a little and somehow slipped away again ? Such dreadful things she had told him ; and he in his sloth had let her go. An unfaithful steward. Would some account of her be asked of him hereafter ? She was too small and frail-timbered a craft to be loosed alone upon the world's dark tides and treacherous undertows. He should have put out like a lifeboat to find her ; but he had not done so ; he had been too slothful and negligent and indifferent to his charge.

What really had happened to Phil Janey ?

CHAPTER SIX

I⊤ was six in the evening when Canon Welcome, dreaming in his chair, asked himself this question, and at that time Phil Janey sat dreaming too, in a house not much more than a mile away. Her day's work over, she sat at the window on her top-floor room gazing, but without clear sight or thought of them, at the houses across the road.

She called this upper room her " flat in Monmouth Crescent ", though her accommodation was bounded by the four walls of the room and her right to use the offices downstairs. The fine word " flat " was brother to the plume she had once carried in her hat and to the ladylike varnish on her fingernails. " Monmouth Crescent " had a distinguished sound too, as of some place up West, but it was not at all what the name suggested. It was an arc of road that swung out of Hebron Town High Street, as if to avoid the beating vehicles, the running gamins, and the dawdlers at the shop-windows, and then, finding nothing of interest in this deviation, nothing but doorsteps and doors and area railings all alike, swerved round again and rejoined the High Street two hundred yards lower down.

The houses which the road thus quickly deserted had been only less quickly left behind by the hurry of Time. Built in the 'sixties for people of middle quality and fair prosperity, they had been captured and occupied in less than forty years by the teeming workers advancing like locusts from the East. You could imagine that they looked grey and gloomy at this treatment and worn out and nerve-wracked by the clamour of numberless children. Like all North London's stucco-dressed houses, they had an indeterminate middle-aged appearance, being neither old like the Georgian houses nor comparatively young like the flats and villas of red-brick and stone.

No. 17, with Phil Janey at the upper window, was almost in the middle of the arc, and since it was exactly the same as all its sisters on both sides of the road, let it serve as the pattern of them all : a high, narrow-chested house with a basement in the earth and three floors above it ; two fair-sized rooms on each floor and an " office " on each half-landing. Mrs. Ansty rented it, living on the ground floor and letting the basement as a flat and the four rooms above as bed-sitting-rooms. Mrs. Ansty, the capable widow of a railway goods porter, had grown, like many tall women, thinner rather than fatter in her fifty years, and now seemed as elongated as an El Greco angel or a modern " Portrait of a Lady " in chiselled wood. On this lean framework she hung neat black clothes and perched a neat black hat ; and in all she was as respectable as any other woman in the Crescent and far more respectable than a few. In the neat clothes and hat she would have been grieved to hear herself described as a charwoman, but she did leave the house at nine in the morning and do daily work for, or in the idiom of the Fields " oblige," certain comfortable ladies on Hamden Hill. And she had a clientele of young wives whose babies she would mind so that they " could get out for a little of an evening."

To her top-floor room under the roof Phil Janey had come three years before. Mr. Carman, we remember, had taken exception to her " sauce " and bashed her one ; and this was definitely a liberty. And Phil Janey, who had disliked liberties when she was as young as twelve years, disliked them all the more at this time when she was seventeen. This bashing, more-over, had provided an excuse she'd long been waiting for, because Phil Janey hated New Victoria Buildings with their cold stone stairways and sour lavatory smells and was a little ashamed of her father's past record and present barrow. So within an hour of the bashing she had walked out of the Buildings with her nose up, stayed a night with her friend, Doreenie Passmore (who was voluble with her sympathy and endorse-ment) and then, having learned of this room from one of her fellow-workers, flew to it like a London sparrow to its hole under the eaves.

§

Her day-dreams this evening, under the slates of Mrs. Ansty's high narrow house, had to do with this search for something better than the Fields and her father. Her mind swept forward into the future and back over the past. But since the future was a mist, although full of spun-gold this evening, she dwelt more easily on the past, which had still the concrete actuality of scenes on a stage before the lights dimmed. She remembered a hundred dances in tawdry halls, but always there had been a sadness, a melancholy, behind the striving gaiety. She recalled at one point her rush, through the Reverend Welcome, towards religion, and what a " real old wash-out " that had been. She remembered this boy and that through whose ministrations on unlit heaths and in dark pathways she had sought the escape. Mrs. Ansty thought of her as a " nice, respectable working girl ", but Mrs. Ansty was often out of an evening, and Phil Janey had sometimes brought her young lover up to this room and here on the old iron bed, with her eyes shut upon all unlovely things, best forgotten, had tried the old escape through the body. She could have wished that it was real love which these young ministrants brought her, but it was never that, alas ; they alighted like butterflies on the honey and, after a wavering, faltered away. Again and again, remembering them, she would tell herself, " I'm not just a tart ; I'm not, relly " ; no, nothing like that, truly ; she was merely a girl determined to find a little happiness sometimes, and in this no one was going to stop her. " If I want to, I will, so there ! "

Most of these boy visitors she had met in the pubs and cafés round the Circus, and she knew them and their mates to be " game boys " who supplemented their wages, or gathered their only money, by the lighter forms of graft. They disposed of crooked stuff for older and suspect hands by pawning or selling it in far-away parts of London. Some went so far as to act as outside men for well-known screwsmen or as stalls for the expert dips. None were indifferent to a little hoisting or dragging on their own ; but only a few could have been described as master screwsmen themselves.

Phil Janey was not greatly shocked by these irregular activities. She was no more shocked, in fact, than her sisters of a more comfortable class would be, when they learned that friends had cheated the Customs by smuggling a silk dress or defrauded the Revenue by concealing some limb of their income. Her view of Law, Justice, and the Police had a bias slightly different from that of her sisters on Hamden Hill who attended St. Boniface Martyr's. Theirs leaned, like well-aimed bowls, towards that jack, the Law ; hers turned away from it. She did not think of the police as wonderful men, ever ready with guidance and protection ; she thought of them as the enemies of her kind—enemies who could fraternize and be generous at times—but, by all accounts, could act very unfair when the war was on :

arresting innocent lads as " sus's " if they wanted them where they could find them ; threatening and bribing them by the offer or withholding of fags, so as to get statements from them, and then swearing before beak or judge that nothing of the sort had been done ; sometimes deliberately framing charges against them ; and often beating them up savagely in the street or in their cells if they had violently resisted arrest.

Her loneliness tonight, in the silence of her high room, had become for some reason or another, a great sadness, and at last in a kind of despair, she got up, pulled on a light coat and a close-fitting hat trimmed with a pom-pom of marabou feathers, and walked out of the house and the Crescent. She hardly knew whither she was walking, or why. Only the vague dream accompanied her, that she might walk into something which would bring a glow into the drabness of her days. If she'd been forced, against habit and inclination, to reduce the misty dream into some concrete shape, she must have said, " Oh well, I suppose I hope to meet with some nice young chap who'll love me without wanting to make too free, and who'll take me places where we'll have lovely times together."

What other door into adventure was open for her ? Sometimes she thought of going as a stewardess on a ship that was bound for wonderful places, but the sea seemed a great way from Hebron Fields ; between the Circus and the sea there stretched a desert of streets and houses, a maze and wilderness of walls, too difficult to traverse. As she walked northward along the High Street, inevitably northward to the old Corners and the scenes of her childhood, she envied all boys who had such far greater chances of adventure. Vaguely she saw them driving lorries through beautiful country scenes; flying aeroplanes over oceans and grounding in romantic lands ; climbing terrific mountains in India; sailing in warships or merchantmen to wildly exciting ports in the East ; or even—yes, there were rebellious moments when she envied them this—enjoying the excitement, the heart-arresting thrills, of burglary or warehouse-breaking, when they crept on tip-toe through the dark. And after many long drinks from this crock of dreams, as she wandered slowly along the High Street, she told herself with angry, up-pressed lip, " I too shall do something dangerous, if something nice or exciting doesn't happen soon. Anything is better than nothing."

But of course nothing happened on this night, and she only came wandering back to her empty room. It was not till an evening some months later that the exciting thing happened. She pushed open the door of the Gentle Shepherd in Greenholt Street, Hebron Fields. The same vague dreams were in her head, as the saloon door swung behind her, but a different hat enfolded the head : a tight green beret trimmed with a brown quill and a brief drooping veil. She walked to the counter and was about to order herself a glass of Douro port when she saw that one of the two young men perched up on stools, leaning on the bar, and talking to Sam Long, the barman, was Len Farrow of Borrett Street. She did not know that it was Len who had razored Reverend Baynes that time ; hardly anyone in the Fields knew this, because Len's gang didn't talk, and Fred Lanark, of Albert's Restaurant, didn't talk either. Phil Janey knew him only as a handsome lad who'd done his three years in Borstal and was reputed to be a very fly boy indeed. Tonight, as on the night when he visited Baynes in the café, his felt hat was thrust far back on his fair hair and had its brim pulled down, ready to be drawn forward over his eyes like a shop's awning in the sun. The hat made a droopy brown halo for his youthful, fair-cheeked, handsome face. This face was perhaps a little less selfish and hard-mouthed than when he had borne down upon Baynes ; he had, in fact, been somewhat shaken, though nobody but himself knew this, by Baynes's refusal to hand him over to punishment, and his public statement, " I forgive this lad with all my heart, and I pray that my blood may be the last he sheds." He had sneered at, resisted, resisted violently, the public words, but—he had not found occasion to use the razor again. And of late he hadn't rowed in so much with the old mob, preferring, he said, to work on his jack. Sometimes he saved his face by saying to himself, " If anyone comes the razor lark on me he'll get some back, but there's not all that sense in slashing a bloke what done you no harm."

Len Farrow, then, was a little less cruel, but he was still a very wide boy. He had no known employment, but he was never without money in his pocket ; and money for Len was nickers and cow's calves and jacksalives—which, in the mother tongue, are pounds, and halves, and five-pound notes.

" Hallo, little stranger," he greeted her, as Phil Janey came to the bar. " Ain't seen you for donkey's years. How's our Phil Janey ? Wouldn't say you look all that good. Been at the game a bit ? "

" What do you mean ? " demanded Phil Janey, her hand on her temper and ready to raise that sharp tool for use.

" Nah then ! Nah then ! Don't get the spike up. I don't mean nothing that you need be ashamed of. We all know that our Phil Janey isn't a twopenny jude, but just a nice girl. I only meant, had you been having some in the ordinary way o' business—not that business is quite the word for a nice girl. I'm saying you look kind'a wore out."

" I'm fine, ta ; thank you, Len."

" Well, you don't look it ; you look pale, ducks—rather as though you'd just been catting over the side of the ship."

" I'm all right ; never better."

" Still in that Monmouth Crescent place ? "

" That's right. Why not ? "

" You been there years and years."

" Certainly I have. I got quite a nice flat there."

" Yeah, but . . . haven't they turned you out yet ? "

" *No !* Why should they ? "

Len appeared to remember something. " Well, what about Wally Bateman ? What happened to him ? "

" Oh, I had enough of him."

" How d'yer mean ? "

" Well, he was no gentleman, relly."

" How d'yer mean ; no gentleman ? "

" He was a sight too fresh and wanted to overstep. He was always trying to, and I didn't care for it."

" Oh, I see ; I see. We can't have that. So you found him out, did you ? Well, we could'a told you a thing or two about Wally Bateman, couldn't we, Ned ? "

" I'd say we could," agreed the other boy.

" Ned, meet our one and only Phil Janey. Phil, meet Ned Horby."

Ned came from the other side of Len, a much shorter and slighter lad, and his exceedingly neat little body was prinked out in such bright colours that it was clear he cared no more than Phil Janey for drabness. Like the youths of Elizabethan London, four hundred years before he trod its streets, Ned was " expressed in fancy ". A puritan eye would have found his suit too vivid a blue, his shirt too bold in its stripes, his brown shoes too red with their ox-blood polish ; and his cap too light a grey and pulled too far to one side. It must have condemned this loud attire as peacockery ; and such it certainly was ; but it was also, like the paint on Phil Janey's lips, and the varnish on her pointed nails, and the genteel mince in her walk, a lavish flowering from unseen roots of hunger and protest and escape. Suit, shirt and tie were so new that they appeared to have been bought but yesterday. A loose fitting of the suit round neck and loins showed that it had come off the rod of ready-mades ; but this was no shortcoming in Phil Janey's eye, who saw nothing but ready-mades on the boys in her streets. She thought he was dressed very posh-like.

" This is Ned Horby, Phil."

Phil Janey smiled, put her head to one side and said, " How do you do ? " very genteel.

" Pleased to meet you, lady. What you ordered ? Port ? No, turn that off. You can't drink Sam's mucky old port. Have something that you'll feel where it hits you. Give her a double whisky, Sam."

" Oh no, I don't like whisky, please. I can't bear it."

" Well, give her a double gin. A gin and Eye-tie, see. That'll make her love me." His words were a showing off, like his wear. So was the wad of pound notes from which he paid. " Take a drink out of it yourself, Sam. Now come here, lady, and sit between Len and me—between Len and I, I *should* say. Who are you, what's your name, and what do you do ? "

" My name's Phillis Jane Carman, if you want to know, and I work in Struwell's Gown Factory, Hoxton Rise."

" Is that so ? " But he wasn't really listening. He was looking at his reflection in the wall-mirror, between the spirit bottles and glittering glasses ; and adjusting the brand-new tie.

" And what do *you* do," asked Phil Janey, who was now seated on a stool between them with her handbag on the counter. " What's your work, may I ask ? Oh no, I'm not nosey, any more'n you."

" Me ? What do I do, Len ? "

" He's a carpenter and joiner, Phil. Yes, that's what he is. A carpenter and joiner. That's correct."

" Well . . . perhaps . . ." said Ned.

" A carpenter and joiner," persisted Len, " and he works

for old Job Hartney in Garrett's Place. A thoroughly respectable lad."

" Officially," said Ned.

Phil Janey turned to him. " What do you mean, ' officially ' ? "

" You don't suppose I'm content with a carpenter's wage, do you ? If so, you're doughy. Less than two bob an hour ? Not likely, sweetheart. I got other ways of raising an income." He lit a cigarette, tossed the match on to the floor for someone else to pick up, and then, gripping the cigarette in the joint of his first and second fingers, drew it from his mouth. " Nor am I going on with the carpentering for ever. Not if I know it," he said, and spat a flake of tobacco away. " I want to get somewhere and *be* someone. Anything wrong in that ? "

" Why, what are you going to do ? " asked Phil Janey.

" *Going* to do ? I done it already."

" Oh you *are* being mysterious," she protested coyly. " Why can't you talk sensible ? I don't know what you're hinting at."

" I just mean that I'm trying out other lines rather than staying on for ever at less than two ogg an hour."

" Well, can't you tell us what they are ? "

" Tell you some time, perhaps."

" Yes," said Len, who'd been musing on a different topic, " he comes from a very respectable family. Chapel, and all. His old dad worked for Job Hartney donkey's years, and now wants the boy to follow in Father's footsteps. So does his ma. Doubt if they'd approve of his palling up with me."

Phil Janey, slightly abashed by this allusion to his Borstal background, dropped her eyes and looked at her handbag on the counter.

" To hell with what they approve," said Ned and, transferring the cigarette to his thumb and second finger, he tapped the ashes from its end with his forefinger, as if committing them to perdition with anything else that might encumber him on his way. Replacing the disencumbered cigarette between his lips, he mumbled while the cigarette danced, " Now drink up, Babe. Put that stuff where it'll do some good, and I'll get you another. Come on : pull out the old plug and let it gurgle down."

" Oh, you do talk dreadful," she chided, and drank. Conscious that he was watching her as she drank, and appraising her, she looked from the corners of her eyes at him and, meeting his eyes, saw for the first time that they were brown and large and singularly beautiful. A small slight lad with small face and small features, his eyes seemed quite extraordinarily large. And quite unnaturally beautiful. The left eye winked at her. She smiled, but instantly looked down again.

" Yes," said Ned, still staring at her profile, " she's sweet and I love her. Len, I haven't seen anything as nice as this for ages. Believe it or not, I love her enough to stand her another drink. Same again, please, Sammy boy."

" Oh no——" objected Phil Janey.

" Same again, Sam," ordered Ned, imperious, unheeding, and very masculine even if (and posssbly because) he was small. " What I want to know, Len, is, When's she going to meet us again, and need you be there when she does ? "

" Oh, don't be so silly," she protested—pleased.

" It's not that I don't like you, Len. You been a good friend to me, and all that, but it's just that I think you'd kind'a dilute things. As you know, I like my liquor neat."

" Oh, don't be such a silly cake," continued Phil Janey.

" She won't want to meet you, Ned, without me to look after her," submitted Len. " She's a very respectable girl— most of the time."

" And what's wrong with me ? I'm a perfectly respectable young carpenter and joiner. You said so yourself. And I go to chapel sometimes with the old man."

" Yeah, good idea that. Puts 'em off the scent. Personally I go to Little Bread Street Church, Reverend Baynes."

" Oh, you *don't* ! " Phil Janey denied, archly.

" Don't I ? Must'a got that wrong."

" Listen, beautiful," Ned intervened. " If you come and meet me tomorrow, I'll take you for a ride."

" That's just about what he will do, Phil. A ride. That's correct."

She turned to Ned, eyes wide open. " A *ride* ? "

" Absolutely," he nodded. " Yes."

" What, in a car ? "

" Absolutely. Yes."

" You're not telling me you got a car ? "

" I certainly am. A last year's Rambler Sixteen. A sweet and lovely thing. A real jammy doughnut."

" But how—how's that ? "

" Oh, hell, it's out now. To tell the honest truth, Babe, I'm a motor salesman on the sly."

" Gawd, that's a hot one," laughed Len.

" Well, so I am, aren't I ? Absolutely."

" Right enough. That's correct. Go on with the tale."

" That's my other line at the moment, honey. I got to sell this car some time—to tell the honest truth, that's what I been talking to Len about—but I needn't do it at once. So I'll take you for a ride if you'll come."

" Oh, do ! Oh, that'll be lovely. When ? "

" Tomorrow. Morrow evening, eh ? "

" But it'll be dark then."

" Never mind. It's fun in the dark. A ride through the night like Dick Turpin."

" Oh yes, yes ! Into some nice country."

" Ach, hell, come away ! " Ned muttered in dropped tones and, resting the half-smoked cigarette on his lips, picked up his glass. " Too many bloody people."

The slack period between six and seven o'clock had passed, and customers were coming into the bar. There were now two other men seated at the counter with their feet on the rungs of their high stools and their knees apart. One was a thin young man in a pork-pie hat and crumpled grey mackintosh ; the other a large man of middle age in a bowler and open blue overcoat. Beyond them was a fat woman in a feathered toque and a fur stole. And all three, side by side, leaned on the counter fingering their glasses and lipping their cigarettes in silence. The smoke from the cigarettes lifted and spiralled into blue haloes above their heads.

" Come away, beautiful," repeated Ned, pushing her by the elbow to a far corner. " Couldn't we go somewhere where we could kiss, not you and Len, and still less me and Len, but you and I ? Do you know the guy in the bowler, Len ? "

" No. Thank God."

" Nor me, either, but you never know who's what in these days. I wouldn't put it past the cow in the pussy being a busy."

" Oh, no, she ain't. I know every bleeding split in this division."

" You don't ! Don't kid yourself. They're always changing 'em."

" Why, are you afraid of detectives ? " inquired Phil Janey, as he pushed her forward. By now she had her suspicions about Ned's money-raising lines, but she didn't want to pursue them too far lest they raised a barrier between her and the night ride.

" Not I, Babe ! They got nothing on little Ned. But they don't love Len, as I think you know. And, between you and me—between you and I, I mean—there's no reason why they should."

" There's nothing they can pin on me," said Len.

They sat themselves at a corner table, Ned and Phil Janey on a settee with their backs against the wall, Len on a chair by the table's side. Ned, looking at the wall-mirror behind him, brushed back his greased black hair, wiped the now greased hand on the plush of the settee, and pulled down his new shirt cuffs so that they and their large gold links should show.

" Tomorrow night then. Is that it, Kiddy ? "

" But couldn't we go on Saturday afternoon and right out into the country ? "

" Take you Saturday too."

" Saturday too ! Oh, would you ? Oh lovely ! And right out'a London ? Into real country ? Out as far as the sea ? "

" Absolutely. I'll guarantee to reach the sea in an hour and a half."

" Oh ! " She just breathed the syllable in her delight. " I only been once to the sea, and I loved it."

" Gee, I been often. Often and often."

" It's a long time ago," continued Phil Janey, savouring the memory, " but there were hills, I remember, running along by the sea."

" That's right. The Downs. We'll see 'em and climb 'em."

" Oh . . . how . . . how marvellous ! "

He put his arm around her and drew her against him. " Give us a kiss, then."

She snuggled into him but did not turn up her face, so he commanded, " Come on, Babe : give us your gob and let's kiss it " ; and she had hardly time to say, " What a way to talk ! " before he had masterfully forced her face round and upward and was pressing his lips heavily on hers. Her heart began to pulse with desire and love.

" If you were a gentleman, Len, you'd leave us," said Ned, drawing her closer.

" Maybe," said Len, as one who had no immediate intention of moving. " And again, maybe not."

" Will you come and fetch me at my flat ? " asked Phil Janey, anxious that Mrs. Ansty and all the other occupants of No. 17 should see her friend with his car.

" No, you'd better come and meet me at the garridge."

" ' Garridge ', ha ! " scoffed Len.

" Well, the place where I keep the old bus."

" Oh no—please—why ? "

" Because—oh I don't know, hang it, you're very sweet, where did you say you lived ? "

" Monmouth Crescent."

" Oh yes, Monmouth Crescent . . . and it'll be fairly dark. I'll come, but for Gee's sake, don't keep me waiting. To tell the honest truth, I didn't ought to be driving this car, because I'm only selling it—that's right, isn't it, Len ?—but it's honest enough if I pay for the petrol, see. I'm not kidding : you come at once when you hear me honk because, see, there's another point. Yes." He seemed more pleased with this explanation than with the previous one. " To tell the honest truth, I haven't got a driving licence."

§

And on the Friday evening the long black Rambler Sixteen was speeding in the dark through North Finchley and Totteridge and High Barnet towards Barnet Common. And within the speeding black box Ned, at the wheel, was showing off before his girl : now driving with one hand while the other picked up her fingers and kissed them, now drawing her into his side and nearly having a collision but still managing to swerve the car into safety without taking his arm from her waist ; and between these acts singing loud and long like a man coming home from an outing by the sea. Now they were at Stirling Corner among the farms, and he turned the car on to a hedged cart-track leading to Rowley Lane and Rowleygreen Farm. He switched off the engine and the dashboard light and, putting his arm round her again, said, " My God, I been waiting for this all day—yepp, and all night too. Beautiful, I love you. D'you love me likewise ? "

" I like you a lot." She nestled into his side gratefully, and soon, the darkness engulfing them, and each stirred by the feel of the other's body, he told her she was the sweetest thing he'd met for ages, and she told him " Don't be soft ", which meant that she liked it and wanted more ; and he said " Soft, am I ? ", and she answered " No, you're sweet ", and pressed harder against him.

Then there was silence in the car to match the dark silence outside and the darkness in their minds where neither had sight, or cared to have sight, of anything ahead of them. But being a man with a receptive female in his arms he soon began to brag about his past distinctions and present powers.

"Do you like this car? I may get another like it after I've sold this one. I'll buy one for keeps and take you out often."

"Oh, lovely," she said, only half believing.

"Yes." A hesitation here. Shut in by this surround of deep and empty darkness he seemed to want to tell her something, but was not yet resolved to do so. "Did you notice anything about this car?"

"No. How do you mean?"

"Anything different, like?"

"No."

"Nothing about its front or its arse?"

"Don't use words like that. You do talk awful sometimes."

"You noticed nothing, back or front?"

"No."

"Oh, well. That's just as well."

"What are you getting at, Ned?"

"Never you mind."

"Oh, tell us. Do tell us." She was looking up at his dark profile silhouetted against the dim grey square of the driver's window. "You must tell us now."

He seemed to ponder something, thrusting his jaw forward and sideways and holding it there. He withdrew his arm from around her, lit himself a cigarette, and replaced the arm. Then, gripping the cigarette in the joint of his first and second fingers, he removed it, blew out a jet of smoke and asked, "How's the old man?"

"What old man?"

"Your dad."

"Oh, he's all right. I don't see so much of him."

"Still giving the straight life a go?"

Abruptly she turned her face from him and drew an inch away. "What do you mean?" she asked sullenly; and he pulled her close again.

"He was a real whole-time screwsman in his day, wasn't he?"

She dropped her head and didn't answer; and he went on: "Don't be a boob, ducky. I know all about it. Len told me. And you needn't be ashamed of him. I'm on his side. Absolutely, yes. My quarrel with him wouldn't be because he

271

was an honest-to-God cracksman but for having had so many tumbles. I don't reckon he used his brains enough."

She shifted impatiently. " It's only luck if you don't tumble every time."

" Oh, no, it isn't, my lovely one. It's just a matter of making use of your loaf. I reckon that, given brains, the odds are all in your favour."

" You don't know anything about it."

" Don't I ? That's your idea, is it ? Well that's where you're a little bit off the map." Relaxed in the darkness, shut away from the living world by this waste of silence, he must complete the braggartry. " Do you suppose I really bought this car ? "

" Why ? Didn't you ? "

" Don't be daft. Where'd I get money to buy cars ? I knocked it off."

" *Stole* it ? "

" Absolutely. Why not ? And I suppose you wouldn't know that I done a nice little job last Sat. ? "

" A burglary ? "

" What d'you suppose it was : a sick visiting ? "

" I don't believe you. You're just sprucing."

" Am I, Baby mine ? Don't you kid yourself. It was a smashing little bust. A hundred-per-cent. success."

Hardly knowing whether she was disturbed by this revelation, but eager to hear a thrilling story, she answered nothing and left him to speak. And his voice went on in the darkness.

" It was the first I ever done, I don't mind telling you. And it come off as clean as a whistle. I used my brains, you see. Most burglars haven't any to use ; that's the trouble. I put in good staff work. Don't think it was anywhere near here ! *Course* not. Nor that it was a house that was occupied. No, my child, it was a dead gaff. And I done it on my own. I'm one of those who never believe anyone can do a job properly except myself. Can't help it : that's me. It was at a place called Horley, a place for nobs who work in London but like to live in the country. And nice posh houses they got. I first cocked an eye on 'em when we was helping out a local contractor there. Strike me blind, I thought, looking down from a sash window I was fitting, those are drums that ask to be screwed. High hedges all round and back doors where they ought'a be—at the back. And everything quiet, because the

272

people's mostly out and ain't got no servants these days. So what do I do? I get the local directory to see who lives in those nice quiet houses. Staff work, see. And I see that one of the nobs is His Honour Judge Charles P. Hendry. And immediately I think, What ho! fun if my first job's at an old judge's. Course he's only a County Court Judge but I'll lay he made it hot for some of us lads when he was a barrister. O.K. Last Sat. I go down to pipe off his drum and if things are favourable to visit it or one of the others. I go in my best suit, you bet, properly mushed up. Very important, that. I take a walking stick and swing it like I'm enjoying my Saturday walk. I get to the road and the old judge's house certainly looks as quiet as a warehouse on Sunday. But I don't sound it yet : oh, no, I go next door and ring. An old cow in an apron comes to the door, and I ask, very polite, ' Is Mrs. Hughes in ? '—no such name in the directory, sweetheart, you see. Staff work. She says, ' No such name here ' ; I looks at a letter in my hand and say, ' But this is Number Eight, isn't it ? I wonder could it be next door ' ; and she says, ' No, that's The Saffrons. That's Judge Hendry's and he's away. There's no one there.' So obliging! Obviously Fate is on my side, so I thank her, walk out of the road swinging my stick, lest she's watching, but at about hah' past four when everybody's more interested in their tea than in little Ned, I come back." Was his constant use of the words " Little Ned " a grasping of the nettle of his smallness? " The rest was just plumb easy. Before they done washing up their tea things I'm coming out of His Honour's gate, bold as brass and carrying one of his suit cases loaded with the stuff. Fine ! Len flogged the stuff for me and got sixty nicker for it. How's that for a first go ? My only mistake was to be too ambitious first time and make the case too blasted heavy. A bit risky to take that load past a ticket collector and be remembered, so O.K., I take a car. And that's what I mean exactly. I squint at every car till I see this one which I can pretend I think is a taxi ; and in I get and off we go. First I think I'll abandon the car in Brixton, but then I think, why the hell ? Len had got me a nice coachhouse in an old mews to hide the hot stuff in—staff work again, lady !—so why shouldn't I stow the car there ? And there it's been, my sweet, till tonight. Len and I changed the number plates. Dead easy ; he'd learned the tin-smith's trade in the Borstal place

273

on purpose for this kind of thing. All he wanted was some tin plate and some black and white paint, and the new ones were on. That's why I asked you whether you'd noticed them. And had you? No. The licence has been altered to match the plates ; the engine number's a goner ; every kind of paper's been cleaned out of the car ; and now there's absolutely nothing to identify it. Absolutely nothing at all. There are thousands of these black Ramblers on the road. Still, I kep' it locked up. I only brought it out for you, because I've fallen for you, see. Pleased, Beautiful ? "

Still not certain what she felt about this tale, Phil Janey could not answer ; and Ned, apparently wondering of a sudden if his braggart tongue had cheated his brains and told too much, said, " All that's absolutely secret, see. You'd never split, would you ? "

" Of course not."

" No, I know you wouldn't." And to make more sure of this, since he was a man of brains who neglected not the smallest precaution in his staff work, he added, " My God, if anyone grassed me I'd mark 'em for life. If I couldn't do it before the bogies nailed me, I'd do it afterwards, even if it was ten years afterwards—yes, and even if they only done it carelessly. No one shops me and gets home with it."

Neither spoke more ; they seemed submerged in the dark silence of the car, and the car in the silence around. He kissed her many times, and she accepted the kisses, but when he tried to take what she held to be liberties, she pushed his enterprising hand half-humorously away, saying, " No, no ; I thought you was a gentleman."

" So I am ; everytime ; but what's ungentlemanly in this, eh ? "

" I don't know you yet."

" But you like me ? "

" Yes. I like you."

" Well, then. Why shouldn't—— ? "

" If I like you, it doesn't mean I make myself cheap."

" Cocky little beast, aren't you ? "

" Oh, I'm not ! No, please, I'm not. I'm not a cocky thing relly. It's just that—well, I'm pretty particular, you see."

" Are you, indeed ? But listen, ducks, you're letting me come home with you tonight, aren't you ? "

" Of course not. What next ? What cheek ! "

" *Not ?* "

" No. No fear."

" But you used to let Wally Bateman. Len told me so."

" Yes, and he learned me not to let anyone else in a hurry.
Besides tomorrow's Saturday, and Mrs. Ansty doesn't go out to
work. She'd know."

" That's all bull and bunk. I'd see she didn't know."

" It isn't bunk. It's just sense."

" Well, are you ever going to let me ? "

" I don't know. That's all according. All according to a
lot o' things, mind."

" Is it ? I see. Oh, very well."

Perceiving at once the new sourness in his tone, she said,
" Have some sense, Ned. It's nice just like this " ; and tried
to sweeten him by nestling closer.

But he did not respond, and his arm about her slackened.
The small dosage of sour resentment which he'd injected into
his veins had now coursed over his whole system and poisoned
it. He sat there, sullen and immobilized ; and she sat impatient and undisposed to offer any more solatiums. She was
quite within her rights in refusing to allow him those liberties.
After all, she had her feelings. She didn't like to feel she was
anyone's pick-up. Sometimes these boys were beyond anyone's patience. They just took a girl for granted, and no girl
worth anything wanted to be taken for granted. Let him
speak first ; she wasn't going to. But he did not speak ; he
did not move for some time ; and then he angrily snapped
on the dashboard light and switched on the engine. She saw
the lit clock on the dashboard, and she was trapped into saying,
" My ! Coo ! Is that the time ? Quarter to eleven ? "

The clock on the dashboard stood at eighteen minutes to eleven.

" No," he replied moodily. " That bloody clock doesn't
go. It's half-past nine, and I'm going home."

" Home ? Now ? "

" Yes, of course. Absolutely. Why shouldn't I ? There's
nothing doing here."

" All right," she agreed, now as sulky as he. " Please yourself. I don't care."

He backed the car out of the lane and turned its head southward. And in a minute the black Rambler was sweeping through
the traffic at dangerous speeds and carrying them, boxed within
it, side by side, in an unforgiving silence. As they approached

Monmouth Crescent, she relented so far as to ask, " Shall
you come for me tomorrow as you promised ? "

" Tomorrow ? "

" Yes. You said you'd take me to the sea."

" No. I can't come tomorrow." He offered no explanation.

" Why ? You said you would. Why can't you ? "

" Because I don't want to."

" All right. Please yourself. I don't care. . . . Shall I see
you again ever ? "

Determined to hit her and hurt, he said, " I shouldn't think
so," and as they swung into the Crescent, added, " Remember,
I'd mark anyone who grassed me. And mark 'em for life.
Not a doubt about that. Here you are. Get out quick."

" All right. I don't need to be ordered about." She averted
her eyes that he might not see the tears. " Good night, Ned."

" Good night." The car door banged and the car raced
guiltily out of the Crescent into the High Street.

§

Her grievances fidgeted and fretted in Phil Janey's heart as
she walked to her work next morning, but they had not so
heavy a tread as those old lodgers, the loneliness and the sadness. Soon it was these two black-veiled widows who held the
floor and did the talking. " You liked him, you really did,
and now he's gone off in a proper huff. He's gone for good,
as like as not. And, say what you like, he was ever so charming,
and ever so handsome." Soon they persuaded her that she'd
liked him better than any fellow she'd met for ages. She was
a little frightened of him, yes, but excited by him and ready to
love. The harshness beneath his gaiety and charm stimulated
her almost as much as it antagonized her. " After all, all men
are like that." Nor had that tale of the housebreaking driven
her away from him ; her attitude to society and the police
was too splenetic for that. No longer would she care much
what a fellow did by trade so long as she could love him. In
the blend of gentilities, umbrages, ambitions, pugnacities and
loyalties that made up Phil Janey, old Carman's daughter,
there was even something that was quite ready to be married
to a desperado. If some other part of her wanted him to make
his money in a more gentlemanlike profession, it was less because

burglary was legally wrong than because it was a mug's game which you couldn't win.

Oh, well, he was gone, and a quick little hope had died. The trip to the sea and the hills was off. Off for good. " There's nothing for a girl unless she allows liberties." And she'd been looking forward to that ride all yesterday. Oh, well. . . . But all the morning, as she sewed and machined at her bench, she sewed up and stirred up her disappointment too, till at last it was an angry despair that drove her, when the day's work was done, to the post office in Hebron Town High Street where she had twenty-two shillings and ninepence in the Savings Bank. She cashed it all, determined to go alone to the sea. She would go tomorrow on a Sunday coach trip. She would sit at the window of the coach and see the country in its autumn dress, and she would walk on those hills she remembered between the patterned landscape and the far blue sea.

But on the Sunday morning, at nine o'clock, when she was hardly yet dressed, the horn of a motor sounded a peremptory summons beneath her high window. Twice, thrice, and, impatiently, emphatically, a fourth, fifth, and sixth time, it called to her or to someone. She looked down and there was the shining black Rambler with Ned at its window, looking up.

An imperious gesture of his hand beckoned her down ; and when she was at the car door, he commanded, " Come on ! "

" But——"

" Come on, I say ! Don't keep me standing about. We're going to the sea, aren't we ? "

" Oh, Ned ! Are we ? "

" Of course. But for Gee's sake be quick."

He was not going to explain his change-about. She could think it was forgiveness, or a dislike of disappointing her ; or she could think what she liked. Actually it was the triumph of desire over anger. Desire for her lips, limbs, and narrow body had had a day and night to swell in, and this morning it had forced him to pull out the car, not without petulance, and bring it to her door. Desire had triumphed also over any fear that the car might be recognized. Not a soul had turned to look twice at it on Friday ; why should they today ? Not a chance in a hundred thousand that it'd be identified. Why—hell !—there was nothing in it or on it or under it by which it could be identified.

It was a gracious October day of clean sunlight and mid-spring warmth, and to Phil Janey the happy sun, the glistening car, and the warm air in which one could already smell green grass and the sea, composed a solvent in which piques and huffs were annihilated. Away with all dudgeon ; away with past and future ; be happy today. She dashed up the stairs for a hat and coat, and dashed down again, hoping that Mrs. Ansty was peering at the car from her ground-floor window.

Opening the door of the car, she saw that Ned was dressed for the holiday in entirely new clothes. Full of new money, he had probably bought them yesterday : brown sports jacket, green shirt, grey slacks, *suède* shoes.

" Golly, you do look nice," she said. " Ever such a gentleman."

And she herself stepped into the car with some dignity and sat herself beside him like a lady.

They travelled down towards the sea at Brighton, one of an endless chain of Sunday cars. They ran into the crowded town and drove along its miles of sea-front. They visited its piers. They drove slowly over the Downs through the weak, frail sunlight ; and then, leaving the car on a chalk road, pressed up into the wind on Ditchling Beacon. From the summit they looked down on an English landscape bathed in the beauty of October : misty but deep blue sky, rose-touched clouds, smoke plumes lifting from leaf bonfires in the chequered fields, and an opal haze along the horizon, veiling a sweep of grey-blue hills.

" Oh its too, too lovely," said Phil Janey.

They walked along the ridge and, hand in hand, ambled back to the car. And not once in the bright daytime, neither in any secret crevice of the Downs nor in the close privacy of the car, did he seek more than a kiss and a tight hold ; but he spent his money on her prodigally that he might be justified in a large request—or angry demand—later on.

Sitting in the car towards evening, in the sweet green somnolence of a lane, she drowsy within his arms, he patting and pressing her breast, she spoke again of his adventure in Horley eight days before.

" Aren't you at all afraid ? " she asked.

" What of, honey ? "

" Of their finding out who it was."

" Not one fear in hell."

" But why ? "

" Because I've absolute confidence in myself, see. There's no reason on God's earth why they should hang that job on me. *I* saw to that."

" I've heard Dad say that ; and they come for him."

" Listen, Babe ; the busies've got no dabs of mine, and in any case I lef' none there. I wore kid gloves like a gent. No one saw me ; *that* I'll lay ; and if they did, they didn't suspect such a nice gentlemenly little lad. The chat's all disposed of. If I'd any fear a week ago, which I hadn't, I got none now. The job's more'n a week old, and in that sort of bust, if they're going to get you at all, they got to get you while it's hot. Everyone knows that."

" But this car ? Aren't you at all afraid about that ? "

" Not one bit, my beautiful. I've lef' nothing inside or out to recognize it by. When I do a job, I do it properly."

" Are you going on with—that sort of business ? "

" Bet your sweet shirt I am ! And I'll give you two reasons for why. First, as your old dad'll tell you, it's the only game where there's any big money for the likes of us, and I intend to have my share. I'm ambitious, you see. When I got all the money and the kind'a position I want, I'll rest. I'll be the good little c'pittalist then. Not 'ahf ! As I work it out, there's no sense in being anything but a c'pittalist or a crook. The c'pittalist makes the mugs create his dough for him, and the crook takes what he can of it back. Both, as far as I can see, are con men and wise guys, bleeding the saps everywhere, and the only difference I can see is that the c'pittalists have the cops on their side. They got Scotland Yard in their pay."

" That's what Dad says and what I sometimes think. But how if you get caught ? "

" I've no intention of getting caught. The cops'a got nothing about little Ned Horby in their cupboard ; and they're not going to have anything ever. They think he's a nice little joiner, and so he is, but not every hour of the day. Secondly, my sweet, it's exciting ; and I need a spot of excitement now and then. One can only live once. If I had bags of money, I'd go to Switzerland, like the swells do, and skee down the mountains or shin up 'em, hanging on by my eyebrows——"

" I've always wanted to go up mountains."

" —but, as I haven't the rhino yet, and till I have, I'll shin up the ivy to the first-floor window and skee down the stack pipe. And one day I'll go to Switzerland too. Cold ? "

" A little, p'raps."

" Yes, it's getting cold. Like to go back ? "

"Oh, I don't know. I love it here. I've never had such a day."

It was but four o'clock, and the late October sun was low and large in a deep blue sky. The shadows of the trees lay in a purple lacework on the cream ground of the lane. Behind the nearer trees with their bronze and copper leaves the distant woods were blue. Every now and then a tired bronze leaf gave up the ghost and sank like a bird to the camber of the furrowed road.

"You're shivering a little. I tell you what. We'll get back and go somewhere where there's a bit of fire."

"Oh, well . . . if you like. All nice things come to an end."

"Where shall it be? What about your flat?"

"Lor' no! Not on a Sunday. Mrs. Ansty'll be in."

"Damn the old mare. I know! I know what we'll do." He started the engine and backed the car towards the mouth of the lane. "We'll get some grub in a pub. and we'll take some skimish with us, and go to our carpenter's shop. There's a gas stove there."

"But isn't it locked? How are you going to get in?"

"My dear sweet simple babe!" They were now running westward towards the high road, where they would join the endless fleet of cars, London bound; and he held up a six-penny fingernail file between her and the apricot sunset sky. "Aren't I a professional?"

§

Messrs. J. Hartney and Son's yard lay behind the small shops of Cornmeal Street. You approached its wooden gates by a long cobbled passage. Cornmeal Street and Jason Road converged upon the Circus, making one of the seven Corners, and this long passage joined the two roads like the crossbar of a capital A. The yard, a square cobbled area, had once been the yard of Garrett's Livery and Bait Stables. In some dead yesterday when the merchants and gentlemen of the Fields (long abed now) had their horses at livery, it had echoed with the stamping of hooves and flushed the air with the scents of corn, dung, and the stale of horses. Now all that remained of Garrett's Stables, apart from the buildings, was the name, Garrett's Place, which had attached itself to the long narrow lane. Now the coachhouses and horse boxes were stores for

Job Hartney's planks, ladders, ceiling boards, paint drums and sacks of Portland cement, while the yard itself was a floor for scaffold poles, hand trucks, drain pipes, chimney pots, stacks of slates and tiles, and bins of sand, lime, and ballast.

Ned stopped the car in the lane by the gates. He locked the door and led Phil Janey through the full and littered yard to an outside stairway which climbed to the door of a long room above the stables. The steps of the stairway were of coarsely-cut wood and might have been the steps of a scaffold. Reaching the top platform, Ned straddled the air with a foot on the handrail and a foot on a window sill and, forcing his nail file through the sashes, thrust back the bolt. He pulled down the upper sash and stepped over it into the darkness beyond. Phil Janey heard him draw back the knob-latch of the door.

She stepped into the long room. It was occupied by a deep gloaming rather than by a complete darkness, and this because of its many unblinded windows and the night's unclouded stars. She could see, one behind another, the heavy carpenter's benches with their vices and their spatter of sawn planks, nail boxes, tool bags, and discarded tools at rest. Under the roof were racks of small timber, and against the walls tilted planks, laths, matchboards and sheets of hardboard and three-ply. The close atmosphere, imprisoned now for the week-end, was heavy with the smell of glue from the pots and of wood shavings and sawdust from the floor.

Taking her hand, he led her past the benches to a screened-off windowless corner which was the office of the foreman carpenter. Here, besides a cheap writing-desk bestrewn with plans and bills, was a rusted gas fire and an old listing upholstered chair, its leather torn and its fibre stuffing spewing forth towards the floor. The smell of the fibre and the dust hung in the cubicle's stale, cabined air.

" Good," said Ned, stooping to light the fire. " No one'll find us here. Come ! " And with the fire for their only light he drew her down to him on the chair.

" Phil," he whispered lovingly, and stroked her cheek, her arm, and her thigh.

She resisted his advances at first as a young lady was bound to do, but he only laughed and said, " You can scream your little head off, Beautiful, but nobody'll hear you here." And he continued the slow craft of a lover—there in the carpenter's shop. There in that dusty corner, on that old broken chair as it might have been a workman's bench, he pressed upon Phil Janey, now soft with love, and yielding, the pattern which in lonely hours he had designed.

§

Outside the car waited. It waited an hour, two hours, three, because a young man does not easily lay aside such labour as Ned was engaged on now. And some time in the third hour, the time being then eight minutes to twelve, a tall young policeman came measuring his beat, at the regulation pace of two and a half miles an hour, along the dark alley. Ian Ramsay, P.C. 965 of the Hamden Division. He looked without suspicion at the car standing against the wall. Like Ned Horby and many another young man, however, he was interested in all cars and would amuse himself identifying their makes, ascertaining their horse power, and guessing their dates. He needed to amuse himself now, for although he'd done only two hours of his night duty turn, he was—not to mince matters about it— bored stiff by the dark, the silence, and the general emptiness of the Fields. So he took his lantern off his belt and shot its beam on the car. " A Rambler Sixteen." But hardly had he said this than he remembered something, and a quaint little hope leapt within him. " GLA 7737 . . . Rambler Sixteen . . . black." Day after day the description had been read from the Stolen Car List to the lads paraded for duty. It had been read to them tonight, for this car was " still outstanding ". This exciting memory carried him back to eight days ago when he was on late turn and saw, at about seven in the evening, the lamp above the police box at Andersen's Corner twinkling like a lighthouse. Thrilled by the thought (for he was still a very young policeman) that similar lamps were beckoning to the police all over the seven hundred square miles of London, proud as a new boy of his Force, with its immense reach and its cold-steel efficiency, he had hurried to the box and heard the message, " GLA 7737 . . . Rambler Sixteen."

Could this be it, abandoned in a dark and empty lane? He looked at the number plates. H'mmm, yes ; dubious, very. The licence ? Not sure. Nothing on the outside to identify it as the wanted car. He tried the door. Locked. But the window on the near side was partly open and, remembering more of the description, he shone his torch on to the dashboard clock. Eighteen minutes to eleven. God! He kept the beam on the clock. The hands didn't move. " GLA 7737, Rambler Sixteen . . . Horley. . . . The dashboard clock has stopped at eighteen minutes to eleven."

Excitement inflated him so that he was at this moment the happiest of all the twenty thousand policemen encamped or on duty over London. The prize had come to him. To him ; and he one of the youngest and newest. What a beginning ! It was like winning a lottery which had twenty thousand subscribers. Surely he would get a commendation for this. He lifted the bonnet of the car, removed the sparking plugs, and hastened, at fully twice the regulation pace, to the box at Andersen's Corner. A lift of the telephone receiver to his ear, and the station was talking to him.

" Reserve here."

" This is 965 here. Is that you, Tom ? "

" Hallo, Mr. Ian Ramsay, how are you ? And what have you got ? A lost dog ? "

" Got ? I've got the Rambler Sixteen. And it's not abandoned either, if you ask me. I have reasons for supposing it's not. Unless I'm mistaken its present owner'll be coming along soon, and meantime I've pinched his sparking plugs."

" Smart young policeman ! "

" It's the bus all right, or I'll eat my hat."

" All right, all right, Rammy, don't be so cocky about it. You're not the first cop that's found a stolen car."

" Oh, you shut your face."

" Now then, now then ! Naughty, naughty. Temper ! O.K., Rammy, I'll report to the station officer. Keep moving, if it's cold out there. It's lovely in here, thank you. Don't disturb me more than you can help. If you want any help or advice ask a copper. 'Bye for now."

" 'Bye, you—— Tell the Sarge I'm keeping obbo on it."

And Ian Ramsay went back to the lane. The car was still there, standing against the wall like a forgotten thing. He placed himself behind it and taking his notebook from his overcoat pocket, made his notes as happily as a poet recording ideas for a poem. Date, hour, position of car : " stationary . . . facing south . . . approximately five feet from the gate of Messrs. J. Hartney and Son's building yard. . . ."

But now, not four minutes since he left the box, another car was coming quietly up the lane, a black Wolseley Fourteen. Good work. It pulled up some fifty feet from the Rambler, so as to be out of sight of the yard. It lay as close against the wall as a shadow. Almost you might say it leaned against the wall : a shy, retiring wallflower. Out of it stepped first the uniformed driver and then, with some awkwardness for he had a paunch to get past the steering wheel, Detective Sergeant Trapnell in an unbuttoned grey overcoat and with a grey hat on the back of his head. Evidence of hurry.

The two came towards him softly.

" Nothing doing yet, Rams ? "

" No, sarge. Not yet. You haven't given them much time."

" That was rather the idea, love. I suppose it can't have been abandoned here ? "

" What ? With its lights on ? "

" Might be."

" But there's a gent's overcoat left in it and a girl's scarf and a box of chocs. And fags."

" Yes ; and those aren't the original number plates."

" No. But they match the licence nicely here."

" Yes. Spot of forgery there, I fancy. Bright lad, our Ian, isn't he, Bert ? "

" I'll say so, sergeant."

" He's right : whoever they are, they'll come back. They've probably nipped in somewhere for a little of the you-know-what-I-mean."

" I suspect they're in there somewhere." Ian jerked his head towards the yard.

" And they've probably no right in there ; those are only sheds, aren't they ? Still, we won't show ourselves just yet, or he may peel off by some back door. We'll wait here and pick him up when he comes out. O.K., Ian, you stand by the car, and the minute you want help, stick up your arm. We'll be along then."

" O.K., sarge."

" All right. We'll be seeing you."

The sergeant and the driver went and hid behind the Wolseley. Ian stood behind the Rambler. All three remained as quiet and nearly as motionless as the cars. Not even the sergeant smoked. A crook at midnight would detect a glimmer at once, and as likely as not smell the tobacco before he'd seen the glimmer. Why, they'd be lucky, supposing it was a real crook, if he didn't smell the police car through the wall.

But now voices—young voices in the builder's yard. Here they were : a small and slight young man and a yet smaller and slighter young lady. They approached the car's off-door, and the youth, having the key in his hand put it to the handle. Ian Ramsay stepped forward, touched the youth on the arm, and immediately, at a word from the sergeant, his driver switched on the Wolseley's headlamps, flooding the Rambler with light.

" This your car, sir ? " said Ian to the youth.

The young man, suddenly blinded by the headlamps and apparently stunned by the sight of a policeman in their beams, had no answer ready. He stared terrified, blanched, sick. If ever a face was guilty——

" Of course it's my car. Howdyermean ? "

Ian changed his tone, speaking sharply. " I have reason to think this car was stolen."

" Stolen ? Howdyermean ? It wasn't. It——"

The youth, all thinking disordered, lugged open the door and tried to dive in, as if to race the car away, leaving all of them there in the dark, including his young lady.

" Oh no, brother ; not that ! Not quite so quick." And Ian put out one arm to stop the fugitive and flung up the other. Instantly, like the genie of the lamp. Sergeant Trapnell was at his side. Each of them, Constable and detective sergeant, grabbed an arm of the youth. He fought in a frenzy of disappointment and fear, and Sergeant Trapnell, who was no tender type with those who played rough, grabbed the boy's throat and pushed back his head. Between them they forced him against the wall. His breast panted, his mouth gaped, and in his eyes gleamed the mad anger of one who'd never believed he'd be caught. Sergeant Trapnell did the talking.

" Is that your car ? "

" Yes. Of course it's my car. Leave me alone."

" Good. It's your car. Sure it is. Well, now, where did you get it ? "

" That's my business."

" Ours too, laddie. Are you going to tell us where you got it ? "

" No."

" Not really ? "

" No. Absolutely, no. Leave me alone. I haven't got to tell you anything unless I want to."

" O.K. Have it your own way. We'll give you time to

think over that. But perhaps just to be pleasant and to keep the conversation going, you'd like to tell us what happened to the original number plates ? "

" Number plates ? Far as I know those are the original."

" I see. They're not nice new ones made to order."

" No. At least, I——"

" Oh, ' at least ' something ! At least what ? "

" I don't know anything about the number plates. I can't say anything about them. The car was given me by a man to sell for him."

" Ah ! You didn't buy it ? You had it given you ? "

" Well, I did, really, yes."

" And of course, for all you know, it may be a stolen car. That's why you tried to grease, is it ? Well, will you tell us, who is this man who gave it to you ? Ian, take the gentleman's name and number. . . . Well, who is he, son ? Don't you know ? Can't you think up something ? Not at once. Pity. Not so sudden, like. Well, why did you try to make a get-away, eh ? Because you knew the car was stolen ? "

" I didn't know that."

" Really now ? Do we know this lad, Ian ? "

" Don't think so, sarge."

" Well, you come along with us, my lad, and tell us a whole lot more. We're quite a bit interested in this car, and have a very good notion why it was stolen. Ever been in Horley, son ? "

They were now marching the youth towards the police car, and very small and fragile he seemed between the tall Ian and the big detective sergeant. His shoulders were hunched upward as he pulled against their hold, and his lower teeth were bared and pressed forward like the teeth of a bull dog. The young girl, running up, walked a few steps beside them.

" Ned ! . . . oh, darling ! . . ." she bewailed.

He shot his head round to her. " Oh, *you !* Go to hell," he cried in something like an agony. " If it hadn't been for you, you little bitch. . . ."

She stopped abruptly in the road and remained quite still.

Sergeant Trapnell shook his arm roughly as a warning. " Now then, you ! No insulting words and behaviour, please. Never mind him, my dear. Lend us a hand, Bert, and take him along. We don't need to trouble you, I don't think, miss. You go home quietly now, like a good girl."

CHAPTER SEVEN

CANON WELCOME was again playing opposite a column of the *Times*. Lying back in his deep armchair, in the after-breakfast hour sacred to work, he was gazing at a column in love. The date above the column showed an April day five months after that October midnight when the police walked away with Ned Horby, leaving Phil Janey in the lane. Certainly he glanced now and again at other columns and other pages, but always he came back to this one, the delight of his eyes. It enchanted him thus because it held a long letter signed " Humbert Welcome ". Ever since that correspondence in the *Times* had made the name of Canon Welcome familiar to the Editor, his letters, which were not infrequent, had been given a fair prominence, but never such a distinguished position as this. The letter stood at the top of Column five on the editorial page. Its first paragraph was in larger type than all the other letters, and one of these came from the Athenæum, another from a deanery. A leading article on the same page mentioned his letter. He, Canon Welcome, mentioned by name in a *Times* leader ! Not since the editors of *Who's Who* invited him to contribute a potted biography of himself had he known an hour as good as this.

Of course the subject in controversy was stirring a great interest. *The New Bishoprics* was the heading under which it was conducted. In the previous year three measures had received Final Approval at the Summer Session of the Church Assembly, each providing for the creation of a new see, or sees, by abstracting certain archdeaconries from an overgrown and unwieldly diocese ; and now these measures were about to come before the House of Lords for its consideration. There was excitement and debate in Church circles, and beyond, as to whether the Lords would pass them for the Royal Assent. And four days ago Canon Welcome, opening his *Times* at the breakfast table, had been chafed and inflamed by the sight of a letter from Tuppy Williams, now Archdeacon of Hamden, and by the prominence which the Editor had given it. It was a typically spiked and combative piece of writing : it scoffed at the " episcopalian reformers " with their enthusiasm for adding see upon see by the dismemberment of ancient historic dioceses ; it attacked the bureaucratic minds which were quite unqualified to estimate, and even possibly to perceive, the imponderable values of history, tradition, sentiment, and local feeling ; it declared with a ruthless lucidity that if Parliament had still the supreme authority over a National Church, then this was indeed a proper issue on which churchmen could appeal to Parliament for protection ; and it closed with an appeal to the Lords to throw out the ill-conceived measures and so save from disruption great and famous dioceses, some of which were older than the nation itself.

Canon Welcome had read this essay over his bacon ; and, because he still smarted at the memory of Tuppy Williams's appointment to the Archdeaconry, he had been outraged by it. It implanted in him the thought of a long, learned, and mordant reply. A reply as caustic and stinging as anything Tuppy could produce. A verbal cane for that bumptious boy. This thought became a worm in the brain which was not to be quieted till its will was done. The next two days he gave to the acquiring and ransacking of the pamphlets of the Additional Bishoprics Committee, so as to use their arguments as his own. For two days the work of his parish (so far as his intervention affected it at all) stood still. Very pleasing the finished letter ! Suave and sardonic, it reproached the Archdeacon for his Erastianism and rallied him for a Conservatism in Church policy that seemed quite unrelated to his revolutionary attitude to the Church's creed ; with a velvet-pawed stroking it complimented him on his distinguished career in the Church but reminded him that, in the main, it had been confined to university or capitular bodies and hardly qualified him to pontificate upon pastoral work ; and in a fine trumpet close it declaimed the writer's belief (as one who had laboured for years among the poor of London) that a score of new bishops, with a hundred suffragans to assist them, was scarcely more than the needs of the nation demanded.

And here, quite splendidly placed on the leader page of the first paper in the land, was the letter. Each time he read it through he approved its substance, organization, and style. It seemed as good at the seventh reading as at the first. No doubt Tuppy in his study had read it and was now sharpening his arrows, and poisoning their tips, for a characteristic reply ;

288

if so, so much the better ! Everybody of importance was reading this controversy ; let its waves beat about the name of Canon Welcome. Let Tuppy and others attack Canon Welcome for this or that ; let others rush to the support of Canon Welcome. In the realm of Advertising, as old Marcus Brumley, that shrewd expert in mundane things, was always saying, it was the name of a commodity, rather than any statements about it, which must be built into the minds of the people. It hardly mattered what was said about a trade name so long as a great deal was said. When one wanted a toothpaste one was certain to select a tube with a name one had heard of (though what one had heard, good or bad, was beyond recall) rather than one whose name was new ; and doubtless it was the same with prime ministers when they had to select from the counter a bishop or a dean. " Canon Welcome " he had always thought an excellent trade name, euphonious, suggestive, and memorable.

Some perhaps would attack him for his Socialism : good ; that was what he wanted. That was particularly desirable now that the Socialists, as astute old Marcus had foretold, had marched into power and looked like sitting enthroned for a decade. Let it be bruited about now, and as widely as possible, that he had joined the Labour Party even while they were still in opposition and when nobody expected their triumph at the polls. One paragraph of the letter he read again, hoping that the Prime Minister, who surely read his *Times*, had been impressed by it.

" The task of the Church does not lie in great historic dioceses, romantic though they are with their thousand years of history, but in the tiny compass of each individual soul whose life is of but seventy years span, and if, as seems certain, the creation of these new and small dioceses, and the diminishing of the old ones, will enable us to bring the full power of the Church to bear upon the souls of the poor in our great congested cities, especially upon the young and the lonely and the lost, then any parish priest like myself, who has to labour in crowded and difficult streets, will maintain that the removal of an ancient historic boundary and the inevitable but temporary distress to local sentiment, will be a small cost to pay."

He rearranged himself comfortably in his chair to read the whole letter again.

§

Shortly after joining the Labour Party Canon Welcome received an invitation from the Anglo-Slav Society to become a " supporter ". Nominally the Society existed to promote friendship with all Slav peoples, but in fact, and inevitably, as was universally known, it worked for a greater understanding of, and a considerable tenderness towards, the Soviet Union. The notepaper on which the invitation came had the names of the Society's supporters tabulated down the left-hand margin, and Canon Welcome recognized among them many well-known names from the sciences, the professions, and the arts. Probably, thought he, they desired more clergy in this list and had therefore asked him, who was a canon and a member of the Labour Party. And since the Society claimed more than fifteen thousand members, and its " supporters " numbered less than a hundred, or some infinitesimal percentage, he had a strong desire to be thus numbered among the saints. It would carry the name " Canon Welcome " into fifteen thousand homes, and he wrote at once accepting the honourable position, though he had no love for the Russians but rather a terror of them.

That was many months ago, and now, three days after the publication of his *Times* letter, came a handsome card requesting his company at a Reception in the Porchester Room of the Mount Park Hotel in honour of the Foreign Minister of the U.S.S.R. who was in London at the time. Canon Welcome, though pretending to be unshaken and unexcited, was as pleased with this invitation as a child. Did not the Foreign Minister of the U.S.S.R. carry one of the dozen most famous (or notorious) names in the world ? Was not his, Canon Welcome's, selection as a guest a great compliment, since out of fifteen thousand only a hundred or two could be invited ? Was not the Mount Park Hotel one of the most expensive and luxurious in Mayfair ? Would not its sherry be the best ?

So at six o'clock on a Saturday he ascended the wide, gold-carpeted staircase of this palace to its famous Porchester Room. He climbed alone, the card having made no mention of a Mrs. Welcome. On the whole he was glad of this because in such an assembly a wife could be something of a shackle upon one's arm when one ached to escape and present oneself to an influential guest in the distance. She might even discern and silently disapprove of these somewhat pushing activities. Women, sheltered from the full impact of a competitive world, so often failed to perceive that one just had to push and shove a little if one was to get anywhere at all. No, best on this particular pilgrimage to travel light.

Mounting such a staircase, one cannot help feeling distinguished, handsome, and well-dressed, His best black whipcord suit was not three months out of the hands of Messrs. Wippell and Co. ; his hair was now all silver and most becoming above his round, pink, and (so he thought) youthful face ; and he had no doubt that even if he could hardly be described as one of the Higher Clergy, he looked more like one than most. He had an episcopal shape, and he stepped upwards with an episcopal air. At the top of the stairs he passed two splendid monumental flunkeys in knee-breeches, scarlet coats, and powdered hair, and if they seemed better suited to the levee of a king than to a party in honour of a Communist Commissar, well, Canon Welcome much preferred them to a revolutionary guard in their red caps of Liberty.

Another such flunkey just inside the great doors asked his name and bawled it to the vast spaces of the room, " Canon Welcome " ; and he passed through and smiled and shook hands with a fat little man and an appendant lady, not knowing in the least who they were ; and they smiled and shook hands with him, not knowing in the least who he was. He passed quickly on lest their ignorance should embarrass them. Recognizing no one in the room, he walked towards the long buffet table under the windows where he could initiate a brief but profitable how-do-you-do with a white-jacketed waiter behind the bottles, cocktail-shakers and glasses. Having accepted a sherry from this merry and obliging fellow, he sipped it and turned to survey the room.

At present it was far too vast for the company it held. A long hall of ivory and gold, it could be divided into three chambers by curtains of ivory and grey at two points where Corinthian columns stood away from the walls. Each of the three sections had a long Aubusson carpet of pink and pale blue on its glistening parquet, and a many-branched crystal chandelier hanging from its gilded ceiling. Slender white-and-gold chairs, upholstered in pink and blue to match the three carpets stood along the white walls as in a ballroom. Standing in such a luxurious and spacious chamber, and sipping a golden Amontillado, he enjoyed a most agreeable gilding and extension of his self-esteem.

Steadily the guests assembled, overlaying the elegant carpets, extinguishing the graceful chairs, and by no means improving the appearance of the room. Their multiplied chatter, to one who was not taking part in it, beat on the ears like the babel of a playground. A few of the men were well-dressed in formal black coats and striped trousers, but others brazenly paraded their Socialism with their slack tweeds and soft collars, and one or two (foolish adolescents from Bloomsbury and Chelsea, he surmised) carried their defiance of the bourgeois so far as to wear polo-necked jumpers or leather lumber jackets, or both. Loathsome little louts. Odious little Socialist oaves who made his mouth to purse and his nostrils to dilate. Why, the faces of some of them were dark and swart, and not even British. Others had young beards, black and gold, like Leonardo apostles. How came this Bloomsbury trash, immature and unwashed, to be invited as well as the distinguished and the important ? The sight of them diluted his pride in his invitation.

It was some comfort to recognize many well-known Labour M.P.s, though he was shocked at their careless, workaday suitings and still more, when he caught their voices, by their cockney or North Country accents. Glancing over the multitude, framed in this large gilded chamber, he asked himself, did not the picture symbolize a junction of two epochs. A palatial salon built and furnished for the gilded dignity of nobles and nabobs was now inherited and overrun by a new barbarian stock. Here was England's fine old mountain-stream of aristocracy and wealth meeting and blending with coarse waters from the lowlands and even with a thick brackish tide from Un-English seas. A pity. A very great pity. Even a disaster.

Now strangers beside him at the buffet were getting into conversation with him, and always his experience was the same : five minutes of formal talk and he descried someone he'd like to greet or be introduced to, and began to wonder how he could shake off his present encumbrance without hurting his feelings. See : the Minister of Health, familiar face of a hundred cartoons ; and now : yes—the Home Secretary ; and now, most famous of all, a portly figure familiar in half the countries and all the journals of the world, England's

Foreign Minister, to meet, on an uncontroversial carpet and with an expansive smile, his fiery opponent of the Council Chambers. Now at last he felt he was nearing the top of the world. If only one could somehow be introduced to these! Yonder were two bishops and a dean, the Bishops of Glossop and Newberry, and the Dean of Arminster, all known as Socialists, and all come together, probably, from the Athenæum. (He must get into the Athenæum.) Laying down his glass he was about to insinuate himself towards these powerful people, desirable as patrons, when a voice said, " Eh, boot it's Canon Welcome, Ah think. Canon Welcome o' Hamden Hill."

He turned to face a very squat and square young man, with features as thick as his limbs and a chin of unshaven baby-fluff ; one of the common young men whose presence at this party was so disappointing.

" Yes, Canon Welcome ; that's me," he admitted, with a deliberate smile, lest he hurt the lad.

" Aye, that's reight. Ah thowt so."

" Yes, it's right." He sustained the smile. " And you are . . . ? "

" Ah, boot you wouldna knaw me, Canon. Arthur Kershaw's me name, and Ah coom fra Hoodersfield—aye, good old Hooders-field—but Ah'm bein' ordained at Trinity and coomin' sah'th to work near you."

" What : in Hamden Hill ? "

" Nay ! " A horse could hardly say " Nay " more em-phatically, or with wider nostrils ; evidently the young man despised the bourgeois on Hamden Hill. " Ah'm goan' to work among the people. Father Anson's given me a title to St. Silas, Hebron Fields."

Father ! " Father " for old Percy Anson ! Then this whippersnapper was a cocky, aggressive, bull-dozing young Anglo-Catholic. A peculiarly repellent type.

" Oh, well then, we shall certainly have you as a near neighbour. That will be delightful, and you must come to the Vicarage and see me sometimes. The most interesting part of my parish is in Hebron Fields."

" Aye, that's so."

The arrogance of him ! Who the hell was he to pronounce on which was the most interesting part ? Still, Canon Welcome was not the man to crush him ; on the contrary he strove to remain the laughing fellow-guest. " There's the Colonial Secretary. Tell me, Mr. Kershaw, what are you and I doing in this *galère?* "

" In this . . . ? Pardon ? "

" In this galley—this very distinguished assembly."

" Oh, Ah knaw why they asked me. Ah'm t' Founder and Honnery Organizin' Secretary of t' Guild o' Christ the Carpenter."

" Guild of what ? "

" Christ the Carpenter. We're a league o' yoon'g Christians who believe that as followers of Christ, a workin' man, it's ahr duty to feight t'battles o't'workin' class, and that inevitably mak's us Socialists. Aye, and good lef' wing Socialists too ! Nowt pink abaht us."

" I see." Canon Welcome disliked the idea of this league intensely. " A good rich red, are you ? "

" Aye, that's aboot it." The young man sipped his Dry Martini and bit on a Canapé Diplomate, as if he'd sipped cocktails and chewed appetizers all his life. Most offensive. " But Ah'm glad to see you're a Socialist too, Canon. Right glad. Ah shouldn'a thowt it, summah."

" Is yours a big league ? "

" We've got seven thah'sand members aw'most and Ah affiliated it with'aht hesitation to Anglo-Slav Society. Ah mean," he added, chewing vigorously, " one's either on t'side o'democracy or one isn't."

" That seems true enough," laughed Canon Welcome, hardly listening to this limpet but watching the doors to see if any other distinguished persons who would be both accessible and valuable to a vicar were coming in.

" Aye. Ah mean, you're either on side of t'Soviets or of International Finance Capital."

" Again ? Say that again ? "

" Ah said you're either on t'side of Russia or of International Finance Capital."

" Are you ? "

" O' course you are."

" Isn't it possible to be on the side of neither ? "

" No, it isn't. It certainly isn't. Ah should'a thowt Karl Marx'd made that perfectly clear."

The damned, insolent, overbearing young blot !

" Aye, seven thah'sand, and still growin'," continued the

young man, chewing and sipping offensively. " We're strong in t'North, Ah doan' mind tellin' you."

" Then, may I ask, why have you come to a London parish ? "

" Ah thowt Ah could serve the interests of t'Guild better if Ah coom to London. It's too provincial like, at present. Besides, we want to wake oop t'Sah'th."

Canon Welcome now felt an itching desire to put the loathly little cub in his place without seriously hurting him. He almost regretted his soft inability to hurt him. If only he were Bettersby he'd excoriate the puppy with a few barbed words. But the best, the most discountenancing, which he could contrive, were, " Have you any strength at the Universities ? "

" Well, noa. Quite frankly, Ah'm no college man. Me feyther couldna afford to give me much schoolin'. Ah'm just a workin' lad fra Hoodersfield, tha knows, and prah'd of it. A grocer's shop i' Hoodersfield were my university, and I dare say Ah learned more there than ever you can learn at Oxford an' Cambridge. An' one thing it taught me, Ah don't mind tellin' you ; and that were to stand by me oan class and reckon 'em the best o' the boonch."

Abhorrent.

" Aye, it did an' all. Have another o' these, Canon. They're champion."

" Thank you. I will. . . . So you went to a Theological College, I suppose."

" Aye. St. Ambrose's. But Ah got me First in me Finals aw'reight, and Ah hope to take me L.Th. at Durham later. Here, mix me another o' these, waiter. Dry Martini it were, and don't spare the gin."

By now Canon Welcome knew all about him. He was a young shop assistant who'd taken up Anglo-Catholic Socialism as an engrossing hobby just as another would take up Art or Pacifism or Gang Thuggery. An unabashful little self-shover, he'd brought himself to the notice of some sentimental Anglo-Catholic vicar who'd collected the money for his Theological training ; and now, having used the North for his ladder, he'd come up to London where the prospects were wider and one's prominence greater. In other words, he was an ambitious young careerist using the Church for his own advancement. Obviously, he'd only come up to talk with him because he thought a local canon and rural dean might be of use to him in his career. Canon Welcome was strongly repelled by him.

And yet all he could say was, " Well, Mr. Kershaw, I hope you'll wake us up successfully."

" Eh, lad, boot Ah'll have a darned good try ! "

Lad ! The egregious young insect !

" Can Ah hope to mak' you a member, Canon ? "

" A member ? "

" Aye ; o't' Guild."

A *member !* A member only ! Not even a " supporter "— he, Canon Welcome ! A rank-and-file member of his filthy little guild. He to sustain with a subscription this band of bumptious young jack-puddings ! The sooner it dwindled and died the better. " No, thank you, my boy. I'm chairman and vice-president of Heaven-knows-how-many societies, and I daren't take on any more obligations. But I wish you all the success in the world." Extraordinary that one could say such a thing when what one really wanted was the earliest possible annihilation of his league and an early humiliation of the young man. " Ah, here he is ; here's the guest of honour ; here's the great man."

A sudden stilling of the manifold chatter, and a muffled stirring of all heads, had announced that the guest of honour was in the room. Aye (Canon Welcome couldn't get the horrible young man's idiom out of his head) there was the familiar little figure of the Russian Foreign Minister, with his round, crushed-in face, his pince-nez, and his brief moustache, shaking hands with the fat little nonentity by the door. Beside him, at his elbow, closer than a bride, stood a very young interpreter ; and behind him, at two paces distance, loafed three enormous, muscular, bear-like men, who watched the courtesies, unsmiling.

" Who on earth, and in the name of Marx and Lenin, are they ? " inquired the Canon of his young companion who, since he was a student of Karl Marx, might know the answer.

" Ah dunnoa, unless they're his bodyguard. Aye, maybe that's what they are."

Whether or not this was their function they followed the Commissar, always two paces behind, and shoulder to shoulder like Siamese triplets, as he walked among the guests ; whenever he stopped to talk with an old or new acquaintance, they stood, powerful, dumb, and unsmiling. He was now talking to the two bishops and the dean, conspicuous figures in their black and gaitered attire ; and these three huge bravoes stood at their two paces interval watching the three churchmen.

" Do they suppose that one of the bishops is going to hit him on the head ? " asked the Canon of the student of Marx.

" You never knaw what the Trotskyists might be oop to," explained the young man.

Canon Welcome, not at all clear who the Trotskyists were, or why they should be up to anything, did not unveil his ignorance by further words. The great little Russian was now chatting and laughing with his old antagonist, the Foreign Minister, much as opposing counsel joke together in the Bar mess. The Minister of Health, the Minister of Labour, the Home Secretary, and the Colonial Secretary stood around the two, smiling. The three toughs stood at hand, ready for any rough play.

But now a second stirring of all heads and a loud murmuration as of starlings in a tree announced another famous guest : the Prime Minister. The Prime Minister was in the room, shaking hands with the little fat man and his lady.

Canon Welcome's heart jumped up like a child from a stool when promised a gift. It trembled with hope. He must manage somehow to display himself to the Prime Minister and speak a few words with him before this admirable party was over.

To the devil now with this pushing young man. " Well . . ." he gave him the friendliest smile . . . " I must go and talk to my brethren over yonder. All good fortune to you and your guild. You must come and see me some time when you're at St. Silas's. I shall be delighted. Remember me to my old friend, Percy Anson."

Happily free of that impertinence, he thrust a shoulder into the jostled throng and gently, apologetically, with tip-finger touches and disarming smiles, worked his comfortably convex figure, now forwards, now crab-wise, towards the two bishops and the dean. They accorded him a merry greeting, all having been enlivened by their cocktails ; and he made it his business to stay with them, since it seemed more than likely that the Prime Minister, walking round among the guests, would pause to speak with two bishops and a dean.

And, in fact, ten minutes had not passed before the Prime Minister, espying the Bishop of Newberry, one of his own creations, walked towards him with smiles.

" Ah, Bishop," he said. " So you're here, are you ? " On these occasions it is the spirit of a great man's greeting that matters, not its sense.

"I am, Prime Minister. You know the Bishop of Glossop, do you, and the Dean of Arminster? Yes, I thought so. And may I present Canon Welcome to you?"

"Canon Welcome? Welcome?" The Prime Minister appeared to recognize the name and to be pleased at this meeting with its bearer. "Didn't I read a letter of yours in the *Times* on the New Bishoprics Measures?"

"Well, I wrote one," allowed the Canon, modestly.

"And it was excellent," declared the Prime Minister. "There was a leader on it too, wasn't there? I remember I agreed with every word of your letter, and with much of the *Times'* article, though I could have wished it had been a little less cautious and facing-both-ways. All that you said about the difficulties of your work in poor and crowded streets made a great appeal to me, because I did some social work, when I was young, in a very poor quarter."

"We all know of your work in East London, Prime Minister," said the Canon, pleased to have learned that this was the way to address him.

"Yes, and I imagine it was a district very like the parts of which you wrote : full of splendid people but also "—he shook his head significantly and smiled—" a hot-bed for some very rough boys indeed. It was heart-breaking work for the clergy, I remember, and that was why I found the attitude of the Archdeacon to whom you replied quite incomprehensible. Surely the more ministers we have in these overcrowded cities, whether bishops or priests, the better?"

"Precisely, Prime Minister. It seems unarguable. But Archdeacon Williams, though of course he's done magnificent work in other fields, has very little experience of pastoral work."

"Is that so? Well, that may explain much. I was discussing the matter with the Chancellor and the Primate—*and*, a little later, with the Leader of the Opposition—only yesterday. As you know, this question cuts across all party divisions ; and we were in complete agreement, all four of us. But of course the matter rests with the Lords now, and we have yet to see what'll happen."

"There was one point, Prime Minister, that I should have liked to elaborate in my letter, but I didn't want to occupy too much of the Editor's valuable space."

"Oh, and what was that, Canon Welcome?"

"Just this : it's not only for the sake of the people that we

298

want to break up these overgrown dioceses, but for the sake of the clergy themselves. I've discussed the matter with my brother priests all over the country and—I'm sure the Bishops and Mr. Dean will support me in this—I've learned just how much they suffer from disheartenment and spiritual loneliness. They need far more of the help and guidance and comfort that only their Father-in-God can give them ; and the help isn't there, because it can't be there, in present conditions."

" I'm certain you're right. He states his case admirably, doesn't he, Mr. Dean? I've a grave fear that I shall start plagiarizing you next time I have to speak about the measures."

" You could do me no greater honour, sir."

" You won't sue me for breach of copyright ? "

" Most certainly not."

" Nor turn the Performing Rights Society on to me ? "

" No, sir. The bishops are my witnesses that any small writings of mine are at your service."

" Thank you, Canon Welcome. Then I shall certainly look up your letter again. I must pass on and say a word to my friend, Harold Pasco there."

Really there was something extraordinarily friendly and unaffected in a Socialist prime minister. For the first time that evening Canon Welcome felt ready to be, in fact, a Socialist.

CHAPTER EIGHT

HE came away from the grand room and the great men with a glow of happiness pervading his whole being. Could the happiness suffusing a man emanate from his body in an aura, then there must have been an effulgence about the rotund and sable-clad figure of Canon Welcome as he hung from a strap in a crowded Underground train, and walked slowly, contemplatively, up his familiar hill. There were songs in his heart as he went up the pavement. He carried his ebony walking-stick with its silver band—a staff which itself had something of the look of a black-clad clergyman in a high white collar—and swung it in time with the music in his heart. Had he troubled to find words for the triumph which the music was sounding, they would have been, " I have conquered good ground today. I must consolidate this fine position and advance from it."

Night sat upon the hill, for it was past eight o'clock on a young April day. Over the gables and chimneys silhouetted against the sky, over the high skeleton branches of the trees that girt the Vicarage, there were suds of white cloud, but above this tumbled lather the stars gleamed in a great congress ; and his heart was exalted almost to the stars. He was seeing again that gilded room and some of the world's most illustrious people moving through it. He was hearing again that kindly commendation from the ruler of the land. " It was excellent . . . I agreed with every word of it. . . . It was much better than the article in the *Times*. . . . He states his case admirably, doesn't he, Mr. Dean ? " Hardly did he see the gates of his vicarage as he passed through them into the deeper darkness of his garden. Since Amy was away, this face of the Vicarage was entirely dark except for a mosaic of coloured lights in the leaded panes of his hall door. Still happily dreaming, he walked towards this panel of broken lights : but he had not taken five steps before he became aware that someone was near him.

Someone was lurking in the darkness. Listen : a stir in the tall laurel bush by the wall. It was no louder than the flutter of a bird ; but it was not a bird. Standing stone-still, except for a new and different drum-beat in his heart, he stared at the bush. His heart seemed to bound from his body as he discerned a figure standing against it.

" Who's there ? "

A small figure—a child's ? a girl's ?—came towards him, and he stepped back with a terror like the terror of a small boy in the dark. It was a figure in a dark winter coat, carelessly open ; a figure hatless and ungloved, with white face and white hands showing.

Phil Janey ! Even in the darkness he could see that her small face was as white as the face of a dead child, and its big eyes wild with fear.

" Oh, sir ! . . ."

" Phil ? . . ." His quick alarm had melted into sympathy and curiosity. " What are you doing here, my dear ? "

" I was waiting for you. I rang once, and the girl said you were out. So I waited."

" But why here in the dark ? "

" Oh, I didn't dare wait in the street. I'll explain."

" You should have stayed in the warm inside."

" Oh, no, no—please—I'll explain."

" Come in then, my dear. You're cold. You're shivering."

" Is anyone there but the girl ? "

" No. My wife's away."

" Oh, well, then . . . if I may, please. . . ."

" There's nothing to be afraid of."

" Don't let anyone see me, *please*. I'll explain."

He left her shivering there, and went to the door. As he turned the key, quietly like a housebreaker, since he must disturb no one, he remembered something in the past and thought, " How curious ! Phil Janey lurking in the garden not far from the place where her father lurked, and almost at the same time. It was about eight o'clock then, and we were at dinner." He waited in the light lest anyone emerged from the kitchen, and then said softly, " Come, dear. It's all safe."

She came quickly and quivering as if afraid to be seen in the light ; and when with his usual courtesy he opened his study door for her, she shot through like a hunted rabbit into a refuge where it could lie and quake.

" Well, now, now, now," he comforted. " What is it ? It's ages since I've seen you, Phil Janey. I'd no idea where you were, or I'd have looked you up. Something worrying you, is there. Yes, you're pale as death. Look." He went to the cupboard under his bookshelves and mixed her a whisky and soda. "That'll help. That'll warm you and stop the trembling."

As she sipped the drink, the glass chattered against her teeth. "Sit here and tell me what it is." He guided her to one of the easy chairs, and himself sat tentatively on the other.

Looking up at him with her big child's eyes, she said, "I came to see you because you were so wonderful with Dad that time. You got him off."

"Are you in some trouble too now?"

"And you were always so wonderful with me when I was getting confirmed. I didn't know who else to come to."

A love ran from his heart to her, because she had run to him. He watched her as she sat there with her white face and staring eyes and overborne by pity, forgetting all about the Prime Minister and the great men and his ambitions and dreams, he had a vision of what might have been if he'd been a faithful shepherd and not lost her on the foothills. And this sharp vision, after his visit to that gilded chamber, was like the words of Nathan, or of one of the old, dauntless prophets, come to rebuke him in his pride.

"Anything in the world I can do for you, my dear, I will."

"Oh, but it's terrible. But I didn't mean it. I didn't mean it. You'll know I didn't mean it."

"Yes, yes. Don't be afraid to tell me anything. Now, what is it?"

But she couldn't say it. Her lips remained closed and her eyes fixed on him.

He encouraged her. "Don't be afraid. We clergy often hear strange and even terrible things. I'm sure there's nothing a girl like you can tell——" but as he said this, he stopped, for he seemed to recall having said exactly the same to her once before.

"I didn't mean it. He drove me mad. I was mad."

"Who drove you?"

"And you won't tell anyone, not any living soul? No one else knows yet. Not yet."

"Of course I won't tell anyone. Come, dear; what is it?"

But still she didn't speak; she just stared at him like a mad girl, or like a girl paralysed and dumb.

So, leaving his easy chair, he drew another beside her, and

sitting down, picked up her hand and pressed it between both of his. " Now tell me."

" I've killed someone."

Keeping a perfect hold upon himself, he only pressed her hand tighter. " I know you didn't mean it. Tell me everything."

" I—he got me so mad—I——"

But at that moment there was a knock at the door. She gasped, " Oh ! " shrivelled into herself, and plunged her face into her hands.

He stepped very quickly to the door, just as Norah, the maid, opened it a little way.

" Will you be having your dinner now, sir ? "

" Oh—Norah—no." A hand on the door, he stood between her and all sight of his visitor. " Not for a little time yet. I'll let you know when I'm ready."

" I see, sir. Thank you."

He closed the door quietly behind her and came back to the chair beside Phil Janey.

" Oh, but I'm keeping you," she apologized, just as if she'd come to speak about some charity. " I'm keeping you from your supper."

" That is nothing . . . nothing," he said, and gathered up her hand again. " All my time is yours. Now tell me everything. You were saying . . . ? "

" I—I'll tell you how it all come about," she began, her arm quivering against her side like a bowstring, her body convulsed ever and again as in a rigor. And she told him of her three days' acquaintance with Ned Horby, of their drive together down to the sea, of what happened in the carpenter's shop, and of his arrest as they came out of the builder's yard. She told how he'd been given a six months' sentence for housebreaking, but as that was more than five months ago he was now out of prison, having earned his remission, and home in the Fields. In that five months she'd learned for certain that she was going to have a baby and so she'd tried everywhere to find him as soon as she guessed he was " out ", but it was only today that she'd found him, because she'd never known where he lived, and he didn't seem to have gone back to work at Job Hartney's yard. But today, getting desperate, she'd tramped through all the streets round the Circus and at last had seen him in Greenholt Street, not far from the pub, the Gentle Shepherd, where she'd first met him. She'd run up

to him and told him everything. " But he just turned from
me and told me to get to hell, sir. He said I was getting
nothing out of him. And I saw at once that he was mad with
me because he believed that if it hadn't been for me, he'd
never have been caught at all. It was because he'd kind'a
fallen for me that he wanted to show off his car and his driving
and all, and it was because of what he wanted to do to me
that he come to leave the car standing so long where a policeman could see it. You see, sir, he was absolutely wild-like, at
being caught within a few days of his first job when others
went for years without being found out, and he fancied himself
smarter than any of them! I went on pleading with him,
because I just couldn't believe he was going to let me down,
but all he done was to almost spit at me and tell me to get away,
like I was a dog. I couldn't have believed it of anyone. And
he turned and walked away like he didn't know me. Then
I proper lost my temper and walked after him, shrieking things
—which frightened him, so he told me to nark it and follow
him, but if I let anyone think we knew each other he'd knock
me out there and then. So I followed him about five yards
behind. . . ."

Here she bit and bit on her lip, and trembled more violently ;
so he encouraged her again, patting the hand which he was
still holding.

" Go on, my dear. You followed him."

She followed him, she said, and he led her to the only isolated place he knew, which was the carpenter's shop in the
yard. Here he again forced the window and opened the door
to her. And in the darkness of the shop he told her " absolutely blankly " that he wasn't going to admit he'd ever seen
her. She could do what she liked ; he'd deny everything.
Nobody'd ever seen them together except another boy, Len
Farrow . . . " and Len knew that I'd had relations with
other young chaps . . . once or twice. When I told him any
decent feller'd marry me, he laughed in my face and said a lot
of awful things. He said, why should he marry me when he
could get all he wanted from a hundred other girls. He said
he'd had hundreds in his time. He said that all a girl wanted
her marriage lines for was so as she could summons him at
any time. He said that once a girl married you, she didn't
care any more what she looked like, to you or anyone else,
unless she got tarting again. He said he wasn't going to be

such a mug as to give a girl marriage lines in exchange for something that was no longer worth having—not in *this* life, he said. And then he got profane, sir, and said p'raps in the hereafter they could summons him. He jeered at me saying it wasn't two days before I give him all he wanted, and if I didn't know what that sort'a thing might lead to, well, it was my funeral. I said, ' No, it's not, it's yourn ! ' And I picked up something from the bench we were standing by—I hardly knew what it was, but it was a carpenter's hammer, ever so big—and I crowned him with it, using all the strength I got. He went down like he'd fainted and—oh, my God ! . . ."

Canon Welcome put his arm around her that she might feel his support.

" . . . I saw he was dead."

" *Dead ?* "

" Yes, yes, yes. . . ."

" But are you *sure* ? "

" I'm sure . . . sure. He wasn't breathing. I waited and waited, praying and praying he'd move or something, but he never. He was dead."

" And what did you do ? "

" I rushed out and left him there. I didn't know what to do or where to go, I wandered and wandered about the streets, and at last I thought of you."

He drew her closer. " Don't be too afraid. I will help you all I can."

" Thank you so much." And she plunged her face into her hands again. " Oh, I just can't believe that it's happened."

" If it has—if he's really dead, let me think, let me think. Isn't there only one thing for you to do, my dear ? "

" What is that ? "

" It might be difficult at first, but we'd all help you."

" Oh, but what is it ? "

" It's to give yourself up—tonight—immediately—and tell them the whole story."

" *Oh, no, no, no !* " she cried, and was hysterical now. " *No !* I'd commit suicide first. I'd kill myself first. Oh, don't let them get me—I couldn't stand it—I should go mad. Don't let them take me. Please. Please."

His pity was so complete that, after a moment of pondering, he said, " All right. All right, my dear. I shall not let anyone touch you," unaware of the tremendous thing he had said.

Rising, he stood before her in his accustomed place, with his back to the fire, and looked down upon her. Her hands and arms were still spasmodically trembling, and the pity, swelling with him, persuaded him to repeat to himself again and again, " They shall not get her, They shall not get her." And, still watching her and wondering what to do, he couldn't help thinking, " One hour ago I was looking into the face of the Chief Ruler of the land and now into the face of this little criminal and runaway. Was ever so complete a change : from the summit to the base, and below the base ? " And he thought further : " An hour ago, while I was in that splendid chamber, those two were in the carpenter's shop. While I was chatting with one famous man or another, she was delivering her blow." Condemnation of her simply would not rise in him. She who'd had so little chance of learning civility had but struck with a violent hand where the more civilized would have slain with words.

He repeated to himself, " They shall not get her. If I can help it, they shall not get her."

He mixed her a second stimulant and as she sipped it through her chattering teeth, he continued thinking, That young man, was he really dead ? If not, shouldn't help be got to him ? But that must involve betraying this child. And he wasn't going to betray her. Her tale had rung with truth, so he could only believe that the young man was bad and the girl far from bad. Here was a case of conscience ; and he made his choice. There before his fireplace he decided to leave a young man, if necessary, to die. Of the two, the girl was the one he would save. Saying this, he remembered the child she was carrying, and he was confirmed in his choice. If that boy would die for want of help, then he must die.

An hour ago talking, laughing and joking with the governors and law-makers of the land ; now committing something like a murder.

" I will save you if I can, Phil Janey, my dear. And I think I can. Just tell me one or two things. Who knew that you knew him ? "

" No one at all, only Len Farrow, and he only saw us

together for a few minutes, and that was months ago, and only
a night or two before Ned was arrested. The cops—the police
saw me with him that night, but they took absolutely no interest
in me."

" Did his parents know anything about you ? "

" Gracious, no ; I only knew him two days, like, and besides, they're very respectable. He'd never have told them
anything about any of his girls. As a matter of fact, as I told
you, he bragged in the carpenter's shop that I couldn't prove
a thing because nobody'd ever seen us together or knew he knew
me. He said that he'd carefully seen to that."

" Good, then. I'm glad he saw to that. He imagined he was
protecting himself, but, as it's happened, he was really protecting
you. Now does anybody know you're expecting a child ? "

" Oh, no ! I left my job for fear the girls might notice something, and because I intended he should do something for me.
I was set on that. That was why I was so mad with him."

" And you're not prepared to go and tell everything to your
father and mother ? "

" Oh, no, *no* ! I couldn't possibly."

" You wouldn't let me go and tell them ? "

" Oh, no, *please* ! They mustn't know. Dad'll let it out to
someone sooner or later, and Mum would break her heart.
If I get arrested for this, she'll go mad. That's why I came to
you. I'd no one else, see."

In spite of all, in spite of his negligence and sloth and selfish
pursuits, she had come to him ; she had come to the Church,
and he loved the Church and was jealous for its honour, however poor and faithless a servant he might be. It should give
her sanctuary.

" Listen, Phil Janey : if by chance he is not dead, everything may yet be all right——"

" He's dead."

" If he is, if he really is, I will—I will save you somehow.
You're sure you couldn't just remain in your lodgings as if
nothing had happened ? That might be the best way."

" Oh I couldn't ! I couldn't. I should go mad. I must
get right away. No, *please* . . . and soon people will see that
I'm going to have a baby."

He understood this desperate need to escape her local streets.
He could see that, were he to thwart it, it might well, in her
present state, turn her reason sour. " All right, dear, I will

get you out of here and hide you somewhere. I will first find out if he's really dead——"

" He's dead, he's dead."

" If I find that he is, I'll come for you tomorrow and take you away. I'll take you to your home now. You must spend tonight at least in your lodgings."

" Oh, must I ? "

" Yes. You cannot disappear tonight of all nights. Come : you must face that. Nothing will be known till the week-end is over. I'll go with you and if it's possible to see your land-lady, I'll tell her that you've been with me all the evening. I'll say it was about—yes, about some work that you'll be going to in the morning. Eh, how will that do ? That will be a splendid alibi, if any question should arise. Tomorrow, if— if necessary, I will take you somewhere. I don't yet know where."

" Oh, sir . . . you are good. And you *do* think everything will be all right, don't you—everything will come all right ? "

" I am going to do everything I can to make it come all right."

" Oh, however can I thank you ? But I will try to somehow."

" You needn't thank me, dear. It's only my duty. That's what I'm here for."

" Oh, but you are good. Others might hate me and not want to do anything."

" No, Phil Janey, I am not good. But I'm so glad you came to me."

And he kissed her that she might not feel cast out.

§

He took her back in his car to her grey Crescent and, con-triving to speak with Mrs. Ansty, whose face peeped from her parlour door at sight of a clergyman, he said with a laugh, " I'm afraid I may be going to deprive you of your little lodger soon. We've been together this afternoon and we think we've found her a very nice job. She was one of my confirmation candidates, you see, and I was happy to recommend her." Mrs. Ansty responded with nice words about Phil Janey, and withdrew into her room. And he whispered to Phil Janey, " You'd best tell her it's as companion and help to a lady,"

308

because this was all he could think of in his hurry and confusion. And now that he had to leave her there, standing in the passage-way and trembling, he laid his lips on her forehead, and said, " Don't be afraid, my love. I will manage it for you. If I'm not back in an hour, just rest for tonight ; and tomorrow I will take you away."

§

He drove the car out of the Crescent and into the High Street, turning south. A long way south of his parish, he turned into the large car-park near the old Lincoln Theatre, and left the car there. Then he walked up the lamp-lit High Street till he came to a telephone kiosk, which he entered. Ringing up his home and hearing his bell trilling in the Vicarage hall-way and then Norah's voice answering him, he said, " It's me, Norah : the Vicar. Look : never mind about that meal. I don't know when I shall be home. I have some urgent visiting to do " ; the customary excuse, always so credible in a priest, but seldom so true as tonight ! He left the telephone box and hurried on to the Circus and the Corners where the lads, as usual, were loitering in the dark—lads among whom Ned Horby might have been seen but yesterday, or even, perhaps, but an hour or two ago.

He turned into Jason Road and walked along it—why not ? It was his parish—till he came to the mouth of Garrett's Place. The long, walled alley, straight as the gaze of a surveyor's eye, stretched for a furlong to the far-off glimmer of a street-lamp in Cornmeal Street. Two lonely lamps standing within it at a hundred yards' distance apart were its only lighting. It was empty—thank God for that : as empty of movements and shadows and sounds as a dead man's brain. Walking up it with an air of innocence, he saw the lane as a stage-set, empty, but ready for the drama which Phil Janey had pictured to him : the stolen car standing against that grey wall, the police car lurking some way behind ; and the policemen, on their cue, issuing from their ambuscade.

Fear began to jump at his heart as he drew near the gates of Hartney and Son's yard. They were ajar, and he turned through them quickly. If anyone surprised him now, and asked what he was about, he'd have to tell his knowledge and give

her up. " Oh God, let no one see me." Standing in the darkness, between a pile of scaffold poles and a stack of tiles, he
saw before him the wooden stairway leading up to the carpenter's shop like the steps of a scaffold. And the steps of a
scaffold it had been for Ned Horby. He went up those steps
as guiltily and fearfully as Phil Janey's father had done when
he climbed the ladder to the first floor of the Vicarage. At
every step his heart protested against what he might see when
he opened the door.

The door ? What a fool he had been. Not once in all this
flurry had he considered what to do if the door had swung
shut and locked itself when Phil Janey rushed out. He tried
it. It was locked.

But the window at the stairway's side was standing open,
where Ned had pushed up the sash. He glanced round once
more and, trusting that he was unseen, clambered towards it
and through it, just as Mr. Carman had gone through his bedroom window long ago.

" Perhaps they'll think I'm visiting," he thought, as his first
foot touched the floor.

A dim dusky light shone on benches and floor from the unblinded windows, and he took a few steps towards the door over
the shavings and sawdust. His heart pulsed sickly and fearfully—and then he saw him, almost at his feet.

He was lying as she had struck him down : one knee at
rest on the other ; arms at his sides quite naturally and peacefully, though one cupped palm was turned helplessly upwards ;
his head collapsed and on its side among the cast-away shavings
and the dust. So small a figure.

Kneeling down, he struck a match, shaded it, and looked at
the face. It was like a death-mask in white soft clay. The
eyes, wide open, were dulled and barely mirrored the visiting
light from the sky. The lips were parted and dead. He peered
closer, and there on the vault of the cranium saw a depressed
fracture, half the size of a saucer, and as deep.

He was astonished at the feminine smallness of the head,
the features, and the upturned hand.

Not a doubt that he was dead and cold. Almost certainly
Phil Janey's blow had killed him instantaneously.

He put out his light and rose from his knees. But as he
rose he saw on the bench among the litter of tools and planks
and splinters a heavy hammer, probably the one she had used

and desperately laid aside. He thought ; then, picking it up with his handkerchief, he wiped any trace of finger prints from it and placed it in a pigeon-hole. He took one more look at that body and, turning, left it to lie there.

Not a sound outside. Very quickly he passed through the door, shutting it silently behind him. A few seconds, and he was in the lane, walking freely and innocently, as a parish priest might in the streets of his parish.

He had seen the thing he wanted to see, and now he was walking back to his car. His mind was free now to worry with the problem, where to hide Phil Janey in the morning. Where place a girl who was carrying a five-months' child ? How explain the suddenness of his arrival with her ? Impossible to do so without awaking surprise and suspicions. How wild, how thoughtless, he had been in his promise to hide her immediately. The only possible thing would be to find someone to whom he could tell the whole truth. But who—who ?

Like a child, as he walked along, he told himself, " I must reach a solution before I reach the car," and he slowed down his step when he came in sight of the car-park, but was still without his answer. He prayed to God for counsel and help. " O God, help me. I know I do not deserve Thy help, but help me to help her, for her sake. She is so weak. It is not her fault. Help me, O God . . . her father." And then, when he was within a few yards of the car, and creeping so as to delay the moment of touching it, the inspiration, the knowledge, came.

Yes, this was possible ; it was the only possible thing. Let him act on it now—immediately. He hurried back to the telephone box he had used earlier ; he telephoned a message that he was coming ; and, returning to the car, got into it and drove it rapidly towards Chelsea.

CHAPTER NINE

AND as he drove through the thinning traffic of a Saturday night, he felt more and more satisfied with his plan. Lilian Eadie, no matter how mischievous and sharp-seasoned her tongue, had a heart : she had the heart of an actress, as capacious and warm as a theatre, and as ready to welcome and stage any drama. She would do this for him, not only without demur but positively with joy and acclamation. As before, he parked his car in the private parking place at the foot of that brick mountain in Chelsea, Whitehorse Mansions, and hurried into the heart of the mountain. Crossing the vestibule, he entered the lift in its gilded cage and with a touch induced it to raise him, like a magic carpet, to the sixth floor, high above the rumour of the world. On this floor he saw her door left agape for him and her light streaming forth in welcome. As he entered she swept out to meet him, her movements as trained and beautiful as ever. She wore a close-waisted ground-length house-coat of dark blue silk, which swayed and sang as she came. Its length made her seem as gracefully elongated as a fashion-plate figure ; its deep, glossy blue accentuated the paleness of her face, the blackness of her hair and eye-lashes and the scarlet of her lips. Face, lashes, and lips had been dressed for his coming.

" What is this ? " she exclaimed. " You come to me at eleven o'clock. This is drama. And so exciting ! Oh, but I'm pleased. I was dull, darling ; like a nun in her convent cell, darling ; so terribly dull."

" I want your help, Lilian."

" But how lovely ! I love being asked for help. And especially at midnight. Come right in, darling. Oh, but you're pale ; you're pale. You look a complete wreck. What *have* you been doing ? Has anything happened ? "

" Of course things have happened," he protested, as he followed her into her theatrical little sitting-room with its mushroom grey carpets, blue walls, and rose-coloured chairs.

" Not to *you* ? Not to *you* ? " she cried ; and Duse could not have registered solicitude in richer tones.

" No, not to me."

" Oh, I'm so glad ; but you look such a wreck. An absolute wreck, but so pathetic and sweet. Sit down, my love, while I go and get you something nice. Don't speak ! " With a beautiful gesture of her palm she banned all speech, as he dropped into one of the rose-covered chairs. " Don't speak till you've been nursed." And she swept to the cabinet under the window and mixed him a strong whisky and soda, just as he had done for Phil Janey. " There, love. . . . Now, darling, if you feel better, what is it ? Do tell me." She sank gracefully to the corner of her sofa, joined her fingers above her knee, and stared at him, eager to be the confessor this time, and he the penitent. " Someone's in trouble, but not you."

" Well, do you remember my telling you all about old Mr. Carman ? "

" Indeed I do. A pet of a man. A wicked old burglar, but such a dear ! And you were wonderful with him. You got him off and made a good man of him."

" Well . . . only up to a point. . . ."

" You rewarded him for coming and burgling your house. You set him up in another profession, so that he shouldn't come and do it again. So much more sensible than putting him in prison."

" You remember his daughter who came to me for Confirmation ? "

" To be sure, I do. You told me all about her. A little girl with a feather. I love her."

" It's about her that I've come."

" Yes ? She's in trouble ? " Lilian's eyes were tied to his, so avid her interest.

" She certainly is."

" What ? The—the usual ? "

" No. Or, at least, that's only the smallest part of it."

" Then what ? What else can it be ? Don't say she's taken to burgling like her father."

" She has committed a murder."

" Oh, my dear ! " It was ludicrous, the suddenness of her shock, and her patting of her breast above the shaken heart. " Oh, my God ! "

" Yes. Let me tell you all about it."

" Please do. *Do*."

He told her the whole story, from the discovery of Phil Janey in his garden that night to his rash promise to take her away in the morning and his clandestine visit to the carpenter's shop. The golden clock on the mantelpiece ticked on, undisturbed, through the whole of the amazing record ; and at one point it struck twelve perfunctorily and as if bored with the talk. Far below, in King's Road, the torrent of the world's traffic sighed and rumbled and rushed ; it hummed and purred and dwindled into silence ; it swelled, and sank into an uneasy nothingness again.

"Poor child, poor child," Lilian breathed, when the last word was told.

"I don't know what to do. She could think of nobody to come to but me, and I could think of nobody to come to but you."

"Thank you, my dear." Her finger-tips touched his hand in gratitude. "But what can I do ? I'm glad she killed him. I'm sure it's very wrong of me, darling, but I'm glad she just stamped on him like a beetle. He needed it. But what can I do ? "

"I know what I want to ask you to do. I want you to take her in tomorrow, and to keep her here with you."

She sat staring into his eyes without moving or answering.

And he continued, speaking rapidly, "You could call her your maid or your help or your companion, or tell whatever lie you like. And you'd have to be very tender with her all the time and nurse her back to sanity. This whole business is too big for her, and she's nearly mad or dead with it. And don't forget : she's pregnant. My God "—he had convinced himself again—" it is something worth doing. Do you remember how, ages ago, you came and asked me to give you some church work to do—and once you said—after I—after we—you said you'd do anything on earth to help me ? Well, this is something worth-while at last. It may not be church work—I don't know—but it's Christian work—of that I'm certain. And when her time comes, in a few months, we'll get her into some maternity home, if she's still free—as she *will* be, if we can manage it."

Lilian was still staring, and he couldn't tell how she was taking the enormous request.

"Lilian dear, we don't often have a chance to save anyone. Someone young and weak. And not only one young weak creature in this case, but two. Will you do it ? "

"Of course I will."

"And you and I will bring her safely through ? "

" Of course."

" Yes, but it's entirely against the Law—to shelter anyone who's committed a crime."

" Oh, I don't mind the Law." With a sweep of her hand she pushed that irrelevance aside. " The Law, as often as not, is completely silly—isn't it ?—wouldn't you say ? "

" Sometimes it's silly, yes."

" And all the silly lawyers worship it as something sacred and untouchable, like God. So stupid, darling."

" I agree, but the fact remains that this is some sort of crime I'm asking you to commit. You can be prosecuted for it."

" Oh dear ! Prosecuted ?—but how absurd ! "

" Of course you can be prosecuted if you've committed a crime. What do you suppose ? "

" Did you ever hear such nonsense ? "

" I don't know what the penalty is for sheltering a fugitive. It can't be anything much, I imagine. But you'd be arrested, I think."

" Oh, I mustn't be arrested. Oh no, dear ; not if I can help it. I could just say I didn't know it was the Law."

" And that would be no help. Ignorance of the Law is no excuse." It was quite unnecessary for him to repeat the statement in its Latin form, but who could resist doing so, if it was there behind his lips. " *Ignorantia juris neminem excusat.* And that's an exceedingly silly rule that they worship and do not hesitate to enforce with a certain amount of supercilious superiority. Why, did you know that on occasions Frenchmen who've acted as seconds in a duel over here have been tried for murder, though they'd no idea that duelling was against the Law in England ? I learned that from the Anti-Duellers."

" Well, now, isn't that just intolerably silly. Upon my soul, men make me tired. No woman would put up with such nonsense for two minutes."

" So it may be, but that's the Law."

" But, darling, it's all quite simple : I could just say that you brought the girl here and never told me anything about the murder. Not a thing ! How was I to know ? How was poor Lilian to know the girl'd been killing a boy ? "

" You could say that. But you'd crumple up in the witness box."

" *Oh* no ! *Oh* no ! " said Lilian with conviction. " I'm a good actress, and I lie beautifully."

" You'd give a beautiful performance, I'm sure, as long as your own counsel was questioning you, but directly the prosecuting counsel turned his heat on to that little tale, he'd make melted butter of it."

" Oh dear. Do you really think so ? "

" I'm sure of it. So for all our sakes, for yours as well as mine, you must never, never, say a word about this, even to your dearest friend. No one is to be trusted with such a secret. Trust anyone, and you may find yourself in prison. For a week or two, at any rate. Just a formal sentence, probably, but distasteful and something of a disgrace."

" In *prison*? Oh heavens ! This is really drama. Murder, and a fugitive from justice, and prison for me. My dear, you've written a rather exciting rôle for me, haven't you ? My parts were generally light comedy parts, not high drama like this."

" I want you to know the worst and count the cost ; that's all. I've no right to ask you to do this, but I feel defeated. I can see no other way of saving this child."

" But won't they find out that she did it, and come for her ? "

" I think there's a tremendous chance that they'll never associate the crime with anything so weak as poor little Phil Janey or, if they do, that they'll never be able to pin it on to her. They *won't* pin it on to her, if I can help it. But if they do, then I shall have to take the rap, whatever it is. And you too, probably. So . . . what do you say ? "

She thought for a long minute, sitting motionless, with her hands joined upon her lap ; and then said, " Bring the child to me tomorrow. And confound the Law. It can look after itself. I'm not interested in it when it's ungenerous and silly."

He rose. " Bless you, Lilian. I must go now. I've had nothing to eat except a sandwich at the Mount Park Hotel four hours ago. Only four hours ago. I didn't tell you I was talking to the Prime Minister."

" You *were*? Oh, darling, how wonderful ! He's extremely *chic*, isn't he, really ? And with exquisite manners, I'm told. So unnatural in a Socialist . . . surely."

" He was very nice to me——"

" Some of the nicest people are Socialists nowadays. I can't understand it. It would have shocked my poor Chesney unspeakably, and finally slain Father. Father was upset even by the sight of a Liberal."

" He couldn't have been nicer. He praised my letter to

316

the *Times*. He wanted to quote from it. He said it was incomparably finer than Archdeacon Williams's. He told me he'd been discussing it with the Primate, and the Leader of the Opposition and they all loved it. . . . Only four hours ago, and it might have been ten years ago, and in another world. . . . Well, thank you, Lilian. I don't think that anyone has ever helped me quite so much. I was desperate ; and now I feel almost happy."

" Then I am happy too, darling. And if you say this extraordinary business is right and good, I'm glad to be doing it. One doesn't do enough good, really, does one, darling ? One just buys dresses after dresses, each of which cost the earth, and it's all so selfish. Oh, I think women are insufferable sometimes. Yes, bring the little girl to me, and I'll be ever so good to her."

§

Sunday morning, brilliant with a first spring sun ; and it was strange in his bright church, flooding with moted sunbeams, and before a well-dressed, law-abiding, happily singing congregation, to lead them in Matins, knowing that immediately after this service he was going to take a felon from her home and hide her in a safe place. And to remember that he alone knew of a body lying undiscovered and uncared-for in a carpenter's shop. " We have left undone those things which we ought to have done, and we have done those things which we ought not to have done." To say these words loudly, leading the people in them, and not to be ashamed of them, because he couldn't believe that what he was doing was wrong. To follow the psalms, as choir and congregation sang them, and to apply, now and again, some oddly appropriate verses to himself. " Be thou my judge, O Lord, for I have walked innocently " ; and " I will wash my hands in innocency, O Lord : so will I go to thine altar." To say the Third Collect, and to be at peace as he said it : " . . . Grant that this day we fall into no sin, neither run into any kind of danger. . . ." To go up to the altar and give the people his blessing, and then to hasten away to commit a crime.

CHAPTER TEN

IT was an established custom at the Vicarage that the Canon lay late in bed on a Monday morning after his exhausting labours on Sunday. So the clocks were climbing to nine when he awoke on this Monday, and his instant thought was, " They are finding him now." Some small anxiety about his part in the affair might be loitering near the threshold of his mind, but the dominant feeling, the master of that mansion, was his pleasure in what he had done. He devoted a few minutes, as he lay there, to self-approval. He recalled Lilian Eadie, yesterday at noon, coming to the door of her flat, extending both hands to welcome Phil Janey, placing a kiss on her forehead and saying only, " Come, my dear ". He recalled bidding good-bye to Phil Janey in Lilian's delicate and fastidious room, encouraging and comforting her with the pressure of his hand, and saying—perhaps a shade too theatrically and rather like a boy in a game of Hide and Seek—" You stay here and don't worry any more. I shall be standing on guard."

Yes, his compassion for Phil Janey had been a real movement of the heart. It had been an overpowering love for one of the weakest of his flock. And, for once in a way, his actions had been those of a good Christian and a good priest. He was able to think, as he lay there under the heavy clothes, and with his hands resting together on his chest for comfort, " I may be unable to believe all, or even much, of Bible and Creeds ; I may be quite unable to abandon my selfish ambitions ; I am idle and negligent, I know ; but say what you like, deep down in me I have that charity which St. Paul implied was the real substance and marrow of the matter. I have the substance and the marrow. . . ."

After breakfast and a study of the *Times* he decided that it would be just as well to learn what small penalty attached to his technical offence. He laid the paper aside, heaved himself out of his chair's soft embrace, and walked to the window. The sun was above the house-tops and shining on the grey-green trunks of the limes and on the silver-green trunks of the beeches. The arch of heaven was blue at the zenith with a long base of translucent light southward under the sun. Crocuses, white, purple, and yellow, thrust themselves up in every part

318

of his garden, and the spears of the daffodils too. The arms of the beech were red-powdered with young growth ; the limes were dusty with a thousand pink buds. Everything cried to him to come out and enjoy the April sunlight. What pleasanter way to spend a Monday morning than to stroll along to the Public Library over sunlit pavements and there consult some legal volume in its Reference Department and then perhaps visit the park and see the daffodils under the trees.

But of course this was officially his most sacred working period so, when he was out in the hall and taking down his hat, he called out, " I've some important visiting to do, and I may not be back for some time." True enough.

Out in the garden the first fine warmth of the year was rising from the ground, loading the breeze, and bringing out the smell of green things, like the warmth in the Palm House at Kew. It filled him with a sense of bodily well-being that matched his spiritual content. Swinging his ebony stick, drinking the English springtime, basking in honeyed dreams because of the sunshine, he walked along the upper slopes of his particular hill, for the Park Street Branch of the Borough Library, like his church, stood on a high place, in the good air and naked sun above the smoking streets of Hebron Fields.

In the Reference Department, a lofty hall walled with heavy volumes from parquet floor to moulded ceiling, he smiled at the assistant behind the counter, a most attractive brunette in a green overall, for whom he felt at once an automatic affection, and inquired, " Could you give me one or two books on Law ? English Criminal Law. I've got to give an address to some of my young people on English Justice. Yes, give me some English Justice, please," he added, joking heavily with the charming girl. " That's all I ask."

" I'm afraid we haven't many books on law." Her voice was soft, gentle, and low, an excellent thing in woman. " It's regarded as a specialist subject rather outside the scope of an ordinary public library."

" Never mind, my dear. Bring me anything you've got. The simplest will do. Something in kindergarten terms for a very mediocre intelligence."

" I'll find what I can. Criminal Law, did you say ? "

" Criminal ? Yes, I suppose so. Yes, certainly : criminal, ha, ha."

" I'll do what I can."

And thereupon the desirable creature, after beaming on him as if smitten with gratitude at being thus interrupted in her work, visited her card catalogue and then went forth to her book-stacks in a neighbouring room. She reappeared with a tapering pile of books.

" We have these," she said. " I could get you others from the National Central Library."

" I should think these would be ample," he answered, beaming no less gratefully upon her. They were *Outlines of Criminal Law, Criminal Law and Procedure, Stone's Justices' Manual, Felonies, Misdemeanours and Offences, Police Law*, and *Police Procedure and Administration*. " Yes, by the time I've read these there's nothing much I shan't know. I shall be able to practise at the Old Bailey. Thank you, my dear."

And he took the pile to an empty table. Others were at the tables with books before them : a girl poring over a vast atlas and taking notes ; a gigantic coloured youth scratching his sprung, black hair over a half-dozen of opened volumes ; a dilapidated man with an old bound file of the *Times* ; and, sitting in comatose peace before a book which no longer inter-ested him, a tattered greybeard who had nothing to do on a Monday morning or any other day of the week.

Walking to his chosen table, he thought, " None of these people have any notion why I too am doing research," and he remembered again, what he had quite forgotten, that body in the carpenter's shop. What was on foot now, down in the Fields ? None of these people knew of this morning's discovery ; none but he, as he moved among them ; and no one in the world knew that he knew. Such was the curtained loneliness of every soul, whether in public or private rooms.

Seated and comfortable and happy, he opened the largest book, *Outlines of Criminal Law*. What should he look up ? In the index he could find nothing about Aiding to Escape or Sheltering. Conspiracy, was that it ? No, here it was : Acces-sory after the Fact. Of course. A familiar phrase.

He turned to the page indicated and read, " An accessory after the fact is a person who, knowing that a felony has been committed subsequently shelters one of the felons in such a way as to elude justice——"

" Yes, that's me," he thought. " That's exactly me."

There were further paragraphs dealing with Principals in

the First Degree, Principals in the Second Degree, and Accessories *before* the Fact, none of which could apply to him, and then came a section on punishments. This was what he wanted to read, so, crossing his knees to study in comfort, he entered upon the opening paragraph. " In modern times the only important surviving difference between the various grades of accomplices "—ugly word, that—" is the fact that a much more lenient punishment is awarded to the man who is an accessory *after* the fact——"

" Good ! "

" —for instead of being, like accessories before the fact, liable to the same heavy maximum sentence as the principal, he is punishable with nothing more than two years' imprisonment with or without hard labour——"

God ! Two years' hard labour. No, *no* !

But that wasn't the end of the sentence, and he read on ravenously. " —except in the case of murder, where the maximum punishment is penal servitude for life."

Life !

It was as if an opponent with whom he had been gently sparring had struck him, suddenly and treacherously, a cannon blow in the stomach.

He read the words again . . . and again . . . and a third time ; and each time they meant the same. His heart a vessel holed and foundered, he desperately opened *Criminal Law and Procedure*, in the impotent hope that it might state something different. Its index directed him to " Accessories, p. 18 " and, turning to the page, he found the section headed " Parties to a Crime ". Such ugly words. Without heart or hope he read, " An accessory after the fact is one who, with knowledge that a felony has been committed, receives, comforts, or assists the felon in order to hinder his apprehension, trial and punishment."

" Exactly what I set out to do and did. Couldn't be better described."

The punishment ? " Accessories after the fact are liable to imprisonment for two years (Rex *v*. Ransford, Rex *v*. Chapple) unless some greater or other punishment is provided by statute, as in the case of murder where the punishment may be as much as penal servitude for life."

Why turn to *Stone's Justices' Manual* ? But he did so, punch-drunk and therefore hardly caring any more ; and, as he expected, he read the same thing almost word for word.

Why worry with Moriarty's *Police Law* ? Surely in the mouth of three witnesses the truth was established. But what did Moriarty say ? " The Accessories and Abettors Act, 1861, declares that an accessory to felony, either before the fact or after the fact, is guilty of felony and may be tried with the principal felon. . . ."

Oh, God !

Shutting the volume, he rose, a pale wistful man, and taking the unstable pyramid of books back to the girl at the counter, said, " Thank you so much. I feel I've got all I wanted."

He was in no state to feel his first affection for her. But he smiled and tried to look happy, as if the world had not overturned since he spoke to her last. And she smiled and pushed the books carelessly to one side, and got on with her work.

The negro, the tattered greybeard, and the student girl sat bowed over their books, as happy and fear-free now as they were fifteen minutes ago. And he—he drifted out into the street ; and the genial air, the sparkling sunlight, and the smell of the springtime laughed at him. He walked on and on aimlessly, in a sick, bemused state, like a boxer who has been hit too hard. Forty-eight hours ago, on Saturday evening, he had been happy ; the future, after his talk with the Prime Minister, had been refulgent with promise ; now that bright prospect had been suddenly annihilated like a picture on a screen, and the future was a blank—a blank on which terrible things might appear. Disgrace. Imprisonment. Hopelessness for the rest of his life. All those ambitions which yesterday had been so alive were now blood-drained and still, as if waiting to die. All the fame, all the publicity for which he had schemed and toiled, was now his greatest enemy. If " Canon Welcome " were charged with a felony it would make a headline for every paper in the land and a holiday for such disreputable journals as *The Week in the Courts* which he studied on Sundays, that he might keep in touch with life. And—how well he knew this now !—just in so far as a man had craved public praise, so would public obloquy, or even public pity, be a sickness unto death.

Walking on wistfully vaguely, he saw a policeman taking notes from two drivers whose cars had collided, and he heard himself saying aloud, " I can't worry about *their* troubles ". Not many minutes later, crossing a road half blind with thought, he was nearly knocked down by a fast, purling car, and as he dodged from the blow, he thought, " I shouldn't mind much if I had been run over ". Worry had depressed his vitality as far as it would go, so that it seemed to him almost certain now that the worst would happen. That landlady, Mrs. Ansty ! He had incriminated himself with her by deliberately providing Phil Janey with a lying alibi. Oh, God, God ! That was perjury, wasn't it ? And after the landlady, the carpenter's shop. Supposing someone had seen him climbing in through the window. Breaking and entering, wasn't it ? As far as he could see, he could be charged with three crimes : perjury, housebreaking and accessory to murder.

Or say that as a result of his lying and his shielding of the real criminal, they tried to hang the murder on someone else ? He'd have to confess then and take the consequences.

Oh, God. . . .

He was on the dead bottom of despair, but he could still feel no anger with Phil Janey, and no regret for what he had done. He was terrified ; he was a vessel stuffed with alarm ; but he was not sorry. Nor for a moment could he contemplate undoing it and giving the child up. To him it still seemed, that he had been technically wrong but a good priest. " No, that I cannot do."

This was his only comfort as he dragged his limbs through this livid slough of fear. Evidently, wretched self-centred creature though he was, his fellowship with a small overwrought and hunted creature was stronger than his love of himself.

Oh, to be able to tell all to someone ! His lawyer, a sympathetic, understanding man ? No, no ; he might recommend a confession. Lilian ? Yes, Lilian : in the first place because she was the natural confidante, in the second because it would be exciting to tell her the worst, and in the third because, by heaven, he must keep her feminine mouth shut. Yes, quickly, before she should be tempted to whisper the truth to anyone. Clambering on to a bus, he was disconcerted to see a policeman sitting in it. The sight of the constable's blue and silver reminded him that he was a felon. For one half of a moment he had a mind to descend and seek a pleasanter bus. Instead he sat himself nearby opposite the constable and tried to be conscious of his innocent dark suit, clerical collar and venerable silver hair rather than of the vesture of guilt around him. But when, in his abstraction, he gave fourpence instead of fivepence to the conductor, and the conductor pointed out the deficiency, he felt as furtive and guilty as if he'd really tried to defraud the London Passenger Transport Board, and he heard with dislike and distrust his voluble excuses and apologies. He wondered if the policemen distrusted them too.

Sitting dumped and miserable in the bus as it lurched along King's Road, Chelsea, he suddenly saw Lilian on the pavement in a broad plain black hat and a long black Spanish cloak so that she looked a little like a dark and handsome villain who had broken loose from one of the old melodramas of the Lincoln Theatre. Only a basket on her arm justified her appearance among the twentieth-century shoppers. Not a few of these shoppers turned to look at her as she sailed proudly by. He sidled and tumbled off the bus to accost her, bethinking himself, as he did so, that in the eyes of the Law she *was* one of the villains of this drama.

" Lilian ! "

" Oh, darling, how you made me jump ! " she cried, beating her breast. " This is death. What are you doing here ? I've been shopping and shopping and look too terrible for anyone to see."

" How is the child ? "

" She's less frightened how, but she's got a terror of going out into the street or even down to the Whitehorse restaurant. So I'm buying the siege supplies. She's quite a dear, really, isn't she ?—I love her—but *maid*, my sweet ! I'm the maid, and enjoying it. I haven't, to tell the truth, enjoyed anything so much for a long time. It, at least, isn't dull. I'm not bored any more ; and, darling, let me tell you this : there are two things I abominate more than anything else ; and both of them are boredom."

" I've been looking up the penalty for what we've done."

" Oh, yes ? " She rearranged the parcels in the basket, more interested in them than in penalties. " And what is it ? "

" It's penal servitude for life."

Her eyes bounded up from the basket, which she now held in front of her with both hands. " Don't be absurd, darling."

" Well, that's the maximum in a case of murder. As far as I can understand it, you may get off with two years' hard labour."

" I ? Two years ? But, my dear, I can't go to prison. I should be miserable."

" They won't take that into consideration. That's partly their idea."

324

" But I couldn't stand it, darling. Not for a week ; much less two years. And ' hard labour '—what does that mean ? "

" I've always understood it's sewing mail bags and picking oakum."

" Oakum ? I don't know what oakum is."

" Nor do I. But you pick it. You pick it in your cell."

" Oh, is *that* what ' hard labour ' is ? "

" Yes, and having a plank bed to sleep on instead of a mattress."

" A plank bed ? It's useless. I can't do it."

" I believe that you as a woman might be allowed a mattress, but I shouldn't be—not for the first week or two."

" It's useless. I can't even do it with a mattress."

" What do we do then ? Do we tell the truth and give the child up ? "

" Oh no . . . we can't do that." She pondered on this denial and confirmed it. " Good gracious, no, darling. Nobody's talking about that. I'm not giving her up to anyone."

" Very good then : don't tell her what I've told you this morning. If she knew it she might feel she ought to give herself up. Or she might be very unhappy, and we want to get her well and strong to be a mother. If the worst happens, I shall deny that you ever knew anything—except that she was pregnant. I've told lies enough already. I can tell a few more."

" But the child knows I know. We've been talking about it all day and all night. I thought it'd help her to talk to someone who wasn't condemning her."

" Oh, well then. I may have to teach her to lie too."

" But they'll never find out. Of course they won't. The more she's told me, the more I'm certain they won't."

" I'm not sure." He did not wish his alarm to be made light of. " I'm not at all sure. It's touch and go."

CHAPTER ELEVEN

YES, touch and go ; and by now, so deep was his depression, he could only believe that Phil Janey's crime and his own were more likely to be uncovered than to stay hid. All the following days were haunted days. Fear stalked, a familiar at his side, as he walked from dining-room to study, or along the streets of his parish, or towards his stall in the chancel before Tim and Bettersby and the congregation. It walked up to the altar with him at Early Service, a phantom second ; it stepped into the pulpit with him at Matins and Evensong ; it stopped his sermons time and again to remind him of its presence before allowing him to continue his exhortations in a voice now shaken.

Never since he was a child has he been so possessed by a fear as now. But before Amy and Norah and his friends on the pavements he kept a gentle smile on his face, and if they pronounced him pale and lined he maintained that this was due to overwork. The only difference they might have remarked in him was that he was now consistently gentle, unselfish, and helpful with all. Once or twice it had happened before, that he was soft and even saintly like this.

A few days ago, abounding in health and hope, he could not hear his telephone ring or the postman treading the gravel without an irrational hope that it meant good news : an offer of preferment, a newspaper cutting praising his labours, a letter full of admiration for last Sunday's sermon, an invitation that would be fruitful of more publicity—well, something pleasant, though he knew not what. Now every ring on the telephone or knock at the front door stayed his hand and his heart so that, stiller than stone, he listened. The police ?

If the police came he would lie and lie. Hadn't Baynes expressed his readiness to " tell a few lies to the police " to save that boy who had slashed him ? " If Baynes, who's a real saint, can lie, I can. And *he* did it to save a foul young brute. I shall do it to save a betrayed and unhappy child."

" And to save yourself too."

" Yes . . . well, of course . . . there's that too."

" Baynes did nothing to save himself."

" No, but . . . I shall be doing it to save her rather than
myself . . . at least . . . no, that's not quite true . . . saving
both. Oh well, I will not give her up, and that's all I know."

To no one else did he tell any lies, almost for the first time
in his life. To no one else, he resolved, would he ever tell lies
again. The strangest and strongest effect of being haunted
by fear was this desire to be good.

Sometimes as day followed day and no danger came near
him he felt a little less fearful and almost at ease again. Tuesday, Wednesday, Thursday passed by without word or message
to him. Friday began as a day of apprehension because the
local newspaper would be on his plate. To any but a local
journal this back-street murder was a one-paragraph affair,
and already the London papers had forgotten it ; but for the
Hamden and Hebron News it was something for the centre of its
window. He glanced at the front page. Two columns of it.
" The Garrett's Place Murder." " Victim's Double Life."
" Mr. Hartney Talks to the *News*." He laid the paper away,
resolved to read it alone, behind the shut door of his study ;
and he picked up the *Times* instead. But he could no more
apprehend what he was reading than what he was eating.

Breakfast over, he took the paper into his study for his sacred
hour of work. He fell with a sigh into his long easy chair and
began to read. The first paragraphs that he read quickened
his nervous heart, but then came parts that were as comforting
as the first work of an anodyne. " One theory of the police,"
so the paper reported, " is that the assailant was a tall, powerful
man. Only a man of some height and considerable strength
could have delivered so severe a blow. This opens the possibility that the murder was some form of gang reprisal. The
unfortunate young man was known to have associated of late
with some of the rougher elements in Hebron Fields. The blow
is typical of the methods used by some of the young hooligans
in this district who are experts in handling the cosh. It may
be that, because of some real or fancied betrayal by Horby,
they were determined to ' get him '. The attack seems to have
been sudden and unexpected. When the police were summoned to the scene on Monday morning they could find no
sign of a struggle and no disorder except what was natural in a
busy carpenter's shop. Robbery can scarcely have been the
motive, since the victim's money was still in his pocket and
valuable rings on his fingers and a pearl tie-pin in place. He

327

had only just come out of prison, and it is possible that the avengers were waiting for him to appear among them. They may have trailed him to the carpenter's shop and there struck him down intending only a ferocious ' crowning ' but in fact, owing to the thinness of his skull, murdering him. Edward Horby's was a remarkable case of a double life. The son of highly respected parents, he would accompany them to chapel and attend church meetings. He was a member of the chapel Men's Institute and would often lend a hand with the Boys' Club, where he was very popular, teaching them to carpenter and helping them make the models of the furniture they wanted. To Mr. Job Hartney, his employer, he was known as an exceptionally keen, conscientious, and industrious young workman, of most pleasing manner, who was well on the road to becoming Foreman Carpenter or even General Foreman one day. But out of his parents' sight, and after working hours, he was capable of committing a daring daylight burglary and stealing and disguising a car. It has also been revealed that he was something of a Don Juan amongst the girls, which opens the further suggestion that jealousy was the motive of the murder. It is well known that the lads of the Hebron Town gangs regard the cosh as the proper answer to anyone who steps between them and their women."

Having read this, and read it a second time, he felt more comfortable than at any time since his researches in the Library. The devil of fear was not removed from the room, but it shrank in size and power. After all, many murders remained unsolved, especially in these days of exceptional violence and inadequate police forces, and why shouldn't this be one of them ? Reading the police theories a third time he began to believe (since one must always hope the best) that the actual truth was the hypothesis least likely to occur to them. Already four days had passed since the discovery of the body, and with every hour the crime was getting colder. He put the paper aside and turned to the *Times*.

The days padded by, heavily at first, then more quickly, then at a normal pace ; and nothing happened. No one came near him with suspicions and inquiries. The devil of fear shrank yet further ; it shrank day by day almost into insignificance.

Friday, two weeks later, in his study after breakfast, he scanned the *Hamden and Hebron News*, spread out upon the table. No mention in it of the murder; and this for the second time in succession. No, nothing there anywhere and a great melting ease took possession of his heart and mind. He could have laughed at his perturbations of yesterday. For his further comfort he did laugh. And he sank into his upholstered chair, whose embrace was sweet, flung his feet up on the stool, and gave himself to the *Times*.

And without a knock, without sound of steps in the passage, the door opened.

Amy was standing in its frame. "Dear . . ." she began. *Amy!* She had caught him with his feet up and the *Times* in his hands at ten in the morning. She had interrupted his sacred working period. How could a man stand it? After all these years; after twenty years of insistence that the morning hours were sacred to work! Did words mean nothing to a woman? Was she incurable? Did shouting, arguing, beseeching, praying, fail to persuade her that he meant what he said? That he meant what he said when he declared that this perpetual interruption of his labours was a Chinese torture?

Hands gripping the arms of the chair, he sprang to his feet —this was as good a way as another of getting out of that compromising chair. "Oh my heaven and gracious powers above! *Ohhhh!*" Never was such a sigh; it was nearer a groan; the prolonged and hopeless groan of one in unremitting torment. "Oh death and heaven and hell! It is beyond endurance. Here am I at work—that I sit in that chair means nothing— I am thinking out and planning my work—I am trying to relate it to the needs of the times, and I alone know how difficult that is. All I ask is quiet to do it. All I ask is to be uninterrupted between nine and noon. As a dentist would be. As a doctor would be——"

"But, darling, it's——"

"I don't care who it is—it's not a case of business or money, is it?"

"No, it's——"

"No." He was pleased to hear it and be justified. "Then

I don't care who it is. I don't care if it's the Prime Minister.
I don't care if it's the Mayor and the Town Clerk and the
Mace Bearer and the whole bl—— the whole Corporation,
together with the Library Committee. Supposing I'd just
been pulling a tooth? Supposing I'd been giving gas? I
might have killed the woman. Supposing I'd been setting some
old gentleman's bones? Could I be interrupted like this?
Could I be burst in on? Could I be startled in the midst of
the most delicate operations? But no : I'm not a dentist ;
I'm not a doctor ; I'm only a vicar, and a vicar's week-day
work is not delicate, it's not difficult, it's not important. The
poor fool can explain and argue and beg, but does he convince
anyone? No. I give it up. Some things in the world are not
attainable, and peace for a parson to do his morning's work
is one of them. I abandon hope. None the less I could weep."
  " But, my dear——"
  " ' My dear's ' no good. ' My dear's ' no help to someone
in the depths of despair. What I want and ask——"
  " But, my dear, it's the police."
He swung round from the table over which his aggrieved
and angry head had bowed. " The who? "
  " The police. An inspector and a sergeant. Two enormous
men, and so nice and pleasant—not in uniform, of course, but
in just ordinary clothes. Detectives. It's exciting, isn't it? "
  " Detectives? What in the world can they want with me?
Did they say what they wanted? "
  " They said they thought you'd be able to help them in
some inquiries."
  " I? Why should I be able to help them? Oh, well, I must
hear what they want, I suppose, but I can't conceive what it
is. Show them in. I'm sorry if I was rude, Amy dear, but I
didn't realize it was—police. You were quite right to tell me."
  " Yes, I thought you wouldn't mind my interrupting your
work if it was the police. You *will* tell me what it's all about
after they've gone, won't you? Two such really lovely men ! "
Was ever womanish vivaciousness less wanted than when
one's heart was pulsing on the rim of death? And the idea of
being charmed by two men who were probably the messengers
of Disgrace, Ruin, Starvation ! He felt very angry with
Amy.
  " Show them in. Show them in please," he rapped at her.
" I must know."

§

They were certainly a fine pair who came into his room, holding their Homburg hats : Inspector Timmins, tall and burly in a dark brown overcoat and with a merry face ; and a younger officer, tall and slight in a suit of well-cut grey, and with a face like a scholarly priest's.

"*Good* morning, sir," said the Inspector, stressing his geniality so as to put everyone on good terms. "This is Detective Sergeant Wayne—not Corbett, who was with me when we picked up old Rick Carman, if you remember. He's gone on— non-stop for a commissioner's job. This is Canon Welcome, Clemmie, of whom you've heard me speak often, I think. I do hope we're not breaking in upon your work, sir."

"Oh well, don't mind that, Inspector." The Canon put forth an equal friendliness ; his smile held both merriment and a Christian love for all brethren, whether official or civilian. "Delighted to see you. What have I done ? Misappropriated the Church funds ? "

"No, we haven't come to arrest *you*, sir."

"I'm indeed glad to hear that. Well, what is it ? The police must be served at once, I'm sure."

"Very kind of you to say so, sir."

"Yes, time must be of the essence of *your* contract. Do sit down. Take this chair. It's made for a big man." The Inspector dropped into the Canon's own chair, and the sergeant into the other and opposite easy chair—the one Phil Janey had sat in when she told all. Canon Welcome stood between them, but this time with his back to his large writing desk, not to the chimney-piece.

His eyes were on Inspector Timmins. There, in his own chair, sat Inspector Timmins who had stood in the garden to arrest Mr. Carman and was now interested in him, Canon Welcome ; Inspector Timmins who had spoken on behalf of Mr. Carman at the Sessions House, and now about to question and examine *him* ! Inspector Timmins who had said : " Come to Mother."

His heart might be palpitating like a wren beneath a cat's paw, but none of this must show. This was the battle of his life, and therefore he, who had always been a good actor, in

331

pulpit, on platform, and in lady's room, must now give the performance of his life. Terror might sit trembling in his private office, but only ease and liveliness must stand in his window and on his counter. More than ease, perhaps : an otherworldly serenity ; a calm as of a man whose citizenship was in heaven ; a—yes—a faint suggestion of sanctity. His very dress at the moment was a picture of his state : quaking knowledge in his heart, and a long, sacerdotal cassock to curtain it. Charity and the cassock must cover his sins.

It was a battle for both of them, side by side, Canon Welcome and Phil Janey. He remembered his dramatic statement to her, " I am standing on guard," and, no less dramatically, he whispered to himself now, " They shall not pass." He stood ready with lies and perjury, and was unashamed. " You have a right to lie and save her for she is your child in God. They shall not pass."

And he remembered Baynes. Baynes had said he was ready, if necessary, to lie to the police. And Baynes was a saintly type. The teaching and example of Baynes were his lance and charger now.

" Well, Inspector ? " he invited, and leaned back comfortably on the brink of his desk. " What is it ? I am at your service. A cigarette ? " He proffered the silver box, but both Inspector and Sergeant declined. He put the box on one side. " Now what can I do ? "

" It's about a murder, sir."

" Murder ! Good gracious ! Oh, well, let me do all I can to help. As a matter of fact, it's incumbent on all citizens to help the police make an arrest, isn't it ? "

" I'm glad you take that view, sir."

" But it's the Law, is it not ? "

" More or less, sir."

" It's certainly the Law," affirmed the Sergeant who seemed to think, not only that he should speak occasionally, but also that by roughening his tone a little he would narrow the gap between a sergeant and an inspector.

" All right, then, if it's the Law, we clergy, above all people, I take it, must set an example of obeying it."

" That's not quite what your colleague Mr. Baynes thought, sir," the Inspector reminded him with a smile.

Disconcerting this ; but Canon Welcome showed no sign of having been unsteadied. " Baynes ? When was that ? "

" After some fellow had slashed him in Fred Lanark's café."

" Oh yes, but he was the victim ; *I've* not been murdered."
The Canon had recovered his footing. " If you remember he
was quite ready to give evidence against those who attacked
others. I, personally, don't want any murderers hanged but,
good heavens, they can't go unapprehended."

" Exactly, sir."

" Right enough," said the Sergeant.

" Good heavens, no ! " repeated the Canon emphatically,
indignantly.

" No, sir," agreed the Inspector. " And not if we can help
it."

" Very good then. Fire away. What's the question ? "

" It's probably only a routine inquiry, sir, but as you will
appreciate, when we're conducting an investigation, we daren't
leave any detail unexamined, however small."

" No," said the Sergeant.

" Just now we're inquiring into the murder of this young
lad, Horby——"

" Oh, yes, I know all about that," interrupted the Canon,
" I made it my business to know all about that. It was in my
parish, you see. I thought of visiting the boy's parents, but
learned that they were good Nonconformists, and Mr. Hamish,
their minister, was looking after them. Rather brutally murdered, wasn't he, in old Hartney's yard ? "

" In the carpenter's shop. And there's just one point on
which we think you can enlighten us."

" Anything I can do, Inspector. . . ."

" Well, it seems this Horby was rather one for the girls,
sir——"

" I'll say so ! " endorsed the Sergeant.

" —and we decided to check up on all the girls he'd ever
known in case there was any clue to be found that way."

" No light task, either," laughed the Sergeant. " A regular
Don June he was ! "

" That's right, Clemmie ; but let me tell the Canon. We
still believe in *shairshay la fam*, you know. Yes, sir ! Almost
our first rule. As often as not, a woman's the cause, if she isn't
the instigator, of a crime. Well, we're going through everything like a tooth-comb "—the word stirred up the fear in his
listener's heart like a cold draught of bellows on a fire—" and
we've accounted for most of them ; but there's one we haven't

333

traced yet. We at last know her name; it's Phillis Jane Carman——"

"What, little Phil Janey? Old Fred's daughter? Did she know him?"

"We have information that he met her once in a pub, and we know that he took her for a ride in the stolen car two days later—the day he was arrested. That seems to have been the extent of his acquaintance with her."

"Then how can she help you?"

"We're just making inquiries, that's all."

"Yes." The Sergeant agreed that this was the position.

"She may have seen something of him after he came out of prison," suggested the Inspector.

"Or on the evening in question," put in the Sergeant, most conveniently, because the Canon had no answer ready to the Inspector's suggestion.

"What evening was that, Sergeant? I forget."

"Saturday, three weeks ago, sir."

"Saturday . . . three weeks ago. . . ." The Canon, still half-sitting on the rim of his desk, thrust a hand through his cassock, brought out from a vest pocket his tiny black diary, and turned its leaves.

Meanwhile the Inspector proceeded, "We found her address and went round to see her landlady, and she told us that the girl had left her lodgings on the Sunday after the crime and went along with you in your car. The landlady also said that she'd been with you the evening before and that you brought her home."

"Saturday . . . three weeks ago . . . yes, here we are. What time was this murder?"

"Almost certainly some time between six and eight. He was last seen alive in Greenholt Street at about half-past five, and he had a Saturday night date with a girl called Goldblatt at eight, but he never turned up and never went home. What's more the police surgeon and another doctor both put his death at about seven."

"Between six and eight. Yes, that's quite right. How interesting!" The Canon shut the little diary and pushed it back beneath the cassock; then thrust both hands into the ease and comfort of the cassock pockets. "Phil Janey was with me that afternoon and evening. As far as I remember I took her home to Mrs. Ansty at about nine. She couldn't

334

have seen anything of him *that* evening. I met her in the afternoon, you see, when I was visiting in my slums "—God grant they didn't question the Prime Minister or the Russian Commissar—" and I was most happy to be able to tell her that I'd found her a very nice job with a member of my congregation. She'd left her job some weeks before, and now she was getting worried because nearly all her money had gone. I offered to take her at once, if she liked, to see the lady—she lives in Chelsea, and I'll give you her address if you like——"

The Inspector produced a notebook from his inside breast-pocket and a pencil from his waistcoat. Canon Welcome, though the sight of the notebook stabbed his heart, did not dare to hesitate and stated the address. Helplessly he watched the words being written down and wondered if they and the subsequent words he must utter would one day convict him.

" Yes, sir ? " encouraged the Inspector, looking up from the notebook, where the address was now secure.

And immediately the Canon perceived danger lights ahead which he had not foreseen. He must act at once ; he did so ; though terror gibbered at his heart. " There's one thing I ought to tell you, perhaps, Inspector. Strictly it's my secret, I suppose, as her clergyman ; but it can't be hidden many days longer. She's pregnant, I'm sorry to say, by a married man."

" Indeed ? " said the Inspector. " Well, we'll be careful not to notice that. That's not our business."

" No." The Canon said it carelessly, as if he'd hardly heeded or heard. And rather dreamily he added, " Yes. About four months pregnant." Was that " four " a quick, saving gift from heaven ? " Yes, in about five months I shall have to get her into a home, and the man responsible shall play his part. That of course was the reason why I have been trying to get her somewhere where she isn't known, and with an understanding woman of my congregation ; Mrs. Buxton used to be a famous actress in her day ; she's acted with Hawtrey and du Maurier and Forbes Robertson."

" *Is* that so, sir ? "

" Yes, she's a most interesting woman. She knew Barrie and Pinero and Sutro and Henry Arthur Jones. As a child she was a pet of Sir Herbert Tree's and Sir George Alexander's."

" *Is* that so, sir ? "

" Yes, and she was so pleased with little Phil Janey that I promised to take the child along to her the next day. Poor

335

Phil Janey was very unhappy, you see, and didn't want to go
back to her father, with whom she'd quarrelled. I'm very fond
of Phil Janey. She was one of my confirmation candidates,
and she always comes to me in any trouble."

The Inspector wrote things down : the Canon could not
see what. Never before perhaps, he thought, had a man suffered
such terrors beneath an aspect so tranquil and smiling.

"Thank you, Canon," said the Inspector, when the writing
was done. "That's fine." And he said it almost as if he were
satisfied !

The Sergeant said, "Thank you, sir," too, possibly that he
might not be overlooked.

"Not at all," demurred the Canon. "I wish I could help
you more. I wonder if there's anything I can suggest. I know
these parts so well, you see."

"Naturally you do, sir," said the Inspector.

"Of course," said the Sergeant.

"Yes, I—we work a lot down there. We have our mission
there. My own feeling is—but of course I've only what I've
read to go on—that it was some confederate, or some member
of a rival gang, who was waiting for him till he came out."

"That's what we suspect," said the Inspector ; and Canon
Welcome was greatly relieved to hear it.

"It's possible," agreed the Sergeant.

"Yes—of course, but I'm only a theorist—but a ferocious
blow like that is so exactly characteristic of the young male
animal between eighteen and twenty-five. Older men adopt
different methods and women are very seldom murderers."

"I see you know a lot about it," laughed the Inspector.
"You should have been a policeman."

"Better have been an actor," the Canon thought ; while
aloud he said, "I should have loved to be a C.I.D. detective.
A fascinating job yours must be."

"So people think who don't have to do it. They imagine
it's just picking up clues with a magnifying glass and then
chasing after the criminal in a fast car, whereas it's just a
weary, weary grind, day after day and often night after night.
That's right, isn't it, Clemmie ? Over this wretched lad we've
had to make inquiries in every house within a quarter-mile
radius of the Garrett Place yard. And what's it yielded. Precisely nothing. Most of the people had seen a suspicious character hanging about the yard that evening, but unfortunately

not one of the descriptions of the man was the same. All right. Then we visit every house within a half-mile radius. That's detective work."

" Oh," and " Oh dear," thought the Canon in some despair ; but he continued, diverting the subject, " Yes, I haven't worked among criminal types all these years without knowing them pretty well. You remember Phil Janey's father, don't you ? "

" We do. Between you and me, sir, we make it our business to remember gentry like him."

" Well, he's quite a family friend now. He's been a pal of mine ever since he called on me through a bedroom window."

" Go on, sir ! Yes, and I remember you spoke up for him at the Sessions. Very sporting of you, if I may say so."

At this the Canon only shrugged. " It helped a little, I think. He's gone straight ever since."

" Well . . . straight enough," allowed the Inspector.

" That's how I came to know little Phil Janey so well. As often happens, she reacted right away from her father's manner of life and wanted to be good instead of bad. And she came to me to be confirmed. Yes, I can tell you all you want to know about Phil Janey. Any time."

" Well, thank you, sir." The Inspector turned to the Sergeant. " O.K., we'd better be moving now, Clemmie. We've other lines of inquiry to pursue " ; and the Canon was pleased to hear it.

All rose ; and he escorted them to his front door, with a very great hope, but no confidence, that he was escorting them out of Phil Janey's life, and out of his own. " I wish you every success. I sincerely hope you get to the bottom of this. There's altogether too much of this gang warfare these days."

" How right you are, sir ! " said the Inspector, on the doorstep.

" Yes, you're in the right of it there, sir," confirmed the Sergeant, " but I'm not sure that the best way wouldn't be to leave 'em to kill each other off."

" No, no, Clemmie ; that won't do," laughed the Inspector. " We can't have murder. A little razoring yes ; do 'em good. But we've got to go on with this. Where it's murder, sir, we never let go."

This was like a final blow as they quitted his threshold, and a blow at the base of the heart, but the Canon did not show that it had touched him. With a smile he said, " Like the Canadian Mounties, eh ? You get your man in the end."

" That's it, sir. Nearly always."

" Good. Well, I hope you get him this time." The three-lettered monosyllable " him " was his last careful indoctrination of the police.

" We'll hope so. Good day, sir, and thank you so much for all your help." And both of them went out into the garden, smiling.

§

He walked back into the study, his brain shaken, churned, and warm and aching under his hair. Had that been perjury ? Deliberate and detailed lying to the police. The lies written down in a book. The Sergeant a witness to them.

And the thoroughness and efficiency of the police. He had never supposed they were as thorough as that. Every house within a half-mile radius ! Surely, if they went on like that, they must come upon the truth. Oh God, God . . . What could he do ? One thing he must do at once, and that was to race to Chelsea and instruct Lilian and Phil Janey in their parts, lest the detectives bore down upon them in the course of the day. He ran from the room—" I must go visiting, Amy "—he raced to Chelsea, but by a round-about route ; and all the way he wondered if he was being shadowed ; all the way he looked furtively behind.

When he had said good-bye to the police on the doorstep he had turned about and walked into an avenue of yet darker and more haunted days. The spectre whose names were Exposure, Disgrace, Imprisonment, and The End of Canon Welcome, stayed even closer to him now than before. One question, and one only, paced and paced the round cell of his mind, like a captive harnessed to the wall : " Had that rearguard action been enough to turn back the enemy from Phil Janey and himself ? " His saner parts argued that it must have been ; the terrified parts, striving to hearten him, repeated, often aloud on his lips—" They did not pass, Phil Janey ; they did not pass. I saw to that." Lilian reported that the detectives had called on her, and she'd been charmed with them—perfectly sweet creatures, she said ; and they'd got nothing out of her. " Such a delightful and intelligent audience," she said. " Two really beautiful men, so huge and comfortable and strong. My dear, I was at my best. They thanked me with the nicest

338

courtesy for my willing assistance. So sweet! And Phil Janey, after watching my really magnificent performance, darling, before such an inspiring audience, was almost convinced that she must be innocent and gave quite a performance of her own. She's ever so much better now, my pet, and a shrewd little thing in her way ; and she sat there looking so small and weak and timid, but giving her answers so readily, that I was quite ashamed, but, believe you me, darling, the idea of *her* bashing anyone to death simply never entered the heads of those nice, capable men. We were really rather splendid, both of us." But then Lilian was always the completely irrational optimist, believing the best because the worst was not to be borne.

He awaited the answer with a smiling face for the world, though fear pricked and goaded him all the daytime and rent his sleep at night. But always, let the fear torment him as it would, he could not regret his action, nor feel other than that it was good.

All his life he had noticed that if he heard some name for the first time, he would come upon it again and again during the next days in his reading or his talk. So now it seemed that, searching his evening papers for any news of the Garrett's Place murder, he was constantly encountering the phrase " accessory after the fact ". Sometimes it was as if the papers kept mentioning it so as to strike hope down, if for a little it had risen to its feet. One afternoon a headline smote him between the eyes : " AIDED A KILLER. MAN ACCUSED." And with a heart that at first stopped altogether (or so he thought) and then pounded with misery, he read :

" This was the charge at Brighton today against Stephen Alfred Makin, 23, a labourer : ' That, well knowing that a man known to you had murdered John Sydney Gane on April 4th this year, you did, on the same day and other days afterwards, receive, comfort, harbour, assist, and maintain the said man.' The prisoner was remanded for seven days, bail being refused."

In custody! In Brixton Prison without bail. He, Vicar of St. Boniface Martyr in Brixton Prison where he visited Mr. Carman years ago, an honoured guest ! Amy visiting him there ! Even perhaps, Mr. Carman visiting him, for Mr. Carman might well seize this chance to revisit the glimpses. In prison while only on remand ! And what would the guilty man get when he was tried ?

The papers never told him, and the days marched on.

Like a cat with a mouse Life left him in peace for a few days, so that he began to walk in hope again, and then, on a Sunday afternoon when he was reading, not unhappily, his *News of the World* so as to keep in touch with life, the claws pounced again. His eye had been caught by a headline, JURY TAKE A MERCIFUL VIEW, and he had read with interest of a girl named Esther May Levinback whom the jury had pronounced "Not guilty" of the murder of her seven-week-old son, but guilty of infanticide. He had been exasperated by the ruthless words with which the Judge had chosen to scourge her. "The jury have taken a merciful view of the facts in this case," the hard old punisher had said, "but in my considered judgment it was nothing but a wild, savage, and unpardonable act. Still, it is not within my power to deal with you save on the basis of the jury's verdict; and I therefore, with regret, sentence you to nothing more than two years' imprisonment." Canon Welcome was just thinking, "Wonder if that old devil has ever sinned himself, and maybe in his youth got a girl into trouble," when his eye travelled over another sentence; and his heart stopped again. "Barnet Aaron Klee, aged 24, was found guilty of being an accessory after the fact and sentenced to eighteen months' imprisonment."

Eighteen months! And this only in a case of infanticide! What in a case of murder?

He leapt upon any legal book that he saw—just as a man will instantly and furtively consult any medical work, when he fears he has heart disease or gall stones or cataract—and in one of these he read how the great Blackstone had defined an accessory after the fact as "a person who, knowing a felony to have been committed by another, receives, relieves, comforts, or assists the felon"—each word exactly and beautifully describing his deeds; nor—not even in the face of God—could he ever regret having received, relieved, comforted, and assisted that desperate and driven child. In another he read, with a dropping jaw, that as recently as within the last three decades sentences of ten, twelve, and fifteen years had been passed on accessories after the fact of murder.

Hope was nearly dead now because his condition was too depressed to sustain it. Each day in his free hours he tramped his study, head down, hands behind his back, and jaw hanging loose, while he considered, between great sighs, what he would

340

do when the skies fell. And always two exactly opposed responses presented themselves as the only possible attitudes. The one : " If I'm publicly disgraced and my career is at an end, I fall the whole way. If Society has nothing but sneers for me then, by God, I have nothing for it ; I laugh at its laws ; I become the complete sinner, caring for nothing on this earth but myself ; I may commit suicide, or I may take my pleasures, and the money for them, where I can." The other : " Is God perhaps going to break me in pieces that he may make me anew ? Perhaps if all hope and ambition were removed from me, I might learn to care, no more for myself, but only for others. I have always rather wanted to do this."

That is to say, he would be either the complete sinner or the complete saint. Despair could go no further.

CHAPTER TWELVE

But the days mounted into weeks, and the weeks into a month, and though the spectres did not depart, hope came back into the company. And as the month doubled itself and became two, it was hope, rather than fear, which was his daily companion. The hope was enlarged when at a public dinner he found himself sitting next to a senior prosecuting counsel to the Crown and snatched the opportunity, between meat and sweet, to inquire about false alibis and the criminals who provided them. And the distinguished man greatly enheartened him by saying, " *The view of the police is quite simple. The value of an alibi is the value of the witness's reputation. No more and no less.*"

No more and no less. Then, oh then, if the police had believed him—and why shouldn't they, a Prebendary, a Leading Light in the Church, a man of unspotted reputation and even, as some chose to think, of considerable sanctity?—then there was no hint of a case against Phil Janey.

Or say they were not absolutely satisfied by his statements (and the impudence of that doubt!) so that some suspicion rested on Phil Janey as on others, might it not be that they had insufficient evidence to justify a prosecution against anyone?

June was now in the great concave of the sky, emptying it daily of all but a froth of white clouds along the rim ; it was on his trees, attiring them in the brightest of young, fresh, soft, and restless leaves ; it was on his garden beds, beflagging them with sweet williams, delphiniums, snapdragons, lupins, anemones, and roses, roses everywhere ; and he felt incapable of anything but hope in this high summer. Yes, the Garrett's Place Murder had surely gone on to the list of unsolved crimes. He had always heard that a murderer, if not found soon, was seldom found at all. " We never let go," the Inspector had said ; but probably this meant that an investigation might go into abeyance, ready to leap into life again, should a new fact emerge. These were violent times, and other murders had supervened. Probably the police were now more interested in them. There had been something in what the Sergeant had said : " Let the gangs razor each other and, if they want to, kill each other."

And then one morning, among the letters on his breakfast plate, he saw a most official-looking envelope with " Private-and Confidential " typed in one corner. The fear laid its death-cold hand on his heart. Postmark ? " S.W.1." Up from the guilty subsoil of his mind, like an evil flower, sprang the idea : " Scotland Yard ! " Scotland Yard was in Whitehall, S.W.1. Oh, S.W.1 was a large postal area, but—" Private and Con-fidential " ? The evil plant was there ; its roots were deep, and there was no plucking it out : this was—this might be—a summons to Scotland Yard.

He did not read it now—not before Amy. She must not see the shivering of his hand or the whiteness of his face if it struck him down. After breakfast he would take it into his study as a dog takes its sickness into a shadowed corner of the field. He was very quiet throughout the meal ; but by no other sign did he disclose his terror ; and as soon as might be he went from the room. He stepped quickly into his study and shut the door on himself. And, standing before the hearth with the envelope in his hand, he said, " Oh God, give me strength to bear it. . . I will bear it. I am ready. I do not regret having lied for her sake and if I am to be undone thereby, well, so be it." A clergyman slips easily into scriptural quota-tions, and he found himself adding, " I am ready to be offered."

For many seconds he stood there like a traitor against a wall waiting to be shot. He drummed the unopened envelope on his left fist, hesitating, and the nails of the clenched fist dug into his palm. At last with a long, deflating sigh and fingers that stumbled, he opened the letter.

And the first thing he saw was " 10, Downing Street, White-hall, S.W.1." The heart within him leapt like a baby about to be born.

A lightning sweep of his eyes gathered the sense of the letter before he had collocated the words : it was the offer of a bishopric.

" Oh, oh ! " Downing Street, the opposite side of the road from Scotland Yard. In every sense the opposite side of the road.

He read the letter carefully now, so far as the bounding heart would let him. " Dear Canon Welcome, You will be aware that as a result of the passing of the New Bishoprics Measures, the new see of Rexborough is to be carved out of the swollen and unwieldy diocese of Great St. Aubyns. The Prime Minister desires me to inform you that, if you would consent, he would be pleased to submit your name to the Crown for appointment to the new see. The diocese of Rexborough will be largely composed of just such urban parishes, with their big working-class districts, as you have served with distinction in the past, and the Prime Minister sincerely hopes that you will see in this new sphere many opportunities for the pastoral work which you desire and do so well. I am to add that he will be grateful if you can give him an answer at an early date so that His Majesty's consent may be obtained and the announcement made. Yours faithfully, Ewart Heathly, Private Secretary."

" Oh, oh ! " He breathed this cry in a kind of orgasm that protests against its own delight. A bishop ! And safe ! Not disgrace but glory. Not exposure but homage. And Phil Janey safe too—safe behind the portly cassock of a bishop-elect ; nay, behind the portly purple cassocks of the whole bench of bishops. For what policeman would dare question the statement of one of these reverend fathers ? The whole forty bishops of the Anglican Communion, with their suffragans and brethren from overseas, had sat themselves in a row before Phil Janey, like a living barricade. Pat on the moment, the Prime Minister had come to the rescue of Phil Janey ; nay the Crown itself had come. *Rex pro Phil Janey.*

" Amy, Amy ! " he shouted, and when she came from the breakfast-room, he showed her the letter, and then hugged her, kissed her, patted her broad back, and waltzed her around in the passage, calling her " Mrs. Amy, Bishopess of Rexborough." He had danced well in his youth, and could twinkle his feet to good effect still. " The Right Reverend Mrs. Amy. You look every inch a bishop's lady—and there are quite a few inches now, aren't there, Magpie dear, but I love them all. And let me tell you this : it's the truth : almost my greatest joy is that I've been able to bring this rank and position to you. No man ever had a better partner. *Pooh-hooh.*" He ended the dance because he was breathless with exercise and joy. " Bless you, bless you."

As soon as he could he got away from her excited chatter and back into his study. One wants to be alone in a loved place for one's dalliance with joy. He flung himself into his chair to dream. A bishop. A father in God. And in gaiters. " My lord." A crozier and deferential chaplains to hold it.

Surpassing Tuppy Williams after all. An archdeacon ? Pooh !
Nothing. Nothing very much : no pectoral cross ; no ring. . . .
Bishop of Rexborough. . . . He was very, very happy, though
not a little shocked at the appointment.

Sinking into a yet more comfortable position and clasping
his plump hands, he went his dreaming way into the future.
What a gentle and benevolent father he would be to all his
clergy, and especially to the young ones like Tim. Not that
he would be weak. Directly the appointment was announced he
would be bombarded with letters from clergy who felt that they
were in every way suited for such and such preferment. Every
diocese had these " sturdy beggars ", as their fathers-in-God
called them. They would not find him soft or easily deceived.
He had but a low opinion of all such place-hunters. No, he
would appoint, so far as was possible, only the good. And—
yes !—his very first appointment should go to old Baynes.
What a pleasure to give it to old Baynes, and how right ! Give
him men like Baynes, for, if he'd learned one thing in his thirty
years of priesthood it was that only the saintly men, and not
the worldly-wise and " practical ", were truly successful. Few
bishops saw this, but he saw it because he had vision. So far
as he could help it, there should be no humbugs in his diocese.

Bishop of Rexborough. . . . A father in God to all ; loving
and kind to all ; quick to understand and forgive. . . . The
substance and marrow of the matter. . . . Nobody with a face
like yours should be less than a bishop. . . . Nobody with a
power like yours. . . .

So leave him.

§

" My good Timothy," said Dr. Bettersby, walking down the
hill from the Staff Meeting at which the Vicar had told them
of his appointment, " would you desire me to say the kind
or the candid word ? "

" The candid, sir, of course."

" Very well, then." The doctor was walking rapidly as
ever, with his head bent and his hat perched insecurely on the
top of it, and his thin, red, frost-bitten nose directed towards
the pavements, as if he were speaking to them rather than
to his companion. " Very good. His elevation I find pleasing

345

because I am his friend, but I must suggest that it is easier to explain than to justify. Our brother—or should I now say, our father elect?—has little real scholarship and only the most rudimentary and irresolute sanctity ; to a disciplined and precise mind his sermons and talk are, God forgive me, as garbage before the wind ; but he has something which may be called a heart ; he loves the Church of England because it is the element in which he flounders ; he is ready to work for it without undue strain, even though he believes in but little of its teaching ; he will offend few of the brethren, because he will avoid any definite pronouncement on any issue which is the least controversial ; he has, you must allow, a presence ; so let us trust, my dear boy, that this singular elevation will lead *ad majorem Dei gloriam.*"

" I see," said Timothy, after a ponder. " Thank you very much, sir."

" ' Bettersby ', my dear boy, ' Bettersby ' ; not ' sir '. Yes, a heart—a redeeming and attractive quality which is also exhibited by his protégé, the penitent burglar and barrow boy. You have not read the *Speculum Ecclesiae* of Giraldus Cambrensis ? No, I feared not. A pity, because I was about to observe that you'd soon be in a position to write another such entertaining work yourself. Well, I have come a little way down the hill with you, and this is where I make my good-byes. You have further work to do, I think, but I—I to my home, where I shall potter a little in my garden. Go you on to a little failure and a little success, for such is the lot of all mortals. My dreams are over, but do thou have joy of thy children and thy people and of Alcinous the king—as the wise Odysseus said to Arete. This last above all : keep the favour of Alcinous, because his garden is famous for its good fruits. That concludes our lesson for today. Fare you well, my young son, Timothy."